A SPY AT DUNHAVEN CASTLE

A SPY AT DUNHAVEN CASTLE

A CATE KENSIE MYSTERY

CATE KENSIE MYSTERIES
BOOK FIVE

NELLIE H. STEELE

A Novel Idea Publishing

CHAPTER 1

Cate shivered despite the warmer spring weather. She pulled her cardigan closer around her as she bit her lower lip.

"It's definitely human," the police officer said, as he bent over a set of white bones exposed in the soil of Dunhaven Castle's side garden.

"We suspected as much," Jack answered.

The man stood and brushed the dirt from his fingertips. "We'll get someone up here to remove the remains. I'm no expert, but I'd venture to say they've been here a while. We'll send them out for analysis, but I wouldn't hold your breath on any major findings. These cases are pretty difficult to make headway on."

"Thanks, Ben," Jack said, extending his hand for a shake.

Ben Thomson nodded and offered to see himself off the estate, disappearing around the corner of the castle.

Cate sighed and pressed her hand to her forehead. "That poor person," she lamented. "Killed and buried in a garden like they were meaningless."

"Well, they've been found now," Jack said.

"Yes, thanks to Riley and Bailey." The two small dogs, who had been shut inside the castle walls after digging up the skeleton, had made the gruesome discovery.

Cate stared at the makeshift grave with its white bones poking through the dirt, contrasted by the bright spring grass. She narrowed her eyes at it.

"Caaaate," Jack warned.

"I wonder…"

"Caaaaaate," Jack chided.

"Who it is," Cate finished.

"Cate! Now, don't go starting your wondering. Every time you wonder, we end up in a whole host of trouble."

"My wondering has solved more than one mystery at Dunhaven Castle and has righted several wrongs."

"And it's also gotten you nearly drowned, both of us shot at, and you nearly killed when that psychopathic supernatural…" Jack stumbled around for the word, "creature," he finally spat out, "put you inside a coffin! We've done our fair share of righting wrongs. Including the last wrong we righted."

"Yes, at least we're no longer in danger of disappearing into another century," Cate agreed. She stared down at the timepiece around her neck – a new pocket watch pendant. It had the ability to control the new universal time portal which had emerged within the castle walls.

After months of slipping in and out of other eras at whim, Cate and Jack, with the help of an odd set of new friends from across the pond who called themselves the Shadow Slayers, managed to tame the time rips.

Jack nodded in agreement. "Yes, thanks to our other unique friends in the supernatural world. Speaking of, did you get rid of that necklace?" Jack referred to the ostentatious sapphire and diamond necklace Duke Marcus Northcott gave Cate when he had held her hostage in the 1700s.

Despite the negative memories associated with it, Cate kept it in her jewelry box. She found herself unable to part with the priceless object, though this had little to do with the value. For some reason, Cate felt a strong draw to it.

Cate avoided his stare, scuffing her foot into the grass. "Caaaaaate," Jack prodded.

Cate pulled her lips back into a half-grimace. "No, I didn't."

"Why not? That madman nearly killed you! Cate, get rid of it."

"I will. I just… I'll give it to Mrs. Campbell for the auction at the Presidents' Ball. I'm sure she'll be thrilled with it."

"No," Jack disagreed. "Get rid of it now. Chuck it in the bin, toss it in the loch, anything. Just get it out of the castle."

"If I do that, I'll need a distraction, so, it's a perfect time to dive into a normal mystery!"

Jack started to nod, then quickly turned his motion into a head shake. He puckered his lips. "Why would you need a distraction?"

"That necklace is… I told you, I feel some connection to it. Getting rid of it will be difficult. So, I'll need a distraction. And this mystery is the perfect thing!"

"Now, Cate…"

"Jack! There's a body in my garden! This will be the talk of the town. And with the upcoming party, we need some answers!"

"That is where you're wrong. The party is in six weeks. All the rumors will have died down by then."

"Yes," Cate agreed, "because we'll have solved the case."

Jack shook his head at her. "Oh, Lady Cate, there's never any stopping you, is there?"

Cate raised her chin and smiled at him. "Nope!"

"Well, I suppose I can hope this is an open and shut case by the police and we've got no investigating to do."

"We'll see," Cate said, as they began their hike back to the castle.

"I'll put some temporary fencing around the crime scene to keep the dogs away from it until they remove the bones."

"Thanks. They've done enough damage already."

"See you later, Cate," Jack said with a salute, as she ducked through the castle's front doors. Her two furry friends, Riley and Bailey, bounded toward her.

"Hello, boys," Cate said, as she crouched to ruffle their fur. "Well, thanks to you two, we have another mystery to solve. Jack's eternally grateful."

Riley kissed her on the cheek in response. "He's putting up a fence to keep you two out of there until the police can remove the bones."

"Oh, what a terrible thing," Mrs. Fraser said, as she passed through the foyer. "Has little Benny left?"

"Little Benny?"

"Aye, the officer."

"Oh, right," Cate said.

"He'll always be little Benny to me. I can remember him being just a wee lad and now he's a police officer. Investigating a body in the garden!"

"He's sending a team to remove the remains and then I guess they'll do an investigation. Try to identify who it is. He didn't hold out a lot of hope since it's a cold case."

Mrs. Fraser shook her head with a somber expression on her face. "Well, I suppose at least once the body's been removed, the poor person can be properly laid to rest."

Cate nodded in agreement. "Will you be taking your dinner in the library tonight?"

"Yes," Cate said, with another nod. "Thanks, Mrs. Fraser."

Mrs. Fraser continued down the hall, disappearing down the stairs leading to the kitchen. Cate checked her timepiece. She had some time before dinner.

She raised her eyes up the massive main staircase, following its red-carpeted stairs up to the next floor. She bit her lower lip as she ascended the staircase, the dogs trailing behind her. Cate stared upward as her fingers absentmindedly caressed the banister on the way up.

She wandered through the halls and pushed through the doors to her private sitting room. She navigated across it and into her bedroom. Her eyes fell on the large jewelry box standing against the adjacent wall.

Cate crossed to it. With a tilt of her head, she gazed down at a drawer just above the curved legs. Her fingers lingered on the drawer pull as her mind conjured an image of the jewelry piece inside. She pictured the eleven sapphires surrounded by diamonds creating the collar of the necklace. From it hung a large teardrop sapphire, also encrusted in diamonds.

She swallowed hard as she recalled receiving it while held captive at Duke Northcott's rented home on the outskirts of Dunhaven in 1792. Her eyebrow arched as she remembered him sweeping her hair away to fasten the clasp. Her pulse quickened as his voice echoed in her mind. "Keep this as a reminder of me."

Cate slid the drawer open. The necklace lay framed by the black velvet inside the drawer. Cate reached for it. Her fingertips glided across the jewels. She stared unblinking at its opulence. The gems sparkled in the light. Her fingers lingered on the large central sapphire.

Cate's breathing turned ragged, and her heart thudded in her chest. Her mind went blank and all she could see was the necklace. The world melted away around her.

Something touched her leg. Cate's brow furrowed, but she continued to stare at the necklace. The sensation on her leg continued. Cate tore her eyes from the shiny object and glanced to her side. In an instant, her mind snapped back to reality.

Riley stood on his hind legs, his front feet planted on Cate's thigh. "Hey, buddy," she said with a smile, as she reached to scoop him up.

"Lady Cate?" she heard Molly's voice call. "Lady Cate? Yoo-hoo!"

Cate slammed the drawer containing the necklace shut and hurried to her sitting room.

A smile spread across Molly's face as she spotted her. "There you are."

"Yes, I just ran to freshen up."

"Must have been some refresh," Molly said. "It's after five!"

"What?" Cate questioned. She glanced at her timepiece. She'd come upstairs shortly after four. She hadn't spent an hour here. The watch's face told a different story. The second hand ticked by, and the others indicated a time of 5:04 p.m. Cate winced at the watch.

"Something wrong, Lady Cate?" Molly asked.

"No, just lost track of time."

"Oh, well, I'm not surprised," Molly said, waving her hand in the air. "You're always doing that with your research and whatnot. Anyway, nearly time for your dinner. I just wanted to check to see if you wanted blueberry pie or cherry. Mrs. Fraser and I made both."

Cate nodded and smiled as she crossed the room. "Uh, blueberry, thank you," Cate said. Her mind flitted back to the blue jewelry steps away. She shook her head, clearing the image from her mind. With it pushed aside, she followed Molly from the room, Riley in her arms and Bailey in tow behind her.

* * *

Cate awoke the next morning with the alarm screaming in her ear. The sun was already peeking over the moors in the distance. Cate slapped the alarm to silence it before pushing up to sit. She dangled her legs over the edge of the bed. Cate's eyelids threatened to close as she rubbed her face.

She sat for another few moments in an exhausted stupor before she finally rose and padded to the bathroom, hoping a shower could help clear her head.

When Cate emerged dressed for the day, she still struggled to stifle a yawn. What had left her so exhausted, she wondered, as she rousted the dogs from their beds? After breakfast, Cate joined Molly and Mrs. Fraser in the kitchen for a cuppa, craving the caffeine.

"When are the police returning for the..." Molly paused, her eyes darting side-to-side before she whispered, "bones."

"Today," Cate announced, after a sip of the sweet tea.

"Ugh, terrible business," Mrs. Fraser said.

Cate nodded. "Yes, I agree."

"I, for one, will be glad when the bones are gone."

"Me too," Cate admitted. "Jack put up a temporary fence, so the dogs don't get at it again."

Molly shivered.

Mrs. Fraser eyed her. "Someone walk over your grave?"

"No," Molly countered, "Cate walked over someone else's and now their bones are laying in the garden."

"Superstitious, Molly?"

Molly pursed her lips and shrugged. "Maybe a little."

Mrs. Fraser chuckled. "Well, the bones will be gone soon enough." She patted Molly's arm.

"Not soon enough."

"You're really worried!" Cate said, peering over her teacup.

Molly's eyes widened. "There is a body buried in the side garden. Someone was probably murdered and dumped in a shallow grave there. And now her sorry excuse for a resting place has been defiled. This is the perfect recipe for a ghost." She slapped her hand against the table with a determined expression.

"There are no such things as ghosts, Miss Molly," Mrs. Fraser said.

Molly didn't respond. Cate narrowed her eyes at her friend.

Mrs. Fraser continued, "In all my years at Dunhaven, I have never encountered so much as a stray wisp of smoke, let alone a ghost. It'll be all right."

"After creepy Douglas and his devil-worshipping, I just feel unsettled." Molly's eyes grew to the size of saucers, and she focused blankly at the table in front of her, before she snapped her eyes up to Cate's. "You don't think… ohhhhh." She groaned and shook her head.

"Don't think what?" Cate asked.

Molly swallowed hard and leaned forward. She whispered, "That Douglas killed her during one of his satanic ceremonies?"

CHAPTER 2

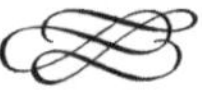

Cate cocked her head and frowned. "No. In all the research I've done, nothing has given any indication Douglas was a devil worshiper, nor that he engaged in any strange ceremonies, *nor* that he killed anyone!"

"But..." Molly flicked her eyes to Mrs. Fraser. "Emily's story..."

"Was just a story, Molly," Mrs. Fraser assured her.

"With Damien's help, I translated all of those journals. They detailed his experiments, all of which were pretty standard scientific stuff. No weird occult obsessions or anything."

Molly's forehead wrinkled as she processed Cate's statements.

Cate bit her lower lip, her face pinching with concern. When the time rips were misbehaving, one had opened and swallowed up an unsuspecting Molly. She had slipped back to some unknown century and encountered a castle resident wandering through the hall. "Molly, is this about the..."

"No," Molly interrupted before she went further. "No. And it's okay. I told Emily."

"Aye, and I convinced her she did not see any woman roaming the front hallway."

"Now that I think about it," Molly explained, "I'm pretty sure I saw a curtain fluttering or something similar. Definitely *not* a woman."

Cate smiled and nodded. "Good. Because this castle is *not* haunted."

"I'll still be glad when the bones are gone," Molly said.

"Mrs. Fraser," Cate said, "do you know of any disappearances? The police said not to expect much in the way of solving this, but my curiosity is piqued."

Mrs. Fraser narrowed her eyes and focused her gaze at a random spot in the air. After a moment, she shook her head. "None that I recall. We haven't had a murder or missing person in Dunhaven in my lifetime."

"At least we're living in a safe town, even if there are ghosts," Molly said with a chuckle.

"There are *no* ghosts!" Cate insisted. "Though, you're right. While it's good to know Dunhaven is safe, it's really puzzling. If incidents are that rare, you'd think this would be easy to track."

"Perhaps it will be, Lady Cate," Mrs. Fraser said, as she began to clean up from their tea.

"Let's hope so! I'd really like to have some closure. And someone else may be looking for it, too."

"I think young Jack would just like the bones out of the garden, especially with the party coming up."

"Ha!" A sarcastic laugh burst from Cate's lips. "He said we have plenty of time before the party."

"Aye, we do. But six weeks will be gone in the blink of an eye."

"I agree. And if this hasn't happened in a while in Dunhaven, it will be the talk of the town."

"You know it, Lady Cate," Mrs. Fraser said, pointing to her.

"Well, I suppose I should get out to the garden. The police should be here soon to exhume the body."

Molly groaned. "Can't be soon enough."

"Why don't you leave the dogs with us?" Mrs. Fraser suggested. "I'll spoil them with a few nice bones. Of the regular kind – *not* the human kind."

"And a few extra treats," Molly said.

"Thank you so much. I'd really prefer them to be in here than bounding around trying to steal someone's remains."

Cate left her two furry friends with her two human friends as she stepped from the kitchen into the bright sunshine. She shielded her eyes as she began her walk toward the side garden.

A bright orange plastic fence was strung around the makeshift grave. Jack stood nearby with the DCI Ben Thompson, who had done the initial assessment yesterday.

"Good morning," Cate called to them.

"Good morning," Ben answered.

"Hello, Lady Cate," Jack said. "No dogs today?"

"Mrs. Fraser and Molly are watching them. So we won't have any rascals running around trying to snag any of the bones."

"I understand it was your dogs who unearthed the remains," Ben said.

Cate nodded, pressing her lips together in a thin line. "Yes, they did. They've been digging in the spot for weeks and yesterday before we called you, they pulled a few of the… well, they pulled some of the remains out."

Ben pursed his lips and nodded. "You know, Lady Cate, you really do not need to be here. I understand this is very upsetting."

Cate forced a weak smile. "It's okay. I'd like to be here."

"All right," he said. "We're going to get started then."

Within moments, Cate's quiet side garden turned into a flurry of activity. An entire crime scene unit descended on the sight. Photographs were taken from every angle. A tarp was laid out, and the crime scene unit meticulously began to lay out the skeleton and recreate the body.

The process took hours. Cate stared at the bones laid on the tarp. She wrapped her arms around her and bit her lower lip. The forensics team continued to poke at the gravesite.

Cate crinkled her brow. "Are they missing something?" she asked Ben.

"Checking for anything else, like jewelry or a weapon. Anything we can use to either solve the case or identify the person."

Cate nodded in understanding and returned her gaze to the bones in front of her. Jack approached her. "You okay, Lady Cate? I can handle the rest if you'd like to head in."

"I'm okay. Just wondering who this poor soul was," Cate answered.

"It is a shame," Jack admitted.

"With any luck, the police can identify her."

Jack side-eyed her. "Her?" he questioned, glancing at Cate.

"The skeleton looks small. I'm just making an educated guess."

Jack raised his eyebrows and cocked his head. "Good assessment. I guess we'll find out if you're right soon enough."

"Mrs. Fraser said she can't recall any murders or disappearances in her lifetime, so if it's not a common occurrence, it should be easy, right?"

"Right," he agreed. "My fingers are certainly crossed. If the police can identify this person, we're in the clear from any of your harebrained schemes."

"My schemes are not harebrained," Cate argued.

"They're half harebrained at best. Plus, I'd like to avoid… well, you know," Jack said, raising his eyebrows at Cate.

She smiled at him. "So, you're already considering it to solve this mystery, huh?"

"I am not. I'm already thinking of ways to avoid it."

Cate arched an eyebrow, a playful grin on her face. She nodded in response.

"What?" Jack questioned.

"Nothing."

"That look was not nothing, Lady Cate."

Cate shrugged and held in a giggle. "Methinks the gentleman doth protest too much."

"Oh, ho, ho, very funny, Lady Cate. Don't quote Shakespeare to me. I'm being serious."

"Shakespeare is always serious. Hamlet was very serious."

Ben wandered toward them, ending their conversation. "We're just about finished. We'll be out of your hair soon."

"And you'll let us know if you find anything?" Cate questioned.

"As a courtesy, yes, I'll let you know."

"We appreciate it," Jack said, shaking hands with the man.

"Well, I suppose that's that. Now we wait," Cate said.

"Aye," Jack agreed. "And I can take down the orange fence."

"Yep," Cate said. "I'll bet the dogs will be all over this on their next trip out."

Jack checked his watch. "I suppose it can wait until after lunch. I'm starving!"

"You're always starving," Cate said.

They began their walk back to the castle's kitchen door. "That's the only plus point to time traveling," Jack said. "Double the meals."

Cate shook her head at him. "At least you're finding a silver lining."

* * *

When Cate sat down at her computer after lunch, she found her mind wandering back to the body in the garden. Her lack of focus made it impossible for her to work on her book detailing the castle's former occupants. Instead, she opted for a long walk with the dogs. She allowed them plenty of time to sniff around the newly disturbed dirt.

"No more bones, boys," she told them, though they now seemed interested in the smells left by the live humans who visited earlier today. "If only you two could give us a hint about who this was."

Riley wandered to Cate's side and stared up at her. "Yes, Riley, another mystery. And I can't stop wondering who this person was and how she ended up in our garden."

Riley offered a small whine in response. Cate tore her gaze from the dirt patch where the body had been only hours ago and ruffled the fur on Riley's head.

"Let's go do some research," she suggested. She called to Bailey and the three of them returned to the castle. Cate threaded her way through the halls to the library.

As she crossed to her desk, her eyes fell on the bookcase concealing the passage to Douglas's secret laboratory. Her mind skipped to a different era. She smiled to herself as she recalled meeting the castle's builder and her ancestor.

The smile slowly faded as she recalled the other events of 1792. A shiver shook her, and she ceased walking. The memory of being entombed alive in the family's crypt by Marcus Northcott embedded itself in her mind. She swallowed hard as she recalled cool stone pressed against her back and the sensation of being confined. His voice echoed in her head. "I'm finished with you, for now." Her lower lip quivered in response to the recollection of being plunged into darkness as the stone coffin's lid slid over top.

She twisted her head and her eyes slid upward. The urge to see the necklace he had given her overcame her. She took two steps toward the hallway before she stopped. Her mind clouded and pain shot across her forehead. She pressed her fingertips against her temples as she squeezed her eyes shut.

Cate blew out a long breath. She opened her eyes to find two furry faces staring up at her. She gave them a weak smile. "I'm okay," she said, in a shaky voice. She wrapped her arms around her midriff and rubbed her arms. Goosebumps pocked her skin.

She shivered again and bit her lower lip as she stumbled to the desk across the room. Cate collapsed in the chair and covered her face with her hands. Being haunted by the disturbing memory of being buried alive was not surprising. However, being drawn to the necklace she wore during the escapade bothered her. Why would she long to see an item associated with so much torment?

A cold, wet nose nudged at her arm and a set of tiny paws rested against her thigh. She uncovered her face and found Riley and Bailey watching her.

No matter the circumstances, her two dogs could always soothe her. She pulled them both onto her lap and snuggled them close. She offered them both a kiss on the head. Riley returned the gesture, giving her a lick on her cheek.

"Thanks, buddy," she said, as she rubbed his back. "I'll be okay. I just need to get some distance from it." She nodded as though trying to convince herself. "Maybe the necklace reminds me that I didn't die."

Bailey cocked his head at her words. "Yeah, even I think that's a weak argument, Bailey."

She sat for another few moments enjoying the comfort of

her two pals. "Maybe what I need is a new project. And maybe the body in the backyard is just the thing."

With another kiss on the top of each of their heads, Cate sent the two pups off for a nap by the fire. She popped open her laptop and waited for it to wake.

As the laptop performed its start-up tasks, Cate swiped at her cell phone. She found a new text message waiting. Cate smiled at the screen as she tapped to read the text from Damien Sherwood. His help during the last crisis at Dunhaven Castle had been invaluable, and the pair had promised to keep in touch.

Hey Cate, just checking in to see how things are going with you. No more trouble with wonky time portals, I hope.

It was nice of Damien to check in, Cate mused, as she typed a response. *No more time portals appearing at random. Thanks for checking! Just a skeleton in my garden.*

She set the phone aside and tapped into her email account, finding it filled with mostly junk. Her phone chimed as she finished deleting her junk mail. She found another text from Damien.

A skeleton in your garden? Seriously? Like a human one? Seems like you have your hands full.

Cate responded: *Yes, a human one. I really hope we can find out what happened and who it was. I feel terrible about it.*

As Cate considered researching her current problem, Damien responded with lightning speed. *Speaking of feeling terrible... I hate to bring this up but... any more nightmares? And did you get rid of that necklace?*

Cate pursed her lips. She hadn't suffered from a nightmare last night, though it may be too soon to tell if she was rid of them for good. The trickier question concerned the necklace. Damien shared the same sentiments as Jack did about the ostentatious object. She struggled to explain away her reasoning for hanging on to the item.

She answered: *No nightmares last night. Let's hope the trend continues!*

Within seconds, she received a response. *I noticed you didn't answer about the necklace.*

Cate puckered her lips. Damien was too clever for his own good, she noted as she typed back to him. *Didn't chuck it yet, but I'm going to get rid of it soon!*

An incoming text popped onto her screen before she could toggle off her display. *Don't wait. Get rid of it NOW.*

Cate clicked off her phone and set it on the desk next to her laptop. She pulled up her search engine, but before she could type a word, her phone chimed again.

I'm serious, Cate... get rid of it, don't wait. And don't ignore me.

The message from Damien was followed by an emoticon with the tongue sticking out. Cate replied assuring him she was not ignoring him and that she would get rid of it. Her mind added the word "eventually", but she left that out of her message.

Her mind turned toward the necklace. No one wanted her to keep it. Why didn't she get rid of it like they asked of her? Perhaps she was too stubborn for her own good. Perhaps it was their insistence that held her back and made her want to keep it until she got rid of it on her own terms.

Perhaps it was something else. Her brain clouded as she dwelled on the necklace, its diamonds and sapphires sparkling in her mind's eye.

CHAPTER 3

She shook her head to clear her mind, pushing images of the necklace away. "I can't get rid of it yet," she mumbled aloud.

With her mind made up, she pushed herself to focus on her laptop. Cate began with a series of Google searches regarding missing persons in Dunhaven. Several results populated on her screen. Several of the top hits were about missing people, but not within the vicinity of Dunhaven. Cate continued to sort through the list of results, finding it offered little in the way of information.

She refined her search and scanned the new list of results. Nothing pointed her toward any information regarding the body. It appeared Mrs. Fraser was correct. People didn't disappear in Dunhaven.

Cate leaned back in her chair, tenting her fingers. She narrowed her eyes as she considered other avenues to pursue. With no news stories from Dunhaven regarding missing persons, who could the individual buried in her backyard be?

Cate pulled a sheet of paper from the desk drawer and jotted down a few notes.

Person not from Dunhaven - no news reports of a missing person - at least not recently

Cate tapped the pen against her lips. She added: *Could the disappearance be older than news reports listed online?*

She made a note to inquire with Mrs. Campbell at their meeting tomorrow. Perhaps they had old news articles predating those on the internet that could identify the person.

A new idea occurred to Cate, and she jotted down the words: *Someone from out of town?*

Perhaps, Cate ruminated, the disappearance was not of a Dunhaven resident. Perhaps the person was visiting on vacation, in town for business or some other reason when they were killed. Then a record of them should exist. Surely, someone reported them missing at some point.

She may need to expand her search into neighboring towns. What if the person came from even further than that? She'd cross that bridge if she came to it.

Cate leaned forward and began to type another search when the doors to the library opened. Molly carried a tray with Cate's dinner.

"Time to quit working and eat!" she announced.

"I wasn't getting very far anyway," Cate admitted, as she stood and stretched.

"Working on the book?" Molly asked.

"No. I was actually trying to see if I could find any information on our former side garden resident."

Molly winced. "I'm not sure I want to know, but did you find anything?"

"Not a thing. Though I'm not sure what I expected to find."

"Well, I'm certain you'll solve it eventually," Molly said. "I've never known Cate Kensie to be stuck for long."

Cate offered her a smile as she settled into her leather armchair. She hoped Molly was correct. She really wanted to solve the mystery of the garden guest.

Cate's heart beat hard against her ribs. Her pulse raced. Her breaths came in short, shallow gasps. She struggled to move, but found herself unable to.

The figure of Marcus Northcott loomed over her. He spoke, promising her he was finished with her. For now. He pressed his hand over the necklace, his icy fingers brushing against Cate's skin.

"Keep this to remember me by," he said.

He grasped the stone lid and began to shift it over the coffin's top. Her lower lip quivered as tears clouded her vision. It narrowed to a pinpoint as darkness closed in around her.

The cold stone of the coffin pressed against her. Her arms were pinned at her sides. The weight of the sapphire and diamond necklace pressed against her collarbone. The pressure from Duke Northcott's hand as he placed it against the necklace lingered on Cate's skin. It felt as though his icy fingerprints were burned into her skin.

"Help!" she screamed. "Help me! Don't leave me here!"

The tears spilled from her eyes and ran sideways down her face, wetting her hairline. "Please, don't leave me," she whimpered again.

Cate gasped as her eyes shot open. She gulped air, her eyes darting around her bedroom. She squeezed her lips together, forcing herself to slow her breath. She fumbled with the lamp on her night table, knocking it over as her trembling hands attempted to flick it to the on position.

The two lumps on her bed shot up to standing. Riley hurried to Cate's side and Bailey offered a yip in response to the crash.

"Sorry, guys," Cate said with a wince. She pushed herself up to sit and dangled over the side of the bed to grasp the lamp. She grabbed it by the shade and hauled it upward, setting it upright on the table.

With a groan, she covered her face with her hands before sliding them over her hair. Cate settled back into her pillows. Out of the corner of her eye, she spotted her dream journal. The details of her nightmare flooded back into her mind. She bit her lower lip as her fingertips glided over the smooth, cool cover.

Cate pulled the book onto her lap and flipped through the pages. Page after page flashed in front of her eyes. Written words in her own handwriting outlined months of terrifying dreams involving Marcus Northcott.

Should she detail this nightmare in the journal? It involved Marcus Northcott. They all involved Marcus Northcott. That was the only similarity to the others, though.

Unable to fall asleep, Cate grabbed her pen and began to write. While she did not find it abnormal to suffer from a nightmare about the frightening ordeal she'd just experienced in 1792 at the hands of that man, she hoped it had nothing to do with the others in the journal.

She desperately wished her bad dreams were over and her latest one was merely a remnant of a terrifying experience. She snapped the journal closed and slid it onto her night table. She reached for the light, but changed her mind, deciding to leave it on as she tried to drift back to sleep.

After a few moments, she braved it, flicking off the light and plunging the room into darkness. In the quiet blackness, she stared out the window at the starry sky.

The glow of the half-moon cast long shadows across her floor. She found herself unable to close her eyes. Fear still coursed through her veins.

She reached toward her bare neck framed by her flannel pajama collar. She rubbed her fingers along her collarbone. The image of the sapphire necklace flashed through her mind. Her thoughts dwelled on the jewelry.

Her eyes flicked to the jewelry box across the room. She focused on the bottom drawer. After a moment, she rose from the bed and wandered to the wooden armoire. The drawer slid open, and she spied the sparkling jewelry even in the darkened room.

Cate reached for it, letting her fingertips glide over the smooth, polished stones. She curled her slender fingers around the center stone and lifted the necklace from the drawer. With it clutched to her chest, she strode back to bed, climbed in, and nestled under the covers.

Holding the necklace close to her heart, she closed her eyes and drifted off to sleep in minutes.

* * *

When Cate awoke the next morning, the sun was already cresting the moors. It painted the sky a brilliant shade of red and purple. Cate rolled onto her back and took a deep breath. She became aware of her hand, balled in a fist with the sapphire necklace still clutched within her grasp.

The memory of her dream and subsequent reaction

flooded back into her mind. Why had she risen and retrieved the necklace? And why had it seemed to calm her?

Cate recalled drifting off to sleep shortly after returning to bed with the necklace. Perhaps she'd just been too weary to do anything but fall asleep then, Cate ruminated. Maybe the necklace was unrelated to her falling asleep.

Cate stretched and climbed from her bed. She deposited the necklace in the bottom drawer of the jewelry armoire, before continuing on to begin her day.

Instinctively, she found herself returning to the spot where the bones had been exhumed the previous day. As the dogs chased each other around a row of bushes, Cate stared at the dirt.

"Who were you?" she whispered. "And what happened to you?"

With no answers forthcoming, Cate returned to the castle for a warm breakfast before her morning meeting with Isla Campbell.

While scheduled for nine, Cate had no doubt she'd see Mrs. Campbell at the stroke of 8:45 a.m. The party planning whiz barreled up the driveway in her sleek black car, her brakes screeching to a halt at precisely quarter to nine.

The slight woman flew from her car and raced to her backseat to gather her materials. "Oh, Lady Cate," she exclaimed, as she pulled folders, fabric swatches, a calendar, a tote bag filled with hidden items and more from her car, "I cannot begin to tell you how excited I am."

"I can imagine. Landing the Presidents' Ball is quite a feat, I'm told," Cate answered. "Can I help you with anything?"

"Oh, no, no, no. I've got it!" She kicked the door shut and turned to face Cate with a grin. "Ready!"

Cate led her into the sitting room. Mrs. Fraser already waited with a tray of tea. "I beat you to it, Lady Cate," she said. "Already brought tea. And Molly's tried her hand at these new lemon crisps. I put some shortbreads out, too, just in case, but I think you may enjoy these."

"Oh, Emily, hello," Mrs. Campbell said. "Got the youngster showing the old dog some new tricks, eh?"

Cate bit her lower lip and offered a slight shake of her head toward Mrs. Fraser. By the woman's expression, she was sure Mrs. Fraser was fuming. Molly would get an earful about the "ninny" the moment Mrs. Fraser returned to the comfort of her kitchen.

"Not really," Mrs. Fraser said. "I'd not be much of a baker if I'd never heard of a lemon crisp before. Just allowing the 'youngster,' as you put it, to spread her wings and bake something of her choosing. She's got to have a signature item."

Mrs. Campbell offered a tight-lipped smile that bordered on a smirk and a shoulder shrug before plopping onto the loveseat. She began arranging her party planning paraphernalia around her, putting a nonverbal end to her conversation with Mrs. Fraser.

"If you need anything else, Lady Cate, just ring."

"I will, thank you, Mrs. Fraser. Please tell Molly the lemon cookies look delicious and, of course, I can't resist your shortbreads."

Mrs. Fraser offered Cate a smile, before retreating through the doors leading to the back hall.

Mrs. Campbell continued to lay out her materials before snatching a large leather folder from her tote bag. She unzipped it, revealing a notebook and pen inside. After removing the pen, she drew in a deep breath, exhaled sharply, and raised her eyes to meet Cate's.

Cate smiled at her. "Where would you like to begin?" Cate asked.

"Well," Mrs. Campbell began, "I hate to begin here, but I feel as though I must."

Cate's mind shot forward, preparing for what she believed was inevitable.

Mrs. Campbell leaned forward and whispered, "The body." She pursed her lips and raised her eyebrows.

"Yes, of course," Cate answered. "The remains have already been removed, so that won't be an issue. And…"

"It's not just the bones," Mrs. Campbell said. "It's the rumors, of course. A body… found on the grounds of Dunhaven Castle." Mrs. Campbell pulled the corners of her mouth into a frown and shivered dramatically.

Cate opened her mouth to respond, when Mrs. Campbell continued. "It's simply ghastly!"

"Well, if anyone can turn this around, I'm certain you can," Cate said. "And as Jack pointed out, we have six weeks before the anniversary party and nearly three months before the Presidents' Ball. The rumors should have run their course by then."

"Let's hope," Mrs. Campbell said.

"On that note," Cate said, before they moved on to other topics, "I wondered if you could be of any assistance with identifying the remains."

Mrs. Campbell furrowed her brow, and she shook her head as though shocked. "How could I possibly help?"

"Well, you are always a wealth of information to assist me with my castle research. I wondered if you may have any information on unsolved disappearances, new or old, that may explain who this may be."

"I don't know of any castle occupants who went missing; certainly none of the earls or countesses," Mrs. Campbell said.

"I haven't come across anything of that nature either. Though I haven't come across anyone who's gone missing in the Dunhaven area," Cate answered.

"No, disappearances are not common here," Mrs. Campbell agreed.

"I can't help but be curious," Cate prodded. "I feel somewhat responsible since the poor person was found on my property."

"Oh, don't be silly, Lady Cate. Certainly, no one blames *you*!"

"Still, I'd like to learn as much as I can. Would you mind helping me track down any news stories that may be relevant?"

"I shall have the assistant librarian gather any materials that may be applicable!"

"Wonderful. Do you mind if I stop in tomorrow to pick them up?"

"Not at all! I'll text her right now." Mrs. Campbell tapped at her phone before setting it down and smiling. "There we are."

"Thank you so much, Mrs. Campbell."

"I am always happy to be of assistance."

"Now, about the party," Cate began.

She was interrupted by Mrs. Campbell's waving finger. "Oh, this is far more than a party," Mrs. Campbell corrected. "The Presidents' Ball is an *event*!" She waved her arms in the air with flourish to punctuate the statement. "It takes place over the span of several days…"

Cate was exhausted already. Mrs. Campbell continued on with her explanation: a formal dinner Friday evening, an auction and ball on Saturday with various other side events, and a brunch on Sunday to close the event. The line-up did little to alleviate Cate's apprehension. She smiled as detail after endless detail paraded through her mind.

Mrs. Campbell seemed to have a handle on everything, as usual. She suggested castle tours, garden tours, a photo opportunity with Cate, a garden tea party, an evening concert, and more. Cate's eyes bulged at the amount of planning it would take the pull this off. The ever-confident Mrs. Campbell seemed unbothered by the level of preparation, stating simply, "I want to make this the best Presidents' Ball the association has ever experienced. I want it to be talked about for years to come."

"Well, I certainly think it will be that!" Cate answered, after she detailed her itinerary.

"Now, I've got a great deal to coordinate, but do you mind if I take up just a tad more of your time to go over a few minor things for your anniversary party?"

"Not at all!" Cate answered.

They spent another hour discussing modifications and details for the party six weeks away. After that, Mrs. Campbell seemed satisfied with their work. Cate showed her out, waving as she shot off down the driveway on a mission to find the perfect something-or-other for one of the parties.

Cate glanced down at her timepiece hanging from her neck. The noon hour approached. Her rumbling stomach also announced the time. She returned to the sitting room and grabbed the tea tray before heading downstairs to lunch with her staff.

She giggled as she heard Mrs. Fraser's voice filtering down the hall as she approached the kitchen.

"... cannae believe she is *still* here. That infernal woman does not understand how to be respectful of other's time. I only hope she won't be joining us for lunch. Or worse, make poor Lady Cate late. The poor girl is likely starving."

"I had plenty of cookies to tide me over," Cate remarked, as she entered the kitchen and set the tray on the counter.

"Ah, Lady Cate, thank goodness she's finally left you alone," Mrs. Fraser said.

"It was a doozy of a meeting, that's for sure," Cate answered, as Molly cleared the tray.

"What did the party czar do today to upset you, Mrs. Fraser?" Jack inquired, as he pushed through the door with Mr. Fraser trailing behind him. "I could hear you all the way outside most of the morning."

The statement elicited another chuckle from Cate.

"She called me an old dog!" Mrs. Fraser exclaimed, snapping her dishtowel against the counter. "The nerve of her. Calling me old and a dog."

Jack lifted his eyebrows at the statement.

"She asked if Molly was showing the old dog a few new tricks with the lemon crisps."

"Ohhh," Jack said, with a nod of understanding.

"That'll be the day," Mrs. Fraser said with a harrumph. "I know all the tricks there are to know. And don't you forget it!" She wagged her finger at Molly.

"I have no doubt, Mrs. Fraser," Molly answered.

Jack plopped into his seat at the table. "And what outrageous requests does she have for these parties?"

Cate sighed as she eased into a chair across from Jack. "Well, she asked how quickly an oak tree grows."

Jack furrowed his brow. "Why?"

"She hoped you could plant one now and that it would grow large enough in six weeks to hang a swing from for a photoshoot."

"Is she insane?"

Cate shrugged. "I told her I did not believe that was likely. Then she asked if it was possible to uproot a large enough tree and transplant it."

"That does it," Jack said, slapping his hand against the table. "She's certifiable."

"At least no snow machine."

"No," Jack answered, "but it will be summer for both parties. I'm surprised she hasn't asked us to harness the sun and pull it closer to ensure warm weather."

"There were some discussions about contingency plans for inclement weather. She has a large number of events scheduled outside. She said since Mr. Fraser seems so talented with his garden designs perhaps he'll enjoy the challenge of creating a magical garden display for each party."

"I suppose I should take that as a compliment," Mr. Fraser said in his soft-spoken manner.

"Wait until you hear what she wants before you decide," Jack cautioned.

"For the anniversary party she requested something along the lines of The Secret Garden," Cate said with a shrug. "And for the Presidents' Ball, she said 'whimsical fairyland, like in Dance of the Sugar Plum Fairies.'"

Mr. Fraser's eyes widened, and he cocked his head. After a moment, he blew out a breath. "I've got some ideas. I'll sketch them up."

"You never cease to amaze me, Mr. Fraser," Cate said.

"As long as you like them, Lady Cate, that's all that matters."

"Because we know Mrs. Campbell will never be satisfied," Jack added.

"It's pretty bad when it's easier to impress a countess than a librarian," Molly said.

"And I'm still raw over her calling me a dog," Mrs. Fraser added, as they set the lunch on the table.

"Speaking of," Cate said, "where are the dogs?"

CHAPTER 4

*E*veryone glanced around the room in search of the two missing pups.

"Oh, there's one," Jack joked, pointing at Mrs. Fraser.

She swatted at him with her dishtowel. "Watch yourself, young Jack, I don't have to hold my temper with you like I do with her."

Jack held his hands up to defend against the flying towel as he laughed. "I'm only joking, Mrs. Fraser. Anyway, I think you'd better ready your fighting skills for Lady Cate. It seems you've lost her dogs."

"Those two rascals are somewhere about," Mrs. Fraser said. "They went tearing out of here about fifteen minutes ago. I assume they heard something."

"Oh, no," Jack groaned. "I hope it's not another body."

"You and me both!" Cate exclaimed as she rose from the table. "That's another thing Mrs. Campbell is having a fit about."

"Really?" Molly inquired.

"Yes. The rumors and all of that after we found a body on

the grounds. She doesn't want it to dampen the festivities. I told her it would die down before the first party."

"News doesn't always die down in Dunhaven," Mrs. Fraser said.

Cate called down the hall to both dogs. "Really?"

Mrs. Fraser gave a slow shake of her head and puckered her lips. "Didnae you figure that out when everyone here knew the story about Douglas and the odd occurrences here?"

"Good point," Jack said, as Cate gave another call down the hall. "Everyone knows about devil-worshipper Douglas and that's been over two centuries."

"Aye, and it still hasn't died down," Mrs. Fraser answered.

"You have a point," Cate answered. The sound of claws and scampering feet echoed through the kitchen. Two small dogs scampered into the room moments later. "There you are! And where have you two been this time?"

"Finding a secret passage?" Mrs. Fraser inquired.

"Digging up bones?" Jack asked.

"Chasing ghosts?" Molly questioned.

"Probably just being rascals," Mr. Fraser ended with.

"Definitely that," Cate answered, pointing at Mr. Fraser. "Look at you two."

A sheen of dust covered Bailey's gray fur, making him a shade lighter than normal and a cobweb clung to Riley's face, haphazardly draped from the top of his head and down his ear before hooking onto a whisker and dangling from his chin.

Cate swiped the cobweb away while Molly dusted Bailey with a rag.

"Ah, they look like you, Lady Cate, when you've been crawling around in a closed-off area."

"Yes," Cate agreed. "I wonder what closed-off area they managed to get themselves off to."

"We may have to follow them next time," Molly suggested. "Maybe they found something cool."

"Looks like all they found is dirt," Mrs. Fraser said. "We may want to have the CLEANING company follow them."

Cate chuckled at the suggestion as she returned to her seat. "I hope the police can figure out who this is. Maybe that will put an end to the rumors."

"They didn't seem to be too certain they'd find anything," Jack said.

"No. I asked Mrs. Campbell to put together a list of articles about disappearances in the area that may connect to it. We'll see what she comes up with."

"Well, if there's a dark secret lurking, you'd better believe Isla Campbell knows all about it," Mrs. Fraser said.

"That's what I'm counting on, Mrs. Fraser," Cate said with a wink.

* * *

Cate spent her afternoon working on her manuscript. After her visit to 1792, she had a wealth of information and insight on the castle's builder, Douglas MacKenzie. Though she found it easy to detail Douglas from a personal perspective and her writing flowed easily, her mind continued to return to the latest mystery.

Even after climbing into bed after a long evening stroll around the property, Cate's mind couldn't settle. It bounced from topic to topic. She began first with the skeleton in the garden. She pondered who it could be and why they were buried there. She wondered if they'd ever determine answers to those questions and strategized ways to search for information.

Her mind turned to another topic, as her fingers absent-mindedly caressed the soft fur on Riley's head. Where had her two friends disappeared to earlier? They usually did not roam around the confines of the castle. What had drawn their attention? Perhaps they'd heard Cate call her goodbye to Mrs. Campbell and sought her out. Cate shook her head. That didn't seem likely. Surely she would have run into them if that was the case.

Cate rolled her head to the side and glanced down at Riley and Bailey. "Where did you two disappear to today?" she whispered. Riley adjusted his head, his dark eyes peeking at her before slowly drifting shut again.

With no answers, Cate closed her eyes. Thoughts whirled through her mind. Images flashed past: the garden, Riley's cobwebbed face, Bailey's dusty back, a skeleton, a mysterious shadow of a person, a lightning bolt, a fireball, the family crypt, a blue satin dress. Cate drifted to sleep as her mind focused on one image. A blue sapphire and diamond necklace.

* * *

The alarm chirped, stirring Cate from a sound sleep. Blindly, her fingers found the clock and silenced it. With a deep inhale, Cate rolled onto her back and stretched.

As she reached overhead, something smacked against her headboard. The scraping sound caused Cate to snap her eyes open. She glanced up at her fist. Something dangled from it. Cate pulled it toward her chest and sat up. She reached for her lamp and flicked it on, squinting against the bright light that filled the room.

Cate's lips parted as she stared at the item in her hand. The large teardrop sapphire gleamed in the light. The smaller sapphires, surrounded by diamonds, dangled from her open palm.

Cate swallowed hard, the crease between her eyes deepening as she stared at the necklace. "How did I get this?" she whispered.

Cate went over the events of the previous night in her mind. She'd drifted off to sleep pondering the mystery of the skeleton and the dogs' disappearance. Her mind had flitted from thought to thought after that.

She recalled thinking about the necklace before falling asleep, but she did not recall rising from her bed and retrieving it.

She must have done it, she assumed. She must have risen at some point and wandered over to get the necklace, then crawled back in bed with it. Perhaps she was half-asleep when she did it. Perhaps she had sleepwalked. A frightening thought, but she couldn't explain it otherwise.

Cate stared down at the sparkling gems. A shudder shook her body, and she discarded the necklace onto her comforter, shoving it away. She drew her knees to her chest and stared at the rejected item.

After a moment, she snatched it and hurried across the room. She shoved it into the bottom drawer of the jewelry armoire and slammed the drawer shut. With a deep exhale, she spun around and leaned against the heavy wooden furniture piece.

Jack's words rang in her mind. "Get rid of it."

Cate shook her head and left the armoire behind in favor of a shower. Her mind could not process disposing of the necklace now.

* * *

Cate emerged into the bright spring sunshine. The dogs raced ahead of her, frolicking in the cool breeze. Cate watched them as they played tug-of-war with a wayward branch Bailey found. Riley snagged it from within his brother's iron-jawed grip and pranced away with his prize as Bailey chased after him. Soon, the branch lost its luster for both dogs, and they scampered away in search of something else to play with.

Cate smiled at them as they danced around the back garden. She raised an eyebrow as she gazed out over it, wondering what plans Mr. Fraser may create to bring a magical theme to her two upcoming events. In six short weeks, Cate would be celebrating her one-year anniversary as the Countess of Dunhavenshire.

She still recalled the moment she'd arrived in the back of Mr. Smythe's black rental car. Even after a year, Cate couldn't believe the turn of events in her life. She twisted to take in the castle behind her. Cast in yellow hues of the rising sun, the castle gleamed at her like a magical fairy tale.

She smiled at it, before turning back to clap her hands and call the dogs back. She'd take a long walk with them after breakfast before she traveled into the quaint town of Dunhaven to pick up the articles Mrs. Campbell put together for her.

After her morning trek around the property, Cate headed into town, parking near the town's center and enjoying a walk along the streets in the brisk air to the library.

"Hi," Cate greeted the assistant behind the desk with a broad smile. It was the same girl who she'd spoken with shortly after she'd arrived. The girl had never quite forgiven her for strong-arming her into borrowing materials from the library that were not meant to be lent out.

"Lady Cate, how can I help you?" she said, her lips set in a firm line, one eyebrow arched.

"I believe Mrs. Campbell had a packet for me to pick up?" Cate said.

"Lady Cate!" Mrs. Campbell called from her office behind the desk. "Good morning!"

"Good morning, Mrs. Campbell. I was just asking Beth about the packet you put together."

"Yes, of course!" Mrs. Campbell swiped the folder Beth pulled from under the desk and held it out toward Cate.

Cate reached for it, but Mrs. Campbell pulled it back. "Now, there's not much," she said, cocking her head and tapping the slim folder. "I told you there was nothing untoward that happened in Dunhaven." She waved a finger in the air. "Well," she added, "nothing untoward except some of those goings-on in the castle." She offered a coy smirk.

"Well, I suppose there has to be some excitement!" Cate said, with a hollow chuckle. "And again, thank you for putting together whatever you could find."

"Have you heard anything about the case?"

"Not yet. I hope to hear soon."

"I certainly hope we hear before the party so the matter can die down."

"I won't let up on them until we get somewhere."

Mrs. Campbell gave a nod of approval toward Cate and relinquished the folder to her.

"See you next week, Lady Cate. Wednesday, 9 a.m. sharp!"

"See you then!"

Cate offered a wave as she pushed through the doors into the cool Scottish morning air. She resisted the urge to claw through the folder and determine if anything could help identify the body removed from her garden. Instead, the shops caught her eye.

She shoved the folder into her tote bag and decided to spend the rest of her morning shopping. She strolled into one of her favorite boutique shops, carrying everything from handmade gifts to mainstream products.

"Lady Cate!" Harry, the shop owner, greeted her. He stared down at the floor, searching around her feet. "Where are my two favorite buddies?"

"Back at the castle, enjoying being spoiled by Mrs. Fraser and Molly," Cate answered. "How are you, Harry?"

"Doing just fine. And you?"

"I'm doing very well, thank you."

"Getting ready for that big party?"

"I am," Cate said with a nod. "Will you and Helen be attending?"

"We wouldn't miss it."

"Good, I'm so glad. I can't wait to see everyone there!"

Harry's wife, Helen, emerged from the backroom. "Oh, hello, Lady Cate," she greeted her.

"Hello!"

"Can't wait to see everyone at the party?" she asked.

"Yep. I'm really looking forward to it."

"Aye, I think everyone in town is. Although, I hope you're prepared for the rumors."

"Helen!" Harry whispered harshly.

"Well, it's best she knows!"

"I assume this is about the latest discovery in the garden."

Helen nodded. "Aye, the body is the talk of the town. And everyone has an opinion."

Cate squeezed her lips together and nodded. Helen leaned closer to Cate. "They've got it pegged to a mistress of Randolph Mackenzie, killed in a fit of rage."

Cate raised her eyebrows and held back a sigh. Randolph's reputation as a womanizer couldn't be further from the truth. She was nearly certain he was not the murderer.

"Or the bones of a human sacrifice of Douglas MacKenzie," Harry chimed in.

Cate's eyebrows fell and scrunched together. Another unlikely culprit, her mind echoed. Douglas had been about as much of a devil worshipper as a priest.

"Or the thief from the 1925 heist met a gory end."

Cate knew this was not the truth. "Didn't the theft turn out not to be a theft, but a misplacement of the jewelry?" she asked.

"So they say," Helen answered, crossing her arms over her chest. "I say they found those jewels and killed the person who took them."

"Now, Helen," Harry began.

"It's all right, Harry. Everyone has a theory."

"Do you?" Helen inquired.

"Sadly, no," Cate said. "I would very much like to find out what happened."

"But those answers may be buried in the past just like that body," Helen said.

Cate nodded. Buried in the past wasn't quite as much of a challenge as most people assumed. She just needed a hint as to when they were buried.

"Well, I hope they find something out," Helen said. "I'm sure either way, it'll be the talk of the town for years to come."

Cate spent another few moments chitchatting with the couple before she said her goodbyes. On her way out the door, something in the display window caught her eye. She cocked her head and studied the display.

Afraid of things that go bump in the night? Catch them on video!

"What's this, Harry?" Cate asked pointing to the small cube.

"Oh, that's a motion cam," he answered.

"A what?" Cate asked. "Sorry, I'm not great with technology."

Harry rounded the counter and approached Cate, picking up the colorful little cube. "It's a little camera. It connects to an app on your phone and alerts you when there's motion. It also records anything it sees and stores it for you to review later." Harry pulled the sign down and tossed it aside. "Ignore that. A bit of left-over marketing from All Hallow's Eve last year."

Cate lifted the cube from his hand and studied it. She handed it back and said, "I'll take one. Are there instructions for setting it up on your phone?"

"Aye," Harry said, as he grabbed a packaged one from under the display and set the display model back onto its perch. "And I can help you if you have a minute."

"Got ghosts, Lady Cate?" Helen inquired.

Cate laughed. "No, but it may be handy to keep an eye on the dogs."

"Oh, a nanny cam," Harry said with a chuckle, as he processed the sale. He pulled the box open and removed a small set of instructions, along with the cube and a short cord. "Now, this is your plug. And this little button up top is how you turn it on and off." Harry toggled it on, and a small blue light bloomed to life on top. He pressed the button again to turn it off and unfurled the instructions. "Now, have you got your phone?"

"Yes," Cate said, readying it.

"Okay, scan this QR code here and it'll take you to the app you need. Okay, good. Press to download it." He continued to walk Cate through the steps to create an account. "Now, when you get home, set it up wherever you'd like. Turn on the camera and open your app. The camera should spring up on here and you can connect them. Oh, you'll also need your wifi password."

"I've got that," Cate assured him.

"If you have any trouble, give me a call, I can talk you through it." Harry packaged everything up into the box and dropped it into a small shopping bag. "Have fun watching the pups!"

"Thanks." Cate accepted the proffered bag and headed out

of the shop. After a bit more window shopping, she climbed into the car and headed back to the castle.

Cate greeted her excited pups with hugs and kisses before settling down for lunch. She stared at the thin folder from the library as she blew on her first spoonful of tomato basil soup. After her first bite of the sumptuous soup, her eyes fell to the bag next to her feet. Foregoing the articles, Cate pulled the miniature camera cube from inside and unboxed it. She glanced at the instructions as she finished her meal.

After Molly collected her tray, Cate grabbed the camera cube, her phone, and the instructions and wandered to her bedroom. The two pups followed her, but disappeared before she reached her suite.

She offered a surprised chortle when she realized she was alone. "Where are those two off to now?" she questioned aloud. She glanced at the blue cube in her hand. "I may need more of these!"

Cate entered her bedroom and glanced around the space. She crossed to a large dresser near one corner of the room and set the cube on the top. She aimed it at her bed, plugged it in a nearby outlet, and toggled it on. She swiped at her phone and selected the camera app she'd downloaded earlier. After a few moments, she managed to get the camera synced with her phone. The display bloomed to life on her screen. A video feed showed her standing in front of the camera, phone in hand.

Cate stepped aside and maneuvered the camera to have a view of most of the room. With the task complete, Cate toggled off her phone display and returned to the library.

The room was empty. Cate narrowed her eyes at the space before she retreated, heading down to the kitchen.

"Oh, hello, Lady Cate," Molly said. "What's up?"

"Are Riley and Bailey here?" Cate peered over the counter.

"Nope, not here."

"Hmm."

"Lost track of the little buggers?" Mrs. Fraser inquired.

"I did. I went upstairs after lunch and lost them some-where along the way. I thought they may have run down here to pester you ladies for a snack."

"No, haven't seen them."

"I'm surprised given that you made tomato basil soup. You know how Riley is about tomatoes. He can't get enough of them."

"That is so funny," Molly said with a chuckle. She wiped her hands on a dishtowel. "Did you want me to help you look for them?"

"No," Cate said. "They're around here somewhere, I'll find them."

"If you don't, let us know and we'll help you look," Mrs. Fraser offered. "Or better yet, get young Jack after them. Riley adores him."

"He really does," Cate said. "I'll let you know if I can't find them, but they couldn't have gotten too far."

"It's a big castle," Molly said with a shrug.

"Yeah, but a lot of it is closed off. Unless they've learned how to open doors."

"There's a scary thought," Mrs. Fraser chuckled.

"We'll find out!" Cate gave them a wave and headed back upstairs. She called the dogs as she walked, checking in the sitting room and the library again. With no sign of them, she ascended the stairs and retraced her steps to her bedroom. She found no sign of them there or along the way.

Cate scanned the hall outside her bedroom as she pondered where to look next. She bit her lower lip, forcing the growing panic down as it rose inside her.

"They couldn't have gotten far," Cate said to herself. Her mind spun in a thousand different directions. Had they found a hiding spot? Were they stuck somewhere? What if they were hurt?

Cate blew out a long breath. They were fine, she assured herself. The castle was huge. She could be missing them. They could be upstairs while she was down and downstairs while she was up. Maybe they climbed to the tower.

Cate roamed around to the tower stairs, continuing to call to them. She stared up the circular stone steps before she climbed them. The tower room door was closed at the top, but Cate still pushed it open and glanced around the space.

No dogs there. She returned to the hall below and descended the back stairs to the main floor.

"Riley! Bailey!" Cate shouted as she snaked through the halls.

She passed another hallway and glanced down its length. At the end, two large wooden doors led to an unused wing of the castle. She'd barely explored this area outside of a cursory walkthrough.

The doors were closed and locked; they couldn't have gotten into the other wing. Cate took another step to continue down the hallway before she backed up. She glanced at the doors again. Was there a crack of light between them? She'd never noticed that before.

Cate hurried down the hall toward the other wing. As she approached, it became obvious one of the doors stood ajar. Perhaps this explained the dogs' mysterious disappearance.

"Riley! Bailey!" Cate shouted as she approached the doors. She grasped the handle and began to swing the door open when two furry faces darted into the hallway. Riley wagged his feather-like tail as he stared up at her. Bailey offered a view of his bottom teeth in an awkward but heart-warming "smile."

"*There* you are!" Cate exclaimed. She placed her hands on her hips and stared down at the two pups. "Is this where you've been sneaking off to?" She glanced into the large hallway beyond the doors. "We're going to have to remind Jack to lock this! He must have left it open."

At the mention of Jack's name, Riley danced on his hind legs, his tail waving rapidly. "Yes, your friend, Jack, has given you some fun places to nose around, but not anymore!"

Cate grasped the doorknob and began to push the door shut. She stopped, her forehead wrinkling. She hesitated with the door still ajar. Something caught her attention. A familiar smell floated past her nostrils. She couldn't place it. Why would any smell other than mustiness be wafting from the closed-off wing?

CHAPTER 5

$\mathcal{C}$ate leaned into the wide hall past the doors and sniffed. Nothing more than stale air sailed through her nose. She straightened and pushed the door closed. She'd caught a whiff of something. But the scent was gone. What was it? And where had it come from?

She couldn't answer those questions. Instead, she opted to return to the library with her buddies to peruse the articles from Mrs. Campbell.

After returning to the library, Cate sank into the oversized leather armchair near the fireplace. She retrieved the folder of articles from the coffee table and flicked it open. Five pieces of paper spilled from it. She glanced at the empty interior searching for more. The minimal amount of results was a disappointing start to say the least.

The first article detailed a missing person's case from the 1970s in the neighboring town of Canberry. The write-up detailed a missing girl, aged eighteen, who disappeared from a local festival. Her absence was first reported by her younger sibling. The child, eight at the time, was found wandering around the festival alone. When asked where her older sister was, the child could not answer. She claimed the sister, named Evelyn, told her to wait near the carousel until her parents found her. The girl, however, was attracted by a large display of teddy bears and left the spot to explore the games. Other details at the time of writing were few.

Cate considered the story. Could a girl from Canberry end up buried in her garden? Perhaps, but by whom and why?

Cate flipped the page and found her hopes were dashed. The next article discussed Evelyn's return. After being found two towns away in the apartment of a man five years her senior, she had reluctantly returned to her parents' house. After a long questioning, Evelyn admitted she had not been abducted, but rather ran away with the man and intended to marry him.

Alive and well, at least at the time of the article's writing, Cate assumed she was not the woman buried on Dunhaven grounds.

She moved to the next article. A routine death in Dunhaven became a mystery when the body disappeared from the morgue. Seventy-two-year-old Duncan MacAllister died from a heart attack while dining alone in his home on 19 February 1958. While there was nothing mysterious about the manner in which he died, when his younger sister appeared at the morgue two weeks after his death to claim his body, she was informed the body was missing. She had been out of the country at the time of her brother's death and only learned of it upon her return.

An investigation was launched, but the body was not found. An obscure reference in the logbook showed an unintelligible name scrawled on 20 February. The attendant on duty recalled the man who collected Duncan's body to have said he was a cousin. The attendant could not recall the man's name nor any other details. The body was never found.

Could Duncan MacAllister have been the man buried? Why? Who would bring a dead body to Dunhaven, and for what purpose? Gertrude's mother, Mary, was the caretaker at the time. She couldn't have done it. Did someone on the property? If the bones turned out to be from a male, Cate decided she would ask Jack's grandfather about it.

She turned to the second to last article. Two tiny paragraphs skimmed over a story about a potential missing woman. Cate scanned it, noting a familiar name. Amelia MacKenzie, her great-grandmother, told the local press the woman, a traveling companion of hers, had merely left her employ. The reporter suggested the story to be more untoward, claiming the woman fled the castle in the middle of the night, though Amelia denied the allegation.

Cate set the article aside. As interesting as it may have been to the locals, she did not believe Amelia would lie to cover up any inappropriate behavior. Most likely, the local gossip mill had worked overtime, turning the small tidbit into an international story, just as they had with both Douglas and Randolph MacKenzie.

She skimmed the last article. This one showed some promise as a potential solution. A local man went missing in the 1840s. Evidence suggested the man may have fallen in with the wrong lot. An associate claimed he saw him leaving town, saying he preferred to lie low for a while. Still, others claimed he was a victim of "something strange at the castle." His disappearance was never resolved.

Molly flitted into the room carrying a tray laden with dinnertime goodies. "Mmm, is that pie?" Cate inquired. She shoved the copies into the folder and set it on the table.

"Yes, it is. Lemon meringue. Wanted to make good use of our lemons."

"I cannot wait to taste it. The lemon cookies are fantastic!"

"Thank you!" Molly said, beaming at the compliment. "Enjoy!"

"Thanks, you too!"

Molly flitted from the room. Cate dug into her dinner as she considered the articles. None of them offered any assistance in identifying the victim. The best option was the centuries-old unresolved disappearance. If the remains were identified as belonging to a male, they may be on to something.

With her meal finished, Cate gathered her tray and headed down to the kitchen.

"The pie was excellent," she announced as she entered.

"Oh, thanks, Lady Cate!" Molly said, as she leapt from her seat to grab the tray. "You didn't have to carry this down."

"It's fine, I needed to stretch my legs."

"Any articles identify the uninvited garden guest?" Mrs. Fraser inquired.

"Not really. There weren't many and there was no smoking gun, that's for sure."

"I'm not surprised," Mrs. Fraser answered. "I told you not much happens in Dunhaven. I cannae even begin to guess who that may be!"

"We may never know," Cate said with a shrug. "Though I hope we find out. Oh, Jack, before I forget, the door to the unused west wing is unlocked."

Jack's brow furrowed as he took another bite of his pie. "Really?" he inquired.

"Yeah. That's where the dogs disappeared to, probably both times."

Jack set down his fork and pushed his plate away. He stood, withdrawing a set of keys from his pocket. "I'll go lock it now."

"I'll walk you up," Cate said.

They climbed the stairs to the main floor. Jack rustled through the keys. "I'm not sure how this happened. I didn't unlock that door recently."

"You must have forgotten to lock it the last time you were in there," Cate said with a shrug.

Jack shook his head. "No, I never forget to lock it. In fact, I remember locking it. I went in there three weeks ago and I distinctly remember locking it."

"Wow, good memory," Cate said.

"Don't credit me too much, Lady Cate. I remember locking it because the damned key got stuck and I cursed it while I tried to jiggle it loose."

Cate raised her eyebrows. "Maybe your curse turned it into a magical door that opens and closes on its own."

Jack gave Cate a sour look. "I'm not magical like our friends across the pond."

"Maybe they enchanted it," Cate said with a chuckle as they reached the doors.

Jack studied them. "You're sure these were open?"

"Yep," Cate said. "Both dogs came running out."

Jack shoved a key in the lock and turned it. He jiggled the doorknob and waved a hand at it. "There we are," he said. "Locked. With you as my witness."

Cate nodded. "Thanks, Jack."

"So, nothing in those articles?"

Cate shook her head and shrugged. "No. One of them was a girl from Canberry who resurfaced – turns out she was with a boyfriend. Another was a man who had a heart attack, and his body went missing from the morgue. But there's no reason to believe someone brought him here. The third was a woman who was presumed missing. It was during World War II, and Amelia said she simply left. The only possible lead is a man in the 1840s who disappeared."

"He sounds like our best lead."

Cate nodded. "And it's tenuous at best."

"Aye. Well, maybe the police will have some information for us."

"Let's hope so," Cate said.

"Well, good night, Lady Cate."

"Good night."

Cate returned to the library for the rest of the evening. She re-read the articles, finding nothing new. After spending some time with a novel, she corralled the dogs upstairs to her bedroom.

Cate bit her lower lip as she stared at the small cube on the dresser in the corner of the room. She licked her lips as her finger hovered on the power button. Perhaps this wasn't a good idea.

She pulled her hand away. It wouldn't hurt, however creepy it seemed to have a video of her sleeping.

"All right, boys," she said, as she crawled between the sheets. "Let's see how much you two walk around at night." She laughed nervously as she shot a glance toward the camera.

Cate flicked the light off and slouched further down the bed, relaxing into her pillows. The blue light glowed across the room. Cate stared at the pinpoint of color. As she pondered what she'd see on the camera the next morning, she drifted off to sleep.

Cate awoke the next morning as her alarm sounded. With a groan, she rolled over and turned it off. She opened her eyes and found Riley staring at her. "Hey, buddy," she said with a yawn. "Sleep well?"

As she stretched, she uncurled her fist. The sapphire necklace dropped from her hand to the duvet below with a thump. Cate sucked in a deep breath as she sat up. She ruffled the fur on Riley's head. "I see we had another active night. I guess I'll find out more when I review my camera footage."

Riley side-eyed Cate as he yawned. "I'm not looking forward to it either, buddy."

Bailey climbed to his feet, stretching, and sitting next to Cate. She gave him a good morning pet before she climbed from her bed and headed into the bathroom for her morning routine.

Cate glanced at her phone several times. It beeped often, alerting her to movement in the room. Each time she considered watching the video feed, her mouth went dry, and her heart skipped a beat. She had no recollection of retrieving the necklace, yet she held it in her hand when she awoke. At some point in the middle of the night, she must have climbed from her bed to retrieve it.

Cate put off the task of watching the video until after she ate her breakfast and took a long walk around the property with the dogs. As she settled in the library with a warm cup of tea, Cate stared at her phone. She blew out a long breath. "Okay, Cate," she whispered to herself. "All you're going to see is you wandering to the jewelry box and getting the necklace. It can't be that bad."

Cate toggled on her phone and selected the app. She had several alerts. Many of them were from her waking hours. She scrolled through the list, finding a timestamp shortly before midnight.

Cate pursed her lips and tapped the button to access the video feed. The video began with Cate sitting in bed. The camera must have detected her sitting up and toggled on. On the video, Cate stared ahead, motionless. After a moment, she peeled back the covers and swung her legs over the side of the bed.

She stood, gawking blindly ahead. After a moment, the video showed Cate shambling forward. Her arms hung limply at her sides as she wandered across the room. She stopped at the jewelry armoire.

With unmoving eyes, Cate reached down until her fingers struck the drawer pull. She slid it open and grasped the sapphire necklace from the velvet interior. Pushing the drawer shut, she straightened, clutching the necklace closer to her chest.

Cate watched as her video counterpart stood still for another moment before she began her slow trek across the room.

On the video, Cate paused at the doors leading to her sitting room. Her head swiveled toward them. Cate's brow crinkled and she squinted at her face on the screen, green from the night vision. On-screen, her forehead wrinkled.

"What was I staring at?" Cate whispered.

As if on cue, her video doppelgänger's lips moved. Cate dropped the phone into her lap as her jaw unhinged.

CHAPTER 6

$\mathcal{C}$ate swallowed hard and recovered the phone, which now showed her continuing on her journey back to bed.

Cate pulled the video's counter back. Her former self sped backward. She played the video again from the spot where she'd stopped at the sitting room doors. Cate stared at the video as her image's lips moved.

Cate rewound again. She squinted at her lips, trying to make out the word. She tried five times before she gave up.

Cate clicked off her phone's display and set it on the desk. She bit her lower lip as she considered the video. Was someone in the other room? Who? What had she seen or heard while sleepwalking?

Cate spent a few more moments ruminating about the source of her speech in the video. A chime from her phone drew her back from the maze of her thoughts.

Did you get rid of that necklace?

Cate smiled at the text from Damien.

I'm working on it, she responded.

His response was delayed a moment. After five minutes, a new text appeared on her screen. *Hmmm... any nightmares?*

Cate responded with a "no" and a smiley emoticon.

That's good news! Damien messaged.

After a moment, he added: *Don't think I won't ask about that necklace again.*

Cate laughed at his message. *I'm counting on it. How are things on your side of the pond?*

Damien responded: *I'm pretty sure I could write another book about our current adventure.*

The comment elicited another chuckle from Cate, and she sent him a laughing emoji before turning her attention to her research. Before long, her focus shifted to the folder with the five articles detailing disappearances in the Dunhaven area.

Cate shuffled across the library and retrieved it. She re-read each article twice more but found no new clues to help her. Perhaps she could use these articles as a springboard for more research. She collected them and returned to her laptop.

She shuffled through and found the article about the disappearance in 1840. Cate scanned the story's details. With a fresh page in her notebook, she jotted down several key pieces of information. The man, named Angus Williams, had moved to the tiny town of Dunhaven ten years earlier. He'd been taken on to work at the Bailey farm and had stayed in his position for the entire decade he'd lived in Dunhaven. Most described him as quiet. Cate noted the dates of his arrival and departure.

A local told the reporter covering the story that Angus had been gambling and made a few enemies. He stated he'd seen the man with a sack tossed over his shoulder, walking out of town. When he spoke with him, Angus told him it was best he leave town for a while.

He was never seen or heard from again. Cate typed his name into the search bar of her browser. It wasn't an uncommon name, making most of the results she found useless. She tried to track down more information by adding Dunhaven to the search. It produced no results.

Cate searched for a more obscure result trying "1841 missing man Dunhaven." She found nothing, not even the article produced by Mrs. Campbell.

She was at a dead-end. If they wanted more information about Mr. Williams, they'd have to travel back to 1841 to get it, she mused. She wouldn't be opposed to the trip, though she was certain Jack would be.

Still, she understood his concern, and if the body buried in her backyard did not belong to Angus Williams, there was no reason to visit that time period.

Cate tried a few extra ill-fated searches before she determined this line of work was a dead end. Her lunch arrived and she abandoned the nonproductive task in favor of eating.

Her phone chimed. A message from Jack awaited her.

Anything from the police?

Not yet, she wrote back.

Jack sent back a straight-face emoji with the message: *Hopefully soon!*

Cate sent a message indicating agreement. Her mind turned from her fruitless search to her odd overnight behavior. Her thumb hovered over the cell phone's power button. After a moment, she swung it over to the screen and tapped to bring up the video. She viewed it several times, still not able to determine what her on-screen self muttered before wandering back to bed.

Cate sighed as she allowed her phone display to time out. Two nights in a row, she had climbed from her bed to retrieve that necklace. What drew her to it? And what caught her attention during her trance-like state?

Perhaps she should take everyone's advice and get rid of the necklace. She bit her lower lip as her stomach fluttered at the thought. Why was she so adamantly opposed to the idea? Was it the mere value of the object that held her back? It must have been. The necklace had to be worth hundreds of thousands of dollars, or rather pounds. This must be the reason for her reluctance, she attempted to convince herself.

The shrill ringing of her phone pulled Cate from her ruminating. An unknown number appeared on her display. Cate considered leaving it go to voicemail. Her finger hovered over the Decline icon.

She shook her head, realizing it may be the police with information about her latest discovery on the property. With a flick of her finger, Cate swiped the Accept button and pressed the phone to her ear.

"Cate Kensie," she said.

"Hi, Lady Cate," Ben's voice answered her.

"Oh, hi, Ben!" she said.

"I figured I'd give you a call and go over some of the information we've come up with on your unwanted garden guest."

"You found something?" Cate asked, as she scurried to the desk and shuffled through her drawer for a sheet of paper and a pen.

"Not really, but we do have some information."

"Oh," Cate answered, the disappointment in her voice obvious.

"I figured I'd pass it along before you called me to ask. I ran into Jackie this morning and he assured me you'd be after me for information."

"He's correct," Cate said, sinking into her desk chair.

"Okay, here goes." She heard a few papers shuffle, before

the detective's voice took on the monotone sound of someone reading the words from a page. "Uh, the vic was… oh that's victim to you as a layperson, Lady Cate."

"Yes, thank you, I realized," Cate said, as she bobbed her head around in an unseen signal for him to get to the point.

"Oh, great. Big true crime fan, huh? Well, anyway, the bones of the victim belong to a female. Adult. On the smaller side, probably about five foot three or four, give or take.

"Uh…" He paused as he shuffled his papers again. "Let's see here. Nothing definitive on age yet but the examiner puts a rough estimate at seventy to eighty years or so, again, give or take."

Cate scrunched her face. "The bones belonged to someone who was seventy to eighty years old?"

"Oh." Ben chuckled before continuing. "No, no, not the age of the vic. The age of the bones. The examiner figures them to have been in the ground for about seventy to eighty years."

"Ohhhh," Cate said as realization dawned on her. She jotted down on her paper: *Adult female, 5'4", 70-80 years ago.*

"Right now, that's about all we have."

"Did the medical examiner determine a cause of death?" Cate queried.

Papers rustled. "Ah, yeah." Another pause. "Blunt force trauma to the head. Skull was cracked and collapsed."

Cate winced at the detail, her stomach rolling.

"Could that have happened postmortem?" Cate said, hope lacing her voice.

"No," Ben answered immediately. "M.E.'s certain it was the cause of death, not postmortem damage."

Cate sighed.

"That's about it, then. Unless you have anything else, Lady Cate…"

"Actually," Cate said, interrupting him. "I was wondering if this coincided with any open cases you had on the books."

"Eh, what do you mean?" Ben inquired.

"Well, you know this was a female from about seventy-five years ago."

"Give or take," he said.

"Right. Were there any missing persons cases opened around that time that could help identify the victim?"

"Oh, ah, right. No, nothing."

"You did go back through the records, didn't you?"

"We did. There were no unsolved cases in Dunhaven from that time."

"So what are our next steps?"

"Well, you have no other next steps, Lady Cate. I will widen my net, see if we can identify this person. Obviously, we won't have DNA on file that could help, but I'll dig deeper to see if there's a missing person who fits the bill in the nearby area."

"Please let me know if you find anything."

"I will do that, Lady Cate," Ben said.

"Great, thank you so much for the information."

"You're welcome, and you have a great rest of your day."

They finished with parting pleasantries and Cate ended the call. She sighed as she stared down at the mostly blank page in front of her. One solitary line graced the top.

Cate reviewed what few details she had gleaned. She added the cause of death to the information, grimacing again as she wrote it.

She realized the information shared by Ben meant her top theory – that the deceased was Angus Williams – was now dashed by the revelation that the body belonged to a woman.

Cate flipped open the folder of articles from Mrs. Campbell.

The missing eighteen-year-old from Canberry was now more likely given her gender, however, she had been found, which ruled her out. Duncan MacAllister, Dunhaven's disappearing corpse, could also be eliminated based on his gender, as could Angus Williams. Which left Cate with only one option. The missing woman with whom Amelia was acquainted.

Cate re-read the article again, noting the date. The date 23 September, 1942, topped the copy of the newspaper article.

Not trusting herself to do the calculation in her mind, Cate used her cell phone's calculator. She stared at the result. The date was seventy-eight years ago. It fit within the time frame Ben had given her.

Could this woman be the one they'd just exhumed from her side garden?

* * *

Cate awoke the next morning exhausted. As sun streamed through her window, she rolled over with a groan. Clutched in her hand for the third morning was the sapphire necklace.

The appearance of the necklace surprised her since she didn't think she'd gotten enough sleep to have sleepwalked.

Cate had spent most of her previous night tossing and turning as she considered the lack of information about their garden guest. Who could she have been? Would they ever find out? The span of a decade was a long time. She and Jack couldn't search the entire time period for clues about the woman.

As Cate rose from her bed and returned the necklace to its drawer, her mind raced through the same questions it had the previous night.

The lack of information stumped her. Surely a missing

person's report existed for this person. Perhaps they were casting too narrow of a net. Perhaps she'd traveled from somewhere further than the towns in the small radius around Dunhaven.

That explanation could be easily remedied by considering a larger net around the town when searching for missing persons cases ranging from 1940 to 1950. Surely with that date range and a larger search area they'd come across something to explain the body.

Another notion occurred to her. What if the body belonged to someone who had never been reported missing? Cate had assumed the person would be missed by a loved one. However, what if the killer was the loved one? Could a jealous husband have offed his wife, buried her at Dunhaven and then told a tale that his wife had run off?

Cate hated to admit it, but it was plausible. And it meant their search would be all the more difficult. With a sigh, she attempted to determine a method for tracking down a missing person who had never been considered missing.

* * *

As Cate strolled around the property following breakfast with the pups, her mind stretched for solutions. She came to none as she approached her favorite spot on the property. Jack stood near the water.

"Hey, what are you doing here?" Cate called to him as he stood under the large tree on its banks.

The dogs raced ahead to give Jack a hearty hello.

"Lady Cate! What are you doing here?" he asked, his eyes wide with surprise.

"Uh," Cate hesitated as she formulated a response to the question, "I always come here."

"But I didn't think you'd be here this morning."

Cate furrowed her brow. Jack was acting a bit strange, she thought. Why?

"Everything okay? You seem… distracted." She noticed his hands hidden behind his back. "What are you hiding there?"

"Hiding? Nothing. I'm not hiding anything." He chuckled nervously as he slipped his hand into his pocket.

Cate offered a confused smile. "Anyway, as I said, I'm surprised you're here and not breathing down Ben's neck about who our garden guest is… or was."

"Oh, I heard from him yesterday, though it didn't seem to help much in identifying the person."

"Oh?" Jack inquired.

"Yeah, I didn't want to bring it up at dinner last night. But Ben called me yesterday afternoon. He said they determined the bones belonged to a female, about five foot four in height. On first inspection, it appears the bones had been buried for seventy to eighty years. And the cause of death was blunt force trauma to the skull."

Jack winced before he nodded. "Do they have any leads?"

"Not a one," Cate said, with a wistful expression. "I went through the articles from Mrs. Campbell, but none of those were helpful."

"Not even a hint of a lead?"

Cate paused for a moment, her face scrunching in thought.

"What is that famous Cate Kensie brain mulling over?"

"Nothing," Cate said. "The only lead I had went up in smoke when Ben said the corpse was female. There was a man in the 1840s who left town. Some people believe he was murdered. I thought perhaps he was our victim, but obviously, he's not."

"He also doesn't fit within the time frame they gave for when the bones were from."

"No," Cate said, as she tapped her lips in thought.

"Is there something else?"

"Not really."

"Not really means something is on your mind."

"There was one article from around that time period. In 1942, a woman went missing. However, Amelia said she merely left for another position. So, it's not much of a lead and apparently the girl wasn't even really missing."

"Amelia, as in your great-grandmother, Amelia?

"Yep."

Jack puckered his lips as his head bounced around. "And it's not likely Amelia would lie. At least, we have no reason to believe so."

"No. She was nothing but honest with us when we met her."

"But?" Jack asked.

Cate shook her head. "But nothing. She probably isn't our gal. We may never know who it was."

"Cate Kensie giving up? I can't believe my ears."

Cate shrugged. "I was up most of the night. Outside of expanding our radius for missing persons reports in the 1940s to 1950s and getting a hit there, we may be dealing with someone who was never reported missing."

"You mean like someone killed them then told a different story to anyone who asked?"

"Right. Maybe a jealous spouse whacks his wife on the head, then tells everyone she ran off with the neighbor or something similar. Which makes it impossible for us to track."

Jack nodded. "That it does."

Cate sighed and they stood in silence for a few moments.

"Well, I suppose the only way to get any answers might be to discuss it with people from that era," Jack said.

Cate crinkled her forehead and glanced up sharply at Jack. "Are you saying…"

"Yes, I'm saying maybe we should do a little time traveling so we can solve this."

Cate stood in stunned silence, her jaw hanging open.

"Yes, I am suggesting time travel."

Cate's eyebrows raised toward her hairline.

"Oh, stop gawking at me and just tell me how much you appreciate my suggestion."

Cate giggled and offered him a smile. "I really do appreciate it," she answered. "But now my mind is spinning in a thousand different directions. Where do we start? With whom?"

"Perhaps Amelia is a good place to start. We know Rory and Anne, Amelia and Lucas. Get the dates from that article and we'll start there. If they have no leads, we'll go forward a couple of years and try again."

"Look at you, Jack Reid! Skipping through time!"

"After what we witnessed in the 1700s, I guess I'm ready to live a little."

"Well, I am pleasantly surprised and very pleased by your suggestion! I'll get the information from the article and try to find anything else that may help. When do you want to go?"

"How's Monday?" Jack suggested.

"Sounds perfect! That'll give me some time to dig up some information so we can tackle this!"

"Sounds like a plan. Well, I'll leave you to your loch. M'lady." Jack gave her an extravagant bow before he retreated toward the castle.

Cate sank to the ground below. Both dogs gathered around her. "Well, what do you think, boys? Do we stand a chance solving this mystery?"

Riley cocked his head to the side and stared at Cate. Bailey offered his paw. "I'll take that as a vote of your confidence!"

Cate spent another thirty minutes staring out over the

loch and watching the clouds meander through the sky. When she became chilled, Cate stood and brushed herself off. "Come on, boys, let's head back and do some work."

Cate, Riley, and Bailey took a winding path back to the castle, pushing through the front door into the enormous foyer. The dogs raced away as they entered the castle. Cate flung her hands out. "Now where are you two going?"

With a roll of her eyes and a shake of her head, Cate navigated to the library. She sighed as she collapsed into the desk chair. She glanced to the folder of articles on the desk as she removed her phone from her pocket.

Her eyes lingered on the cell phone. After a moment, Cate illuminated the display and swiped at the screen to access the cube camera's app. A colorful circle spun around the screen as Cate waited for the list of recent videos to load. She bit her thumbnail wondering what she would find. She assumed the list would be long since she'd spent a large portion of the night tossing and turning.

The screen darkened for a moment before a list of videos filled it. Cate sucked in a breath as she scrolled through the list. She deleted any before midnight since she had definitely been awake through those, and she had no inclination to watch herself toss and turn in bed.

Cate tapped the first video available after midnight. She viewed the short clip of her rolling from one side to the other before smashing her pillow into a ball and squeezing her eyes shut.

She clicked the trash can icon to delete the less-than-useful video. She moved on to the next to find a similar episode replaying on the screen. With a sigh, Cate trashed it along with the third video.

She tapped the next one listed. Occurring just after two in the morning, Cate stared at her sleeping self. Her eyebrows lifted as her on-screen self's eyes shot open. Two eerily lit, glassy balls stared at the ceiling before she slowly rose to a sitting position. Staring straight ahead, her form peeled back the covers and swung her legs over the side of the bed. She hesitated a moment before standing and shambling to the jewelry armoire.

As usual, the video version of Cate pulled the lower drawer open and retrieved the ostentatious necklace. She clutched it in her hand, holding it close to her chest as she wandered back across the room. She froze in front of the doors leading to the sitting room.

Cate tapped at the screen, wondering if the video was frozen as her counterpart stood stock still. Still playing, the video showed her frozen for several seconds, before her head whipped in the direction of the sitting room.

Cate bit her lower lip as she squinted her eyes at the scene unfolding on her phone's display. On-screen, Cate's lips curled into a partial smile, and she reached her hand toward the sitting room. A moment later, she disappeared from the camera's view.

Cate's heart pounded in her chest as she watched herself disappear from view. The video clip ended, and Cate shook her head as she hurried back to the list of videos.

She tapped on the next video. The timestamp indicated it occurred about twenty minutes after the one she'd just viewed. Cate watched the short clip of Riley stretching before he settled back down into a ball with a sigh.

Outside of Riley and Bailey, the large bed remained empty. She'd disappeared in the wee hours of the morning for more than twenty minutes.

Another video occurring about thirty-five minutes after her disappearance appeared next. Cate played it. A shadow crossed the bed and within seconds, Cate's wandering form reappeared on camera. Still carrying the necklace, she crossed the room and climbed into bed, pulling the covers over her and drifting off to sleep.

Cate toggled off her phone's display as she let her gaze drift out the window. Where had she been for thirty-five minutes? What or whom had she smiled at before she disappeared? She shuddered as a chill passed over her. What was happening to her?

CHAPTER 7

The arrival of her lunch roused Cate from her pensive state. She'd made little progress on determining where she may have roamed to in the wee hours of the morning. And she'd done absolutely nothing regarding gathering information on the lead Jack suggested they follow about the garden guest.

Cate slumped into the armchair as she poked at the food on her plate. She eyed her cell phone warily, as though it caused the disruption overnight. The flames leapt in the fireplace across from her, catching Cate's attention. The dogs had returned from wherever they'd raced off to as she worked her way through the videos and were now snuggled near the warm fire.

An idea formed in her mind as she polished off the last bites of her meal. A smile spread across her face, and she sat up straighter. "What do you say we take a trip into town, boys?"

Riley perked up when Cate asked again, this time mentioning the car. After Molly retrieved her lunch tray, she headed to the car with both pups and drove the short distance into town, finding a parking space near the town's center. She took a leisurely stroll through the streets, allowing the dogs to explore even though she had one destination in mind.

They reached their target and Cate ushered the dogs inside.

"Well, Lady Cate!" Harry greeted her. "Back again so soon? And with the two laddies this time. Hello, boys." Harry rounded the counter and offered two treats to each dog. They scarfed them down in seconds.

"I figured I owed the boys a visit," Cate answered.

"Aye, I missed them last time."

Harry squatted down to give both dogs a hearty ear scratch.

"Did you get your camera set up?"

"I did," Cate replied. "I actually came in to purchase another one. It works like a charm, and I'd like to set a few more up."

"Oh? Well, we've got plenty in stock," Harry said. He straightened and grabbed another from the display.

"And do you happen to have any of those cameras that hang from a dog's collar?"

"We do," Harry said. He wandered across the store and pulled an item from a hanger. "Dogs running off on you?"

"Not really," Cate said. "But it's a big place and I'd like to see what they do when they're not lounging in front of a fireplace."

"Well, this'll do it," Harry said, waving the packaging in the air. "Did you want one or two?"

Cate considered it. "I'll take the one for now," she answered. "So far, I think they're sticking together. If I find out otherwise, I may be back."

Henry nodded and rang up the purchase. "Which one of you nice laddies is going to be the volunteer for this?"

"Probably Riley. Bailey gets a bit fussy about clothes and collars. He won't move very far if he has to wear a tie or a shirt."

"Oh? Do you mind your clothes, Bailey?" The little dog wagged his pigtail at the mention of his name. "But not you, eh, Riley?" Riley cocked his head.

"No, Riley enjoys dressing up," Cate said with a chuckle.

"No wonder," Harry said, eyeing Riley. "You looked very dapper at the Christmas party, young sir."

Riley cocked his head at Harry and gave a small yip. "I agree," Harry said.

Cate raised her eyebrows.

"The laddie says he looked so fine he deserves another treat," Harry explained.

Cate chuckled. "Oh, I'll bet he did."

Harry bagged Cate's purchases and gave another treat to the two dogs before they said their goodbyes. "Now you two behave yourselves. Your mam has a way to keep an eye on you now."

"Listen up, boys," Cate said, "I can follow you wherever you go!"

After a few moments of small talk, Cate left the shop with her purchases. She found herself both excited and frightened. The prospect of seeing who or what was beyond her bedroom in the middle of the night was daunting, however, being able to follow the dogs to their secret spot could prove fun.

After a brief walk through town, she returned to the castle. Cate spent the remaining time before dinner setting up her additional camera in her sitting room. When she had it finished and set on the mantle to capture both the door to her bedroom and the door to the hall, she stepped back and stared at it.

"What will you show me, I wonder?" she said aloud. Two

tiny feet pressed against her thigh. Cate glanced down to find Riley standing on his hind legs. Bailey stood next to him. "Don't worry, I'll save your camera setup until tomorrow. You're off the hook."

Riley's tail waved back and forth. Cate scooped him into her arms and wandered to the chaise. Bailey jumped up next to her and she pulled him onto her lap. She balanced both dogs on her legs as she pondered what she might find on her video list tomorrow morning.

With no answers forthcoming, she left her room behind in favor of the library for her dinner. When she returned, she eyed the new camera warily. She bypassed it, trying to push it out of her mind as she continued to her bedroom.

As she slipped between the sheets, she focused on the blue light shining at her. She swallowed hard and closed her eyes.

* * *

Cate stretched as her Sunday morning alarm beeped. With an hour's extra sleep on her staff's day off, the sun was already beginning its ascent into the morning sky, painting it deep shades of purple and red.

Cate reached her arms overhead, uncurling her fingers. She glanced toward her headboard. Her hands were empty. No necklace lay discarded on her pillow. She glanced at her sides, finding nothing. The fleeting idea that she had remained abed for the entire night flitted across her mind.

The hope was short-lived as Cate pushed herself to sit, feeling something shift on her neck. She glanced down, reaching to her collarbone.

Her fingers caressed the thick gemstones comprising the necklace. Cate's heart sank. Not only had she arisen from her bed and retrieved the necklace, but in this instance, she had donned it during her sleepwalking escapades.

Cate reached to the nape of her neck and worked to unclasp the necklace. She pursed her lips as she stared down at it after freeing it from her neck. She shook her head. What would the cameras show her? She wasn't certain she wanted to find out what they'd caught.

She put it off, electing for breakfast and a morning walk. As she settled in at her desk in the library for a check of her email, Molly popped her head in.

"Hey, Lady Cate!"

"Hi, Molly. Going to join me for some reading on your day off?"

"Nope, I'm heading out. I just wanted to see if you wanted to come with me."

"Where to?"

"I'm going to head to…" Molly paused as she consulted a marked page in her tour guide. "Fyvie Castle. It's a bit of a drive, but I'm up for it!"

Cate glanced at her laptop and took a deep breath. "Well, I had planned…" She stopped short and narrowed her eyes. She twisted to face Molly. "To heck with what I planned! Sure, I'd love to go with you. As long as you're driving."

"Still worried you're going to drive on the wrong side?" Molly asked with a laugh.

"Something like that. Also, I'm terrible at following those GPS things."

"I'd be happy to drive."

Cate glanced at the bag sitting next to the desk. "Would you mind giving me a few minutes to set up this camera?"

"Sure! I'm in no rush! What is it?"

"A pet camera. It goes on your pet's collar, and you can see what they're up to and where they're going."

"Oh, neat!" Molly said. "Worried the boys will get up to something naughty when we're gone?"

"Mmm, no," Cate said, as she pulled the camera from the

package along with the instructions. "Just curious as to what they get up to."

"Oh, gotcha."

"Let me run up and grab Riley's bowtie collar to slip this on."

"Okay, I'll read the instructions."

Cate hurried up the stairs and dug through Riley's things in her bedroom, retrieving his plaid bowtie. When she returned to the library, Molly had the camera in setup mode. With her help, Cate connected it to her phone's app. She slipped it onto the collar and snapped it around Riley's neck.

"All right, boys. Behave yourselves! Molly and I will be back later!"

With kisses on their furry heads, Cate and Molly headed out to the car for the drive to Fyvie Castle.

"So, have you been to Fyvie Castle before?" Molly asked, as she aimed the car toward Dunhaven.

"No," Cate answered. "I haven't done much traveling. We came straight to Dunhaven with Mr. Smythe, and I never left."

"Lady Cate, seriously?" Molly inquired. "You've lived in this amazing country for almost a year, and you've never gone further than Dunhaven?"

"I'm not very adventurous," Cate said. "Driving around in a foreign country is a little overwhelming to me."

"Not me! You couldn't hold me back!"

Cate chuckled. "I don't intend to! Though, on a serious note, I am glad you are enjoying the country so much."

"Oh, I am! And now I can strong-arm you into enjoying it, too!"

"I do enjoy it! I enjoy Dunhaven Castle and its grounds. And it's even got a loch. What more could I ask for?"

"It's still nice to see other things. Oh, speaking of lochs – how about a trip to Loch Ness?"

"That's quite a bit further than Fyvie," Cate responded.

"It is, but not *that* far!"

"I guess compared to some of the drives across the pond, it is relatively close," Cate answered.

As they fell into silence, Cate checked her phone.

"Are the dogs exploring?" Molly questioned.

"Nope," Cate answered. "Those two lazy boys are lounging in the library."

"Sounds about right."

Cate clicked off the display and returned to enjoying the scenery. As the trip progressed, she and Molly discussed the Scottish countryside, castles, Molly's move, and Scottish cuisine.

Molly followed the signs for Fyvie Castle as they approached. They drove down a narrow street lined with box hedges. Molly slowed as they reached the entrance where a green sign announced Fyvie Castle & Garden.

The car passed through the open black iron gates between two stone pillars. They continued up the winding road.

"Look, Lady Cate!" Molly said, pointing out her window. "They've got a loch, too!"

"So they have," Cate replied. "I think Dunhaven's loch beats this one."

Molly chuckled. "But they've got ducks!"

"They can keep the ducks. Riley and Bailey would have a field day chasing those poor things around if we had them."

Molly continued up the road. The paved portion gave way to a gravel drive, reminding Cate of her own driveway. Molly navigated to the car park.

The large, beige, stone structure rose in front of them as they walked through the garden to the castle entrance. Cate glanced out across the flat grounds. It was so different from Dunhaven's rolling hills.

After paying the entrance fee, they began their self-tour of the castle's interior. They wandered through the ornately decorated rooms one after another.

"Hmmm," Molly murmured about halfway through their tour, "I think I prefer Dunhaven."

Cate smiled. "I'm glad. And to be honest, so do I!"

"It's beautiful here but…"

"It's not home."

"No, and that hallway with the huge tapestry is kind of tight. As is this bed." Molly grimaced at a rather uncomfortable-looking four-poster bed.

"Well, now that we're sure we've cornered the market on castles compared to Fyvie, should we head outdoors for a walk?" Cate suggested.

"Absolutely. And we'll stop in the tearoom before we leave for a nice meal before heading home."

Cate answered with a nod as her phone chimed. Molly raised an eyebrow, but didn't pry.

"Oh, it's an alert from the doggie cam," Cate said, as she tapped the notification.

"On the move?"

"Probably stretching," Cate said with a laugh, as they exited the castle into the bright sunshine.

The camera loaded and Cate stared at the screen. An awkward bobbling video played on the screen.

"Still in the library?" Molly inquired, as she peered over Cate's shoulder.

"No," Cate said, "I don't think so." Her brow furrowed as she attempted to make out the image on the screen.

"Wow, this is harder than I expected."

"Yeah," Cate admitted. "I don't see things from floor level so I'm really having trouble figuring out where they are."

"Oh, there's Bailey!" Molly said, pointing at the furry form jetting past Riley on the screen.

"Where's he in such a hurry to go?"

The camera darkened as Riley put his nose to the ground, tilting the lens toward the floor. The angle snapped upward before abruptly changing directions to race down a hallway.

"What was that?" Cate inquired.

"What?"

"When the camera angle changed from the floor view, I saw something."

"What did it look like?"

Cate shook her head, staring off into space.

"What? Furniture leg? Wall?"

Cate pursed her lips, before she said, "No. It looked like a person's feet."

"What?" Molly asked, slowing to a stop as Cate continued to stare at her screen.

"It looked like someone's feet and legs."

"It couldn't be."

"No, unless…"

"Unless what?"

Cate tapped around on her phone. "Unless Jack's at the castle. That would explain their sudden urgency to run around. I'm texting him now."

"Oh, yeah, that could be it."

They wandered around the property as Cate waited for a response. Cate's phone chimed as they strolled past the loch. She stopped mid-stride.

"What?" Molly asked.

"He's not there." Cate snapped her gaze up to Molly's face.

Molly winced, then shook her head. "Wait. No one could be there."

"No one *should* be there."

"No one can be, right? Who would be there?"

"I'm not sure, but I swear I saw someone's legs."

"Do you want to head back?"

Cate pressed her lips together as she gazed over the water. She swiped her phone open and accessed the pet cam app. Her eyebrows raised. "Well, it looks like they're back in the library, lounging by the fireplace."

Molly nodded and gave Cate a closed-lipped smile.

"So, I guess we're good!"

"We can go if you want…"

"No," Cate said, with a shake of her head. "I probably saw something else entirely, like a table leg or something. I'm not ruining our trip. They seem fine. And if someone was in the castle, I don't think they'd be lounging in the library."

"No, they'd be barking at the top of their lungs."

"Yep," Cate said with a chuckle. "So, let's keep enjoying the scenery, and then I believe you promised me a trip to the tearoom."

"I did indeed!"

They wandered around the property, taking in all the sites along with several pictures and selfies, ending their meandering at the tearoom for sandwiches and indulging in dessert. The trip wasn't complete without a stop in the gift shop. Molly made a few purchases before they strolled to the car to return to Dunhaven.

* * *

"Well, that was a nice trip," Cate said, as they climbed from the car back on the grounds of Dunhaven.

"Yeah, it was!" Molly agreed. "I'll make a traveler out of you yet."

"Oh? Got another castle trip planned already?"

"Give me the week to figure it out. I've got an entire list for us to get through, and now with the weather improving, I'm going to hold you to that promise to explore Scotland with me!"

"Okay," Cate laughed.

"I've even got some dog-friendly spots for us."

"I'm sure the dogs will love you for that."

They pushed through the front door of the castle. Both dogs plowed toward them, leaping up on their hind legs as they excitedly wagged their tails.

"Well," Molly said, as she knelt down to greet the dogs, "everything looks okay."

Cate nodded. "I must have been seeing things."

"I doubt that. I just think things look so different from their perspective that it was easy to think that's what it looked like."

"Well, how about a nice walk, boys?" Cate asked.

"Whew, I'm beat from walking, so I'll leave you to it. I'm going up to make a plan for the summer months for us using my guidebooks!" Molly flashed her a grin.

Cate returned the expression. "I'll look forward to seeing your proposal."

After removing Riley's bowtie, she ushered the two dogs out into the late afternoon air, allowing them to frolic as the sun marched toward the horizon. The two pups wrestled around on the ground before darting off to chase each other around the grass.

Cate stared at the camera she'd shoved in her cardigan pocket as she allowed the dogs some time to run. What had she seen on the camera that she'd mistaken for someone's legs?

Table legs didn't make sense. It looked like shoes and pants, not wood. The glimpse had been fleeting; perhaps she's misconstrued it. Though, with no expectation of someone being in the castle, she couldn't imagine she had concocted the image in her mind.

She scrolled to the footage on her phone and replayed the video. She paused it when the supposed person appeared. It looked like a blur on her screen. Cate played that portion of the video five more times. She couldn't make anything out. The scene played out too fast to be certain of anything.

With a sigh, Cate clicked her phone off and returned to watching the dogs play. Her mind listed the things she needed to do before she turned in for the night. One of the tasks was to watch the camera footage from her two cube cameras. She dreaded it.

She allowed the dogs as much time as they wanted, putting off making any discoveries of her overnight excursions. When the chill in the air finally drove them in, Cate settled in the library. She shoved her phone aside, deciding to summarize the information from the news clipping on the missing woman from 1942.

Cate noted the article was written in late September. The woman, named Ruth Harper, had not been seen in several days. She had traveled to Dunhaven Castle as a companion to Amelia MacKenzie. The servants reported they had not seen her since Thursday, four days prior to the article's writing. Cate noted the date of her disappearance along with her name and connection to Amelia.

The gossip in town prompted the reporter to inquire at the castle. Servants claimed the woman had not returned one evening, despite all her things remaining in her room. Her personal belongings had later been removed, though no sign that Ruth had returned existed. The household staff believed her disappearance warranted investigation, though the family disagreed.

Amelia MacKenzie had volunteered the information that the woman had sought employment elsewhere. The matter was dropped by the police after this admission.

It wasn't much to go on, Cate thought, as she stared down at the minimal scrawl on her paper. Questions filled her mind about the woman. Perhaps she and Jack should return to the castle before Ruth's disappearance. This may be the fastest way to gather information about her.

Cate noted that they should return in mid-September. She folded her notes and stuffed them into her cardigan pocket. As she flicked the folder containing the articles closed, Cate eyed her phone with antipathy.

With a deep inhale, she pulled it over and opened the camera app. "Moment of truth," she said, as she selected the camera in her bedroom first. Cate dismissed a few videos from her waking hours before she found one from 12:46 a.m.

With pursed lips, she tapped to play it. Once again, she slowly sat up in her bed, staring straight ahead. After a moment, she rose and wandered to the jewelry box, removing the sapphire necklace. As she strode across the room, her on-screen self stopped at the doorway to the sitting room. Her head turned slowly toward it, and she wandered off camera. The video ended.

Cate returned to the list of videos. The next one in the list had a timestamp of 1:34 a.m. She tapped it and watched as her former self wandered back into the room. This time, the necklace was no longer clutched in her hand. Instead, she now wore it around her neck.

Cate shook her head. She'd been gone for almost an hour. Where had she gone for that amount of time?

CHAPTER 8

*S*he backed out of the video and selected the other camera. Cate scrolled to the video at 12:49 a.m. The footage showed her wandering from the bedroom into the sitting room. She ceased walking for a moment, freezing next to her chaise. She continued to stare blankly ahead, her arms hanging limp at her sides. The necklace sparkled in her hand even in the dim light.

After another moment, on-screen Cate resumed her shambling, continuing across the room to the closed doors leading to the hallway. She stopped at the obstacle, her face inches from the closed door. After a moment, she pawed at the handles, fiddling with them blindly until the door popped open.

Cate swung the door open and disappeared into the hall. She lost sight of herself, and the recording ended. She shook her head as she played the next video, occurring around one-thirty in the morning. She, now necklace-clad, wandered through the open door and the room.

Cate bit her lower lip as the recording offered her little

information. The only thing she'd gleaned was that she was roaming around the castle farther than she'd expected. But she had no indication of where she may be going or what was drawing her there. Whatever it was, it was not in her sitting room.

Cate contemplated her next steps as she gathered the dogs for one last romp outside before retiring to her suite. She could place the camera in another location, but where?

The nightmares she'd suffered from for the past several months all occurred in the library. Perhaps that was a prime place for the second camera.

When Cate returned to the castle, she collected the camera from her sitting room and moved it to the library. The blue light glowed at her, bathing the bookshelf around it in blue. She checked the display on her phone. Positioned across from the door, she could see most of the room including the entrance.

Satisfied with her work, Cate returned to her bedroom to turn in for the night.

* * *

Cate awoke early the next morning with a small ball of fur nestled next to her. While Bailey remained curled in a ball near her knees, Riley had snuggled under her chin. As she stretched and opened her eyes, Riley tilted his head and glanced at Cate, offering a lick to her cheek.

"Good morning, buddy," she said, before kissing him on his furry head. "What's with the snuggles? Not that I'm complaining."

Cate propped her head up on her hand as she gave Riley a nice belly rub. As she settled into her lean, a bulky item shifted on her neck. Cate reached for it, discovering the necklace hanging around her neck again.

"This is getting old," she said to Riley with a sigh.

Cate reached behind her for her phone. "Let's see what I did last night."

In short order, Cate found the usual video of herself wandering to the jewelry armoire, retrieving the necklace then leaving the room.

Timestamps indicated she returned almost an hour later. Riley had snuggled near her after her escapades, likely wanting to ensure she didn't sneak away again without his knowledge.

Cate shook her head as she toggled to the other camera. "Let's see if I'm wandering in the library."

Riley cocked his head at her statement. The video list loaded. Cate frowned at the screen. She tilted her head and swiped down to refresh the list. No new videos appeared. The list of videos from today remained empty.

Cate clicked her phone off and bit her lower lip as she tapped the phone against her chin. "Not to the library," she murmured. "So, where did I go?"

Cate pondered other places to position the camera. Did her roamings have nothing to do with her nightmares? If they were unrelated, she had no clues as to where she could be disappearing during her midnight romps.

After a few more moments spent petting Riley, Cate rose and readied for her day. Jack proposed they travel back to 1942 today. She felt ill-prepared for the trip. They had no idea if the lead they were following was even relevant.

Cate hadn't created a plan of action for them to follow. They'd merely be gathering some information, though what information was relevant, she couldn't say. They couldn't very well ask the woman if she planned to disappear in a few days.

Still, perhaps there would be something that would point to the impending trouble.

After a romp outside with the dogs, Cate shuttled them into the kitchen.

"Good morning, Lady Cate," Mrs. Fraser said. "I heard you explored the Scottish countryside yesterday!"

"We did!" Cate said with a grin.

"And we'll be doing more if I have anything to say about it!" Molly exclaimed.

"She'll run you ragged, Lady Cate," Mrs. Fraser teased. "I hope you saved up your energy over the winter."

Cate chuckled.

"Don't worry," Molly said. "I've built in rest days that coincide with some of the parties. We don't want Lady Cate too tired to celebrate her one-year anniversary!"

"Nay, we don't," Mrs. Fraser said. "Mrs. Campbell will never forgive us!"

"I'll save Loch Ness until after the anniversary party. You know, in case the monster gets us," Molly said with a giggle.

"Oh, Loch Ness, I haven't been there in a long time. Perhaps Mr. Fraser and I will tag along with you on that one. If you don't mind, that is."

"Oh, that would be so fun!" Molly said.

"I think so, too!" Cate agreed. "We could make a day of it. Maybe even a weekend. We'll invite Jack, too. My treat!"

"Oh, no, Lady Cate. We cannae take you up on that."

"You most certainly can!" Cate countered. "We'll do it to celebrate my anniversary – *after* the party, of course."

"Of course," Molly and Mrs. Fraser agreed.

"It'll let all of us have some time off. No cooking for either of you, no yard work for Mr. Fraser and Jack. Just a nice peaceful weekend."

"Wow, Lady Cate!" Molly squealed. "You're getting wild and crazy!"

"Lady Cate, wild and crazy?" Jack inquired, as he entered with Mr. Fraser. Riley and Bailey raced to greet the two men.

"That she is!" Molly confirmed. "We went to Fyvie Castle yesterday and I'm planning more outings for us over the spring and summer. Lady Cate suggested we take a weekend to Loch Ness. Give everyone a little getaway and break."

"Wow, Lady Cate leaving the county! Get out! I can't believe my ears."

Cate turned from ladling her oatmeal into her bowl. "Very funny, Jack," Cate groaned. "I left the county yesterday!"

Jack retrieved a bowl of oatmeal, saying, "That's the first time since you got here!"

"I'm not very adventurous," Cate said with a shrug.

"Mmm-hmm," Jack murmured, giving Cate a knowing glance.

"Speaking of adventurous," Molly said, as they all sat down with their breakfast. "Any word on that body?"

Cate nodded. "Yes," she said. "I spoke with the police, and they don't have many leads. They identified the body as belonging to a female from about seventy to eighty years ago. That's about it."

"They can't connect it to any unsolved disappearances?" Molly asked.

"Not yet," Cate answered.

"I cannae imagine they would. I told you, there have been no disappearances in the area for as long as I can remember."

"Seventy to eighty years ago is a bit beyond your memory, Emily," Mr. Fraser said with a chuckle.

"Aye, it is, but in a town like Dunhaven, they'd still be talking about it into my teen years if it occurred a few years before my birth."

"You're right there," Mr. Fraser agreed.

"Nay, you're not," Jack argued.

Mrs. Fraser glanced sharply at him as he ate a spoonful of his oatmeal.

Jack swallowed and said, "They'd still be talking about it to this day."

Mrs. Fraser chuckled. "I dare say you're right, young Jack."

"You know it," Jack said with a wink.

"So, what now? Are they just giving up?"

Cate shook her head. "No. They'll expand their search, but it could be quite a process."

"Well, I hope they figure it out. That poor girl deserves better," Molly said.

The conversation on the body wound down and they discussed their trip to Fyvie Castle. The Frasers and Jack chimed in with suggestions for other locations to add to Molly's list.

As breakfast ended, Jack stood and said, "Lady Cate, might I have a moment of your time for some, uh, estate business?"

"Sure," Cate said, understanding his statement to mean much more than estate business.

They made their way upstairs to the library. Jack shut the doors behind them as they entered. "I figured we'd better discuss a plan before we jump back to the 1940s," he said.

Cate nodded. "We don't have much to go on, I'm afraid. I'm not even certain the woman in question will be there when we hop back. But we have to start somewhere."

"What date do you propose we go to?"

"I'm thinking mid-September. The woman, Ruth Harper, travels to Dunhaven with Amelia sometime in September. The article was dated September twenty-third, and stated she hadn't been seen in several days. So, she had been there since September nineteenth at least, and I don't think she disappeared on her first day in town. At least, that's not the impression I got."

"Okay, so we head back around maybe September

sixteenth?" Jack asked. "That's three days before her disappearance."

"Okay, yes, they should be there."

"And we'll gather some information. Maybe speak with the family?"

"Yes, although…"

"What?"

"We'll be talking to Rory and Anne again," Cate said. "And Amelia. They should recognize us. But they've aged. We have not. It's been almost twenty years and we don't look any older."

"Rory will understand."

"Yes, though I'm not sure how to handle Amelia and Anne."

"We're going to have to do the best we can do. Perhaps we should avoid them at first. We may be able to determine what's going on just by speaking with Rory."

"Okay, let's go with that plan for now," Cate agreed with a nod. "And obviously, I'll have to play Mrs. Jack MacKenzie again, since it would be a terrible shame if we'd gotten a divorce before 1942."

Jack chuckled. "It would be. Especially given what a lovely husband I am."

"Exceptional," Cate agreed.

"All right, seems we have our plan. Should we go after lunch?'

"Sounds like a plan!"

Jack gave her a nod and spun to give the dogs a goodbye pat. His brow furrowed as he caught sight of the blue light shining from one of the bookshelves.

"What's that?" he questioned, approaching it.

"Oh, uh, doggie cam," Cate answered. "I can access it from my phone and check on them."

"Ah, okay then," Jack said with a nod. "You two had better

behave yourselves. Lady Cate has eyes on you even when she leaves the county."

Cate shook her head at him. "I'm never going to live that down, am I?"

"Never, Lady Cate." Jack strode to the door. "Oh, one last thing," he said, turning to face her. "Did you order the fish and chips while you were out?"

"No!" Cate answered. "I had a sandwich and a piece of cake."

Jack's eyebrows shot up. "Why, Lady Cate, I'm not certain I even know who you are anymore."

Cate chuckled at him. "I'll see you later, Jack."

"You know it," he called, as he disappeared down the hall.

Cate stared at the camera for a moment longer. A pang of guilt settled over her as she realized she'd just lied to Jack. She didn't really lie, she told herself. She could use the camera to check on the pups. And she didn't see a point in telling him about her sleepwalking. When she had something solid on the matter, then she'd tell him, she reasoned. Until then, it would remain a pet camera.

Cate spent the morning hours attempting to find more information about Ruth Harper. She located birth records for several Ruth Harpers, but could not pinpoint which may be the correct one. With no knowledge of the woman's age, Cate could not determine which belonged to their target.

She spent another hour searching for photo albums to find any clue as to the woman's identity, but she found none. With a sigh, Cate settled in for lunch, and her mind turned to another mystery.

The blue light on the camera across the library glowed at her. Where was she disappearing to when she roamed the castle at night? Perhaps she should move the camera to a hallway or the foyer.

Her brow furrowed as she tried to discern her sleep-walking target. If not the library, which her subconscious mind had dwelled on for months, where?

After her lunch, Cate snatched the camera from the shelf and strolled down the hall to the foyer. She set the camera on an entry table, aimed at the main staircase.

"Lady Cate," Jack said as she adjusted it, monitoring its view on her phone. Startled, Cate jumped and pressed her hand to her heart.

"Oh, Jack, you startled me."

"Moving the puppy cam?"

"Huh?"

Jack pointed toward the camera cube.

"Oh, right, yeah."

Jack cocked an eyebrow.

"I just wanted to see if they come through here while we're gone."

Jack pursed his lips and nodded.

"Anyway," Cate said, "ready?"

"I just need a change of clothes," Jack said, as they mounted the stairs.

"I found some," Cate said. "I'm not sure if they're 1942, but they'll definitely pass for the 1940s. There must have been a rip to the 1940s somewhere in the castle."

"Ah, good."

"I set them out in the bedroom you normally use," Cate said.

"Okay. I'll change and await your call, m'lady," Jack said with a bow.

"All right. Go slow, I've got to tame this hair into some sort of 40s style."

"Don't forget your wedding ring and a few fake wrinkles so we look older."

"I'll skip the wrinkles, but thanks for reminding me about that ring."

Jack and Cate parted ways. Cate hurried into her suite and to the bathroom. She began with her hair, forming rolls on each side of her face. She uncapped a tube of red lipstick, popular during the era, and smeared it across her lips.

When she was finished, she pulled on a belted navy skirt suit and pair of peep-toed t-strap heels. Cate glanced in the mirror as she made her final adjustments. Satisfied, she hurried out to the jewelry armoire and found her faux wedding band, slipping it onto her finger.

She paused for a moment. Her fingers fell to the bottom drawer. Her breathing slowed and her vision narrowed to a pinpoint. Her fingers curled around the drawer pull.

A knock roused her from her trance. She shook her head, blinking her eyes as she sucked in a breath. She ripped her hand away from the knob and adjusted her skirt. "Coming!" she shouted.

With a deep breath, Cate left the jewelry armoire behind and hurried across her sitting room after she grabbed her envelope-style purse from the bed.

Cate pulled the door open to find Jack waiting in his 1940s duds complete with a boxy jacket, cuffed pants, and fedora.

"I feel like a gangster," Jack said.

"Come on," Cate said. "This has to be much better than the 1700s."

"Oh, aye," Jack admitted. "I'm much more comfortable without my short trousers and tights. And you, Lady Cate, seem to look stunning in any era."

"You're such a charmer," Cate said.

"Let's sneak down the back stairs and into the hidden passage."

"Okay," Cate said with a nod.

They wound through the halls and down the back stairs. Cate pulled the wall sconce, popping open the secret passage. A damp chill swept from within the passage as they stood in front of it. Cate shivered. The memory of hiding here from Marcus Northcott swept through her.

"You okay?" Jack inquired.

She forced a smile on her face and nodded. They stepped into the passage and pulled the panel shut behind them. Jack toggled on a pocket flashlight as Cate set the timepiece to September 16th, 1942.

"Ready?" she asked.

"I guess," Jack said.

"Second thoughts?"

Jack wiggled his eyebrows. "No, but time travel gives me the willies."

"Easy trip, remember? Information gathering only."

"Right," Jack said with a nod. They both wrapped their hands around the timepiece and, with a deep inhale, rubbed it, opening the time rip and slipping back to 1942.

In the darkened passage, Cate and Jack struggled to determine if the shift had worked.

"I guess we're back," Cate said.

Jack clicked off the flashlight and wandered to the panel, blindly feeling for the release. After finding it, he inched the panel open and peered into the hallway. With a shrug, he closed it. "I guess," Jack said. "Everything looks eerily similar."

"The price we pay for only traveling back seventy-odd years."

Jack snapped the flashlight on and shined it under his chin. "To a time with modern amenities."

Cate chuckled at his fearsome expression. "Come on, we

can head out through the crypt, and no one will be any the wiser."

"No more sneaking around the hallways and risking getting caught!" Jack exclaimed.

"Nope. Instead, we get to sneak through a dark, creepy cave and into a crypt."

Jack ceased his walking for a moment and grasped Cate's hand. "Hey, are you sure you're okay going that way? We can sneak through the halls if you'd rather."

Cate smiled weakly at him and squeezed his hand. "Thanks, but I'm okay. Ancient history, right?"

"Yes and no," Jack said. "It may have occurred in 1792, but it was only days ago for us when that bastard put you in a stone coffin and left you to die."

"Technically he put me in there and then gave you the clue to find me," Cate said, as they started down the passage.

"Bull," Jack retorted. "I'm not falling for that excuse. He's not forgiven on a technicality."

"Well, either way," Cate answered. "I didn't die."

"Thank heavens," Jack said, with another squeeze to her hand. "Wow, it's dark in here. How did you make it through in 1792 without a flashlight?"

"Celine's magical version of a flashlight is actually much brighter than the one you've got," Cate explained, referencing the ethereal blue-white bulb Celine was able to create from thin air. "One of her many talents."

Jack screwed up his face. "I'll say. This is an LED!"

"She's got that beat."

They continued through the dank passage. "It should start sloping upward when we're approaching the crypt," Cate said.

Within a minute, Cate's legs worked to walk uphill.

"Should be getting close," Jack said.

They approached an enclosed space.

"Okay, where's the crypt?" Jack inquired.

Cate adjusted Jack's hand to aim the flashlight above them. A block protruded above their heads with a ring. "Pull that and we're free."

Jack yanked the ring down. A clank sounded followed by a screech. Fresh air rushed in, and daylight lit the chamber. Jack clicked off the flashlight and they stepped into the next chamber.

Jack side-eyed Cate as she stared at the coffin where she'd been buried alive. She swallowed hard and offered another weak smile. "I suppose Douglas is in there now."

"Doesn't make it any easier, Cate."

"I'm okay. But let's not linger here."

Jack nodded and they exited the mausoleum onto the gravel path outside. Jack removed his hat and dusted it off. "Got dirt on my gangster hat."

"Perhaps we should take an indirect route to the castle. We'll just look around and see if we can determine who's here."

"Sounds like a plan."

They strolled down the path. The castle rose on the horizon as they wound away from it toward the back of the property. Cate's brow furrowed as she glanced down the hill behind the castle. "What's that?" she inquired.

"Why, Lady Cate, don't you recognize your own loch?"

"Not that," Cate said with a shake of her head, and a tongue-in-cheek annoyed glance to Jack. "That!" She pointed to another structure tucked behind the castle to the right of the loch. A large, green tent-like structure stood on a flat area of land.

Jack scrunched his eyebrows together as he ceased walking. He shielded his eyes staring at it. "I'm not sure."

"It looks like a tent," Cate said.

"Aye, but a rather large one. Like for an event."

"Yes and no," Cate answered.

"What do you mean?"

"Can you imagine Mrs. Campbell putting up a green tent?"

Jack considered it. "No," he admitted, "I can imagine the sheer shock on her face when she saw that color."

Cate giggled. "And then the green-around-the-gills panicked expression when I suggest we use the red napkins anyway, despite the green walls."

"Lady Cate, if we put a green tent like that up for a party, we'd be wallpapering the inside."

"I have no doubt."

"Maybe we can get a closer look from the loch."

Cate nodded and they wandered down the path to the loch. The large tree nearby, full of foliage, provided the perfect hiding spot to spy on the temporary structure.

Cate and Jack sheltered behind it, eyeing the large green blob. After a few moments, two women emerged from inside. They strode purposefully toward the castle. A man wandered out ten minutes later.

"Who are those people?"

Jack shrugged. "I'm not certain. They certainly aren't anyone we know."

"No, that wasn't Anne or Amelia. Nor is that man Lucas or Rory."

"Could it have been Oliver or Charles?"

"I suppose the man could have been Oliver. He'd be twenty-eight by now. My grandfather, Charles, would be seventeen. He may or may not be here. But that still doesn't explain the women."

"Nor what they're doing there." Jack pressed his finger to his chin. "Could one of the women be Mary?"

"Oliver's wife?" Cate inquired. "I'm not certain when they met, but if I recall their age difference correctly, she'd only be eighteen right now. I can't recall exactly the age she married, but I'd be surprised if it was this early."

"We'll ask Pap when we go back."

"Okay," Cate said.

"Oi! What are you two doing there?" a voice from behind them called.

CHAPTER 9

Jack and Cate spun around to find a small child, about five or six, staring at them. He pointed a stick menacingly in their direction.

"I said, what are you two doing there?"

"Oh," Jack said, approaching him slowly, "hello, there, little fellow."

"Don't little fellow me!" the child said with his eyes narrowed. "I asked you a question!"

"We were just enjoying the view," Jack said.

The boy narrowed his eyes further. "You were looking at the tent, weren't you?"

Jack squatted down as he spoke. "We were. You're a very perceptive laddie."

"Aye, that I am. Why are you so interested in that tent?"

"Do you know what the tent is for?"

The child eyed Jack for a moment before he answered. "Aye, I do. Why?"

"Would you like to share that information?"

"Are you Nazis?"

Jack's eyes went wide at the question, and he glanced

back at Cate. With a scrunching of his eyebrows, he returned his attention to the boy. "No," he answered with a chuckle.

"It's not a joke. If you're not a Nazi, why aren't you volunteering for your country, strapping lad like you?" The boy gazed down at Jack's feet. "Got flat feet?"

"No, I haven't got flat feet. You ask a lot of questions for a little boy."

"Then why aren't you fighting for the crown?"

"Ah, well," Jack began.

"He's nearsighted," Cate interjected.

"Oh," the boy said. "Can't fly with the RAF then. But you could volunteer for the army. I would if I was old enough. I'd be right there on the front lines killing them Nazis right and left." He swung the branch around to showcase his fierce skills.

"Well, I have other contributions to make," Jack said.

"Oh, intelligence, are you? That why you're asking about the tent? What're your names?"

"I'm Cate and this is Jack. And yes," Cate said. "Is that a group of codebreakers in there? That's what we're looking for."

"Aye, codebreakers, they are. Working on the Enigma code."

Cate smiled, not just at the answer, but at the idea. Dunhaven Castle was a miniature Bletchley Park. Codebreakers were given room and board along with security here while they worked to keep allied convoys safe by decoding intercepted German messages.

"Thank you," Cate said. "You've been very helpful."

"You sure you're Allies?"

"Certain," Cate said. "I'm an American!"

"Aye, that you are, lassie. About time your lot joined our efforts. Say, what time is it?"

Jack glanced at his wristwatch. "It's quarter to four," he said.

The boy winced. "Yikes. I've got to get back before my Da leaves! Good to meet you!"

The little boy trotted down the path. Jack rose to stand and called after him. "Before you go, what's your name, son?"

The boy spun around. "Stanley!" he shouted, as he offered a salute. "Stanley Reid!" The boy spun back toward the castle and darted down the path.

Jack's jaw dropped open as he stared after the boy. Cate covered her mouth which hung agape. She grasped Jack's bicep and squeezed.

Jack whipped his head to stare at her. He blinked as he processed the statement. "My Pap just called me a Nazi and asked if I had flat feet."

"Well, he is only five," Cate said, barely holding in a chuckle. "But he called me lassie, just like he always does."

"I can't believe he's always been that ornery. I thought it was old age."

"Apparently not," Cate answered. "I guess he's always been a character."

"I'll say," Jack said with a shake of his head.

"At least he told us what the tent is for," Cate said.

"I'm not quite sure I understand what he meant."

"It's an intelligence hub. Think Bletchley Park. Large properties like this offered a place for a group of code-breakers to stay and live while they worked to decipher coded messages from the Germans. Sometimes they even served as airbases. The codebreakers worked to prevent attacks on Allied convoys by the U-boat Wolfpacks. Dunhaven Castle must be assisting with the war efforts. A property this far north was probably a great area to house them for safety. Plus, in 1942, the messages became indecipherable for a period. They needed all the codebreaking help they could get."

"Oh," Jack said, with a nod of understanding. "So our girl could be one of the codebreakers."

Cate's brow crinkled. "Amelia said she worked for her, so probably not. But she could have been killed by someone in that tent. Still, it doesn't provide us with much information."

"No, it doesn't, but we've now got a new lead to follow."

Cate nodded. "Maybe we should head back."

"Okay. You follow up on this while we decide how best to explain our youthful appearances to people who aged twenty years."

Cate nodded in agreement. "I suppose we should sneak back in using the crypt, though we'll have to figure out how to open the passage from this side."

"No time like the present," Jack said, offering his arm.

"Technically, we're in the past, but sure," Cate said as she accepted it.

"Witty, Lady Cate. My humor is rubbing off on you."

They returned to the crypt. Cate's eyes roamed over the stone interior. "I've never actually entered the passage from this side," she admitted.

"I suppose now's as good a time as any to find the opening," Jack replied.

"It's a ring on the other side."

"The only ring I see in the lion's mouth there." Jack pointed up at the decorative lion.

Cate smiled and nodded. Jack reached up and tugged. His grin turned upside down into a frown when nothing happened.

"I really thought that would work."

"Me too," Cate answered. "It always works on TV."

"We live wilder lives than people on TV," Jack said, as he tugged on his collar.

"I beg to differ," Cate said. Any further comment was drowned out by a droning overhead.

"What is that?" Jack asked.

Cate stepped out through the gate and glanced upward. "Jack, look!" She pointed skyward as Jack joined her.

Four RAF fighter planes flew overhead. "Are those…" Jack asked, as he shielded his eyes against the bright sun.

Cate nodded, her skin turning to gooseflesh. "Royal Air Force."

"What are they doing here?"

"Protecting the intelligence post, perhaps," Cate suggested.

Moments later, the squadron, flying in finger-four formation, split apart. The planes darted in different directions.

"What's going on?" Jack inquired.

A new sound joined the buzzing of the RAF fighters. "There!" Cate exclaimed. Four differently configured planes sped in from the south.

"Who are they?"

"By the looks of the planes, that's the Luftwaffe!" Cate exclaimed. "Oh, Jack, we're about to see a dog fight up close and personal!"

Jack's eyes went wide as the four German planes split apart in pursuit of the RAF. Bullets strafed from the eight aircrafts. The planes darted through the sky, diving and climbing, doing barrel rolls, and chasing each other in hot pursuit.

Two RAF fighters managed to corner one of the German planes. One plane open-fired. A black line of smoke trailed from the German plane as the pilot fought to bring the plane down safely in enemy territory.

"Oh, a hit!" Jack exclaimed. "Now they've got the advantage."

Cate nodded and continued to watch the fray. Another

pair of pilots battled it out on the far side of the castle. Again, the RAF pilot outmaneuvered the less-agile German fighter. Another black streak smoked through the sky, this one ending in a fiery explosion as the plane hit the ground.

The remaining Luftwaffe planes hightailed it away in the direction they'd come. As the skies quieted, Jack murmured, "Wow," in an astonished whisper, adding, "I can't believe we just saw that."

"Yeah," Cate answered. "I still have goosebumps."

"Good job by our boys!"

Cate nodded as they ducked back into the crypt. "The RAF planes were far more agile in dog fights. They had an advantage. It was still an awesome sight to see some of those maneuvers."

"I agree, Lady Cate," Jack said. "Maybe this time travel stuff isn't all that terrible after all."

Cate lifted her eyebrows and grinned at him. "I'm so glad it's growing on you."

"Now if we can only find the entrance, we can enjoy it from our own time.

"I really thought the ring in the lion's mouth would be it," Jack said with a shake of his head.

Cate pressed a finger to her lips as she surveyed the space. "Too obvious, I guess," she murmured.

"I was okay with how obvious it was," Jack said, as he poked around searching for another option.

Cate chuckled at the statement as she zeroed in on a large ring attached to the head of the middle stone coffin. "Maybe this," she said.

She wrapped her fingers around the ring and tugged. It gave way slightly. Her features scrunched as she struggled to pull the ancient mechanism further. Jack grabbed hold of the ring to assist.

It broke loose and triggered the doorway into the

passage. "Success," Jack said, as they darted inside and closed the panel.

They wandered through the tunnel back to the house, resetting the watch and returning to their own time. They emerged from the secret panel and took a back stairway upstairs to change.

"Well, I suppose there's no need for our usual post-time travel trip analysis meeting," Jack said, as they traversed the halls.

"Not unless you'd like to discuss running into your grandfather when he was five."

"I'd really rather not. I found it a little disturbing. Pap was a tough little bugger."

Cate giggled. "He was. I can't believe he accused us of being Nazis."

"At least he didn't insult your feet."

Cate continued her chuckling. "Anyway, you're off the hook. I'll get started on researching the intelligence base at the castle and see if I can find any leads there."

"Let me know what you come up with, Lady Cate," Jack said.

"I will."

After donning her twenty-first-century clothes, Cate wandered to the library for a brief research session before her dinner. Much of what she read she already knew. Deciphering German messages was a large focus of the war efforts. So-called Wolfpacks of German U-boats prowled the waters and attacked allied supply ships. Determining the location of these Wolfpacks on any given day could help turn the tides of the war or could sink the Allies' efforts, quite literally.

As such, mathematicians were housed at estates such as Bletchley Park and put forth phenomenal efforts to break the German Enigma code. Submarine crews often risked their lives to overtake a U-boat and retrieve the Enigma machines for codebreakers to study.

While having Enigma machines was helpful, the machine settings were changed daily and based on secret keys distributed in advance, making messages difficult to decrypt.

On her initial search, Cate found little information specific to Dunhaven Castle. However, she became swept away with the fascinating stories of the work intelligence analysts did to aid the war efforts. She marveled at the lengths some people went to to help the war efforts.

When dinner interrupted her research, she set the laptop aside for the day and enjoyed her meal. After an evening walk with her pups, Cate settled in her sitting room with a hot chocolate and a mystery novel.

As she readied for bed, Cate bent down to remove the bow-tie collar she'd placed on Riley earlier. "Did you get up to anything interesting today, Riley? I forgot to check your camera feed. Well, tomorrow's a new day."

The small camera dangled from Cate's fingertips as she crossed the room. The blue glow of her own monitoring device caught her eye. She stared at it for a moment, wondering if she'd wander around the castle again tonight.

"Where am I going?" she murmured to herself. Cate glanced down at the collar camera still clutched in her hand. An idea formed in her mind, and she narrowed her eyes at the small device.

Within twenty minutes, Cate was climbing into bed with the pet collar camera dangling from her wrist on a bracelet. As she lay back amidst her pillows, she stared down at the small item strapped to her.

"I wonder what you'll show me tomorrow," she asked aloud, as she relaxed into sleep.

CHAPTER 10

*C*ate awoke with a start. Sweat beaded on her forehead and she gasped for breath. The sun painted the morning sky a deep shade of red. Cate grasped her clock and checked the time. Fifteen minutes remained before her alarm would signal her to get up.

Cate collapsed back into the pillows as she caught her breath. She searched her mind for what disturbed her sleep. She didn't recall having a nightmare. What caused her to break into a sweat? What caused the shortness of breath?

With no answers in sight, Cate stretched and climbed from her bed. She blew out a long breath as she clutched at her neck, finding the familiar sapphire necklace hanging there. As she pulled on her robe, she caught sight of her other accessory.

Cate bit her lower lip as she stared at the camera attached to her wrist. Perhaps she'd get some answers from the video feed this morning.

Cate delayed her findings into her overnight excursions until after breakfast. After moving the camera from the foyer back to the library, she settled into her desk chair. As she slouched down, she eyed her phone. She stared at the blank screen. Her finger tapped against the power button as she attempted to muster the courage to view the video.

After a hard swallow, Cate toggled her phone on and navigated to the camera's app. A list of videos filled her screen. She clicked on one showing Dunhaven Castle's estate from a dog's perspective. The camera bobbled around as Riley frolicked through the back garden.

Cate smiled at the video as she caught sight of her legs and a bashful Bailey trotting next to them. Her brow furrowed and she stopped the video. This had been a similar angle to the video she'd swore she saw legs in while she and Molly were visiting Fyvie Castle.

She stared at it for a few more moments before she realized she was stalling from the task at hand. Cate pursed her lips as she returned to the video list and scrolled through it. She found one with today's date. The timestamp read 1:37 a.m.

Cate sucked in a breath and tapped on the video. It took her several seconds to acclimate to the video's perspective. At her hip level outside of some bobbling around of her right arm, things appeared very different.

Cate squinted at the phone as her bobbling hands settled back at her sides, following what she assumed to be clasping the sapphire necklace around her neck. She recognized the sitting room as her on-screen-self wandered through it. The camera angle became frenetic as Cate turned the door handle and pulled her suite's doors open.

Cate stared down the length of the hall as the bobbling video continued. "Where am I going?"

She covered her mouth as the video captured her threading through several hallways in a seemingly random pattern. Cate wandered down a set of back stairs. She continued her aimless wandering until she reached a set of doors to the closed-off west wing. She paused for a moment before she continued along the hall.

After a few more moments of wandering, the camera faced another set of doors. Cate recognized the entrance to the ballroom. The camera approached the large double doors. The picture bobbled again as Cate flung the doors open. The turning of her wrist spun the camera. It caught on the ring used to attach it to the bracelet. Now angled upward, Cate could see bits and pieces of her face.

The night mode toggled on as Cate stepped into the darkened ballroom. Her face lit in an eerie green, her eyes forming two piercing dots as they scanned the space.

The video moved as Cate wandered to the center of the ballroom. She spun in a slow circle, her eyes searching. After two full turns, she stopped.

"I'm here. Where are you?" her on-screen counterpart said.

Cate's brow furrowed as she pondered the meaning of her sleepwalking-self's statement. Another moment passed, before the Cate on screen whipped her head toward something. From the odd angle of the camera, Cate detected a smile forming on her lips. She took a step toward whatever she focused on when the camera froze.

"What?" Cate asked, tapping at her phone's screen. "No!"

Her heart sank as she attempted to find more of the video. No other footage existed, including her return trip to bed. The next video on the list was of her awakening earlier this morning.

Cate sat in stunned silence for several moments as she pondered the meaning of the latest revelations. Who was she searching for? Her mind leapt to an answer. It was one she did not like.

A knock on the library's open door snapped her out of

her ruminating. She glanced at the door to find Jack leaning in.

"Lady Cate, lost in thought?"

Cate didn't respond for a moment. She flicked her gaze to the phone. The wrinkles in her forehead deepened as she directed her gaze back to Jack.

"Cate?" he questioned, his face quickly turning to a mask of concern as he approached her. "Are you okay?"

She shook her head as she rose from the chair.

"Did you find something on our lady?"

"No," Cate answered. "We've got another problem, Jack."

"Oh? Find another body in the garden, did you?"

Cate tried to force a smile at the terrible joke as she shook her head, but it faltered, and she glanced down at the phone still clutched in her hand.

"Cate, you're scaring me. What's wrong?"

Cate swallowed hard, bringing her eyes to meet Jack's for a brief second. She licked her lips as she pondered the words.

"I've been sleepwalking," she settled on.

Jack's brow furrowed and he blinked his eyes a few times before cocking his head. "Oh," he said, after a moment, "so you're tired? Is that what's got you so down?"

Cate shook her head. "No," she admitted. "It's not that."

"Then what?" Jack prodded as Cate continued her reluctance.

She glanced to her phone again before returning her gaze to Jack. "It's not normal sleepwalking," she reported.

Jack's eyes widened and darted around the room. "Ooookay," he said. "Are you doing strange things? Like wandering around naked or something?"

The comment made Cate chuckle despite her trepidation. "No," she gasped out.

"Then what? Maybe you should sit down and explain it to me," Jack said, leading her to one of the leather armchairs near the fireplace. He eased her into it and plopped into the chair adjacent to hers.

Cate bit her lower lip before she proceeded with more details. "I keep getting up and retrieving that necklace…" she began.

Jack let his head fall onto the chair behind him with a sigh. "Oh, Cate, you need to get rid of that damn thing."

"Yes, I'm starting to agree with you," Cate admitted.

"Although, it's not that terrible. Why has it got you so disturbed?"

"Well, there's more," Cate said with a frown. "It started with me simply wandering in my sleep to the jewelry armoire, retrieving the sapphire necklace and returning to bed. I'd wake up with it clutched in my hand. But then…" Her voice trailed off.

"Then?" Jack prodded.

"Well, then things took a turn for the stranger. And after I pick up the necklace from the jewelry box, I wander around the castle for a while."

Jack sat for a moment, processing the information before he shook his head. "If you're sleepwalking, how do you know what you're doing? Do you wake up somewhere else?"

Cate shook her head and waved her phone in the air. "No. Those doggie cams aren't really for the dogs. I've been using them to track my movements around the castle. And last night I strapped the collar cam to my wrist, so I had a record of where I went."

Jack leaned forward, placing his elbows on his knees. "How long has this been going on, Cate?"

"Since our last trip to 1792."

Jack scrubbed his face with his hands.

Cate continued her explanation. "I started out with a camera in my bedroom." She toggled it on to show Jack the videos. "At first, I just wander to the jewelry armoire and remove the necklace and go back to bed." She toggled into a video showing her zombie-like self wandering around her bedroom.

"But then," Cate continued, "I saw this one." She tapped the screen to display the video where she wandered into the sitting room.

"So I bought another camera." Another video played on the screen, showing her wandering through the sitting room and out into the hall.

"Which led me to move the camera here because I assumed this phenomenon was tied to my nightmares about the bookcase. Or rather, I assumed this replaced those nightmares since I haven't suffered from them since this began."

Jack gazed over at the camera cube now across the room. "So, did you come in here?"

Cate shook her head. "No. No video of me coming to the library. I wasn't sure where to put the camera next, so I tried the foyer, but nothing there, and then last night when I was removing the collar cam from Riley, the idea struck me to attach it to myself. Then I could essentially follow myself around at night."

Jack gave her a sideways glance. "It disturbs me how scientific you are about this, Cate."

Cate shrugged. "It seemed the best way to collect evidence. Anyway, this is the video from last night."

"And this is the collar cam?" Jack inquired.

Cate nodded as she pressed play on the video. Jack accepted the proffered cell phone and watched the video play. Cate leaned over his shoulder as she offered commentary.

"Okay, likely I'm fastening the necklace," she said, as the camera bobbled around, covered by her hair at times. "And now, here we go into the sitting room and down the hall."

The camera bobbled around as Cate plodded down the hall past Molly's room and turned into another hallway.

"Where are you going?" Jack inquired.

"Same question I had," Cate said. She speeded the video until she arrived at the ballroom doors.

"Ah," Jack exclaimed, as Cate allowed it to play at normal speed. "You want to have a party."

The video continued as Cate entered the ballroom and began to spin in a slow circle. "What are you doing?"

"Just keep watching," Cate said.

Jack returned his attention to the screen and watched as Cate stopped. "I'm here. Where are you?" her voice questioned from the phone.

Jack's face became a mask of confusion. "Where's who?" he asked. A moment later, the corners of Cate's mouth turned up and she stared at something. Or someone. As she took another step, the video froze.

"Why did it stop?"

"I'm not sure. But there are no other videos after that. Not even of me returning to bed."

"Did you?"

"Yes," Cate said with a nod, as she plopped into her armchair. "I woke up in my bed this morning, so I got back somehow."

Jack pursed his lips and stared at the image frozen on the screen. "Who are you looking for, I wonder?"

Cate stared blankly ahead as he spoke. "Him," she murmured.

"Huh?"

Cate blinked slowly as she focused on nothing in front of her. Her senses dulled and her world slid away.

Suddenly, her body jolted. She blinked a few times as she focused on what was in front of her. Jack knelt in front of the chair. His hands gripped her upper arms tightly. The wrinkles on his forehead and the pained expression on his lips hinted at his worry.

"Cate?" he said.

"What?" she answered. "What's wrong?"

Jack's eyes widened. "What's wrong? I asked who you may be looking for, and you murmured some response and then you just turned into a zombie! I couldn't get a response from you."

CHAPTER 11

ate drew in a deep breath. "I don't remember any of that."

Jack crept back to his armchair and perched on the edge of it. He shook his head. "Cate, I think we need to get rid of that necklace."

Cate nodded. "I'm inclined to agree with you. It obviously has some strange effect on me." Cate pondered for a moment before adding, "I guess I could call…"

"Cate, no," Jack interrupted. "Get rid of it. Stop putting it off, or letting someone else handle it."

"I'm not putting it off but… what am I going to do with it?"

"Chuck the damn thing into the loch."

Cate winced. "I hope I don't try a midnight diving excursion to get it back."

"That settles it," Jack said, pounding his palms on the chair's arms. "I'm going to stay here until we're sure you're back to normal. We'll make sure all the doors are locked so you can't get away and harm yourself. And we're tossing that necklace right now."

Jack stood and held his hand out to Cate. "What, now? Like now, now?"

"Yes, like now, now, Lady Cate. Hop to it and get that cursed thing out of your jewelry box." Jack shook his head. "No, scratch that. I'll go with you. Before you put it on and start wandering around again."

Cate grasped his hand, and he pulled her up to standing. She offered a defeated nod and led the way from the room. They traversed the halls to Cate's suite.

"How will you explain staying here?" Cate inquired.

"I suppose I'll invent another problem to deal with," Jack answered.

"Another leak, huh?" Cate said.

"Something like that," Jack answered.

"Darn leaky roofs on these old places," Cate said with a chuckle.

"At least it works in our favor," Jack replied, as they reached Cate's sitting room. Jack hovered at the door to her bedroom as she stalked across the room and pulled open the drawer. Her eyes fell onto the extravagant necklace. Her fingers reached out to caress the gems. She arched an eyebrow as the world around her seemed to fall away.

After a moment, she blinked several times. Only black velvet stared back at her.

"We'll have none of that," Jack said, as he swiped the necklace from the drawer. "I can't wait until this thing is gone." He dangled it in the air before shoving it into his pocket. "Let's go."

Cate nodded and they snaked through the halls and onto the grounds after collecting the dogs. Cate took a deep breath as they began their walk to the loch. When they arrived, her stomach filled with butterflies. She bit her lower lip as Jack removed the jewelry piece from his pocket.

He closed his fist around it and raised his hand high.

"Wait!" Cate exclaimed.

"What?" he asked, lowering his hand to his side.

Cate grasped hold of it and pulled his fingers back. "Maybe we shouldn't throw it into the loch. It really is beautiful. Perhaps…"

Jack yanked his hand away. "No more, Cate. It's going to the bottom of that loch today. It's a cursed thing, no matter how pretty it is."

Jack pulled his hand back and threw it overhand. Cate's heart somersaulted with the necklace as she watched it arc in the air before descending toward the water. It plopped into the still surface. Concentric circles radiated from where it bobbed for a second before slipping below the water.

Jack nodded his head as the waters calmed again. "Done."

Cate stared at the spot where the necklace had disappeared. Jack glanced at her. "How do you feel?"

Cate raised her eyebrows and drew in a deep breath. "Better," she said. "I think."

Jack smiled at her. "Good. And I'll stay the night just in case. But let's hope that puts an end to your troubles."

Cate returned his smile and nodded. "Yes. Let's hope my sleepwalking days are over. Maybe now I can make some progress on our girl."

"Nothing yet?" Jack asked, as they began their walk back to the castle.

Cate shook her head. "No. Though, I'm afraid I got caught up in reading some of the history of the time. World War II is one of my favorite periods to study."

"A war buff? I'd never have guessed."

Cate nodded with a coy grin. "Maybe you'd like to borrow my Battle 360 DVDs," she said.

Jack chuckled at Cate's comments as they reached the castle.

"All right, Lady Cate," Jack said, as they stepped into the

foyer. "As long as you feel okay, I'll leave you to your work. I expect a full report on Ruth Harper later today."

"Aye, aye, sir!" Cate said with a salute. "And yes, I feel fine. I only seem to have an odd reaction when I see that necklace. Now that it's gone, let's hope that's all behind me."

"Fingers crossed, Lady Cate," he answered as he backed down the hall.

Cate ushered the dogs into the library. With a short amount of time before lunch, Cate opted for busy work rather than diving into any research on Ruth Harper. Instead, she grabbed her cell phone.

She frowned at the picture on the screen. Her frozen image standing in the ballroom faced her. She quickly tapped her home button to remove the image and navigated to her text app. After selecting the appropriate message thread, Cate typed: *You'll be happy to hear we've gotten rid of the necklace.*

She tapped the arrow button to send the message. Within a few moments, a bubble appeared with three dots, indicating a response being typed. Cate smiled as Damien's answer appeared: *Way to go, Cate!*

The two conversed through Cate's lunch. She avoided telling him about her sleepwalking drama, feeling a bit guilty keeping it from him, particularly after he asked about her nightmares.

She reported she had no trouble with them after her return from 1792.

Celine says hers never stopped. She thought I should warn you, just in case you experience a similar thing.

Cate responded: *Really? I had one nightmare about being trapped in the coffin, but nothing since.*

Damien's answer confirmed his earlier message. *Yeah. Celine said she's had the nightmares for over two centuries. I hope you don't. Not have them for two centuries, that would be impos-*

sible for you as a human. I mean I hope you don't have them anymore. Celine's are on and off, though, so if you start having nightmares again, it may be normal.

Cate's forehead crinkled as she processed the message. What about Duke Northcott affected both her and Celine? Perhaps she should say something to Damien about the sleepwalking. Maybe he could tell her how to stop it.

Cate began to type a message but then erased it. She'd sleep on it and decide about sharing the information with him later. She toggled off her phone after sending a simple "Thanks!" and finished her lunch.

She settled in at her desk after a hearty meal, prepared to work. She spent the better part of the afternoon attempting to track down information about the intelligence base on Dunhaven Castle's grounds or anyone named Ruth Harper.

Cate found a number of references to women named Ruth Harper. She sorted through the hundreds of results, removing those who did not fit the time frame first. She trimmed her list down by removing anyone who could not have been at Dunhaven Castle in 1942. When she finished, she had a handful of women left.

Cate stared at her list of four women. She'd dive deeper into researching each of them tomorrow to determine if any could be the Ruth Harper buried on Dunhaven's grounds.

Cate closed her laptop as Molly delivered her last meal of the day. She spent the meal and her evening pondering if she'd wander the castle again tonight. Jack followed Molly into the library when she arrived to remove Cate's tray.

He waited for Molly to disappear down the hall before he spoke. "How you feeling?" he asked.

"Fine," Cate said. "No ill-effects. Jack, you really don't have to stay if you don't want to. I can put the camera on myself again and…"

"I'm not going to argue with you, Cate. I want to stay. I've already told everybody about our leak."

Cate smiled at him. "Okay. Thanks, Jack. Hopefully, we'll have a quiet night."

"My fingers are crossed. I'd still put the camera on. Just in case."

They spoke for a few more moments before Cate retreated to her suite with her book, hoping to relax before she went to bed.

As she crawled between the sheets, her camera accessory hanging around her wrist, she hoped for a good night's sleep.

* * *

Cate awoke the next morning before her alarm. After a stretch, she reached to caress her neck. The memory of Jack tossing the necklace into the loch flooded into her mind. She must have had a peaceful night's rest, she thought with a smile.

She rose from her bed, humming as she went about her morning routine. As she pulled on her boots, she pondered the song she'd been humming. It occurred to her that she couldn't recall the name of the tune, nor where she'd heard it.

With a shrug, she finished dressing and took the dogs out. As they romped in the yard, Cate checked her cell phone. A few videos existed on both cameras. Cate swallowed hard as she saw the list. Had she climbed from her bed despite the absence of the necklace?

She toggled off the phone, putting the discovery off until after breakfast. Following the meal, she settled in the library. Rain pelted the windows outside and thunder rumbled in the distance. Cate sighed as she toggled on her cell phone.

She jumped in her seat as a knock sounded at the door.

"Sorry," Jack said, holding his hand out. "You okay?"

"Yeah, you just startled me."

"How did you sleep?"

"I'm about to find out," Cate said, wiggling her cell phone at him.

"Want me to leave?" Jack inquired.

Cate shook her head. "No. In fact, I'd prefer you to stay. I'm interested but more than a little nervous to find out what happened last night."

"So, there are videos?"

"Yes. Though they could be as mundane as me turning over in bed or Riley stretching."

"Let's find out."

Cate accessed the cube camera first. The few videos from overnight showed Cate rolling over, fluffing her pillow, and adjusting her covers. One video showed Bailey climbing to his feet and stretching before curling in a ball to continue sleeping.

Cate smiled as they played the last video. She had not climbed from her bed. She had not roamed the castle. She hadn't tried to dive into the loch to retrieve the necklace. She breathed a sigh of relief. "Thank goodness," she said, as she tossed her phone onto the desk.

"Looks like our leak is fixed!" Jack exclaimed. "Now we can focus on our 1942 problem."

"On that note, I've got some research to do! I narrowed down the Ruth Harpers from the United Kingdom to four possibilities. I plan to flesh out the details on each today to see if they could be our girl. Of course, Ruth could be from another country, so if none of these pan out, I suppose I should expand my search." Cate pressed her finger to her lips as she vetted her thoughts.

"Well, I'll leave you to your work, Lady Cate," Jack said with a smile.

Cate smiled. "Wish me luck!"

"Good luck, Lady Cate." He offered her a wave as he backed through the door. Cate took a deep breath as another clap of thunder boomed. Riley climbed to his feet, his tail between his legs instead of arched high above his back in its usual position. He scampered across the room to Cate with a whine.

"Aww," Cate said, as she scooped him up. "It's just a little thunder, buddy. Nothing to worry about." He licked her cheek. She smiled at him and kissed the fur on top of his head.

A loud bang sounded. Cate jumped again, before realizing it was her door knocker. "I'm getting as jumpy as you, Riley," she said, as she carried the small dog with her to the front door.

"Who could that be?" she asked him as the knocker sounded again, echoing in the foyer. "Coming!"

Cate pulled the door open to find the mail carrier.

"Top o' the morning to you, Lady Cate," Otto said. "And hello. Riley, right?"

"Hi!" Cate greeted him. "Yep, this is Riley. For once he's not barking at you."

Otto chuckled. "Oh, I dinnae mind. Little fellow's doing his job and protecting his castle, aren't you, little fellow?"

"I'm certain he'd agree."

"I've got a package for you. Special delivery. Marked 'Handle with Care,' so I dinnae want to leave it out in the rain. I suppose I could have run it around back to Mrs. F but…" His voice trailed off as he glanced to the skies.

"I'll save you the steps and keep you dry," Cate said.

"I much appreciate that, Lady Cate." He handed the package over to her.

"Thank you," Cate said with a smile. "Stay dry!"

He nodded and hurried back to his car as Cate closed the front door. She stared down at the wrapped box. Brown paper covered it. Her name was scrawled on top. No return address was written.

Cate turned it over, searching for the sender. She found no other marks outside of her address and the postage.

"Wonder what this is?" she asked Riley, as she juggled both him and the box on their way back to the library.

With the small dog balanced on her lap, she settled at her desk. She rummaged through the desk drawer for a pair of scissors and flipped the box over to begin removing the brown paper.

Riley became restless as Cate jostled him around working to remove the wrapping and leapt down. With no hints of thunder in the past few minutes, he decided to brave it and settle in for a nap near the roaring fire.

Cate freed the box from the paper and studied it. The nondescript brown cardboard container gave no clues as to the contents. Cate sliced open the packing tape sealing the top. A few packing peanuts spilled over the top as she pulled it open to find a cream-colored box wrapped in a blue satin ribbon inside.

"What is this?" Cate inquired aloud, as she lifted the fancy packaging from within the plain cardboard box. A few more peanuts spilled to the floor. Cate scooped them up before continuing, afraid the dogs may find them an interesting snack.

She pushed the box to the side and stared at the ribbon-adorned cube. Cate grasped one of the tails from the bow and pulled, unfurling the ribbon. She shimmied the thick box top off of the package and peeked inside.

Blue tissue paper obscured whatever object lay there. As Cate pulled it back, the crease between her eyebrows deepened. A miniature wooden piano sat inside.

"Where did this come from?" Cate asked herself. Riley

popped his head up and sniffed. The object didn't seem to faze Bailey. "I didn't order this."

Cate checked the brown paper to verify her name and address before she removed the item to examine it further.

A winding key protruded from the underside of the piano. Cate wound it. No music played.

"Hmm," Cate murmured. "Oh, maybe the lid has to be open."

Cate traced the outline of the lid, finding a finger notch to open it. As she lifted the lid, tinkling music began to play. The tune seemed familiar, but Cate couldn't place it.

She lifted the lid a bit further when something inside caught her eye. Cate's jaw dropped open and her heart pounded. She gasped, leaping onto wobbly legs as she backed away from the desk. Her sudden movement brought both dogs to their feet and knocked the piano-shaped music box off its perch on the desk.

It clattered to the floor, landing on its side. The lid popped open, and the contents of the interior spilled out, skittering across the hardwood floor and landing next to Cate's feet.

Tinkling music filled the air again as Cate stared in horror at the item below.

"No," she whispered. "It can't be."

Cate squatted down and scooped up the object. With trembling hands, she brought it closer to her face. Her breathing turned ragged as her mind confirmed what she suspected.

In her shaking hands, she held the sapphire necklace she and Jack discarded less than twenty-four hours ago.

CHAPTER 12

$\mathcal{C}$ate's lower lip trembled, and she pressed a palm against her forehead. She stood motionless, the latest turn of events rendering her speechless. Her brain failed to process what she stared at or comprehend how it could happen.

Cate collapsed into the desk chair as Riley and Bailey joined her. She dropped the necklace on the desk in favor of cuddling the two dogs. A tear fell onto her cheek and Riley offered her a kiss, sensing her upset.

"I'm okay," she said with a sniffle. "Thanks, buddy."

Bailey stared at her, his ears wiggling up and down as he attempted to determine the source of Cate's distress.

She stared over at the music box, still playing its tune. She leapt from her seat and snapped the lid shut as she realized why she recognized the tune. The little music box played the same tune she'd been humming this morning.

Cate bit her lower lip hard as tears filled her eyes. Emotions overcame her and a sob escaped her lips. Tears flowed down her cheeks as she clutched the piano against her chest.

Warm arms embraced her, and she glanced up to find Jack. The concern on his face was obvious. "Cate?" he whispered.

Cate gave in to another moment of weakness, squeezing her eyes shut, causing more tears to fall to her cheeks as she let her head rest against Jack's shoulder.

"Oh, now, it can't be as bad as all that, can it?" Jack inquired as he rubbed her shoulder.

Cate swiped at the tears glistening on her cheeks. "Sorry," she choked out. "I'm sorry."

"It's okay, Cate," Jack said as she pushed away from him. He gave her back a gentle rub. "What happened?"

Cate swallowed hard and blew out a long breath. She retrieved a tissue and composed herself. "I'm sorry," she said again. "I don't know what came over me. I just panicked." She held up the piano with both hands. Jack studied the item.

"A package arrived this morning. Addressed to me. This was inside," Cate explained.

"And it brought you to tears? Is it from one of your parents?"

Cate shook her head. "I've never seen it before in my life. But that's not what brought me to tears. It was what was inside of it."

Jack grabbed the piano from Cate and glanced at it. He lifted the lid and music filled the air again. "Close it, please," Cate said. "Something about that song bothers me."

Jack snapped the lid closed. "I don't see anything inside."

Cate pulled the item off the desk. "It fell out when I had my moment. This was inside."

Cate raised her arm, letting the sapphire necklace dangle from her fingers. Jack's eyes went wide and his face blanched three shades lighter than normal. "No," he said with a shake of his head, his jaw gaping open.

"That's about the reaction I had. And then some," Cate said, still sniffling.

Jack set the music box down on the desk and grasped the necklace. His head shook as he studied it. After a moment, his eyes met Cate's. "No, this can't be."

"And now you know why I was so upset," Cate said. "I watched you throw that into the loch yesterday. And today, it arrives in a music box. A music box playing a song that I happened to be humming this morning *before* I received it."

"I need to sit down," Jack said. Jack wandered to the leather armchair and plopped into it. He stared straight ahead, the necklace still threaded through his fingers. His brow wrinkled. "I threw it away. I know I did. I watched it sink."

"I was a witness," Cate said, as she eased into the armchair next to him, tucking her feet under her.

Jack stared wide-eyed at the necklace again. "How could this happen?"

Cate shrugged.

"There couldn't possibly be two of these, could there?" Jack inquired. "It's identical. And worth a fortune. Who would have *two* made?"

"What are the chances even if there are two that the second one arrives the day after we discard the first? This can't be a coincidence."

"I'm afraid it's not," Jack said. "But I have no idea what to do about it."

Cate pursed her lips as she sorted through options for tackling the problem. No solutions came. "If we throw it away again…"

"I'm afraid it'll come right back like a boomerang," Jack said, as he grimaced at the necklace. "There's no guarantee that will work. In fact, I'd say we're inviting more trouble by doing it."

"Inviting more trouble?"

"Cate, *someone* sent you that package. And you've been roaming the halls looking for someone. Who? Him! Northcott! Who else can do this?"

Cate sucked in a shaky breath as she shook her head. "So, what do we do?"

"Call Damien," Jack said. "Maybe he knows how to handle something like this."

Cate hurried across the room to grab her phone. Jack tossed the necklace onto the coffee table in front of him. "You're right. He's the best resource we have for anything Duke-related. Although I did tell him we got rid of the necklace yesterday and he didn't warn me about this. He did warn me my nightmares may continue." Cate tapped around on her phone.

Jack screwed up his face. "He warned you your nightmares may continue?"

Cate nodded as her thumbs flew across her virtual keyboard. "Yes. He said Celine's have never stopped and she wanted me to know now that I've had a… negative experience with Duke Northcott, I may be haunted forever by it."

Jack sighed as Cate toggled off her phone. Seconds later, it rang. "Wow, that's service," Cate said, as she swiped to answer the call.

"Hello," she said.

"Hey, Cate. Got your message. What's up?"

"Hey, Damien. Thanks for calling. Is it okay if I put you on speakerphone? Jack's with me."

"Sure, Cate," Damien answered. "Everything okay?"

Cate toggled on the speakerphone and Jack offered a hello. After Jack and Damien exchanged pleasantries, Cate launched into her story.

"Everything's okay, sort of. We've just had an… incident

and I wondered if you may be able to offer us any insight on this."

"Incident?" Damien questioned. "That sounds ominous."

"Well, I told you yesterday that we got rid of the necklace."

"Yep," Damien answered. "Best thing you could have done."

"Well," Cate said with a sigh, as she considered which details to reveal first. "Yes and no."

"What do you mean?"

"The necklace was having an odd effect on me, which is what prompted us to take rather extreme measures to rid ourselves of it." Cate recounted the tale of her sleepwalking, increasing from retrieving the necklace and returning to bed and ending with her search for someone in the castle's main ballroom.

"Like I said," Damien responded, "best thing you could have done is get rid of it."

"There's more," Cate said. "And this is actually what prompted the call."

"Okay?"

Cate took another deep breath. "Jack threw the necklace into the loch yesterday. I watched him do it."

"Way to go, buddy," Damien cheered him.

"Thanks. Unfortunately, it failed to solve the problem," Jack answered.

"Are you still sleepwalking, Cate? Oh, no," Damien said. "You didn't sleepwalk into the loch, did you?"

"No," Cate answered. "But this morning a package was delivered. It contained a piano-shaped music box. And inside the music box, I found the necklace."

"What?" Damien exclaimed. "Are you sure?"

"Positive. Same necklace. Same design, same sapphires. If it's not the same necklace, it's a carbon copy of it."

Cate heard rustling on Damien's end of the line. "Can you hang on the line for a sec? I'm going to run this past Celine."

"Sure. And thanks."

"No problem, Cate."

Cate heard a knock and then Damien and a woman conversing. "Okay, I've got you on speakerphone with Celine and Alexander. Can you tell them everything you just told me? Sorry to make you go through it again but, it's best if the details come from you."

Cate relayed the odd tale of the reappearing necklace to the newcomers on the line. At the conclusion of her tale, the line went quiet for a moment before Celine spoke.

"I'm really not surprised. This fits pretty well with Marcus's standard operating procedures. What puzzles me is why he's pursuing this, though."

"Has the necklace had any odd effects on you since its reappearance?" Alexander inquired.

"Other than my fleeting moment of panic when I saw it again, no. But I've had it less than an hour."

Another pause before Celine spoke again. "I can speak with Marcus about it. I'm certain he won't admit to anything, but perhaps if he's warned that we're aware of the situation, he won't pursue it further."

Cate's brow crinkled at the comment. "I really don't want you to have to deal with him, Celine."

"It's fine," she answered. "He won't hurt me. Though, as I said, I doubt he'll admit anything to me."

"Anything you'd suggest in the meantime?" Jack asked. "I'd throw this bugger in the loch again, but I'm not certain it would do any good."

"You have a safe, right?" Damien asked.

"Yes," Cate answered.

"Lock it in there for the time being? You can't get to it

then, so if it's causing your issues, maybe not being able to retrieve it will help."

"Excellent idea, Damien," Alexander said. "And we'll work on things on our end. I'll search for a way to destroy an enchanted item."

Cate's shoulders slumped at the conversation, both in exasperation at the words "enchanted item" and with relief for the help. "Thank you," she murmured.

"You're welcome, Cate," Damien said. "And try not to let it bother you. I know that's a weird thing to say, but we'll figure it out. And remember, not every enchanted object is bad. You're wearing one of the good ones around your neck right now." There was a brief pause, before Damien added, "Oh, not to creep you out. I can't see you. I'm just assuming you're wearing the timepiece Celine enchanted."

The extra explanatory comment gave Cate a chuckle. "Thanks, Damien. I needed that laugh."

"Hang in there, Cate. We'll get back to you soon."

They said their goodbyes and Cate ended the call. She sat with her brow crinkled as she held the phone in her lap.

"You okay, Cate?"

She nodded. "Yeah, I'm just again blown away by how odd their lives are."

"Yet they act like it's totally normal," Jack voiced in response.

"Yes!" Cate exclaimed, pointing a finger at Jack to punctuate her statement. "I don't understand Celine talking to Duke Northcott. They seemed to be extremely acrid toward each other when we saw them last. Then again, I don't understand any of this."

Cate popped up from her seat and paced the floor behind the chairs. "The natural assumption is I'm seeking Duke Northcott, right?"

"I can't figure out who else it would be," Jack admitted.

"But why would I seek him out? Why am I seeking a man who almost killed me?" Cate asked.

Jack rose from his chair and stopped her pacing. "I don't know, Cate. But I think we should do what Damien suggested and lock this necklace up in the safe. It seems to have some strange effect on you. And I also think I'd better plan on staying another night or two."

Cate nodded in agreement. "Why did we ever think it would be as easy as tossing that thing in the loch?" Cate asked.

"Well, I must admit, I never expected this turn of events," Jack said, motioning toward the necklace laying on the table.

"Neither did I. Let's hope locking it up produces a better result."

Jack swiped the large necklace off the table. "What about that?" he asked, pointing to the music box still on the desk.

"Maybe we should take it, too," Cate said.

Jack nodded as Cate grabbed it from the desk. Leaving the pups behind, they ambled down the hall to the first-floor office. Cate unlocked the password- and thumbprint-protected safe and they stowed the items inside.

As Jack closed and locked the door, he shot Cate a sideways glance. "You okay?"

"Better now, actually," Cate said. "At least they're locked away where hopefully they can do no harm."

Jack nodded at her.

"Time to do some work on our mystery!" Cate exclaimed, forcing a grin onto her face.

"If you need anything, Cate, and I mean anything – even if something just feels slightly off to you – call me, okay?"

"I will," Cate promised.

Jack gave her a closed-mouth smile and a nod. He stepped toward the door. Cate remained still, staring at the safe. "You coming?"

"Yep," she said, as she spun around. She smiled at him as they made their way into the hall and parted ways.

Cate arrived at the library and plopped onto the desk chair with a sigh. The packaging from her surprise gift still sat on top of the desk. With a frown, Cate gathered it and delivered it to the kitchen trash bin. She collected a cup of tea and returned to her work.

With her laptop open, Cate shuffled through the notes she'd compiled yesterday on Ruth Harper. She began with the first woman on her list. Born in 1920 in Edinburgh, this Ruth Harper lived with her parents, Elizabeth and William Harper, until her marriage in 1941, when she became Ruth MacArther.

Cate frowned at the marriage certificate information. After an hour of seeking reports, she'd been led to a dead-end. To be thorough, Cate checked that the woman remained married in subsequent years. She managed to follow her through the 1970s, when Ruth Harper MacArther passed away.

Cate scratched the woman off her list. If she married in 1941, she almost certainly wasn't at Dunhaven Castle as a traveling companion in 1942 using her maiden name, particularly if her spouse remained alive.

"On to the next," Cate said aloud.

She spent the rest of her morning tracking down information on her next potential suspect. She found nothing definitive before her staff lunch in the downstairs kitchen, and left the project in favor of her meal and a walk before returning in the mid-afternoon.

Cate stretched and settled in at her laptop. She found her eyelids growing heavy and a yawn escaped her lips. As the afternoon hours waned, she managed to find a death certificate for her current person of interest.

The second Ruth Harper had died in 1962. Given this

information, she couldn't have been killed and buried at Dunhaven Castle in the 1940s. And since they clearly had this Ruth's body with a cause of death listed as "Stroke," she had not gone missing and been declared dead.

Cate put a thick strike through this woman's name and stretched before moving on to the next. As she pulled up the third Ruth Harper's birth records, a chill passed through her.

Cate shivered and wrapped her cardigan around her. She glanced to the fire, expecting to find it dying. Instead, a healthy orange glow emanated from inside the hearth.

Perhaps the steady rain that now fell from the gray skies added an extra chill to the air. Cate tossed another log onto the fire before returning to her work.

After several minutes of pawing through census records, Cate shivered again. She wrapped her sweater around herself again and moved closer to the fire, pulling a blanket over her lap.

Before she could settle in again, both Riley and Bailey leapt to their feet. "What is it, guys?" Cate inquired.

Both dogs stared at the closed library doors. Cate set her laptop down and flung her blanket to the side. She crossed to the door and peeked into the hall.

"Nothing's there!" she said.

Riley cocked his head at her before he stared into the hall again. Bailey sidestepped to get a better look into the hall. An icy blast of air washed over Cate, originating from the hall. As Cate peered through the doors again, both dogs bolted into the hall.

"Where are you two going?" Cate inquired, as they darted past her and fled down the hall.

"Riley! Bailey!" she shouted after them. The two pups turned the corner and continued to run headlong toward some unknown target.

Cate's shoulders slumped and she followed them into the hall. "Riley! Bailey!" she called again.

She turned the corner, finding them nowhere in sight. "Where did they run off to?" she asked herself, as she continued down the hall's length in search of them.

As she passed the office containing the safe, her footsteps slowed. She stared through the open door at the large black object.

Her head lolled to the side as she focused on the dark vault. The world melted around her. Her vision outside of her focal point blurred. Noises faded away, replaced by a light tinkling. She hummed along with the tune as she took a step toward the safe.

Her senses dulled as the music filled her mind.

CHAPTER 13

The corners of her mouth turned up as she lost herself in the tinkling tune that played in her mind. She closed her eyes and reached her hand out. An image formed in her mind. A room. Soft light glowed from above her.

"I'm here," she mumbled.

"Lady Cate?" Jack's voice called.

Cate's smile faltered and her brow furrowed as the image splintered. In an instant, everything faded away. She jolted back to reality with a start.

The fog cleared from her mind, and she twirled to find Jack standing a few paces down the hall from her.

She sucked in a few breaths, her eyes darting around as her mind recovered.

Jack approached her. "Cate? You okay?"

"Yeah," Cate assured him.

"What are you doing here?" Jack asked, his gaze flicking toward the safe.

Cate swallowed hard, following his eyes before she returned her gaze to Jack. "I was looking for the dogs."

Jack's eyebrow arched. "In the office?"

Cate offered a chuckle. "Ah, no. Well, yes. They darted around the corner, and I haven't seen them since. I'm not sure where they are."

"Well, they're not in here," Jack said, pulling the office door closed. "Want me to help find them?"

Cate pursed her lips and shook her head. "No, I'm sure they'll turn up. I'm happy to wander the halls for a bit in search of them, though. I'm not making it very far with my Ruth Harper research."

"No progress?" Jack inquired as they strode down the hall.

"Yeah, I crossed two of my four off the list so far. I guess that's progress. Of the negative kind."

"Progress is progress, I guess," Jack said, as they rounded the corner into another hall.

"Well, two down, two to go. I think I'll take a break for the night though and try again tomorrow."

"Sounds like a plan," Jack said.

The sound of skittering paws reached their ears. Riley and Bailey bounded around a corner and down the hall.

"There you are!" Cate exclaimed, as they raced toward them.

"Hey, Sir Riley, just where did you and your brother get off to?" Jack inquired, lifting the small dog into his arms. "You had poor Lady Cate worried!"

"Not worried, just curious!" she said as she scooped up Bailey.

"It's almost time for dinner. Heading back to the library?" Jack asked.

"Do you think anyone would mind if I joined you for dinner?"

"No, not at all, Lady Cate," Jack said. "Are you sure you're all right?"

"I guess I'm just a little spooked by the events earlier today, to be honest. I'd love a distraction. *Not* that dining with everyone is just a distraction but…"

"I understand, Lady Cate. You don't need to explain."

They snaked through the halls and down to the kitchen.

"Hi, everyone," Cate said, as she set Bailey on the floor near the warm stove.

"Lady Cate! To what do we owe the pleasure?" Mrs. Fraser inquired. "I hope you haven't come down here in hopes of wrangling your own tray from Molly and carrying it upstairs."

"No. I've actually come down in the hopes of saving everyone a trip and eating here." Cate paused for a moment. "That is if no one minds."

"Not at all," Molly said with a smile.

Mrs. Fraser flicked her gaze to Cate and arched an eyebrow. "I dinnae mind. Are you sure you're feeling all right, Lady Cate? You look a bit pale."

Cate planted herself at the table. "Mrs. Fraser, I always look a bit pale."

"Paler than normal," Mrs. Fraser corrected, shooting her another look.

"Too much work and no play," Jack said as he settled across from Cate and rubbed Riley's belly.

"Probably," Cate said.

"Well," Mrs. Fraser said. "Young Jack told me about the leak. I'm concerned your worry over this old place is going to have you down with something, Lady Cate."

"Oh, I'm sure it'll clear up. I trust Jack."

"Mmm, I'm not saying you don't, but it is a lot to carry."

"Oh, Mrs. Fraser, just tell her," Molly said.

Mrs. Fraser harrumphed at Molly.

"Tell me what?" Cate asked, a concerned expression on her face.

"Miss Molly and I were discussing the leak. And I was concerned about something happening in the middle of the night. Young Jack would have his hands full. And…" Her voice trailed off.

"Oh, Mrs. Fraser," Molly said with a chuckle, as she set a salad in the center of the table. "Lady Cate, she wants to stay in the castle with Mr. Fraser in case the leak springs up."

"Oh," Cate said, "why didn't you just say so! Of course, you can. You know you're always welcome here."

"Well, I dinnae want to invite myself into your home," Mrs. Fraser said.

"Don't be ridiculous," Cate said, with a wave of her hand. "You don't need to ask. You can stay anytime you'd like! Bad weather, good weather, leak, no leak. I'm happy to have people here!"

Mrs. Fraser smiled at her as she settled in at the table.

"And I'm busy making sure Cate's not all work and no play," Molly said. "I'm almost done with our itinerary for the next few months!"

"What's on it?" Mr. Fraser inquired.

Molly rattled off several places. "And there's tons more. That's just what I remember off the top of my head. If anyone is interested in going with us to any of these, just let me know!"

"When do you have Loch Ness scheduled?" Jack inquired.

Molly responded, "September. Is that good for everyone? I figured after both parties would be a good time for a rest."

"Aye, perfect," Jack agreed.

"Yes, a nice respite after the Presidents' Ball and before the second annual Halloween Ball," Cate said.

"Oh, no, please don't tell me she's already brought that up," Jack said.

"She has," Cate said with a laugh. "Her words were 'bigger and better.'"

"Oh, I'll bet they were," Jack said with a groan.

The conversation centered around the upcoming events and how Dunhaven Castle was quickly becoming the party capital of the area.

"Soon, you'll be renting out for weddings," Jack said.

"No," Cate answered, with her eyebrows hiked high. "That's where I draw the line."

"Aw, come on, Lady Cate," Jack teased. "Every little girl dreams of a fairy tale wedding at a castle. Are you going to crush their dreams?"

"I just might," Cate said with a chuckle. "I'm not certain that's something any of us want to get into."

"Not me," Mrs. Fraser said. "I would want no parts of people traipsing everywhere here for their wedding."

"Aye, I agree with Emily," Mr. Fraser said. "These grounds are unspoiled. And I like them that way."

"Me too," Cate said with a smile. "While I don't mind the parties, I'm not sure I want those interruptions on a regular basis."

"Well, you have our support on that decision, Lady Cate," Jack said with a nod.

With the matter settled, they steered the conversation to other topics. The shared dinner allowed Cate to push both mysteries from her mind. She hoped the meal provided her with enough relaxation to fall asleep quickly. She'd even avoided asking Mrs. Fraser about the intelligence base so as not to stir up her mind.

She spent the rest of the evening helping Mrs. Fraser settle in while Mr. Fraser retrieved their things.

As she climbed into her bed and slipped between the sheets, she worked to push any remnants of the two dilemmas away.

The moon hung low in the night sky as Cate stared out over the moors, bathed in an ethereal white light. She turned onto her side, squeezing her eyes shut. Within moments, she was spinning the other way. She spent the first hour tossing and turning in search of a comfortable sleeping position, but found none.

As she flopped onto her back, Cate's mind centered on one thing. The piano-shaped music box currently housed in the downstairs safe. The little tinkling tune ricocheted in her mind. It was a lovely little tune, Cate thought. Perhaps it could help her sleep. Yes, she mused, the little tune may help her fall asleep.

Cate rose from her bed and wrapped her robe around her, shoving her feet into her fluffy slippers. She shuffled across her room and threaded through the halls toward the back stairs. After padding down them and to the office, Cate flicked on the light, her attention focused on the safe across the room.

Movement caught her eye, and she leapt back a step, her eyes wide with fear and her heart pounding. After a moment, she breathed a sigh of relief with her hand pressed against her chest.

"Lady Cate," Jack said, as he rose from the desk chair. "Fancy meeting you here."

"Oh, Jack, you scared me. What are you doing here?"

"What are you doing here?" Jack shot back.

"Uh," Cate said, giving a hard swallow. "I was just going to double-check that the music box and necklace were still in the safe."

"They are," Jack assured her, stepping between her and the safe.

Cate smiled at him. "Good. That's good."

"You can sleep soundly knowing they are still locked up tight."

Cate licked her lips and nodded but didn't budge. Jack

raised his eyebrows at her, crossing his arms over his chest. "Did you need something else?"

"No," Cate said, with a slight shake of her head. After a moment, she added, "I couldn't sleep."

Jack's expression softened. "Care for a cuppa and a biscuit?"

"Umm," Cate hedged. "No, thanks."

"Okay, though I can't believe you're turning down one of Mrs. Fraser's shortbreads. But okay. How about if I walk you back to your room?"

"That's not necessary," Cate said with a chuckle.

Jack narrowed his eyes at her. "Cate, did you come down here for the necklace?" he asked.

"No," Cate said with a shake of her head. "You know what, I think I will take you up on that offer."

Jack nodded his head and led Cate from the room to the kitchen. Cate gave one wistful glance at the safe as Jack flicked off the room's lights.

"You sure you're okay, Cate?" he asked, as they traversed the halls.

"I'm sure. Just couldn't sleep," Cate admitted.

Jack bustled about the kitchen making Cate a late-night cup of tea. As they cleaned up, Jack inquired, "Do you think you can sleep now?"

Cate stretched and faked a yawn. "I think so. Thanks, Jack." She took a few steps toward the door.

"Wait just a moment, lassie," Jack said. "I'll walk up with you."

Cate shoulders slumped, but she twisted to face Jack, plastered a smile on her face and nodded. Jack accompanied her on the walk upstairs, eyeing her as she waved goodnight and closed the door to her suite.

The smile quickly faded from her face as the door shut. She puckered her lips and narrowed her eyes. She inched sideways away from the door but remained with her ear pressed against the wall leading to the hall. After a few moments, she heard the click of a door closing.

A grin formed on her lips. She waited an extra few seconds before she crept back to her door and eased it open. She peered into the hall. Jack's door was closed.

Cate swung her door open further and tiptoed into the hallway. She crept past the bedrooms used by Jack, Mr. and Mrs. Fraser and Molly. As she slipped past the last doorway, she picked up her pace, hastening down the remainder of the hall and around the corner.

She skidded to a halt, her arms held up in defense, as a large dark figure approached her. Hands clamped down around her shoulders and she was driven back several steps. She let out a yip as she fought to free herself.

"Going somewhere, Lady Cate?" Jack inquired.

She gasped in a breath before she explained. "Yes, I thought we may have left the stove on…"

"No, you didn't," Jack interrupted.

"Yes, I…"

"You know very well I turned the stove off. And the water. And put everything away."

"I didn't…"

"Cate," Jack said, his hands still firmly clasping her shoulders, "you're not telling the truth. You're after that necklace, aren't you?"

"No, I'm not!" Cate exclaimed, wrenching herself free from his grasp.

"No? Then what? Why are you sneaking around the halls at this hour?"

"I'm hardly sneaking," she said, crossing her arms. "I couldn't sleep, and I often walk the halls. I'm usually not policed though."

"I'm sorry," Jack said. "I don't mean to police you. I'm just worried, that's all."

"There's nothing to worry about," Cate answered. "I'm just restless."

"That necklace is having a terrible effect on you. I think we should remove it from the house. I'm not sure Damien's suggestion is helping."

"No!" Cate shouted. She lowered her panicked voice before continuing. "I mean, it's not that. It is, but not in the way you think. And even if it was, is it really hurting me? All I do is put it on and wander around."

Jack cocked his head and narrowed his eyes. "Cate, you have no memory of anything you do while you're wearing it. You're wandering could get you harmed. And who are you looking for? What happens if you find him? I don't want you lost for days again. Cate…" His voice trailed off.

Cate bit her lower lip as tears formed in her eyes. "I don't want that either."

Jack put his hands around her shoulders again. "Oh, Cate. If the necklace is bothering you, just tell me."

"It's not," she admitted. "I'm being honest. I just…" Cate's voice trailed off as she considered admitting her desire to hear the music box. "I guess in a way, it is. I just want it dealt with and off our minds."

Jack nodded and sighed. "Me too, Lady Cate, me too. And until then, I don't want anything to happen to you."

Cate stared up at him for a moment. "Well, I guess roaming the halls isn't helping to solve anything. I'm going to go back to bed and try to get some sleep."

"Okay."

"You should, too. Really, I'm fine. I feel terrible keeping you awake."

Jack smiled at her. "I'm okay, but I am going to bed. I hope you sleep, Lady Cate."

Cate smiled at him before she strode down the hall and entered her bedroom for the third time that night. She leaned against the door as she sighed and stared up at the ceiling.

A thudding pounded at her temples. She hated lying to Jack, but she couldn't tell him the truth. He'd never let her near the music box even if she was honest.

Cate stalked to her chaise and sank onto it. She cupped her chin in her palm and steadied her elbow on her knee. She checked the timepiece before she returned to staring at the door.

Cate waited an hour before she crept to the door again. With a quick peek into the hall, she stepped out and eased the door shut behind her. Her eyes studied each door. Satisfied no one lurked behind one waiting to spring out at her, she tiptoed down the hall.

She approached the corner slowly and peered around it. No one stood in the hallway this time. The corners of her mouth turned up again as she hurried down the hall, back stairs and to the office.

Devoid of anyone, she flipped the lights on and hurried to the safe. She tapped in the five-digit code and pressed her thumb against the scanner. A beep sounded and the light changed from red to green. Cate's heart skipped a beat as she anticipated collecting the music box. Her breathing increased and she grinned as she pulled the safe door open.

CHAPTER 14

Her smile faded, concern creeping into her features as the interior of the safe came into view. Her lower lip trembled as her brow furrowed. Her breath caught in her throat and her stomach turned over.

"No!" she exclaimed, reaching into the safe and shoving items around. "Where is it?"

She stared in at the nearly empty interior. Her old timepiece sat on the top shelf, a few folders of important paperwork lay below. But the music box and necklace were gone.

"Looking for something, Lady Cate?" Jack inquired from behind her.

Cate spun to face him, a frown on her lips. "Where is it?" she demanded.

"Somewhere safe."

Cate pressed her lips together into a thin line. Her hands balled into fists. "Where?" she asked again, her voice quavering.

"Cate…" he began.

"No!" she interrupted. "I want it."

Jack approached her, holding his hands in front of him.

He shook his head. "Cate…" he tried again, keeping his tone as even and soothing as he could. He placed his hands on her shoulders. "Leave it alone."

Tears formed in Cate's eyes. "I want it. I need to see it!" she said, as a sob formed.

"No, Cate," Jack answered. "It's not safe for you to see it."

"I just want the music box, that's all," Cate said.

"I realize you're going to hate me for this, Cate, but I don't think I should."

Cate bit her lower lip as she sucked in a shaky breath. "I know," she said, her face a mask of pain. After a moment, she grasped Jack's arm. "What's wrong with me?"

"Nothing," he assured her, as he pulled her into an embrace. Cate laid her head on his chest as she fought back tears. "Let's get you another cup of tea."

She pulled back and shook her head. "No, I've kept you up half the night already. I'll just go back to my room."

"It's fine, Cate," he assured her, grasping her hand and tugging her from the room.

"Wait," she said, stepping back to close the safe.

After making a cup of tea, Jack and Cate settled in the generous leather armchairs in the library. Jack built a fire. They attempted to sort through some of their mystery from decades ago. With the conversation, Cate eventually dozed off in her armchair.

* * *

Cate's eyes opened slowly as dull light streamed in through the large library windows. She blinked several times as she oriented herself. After peeling her face from the leather chair, she stretched and yawned.

She peered around in the dim light. Jack's sleeping form huddled in the armchair next to her. With another stretch,

Cate pulled back the blanket Jack must have draped over her at some point and rose to stand, her arms reaching high overhead.

After another yawn, she rubbed at her face before folding the blanket and giving Jack a soft shake.

"Huh? What?" he asked.

"Jack," she whispered. "It's morning."

Jack's eyes opened and he blinked a few times, searching the space. He offered a sleepy sniff before he stretched and yawned. "Good morning, m'lady," he said as he stood.

"Good morning," she said, as she folded his blanket. "Thanks for covering me last night."

"You're welcome. You finally fell asleep around one."

Cate heaved a sigh. "I'm sorry," she said. "I just couldn't get my mind off that music box."

"It's okay, Cate. It's not your fault. With any luck, we'll get some information from Damien today, and maybe we can put this thing behind us."

Cate yawned again. "Gosh, I hope so. I don't want to keep you up for another night."

"Don't worry about that Lady Cate," Jack said with a half-smile. "I just don't want to see you so upset."

"It's odd," Cate admitted. "At times it doesn't bother me, but then it will pervade my thoughts. I can't stop thinking about that music or hearing it in my head. It's like a craving where I need to hear the music box."

Jack narrowed his eyes. "What about the necklace?"

Cate shook her head. "That didn't seem to be on my mind. Just the music box."

"That's odd," Jack said. "Are both enchanted?"

Cate shrugged. "Maybe once I had the music box I would also want the necklace. I'm not sure."

"I'm not sure I want to find out," Jack admitted.

"Me either."

"Will you be all right for now?"

"So far, so good," Cate said. "I feel fine. No overwhelming urges to claw through the walls to find the music box."

"Well, given the rain today," Jack said, eyeing the dark clouds, "I can keep an eye on you."

Cate sighed and rolled her eyes. "I never thought at this age I'd need a babysitter."

"You also never thought you'd time travel or meet a warlock, but here we are."

The last statement earned a chuckle from Cate. "Very true," Cate said. "Anyway, I'm fine for now, but I'll see you later for whatever it is you're doing inside today."

"Maybe I'll build a puzzle," Jack quipped.

Cate raised her eyebrows. "Oh, taking a vacation day, huh?"

"Sick day. Someone kept me up half the night."

Cate offered him a wry glance and a head shake. "See you later, Jack."

Cate wandered up to her bedroom, finding her two furry friends still sprawled on her bed. Bailey lay stretched on his side, and Riley, in true Snoopy style, lay on his back, his front legs stuck in the air, his floppy ears flung out across the duvet.

"Glad to see you two had no trouble sleeping without me," she said, as she stalked into the room.

At the sound of her voice, Bailey's tail gave a weak wag. Riley spun onto his belly and glanced up at Cate. "I'll be ready soon," she announced, as she sauntered around the room for her morning routine.

When she was finished, she ushered the dogs outside before her breakfast. The warm smell of cinnamon greeted her the moment she stepped back inside through the kitchen door.

"Mmmm, that smells amazing, whatever it is," Cate said.

"Snickerdoodles," Molly reported, as she peered in through the oven's window.

"That's what happens when I stay at the castle," Mrs. Fraser said with a nod. "I'm up early baking."

Cate crinkled her forehead. "You're up early baking even when you don't stay," she said.

"Aye, but I'm baking more. Snickerdoodles *and* short-breads. Seems someone's been robbing my tin! I'd wager it's young Jack."

Cate winced. "And me," she admitted. "I had a sleepless night, and Jack and I may have hit up the cookies once or twice."

Mrs. Fraser's eyes went wide in mock surprise. "Lady Cate! I'm shocked!"

Cate chuckled.

"More problems with the leak last night?"

"No," Cate admitted. "But both of us found ourselves roaming the halls just in case."

"Well, I hope my shortbreads helped put you back to sleep."

"They did," Cate assured her, as she collected her tray before ascending to the library to eat.

Cate stared out over the gray skies as she ate. Thunder rumbled in the distance, giving Riley a start. When the grumble died down, he flopped back down for a morning nap next to Bailey, who remained unbothered by the noise.

Cate popped her laptop open as she ate to check her emails. She fought to keep her mind off of her evening escapades the previous night. Where had Jack hidden the necklace and the music box, she wondered? And how had he anticipated that she'd search for it?

She supposed her recent obsession with the necklace, coupled with its mysterious reappearance was enough to warrant his actions. She hoped it didn't make the situation worse. Cate leaned back in her chair, studying the clouds zipping past the window. Images of her roaming the castle, pawing through every imaginable hidden area bounced around in her mind. She pictured herself returning to her bedroom with cobwebs in her hair and dirt smudges on her cheeks.

She shook the images from her mind as a knock sounded at the door.

"Still feeling okay?" Jack asked as he strode in.

"Yes," Cate answered with a nod.

"Molly'll be up soon to get your tray. She's taking cookies out of the oven. I didn't wait in case..." He didn't finish the statement.

"It's fine," she said, with a wave of her hand. "I was just pondering my behavior last night and wondering if it will worsen."

"How so?" Jack asked, as he opened a cabinet in the library and removed a box.

"Obviously I was intent on finding that music box last night. How far will I go? Will I begin roaming the halls and secret passages? Clawing at the walls?"

"Hmm, good question. I hope not, but now that you know it's hidden, will you go to extreme measures to find it?"

Molly flitted into the room as Jack finished his statement. "Good morning, again," she said in her cheery voice. "Looks like you won't be able to take your morning walk of the property."

"No," Cate said, with a dejected shake of her head. "Oh well, maybe I can make a killing on my research."

"What are you on to now?" Molly asked.

"World War Two era Dunhaven," Cate reported. "I think there may have been an intelligence base here."

"Really?" Molly asked, her eyebrows shooting upward. "That's interesting."

"Yes, I'm only just scratching the surface, so I have plenty more to learn."

"Well, I'll leave you to it. That is if Jack doesn't take up all your time discussing estate business."

"Estate business is just as important. Perhaps more so!"

"Uh-huh," Molly said, with a wry glance at him. "Better you than me, Lady Cate." She winked at Cate before disappearing through the door with the tray.

Cate closed the doors behind her as Jack settled into his favorite armchair.

"I sometimes feel bad about how good we are at lying to people," Cate said with a sigh.

"I'm not lying. I'm working on Dunhaven Castle."

Cate scrunched up her face at the statement. Jack pulled the lid off his puzzle box and flashed it at Cate. A large picture of Dunhaven Castle graced the front. A printed yellow puzzle piece announced the one thousand pieces to be found inside the box.

"Where did you get that?" Cate inquired.

"Mr. Smythe gave it to me for Christmas," Jack answered. "Him and his puzzles. I think he was rather regretful to give it away and not complete it himself."

"When you're finished, you can break it apart and put it back in the box for him to complete the next time he's here," Cate said.

"*If* I finish, Lady Cate, if."

Cate chuckled at his statement as she settled in at her desk. Jack twisted to eye her. "I thought you'd help me," Jack said.

"Maybe later," Cate said. "I hope to figure out if one of these Ruth Harpers is the one we found in the garden first."

"Oh," Jack groaned, heaving a large sigh. "I'm on my own. I hate puzzles."

Cate glanced over her shoulder. "Get all the edge pieces out first and build that. Maybe by then I'll be finished."

Jack offered another sigh as he sorted through pieces. "You know, I feel perfectly fine. You don't have to stay and build that puzzle."

"Sure, sure," Jack said. "And then I'll be changing a light bulb and see you wandering past in search of the music box."

"Just hop off the ladder and grab me then."

"Very funny, Lady Cate," Jack said. "No chance. I'm not taking a chance I don't see you in time and you get hurt. Plus, I'd like to gather as much information about what's happening from the moment it happens."

"What do you mean?" Cate asked.

"I mean, is there some trigger that causes you to turn from Lady Cate to Zombie Cate? A noise, a scent, something you see."

"Oh," Cate said, nodding in understanding.

"I hope Damien and his friends come up with something for us, but if they don't, I want to have as much information as possible to create a backup plan."

Cate nodded again. "Thanks, Jack."

"Well, I'm tasked with protecting you and I'm not about to fall down on the job."

"I think when that pact was made, they didn't anticipate enchanted music boxes and warlocks."

"Doesn't matter," Jack said, as he dug through pieces in the box. "Time travel, warlocks, enchanted music boxes, white water rafting, rock climbing…"

"Whoa," Cate said, waving her hands in the air. "I'm drawing the line at enchanted music boxes. No white water rafting or rock climbing for me."

"Fair enough," Jack said. "To be honest, I'd rather not rock climb either. I don't even like flying, let alone dangling from a rock."

Cate chuckled. "Okay, I'll leave you to your edges." She spun to face her laptop, tapping around to open her notes and several websites.

Cate spent several of the morning hours tracking down information on her last two leads. The first woman married in 1947, had three children, and passed away in the 1970s. Cate scratched her name off the list and moved on to her last Ruth Harper.

Born on 1 February, 1919, Ruth Harper disappeared shortly after. Cate's pulse quickened as she searched for records and found none. Perhaps this was her Ruth Harper. No marriage records existed for the woman, so her name had not changed. No death records existed in the UK. Could this Ruth Harper have come to Dunhaven and disappeared, therefore never having a death certificate recorded?

CHAPTER 15

Cate bit her lower lip as she searched for more information on the promising lead. A sigh emanated from the other side of the room. Cate glanced at Jack, who frowned down at the pieces spread across the table in front of him. Riley lounged on his lap.

"I hope you're having more luck than me," Jack said.

"I may be!" Cate answered. "I have a Ruth Harper who has disappeared."

"That sounds promising!"

"I have a few more places to check for her, but I think so. No luck with the puzzle?"

"The edge pieces all look alike. I can't even tell the corners apart. And Riley isn't much help."

"Sorry," Cate said. "I think Bailey is more of the puzzle solver."

"Do you want to help, Bailey?" Jack prodded. The dog lifted his gray and white head and glanced sideways at Jack before he lowered his head to the floor. "I'll take that as a no."

"I'll help you as soon as I've finished here."

"Thank goodness," Jack said. "Otherwise, I'm fairly certain I'll fail miserably."

"If I've found our lady, I will happily help!"

Cate returned her attention to her laptop. With no marriage records or death records in the UK for her latest Ruth, she double-checked the census reports. Born in 1919, her first census report following Ruth's birth was dated 1921. Nearly two-year-old Ruth was reported as living with her parents, Theodore and Elizabeth Harper. Other children listed within the home included Ruth's six older siblings: Stephen, Lois, Henry, Harriet, Evelyn, and Eleanor.

No mention of the Harpers was made in the subsequent census of 1931. Cate expanded her search to several other venues. A frown crossed her face as she came across Ruth Harper's name in another database.

She pulled up the record and compared it to the 1921 census. One Ruth Harper was listed arriving at Ellis Island in October of 1925. She traveled with her mother, Elizabeth, and six siblings. They were to join their father, Theodore, already stateside since 1922.

Cate's shoulders slumped. No marriage or death records existed in the UK for this Ruth Harper because she had emigrated to the United States at the age of six.

Cate followed up on US records, finding that Ruth did not return to her home country, but remained in the United States for the duration of her life.

With a groan, she closed her laptop and scratched the last name off the list.

"That sounded terrible," Jack said, as he studied the table, his chin resting in his palm.

"There goes my last Ruth Harper," Cate said, as she stood and stretched.

"What happened to her?"

"She went to the United States at the age of six."

"Darn her," Jack said, sliding puzzle pieces aimlessly around.

"She was my best lead," Cate said as she flopped into the other armchair, pulling her legs underneath her.

"None of the others are any good?"

"Nope," Cate answered. "They've all got solid death records and marriages that rule them out." She shook her head. "And now this one had to go and move on us."

"Traitor," Jack said, with a shake of his head.

"So, as usual, we'll be exploring in the past with little to no clue as to what may have happened."

"No different from usual. Hey," Jack said, snapping his fingers, "you don't think she's…"

"She's what?" Cate inquired, screwing up her face as she picked up the puzzle's box top.

Jack pursed his lips before continuing. "Maybe I'm way off-base but… the last time you couldn't find anything about the people from the past, it was because half of them were immortals, and the other half were time travelers."

Cate furrowed her brow. "But…" She shrugged as she parsed through it. "Okay, she couldn't be an immortal, otherwise…"

"She wouldn't be dead," Jack said.

"Right," Cate answered. She connected two edge pieces together and slid them to attach to a corner piece.

Jack wrinkled his nose at Cate's progress.

"But…" Cate continued, the crease between her eyebrows deepening as she stared at the pieces. "I suppose Ruth Harper could be a time traveler."

"Which means Ruth Harper could be a fake name and you could be looking for the woman in the wrong century."

Cate snapped another three pieces together and slid them

across the table. "How common do you think time traveling is?" she questioned, pulling several puzzle pieces toward her and studying them.

"I'm not sure," Jack answered. "Maybe this is a question for Damien. Do you think he'd have any insight?"

"Maybe," Cate said, adding more pieces to her three-piece chain.

Jack's jaw unhinged. "How are you doing this?"

"Doing what?" Cate asked, as she shoved a lock of hair behind her ear and crossed the room to retrieve her phone from the desk.

"Building this puzzle? It's impossible."

"It's definitely difficult," Cate admitted, as she swiped into her phone, "but not impossible."

"All the pieces look the same!"

"No they don't," Cate replied with a chuckle. "See, these two fit – see how the shapes are the same?"

"No," Jack said, with a shake of his head.

Cate shrugged as her thumbs flew across her virtual keyboard. "I'm good at puzzles."

Jack continued to try his hand at fitting edge pieces together while Cate fired a message across the pond. "I sent a message to Damien about your theory."

Cate managed to finish one entire edge before her phone chimed.

"I'm really starting to detest your puzzle-building skills, Lady Cate," Jack said as she fiddled with her phone. "You make it look way too easy."

Cate shook her head at him and studied her phone. "Okay, Damien says it's not very common, though given the history surrounding Dunhaven, he wouldn't be surprised." Cate frowned. "Which means we'll be doing most of our work back in the past."

"No change from normal then," Jack said with a sigh.

"It's amazing how much history is lost over the years," Cate said in agreement, when her phone chimed again. "It's another message from Damien. He says that reminded him of another solution to our problem. Getting rid of an enchanted object is no small feat, but lessening the effects may be possible if we simply go back to another time period."

"What?" Jack said, his expression incredulous.

Cate lifted a shoulder and offered him a confused glance. "He's typing again. But yes, his first message says they haven't made any progress so far because enchanted objects are difficult to destroy. He's assuming the duke's enchantment would be fairly powerful given what they know about him. He also says Celine's inquiry fell flat."

Jack pursed his lips as they waited for the next message to come through. A new bubble popped onto the screen and Cate studied it. Her posture stiffened and her jaw dropped open.

"What is it?" Jack inquired.

Cate shook her head and blinked her eyes at the message as if to confirm what she was reading. She stammered around for a moment, before she explained her shocked expression to Jack.

"He says…" Cate paused and gave another shake of her head. "I can't believe I'm about to read this statement to you. He says, and I'm quoting here, 'It worked for Michael when he was bitten by a vampire. We went back to the 1790s and he had no ill-effects like he did in our current time.'"

"What?" Jack exclaimed. "Bitten by a vampire? Is he joking?"

"I don't think he is," Cate said, with a shake of her head.

Jack took a deep inhale, his eyebrows raised high. "Well, I suppose that's a solution then," he said, after a few moments of silence. "We can hope our time travel keeps the enchantment at bay."

Cate nodded in silent response. Another moment passed before Jack spoke again. "Why do they say those things like it's completely normal?"

Cate chuckled. "I'm not sure, but they must lead fantastically interesting lives. I cannot even imagine."

"I don't want to imagine. The revelation of time travel was enough for me. I nearly lost my marbles when we added the existence of supernatural creatures. And now this?"

Cate shrugged again. "I suppose vampires are not much of a stretch when you consider we've met supernatural creatures in the form of witches and warlocks."

"I hope they keep them on that side of the pond," Jack said with a shiver.

Cate returned to working on the puzzle after sending a brief reply text to Damien.

"I suppose given your lack of progress on research and Damien's latest message, we should discuss returning to 1942," Jack said.

"Yes," Cate agreed. "And it seems like we'll have to take our chances with showing our too-young faces to the family."

"Aye. Information is in short supply," Jack agreed.

"Should we go today?" Cate asked. "Or are you calling in sick for that, too?"

Jack sucked in air before he replied. "Well, I usually like twenty-four hours' notice so I can fret for a full day before a trip, but I suppose there's no time like the present. Particularly if it prevents you from going haywire over that music box and necklace."

"After lunch then," Cate proposed.

Riley lifted his head from Jack's knee and glanced at the closed library door. His nose wiggled as he sniffed the air.

"What is it, Sir Riley? Lunch on its way already?" Jack asked as he stroked his back.

Bailey rose to his feet, stretched, and stared at the door. Riley leapt from Jack's lap and circled around the chairs to stare at the door again. His feather-like tail gave a slow wag as he continued to sniff.

"What's with you two?" Cate asked.

"They must smell something fantastic from the kitchen," Jack suggested.

"This is the first time they've ever acted like this," Cate said.

Riley raced to the closed doors and scratched his paw against it. He stuck his nose in the small crack between the doors and sniffed. Bailey hurried toward the doors, sticking his nose underneath to sniff.

Cate crinkled her brow before she glanced at Jack and shrugged. She shuffled to the doors and pulled them open. The dogs raced from the library and disappeared down the hall.

"Headed for the kitchen?" Jack inquired, as he snapped two puzzle pieces together.

"No, the opposite way, actually," Cate said as she stared after them.

Jack glanced at her and raised his eyebrows. "Why?"

"I have no idea," Cate answered.

Jack stood with a huff. "And just as I was making progress on this puzzle."

"You can stay and keep working," Cate said.

"No thanks, Lady Cate. I'd rather find out why your dogs are racing around the castle."

"Maybe you don't," Cate said, as she stepped into the hall. "Last time they were interested in something, they found a body."

"Very true, Lady Cate, very true. Let's hope they haven't found another."

"Though I suppose it's best to know if they have," Cate said, as they rounded the corner into the hallway containing the office she'd raided last night.

They continued through the hallways as Cate called to the two pups. They turned the corner and passed through another hall. The dogs raced toward them. Riley leapt onto his hind legs, dancing in front of them with excitement.

"What's got you all riled up, buddy?" Cate inquired.

Bailey pranced around at their feet, before letting out a long howl and jumping to his hind legs to wave his front paws.

"My goodness, Bailey! Why are you singing?" Cate inquired of him.

His curly tail wagged excitedly.

"What's got them so wound up?" Jack inquired.

"I'm not sure," Cate admitted. She continued a few paces down the hall toward where they'd come from. Her footsteps slowed as she approached the end.

"What is it?" Jack asked, noting her hesitance.

"The door to the west wing is open again!"

"What?" Jack exclaimed, hurrying down the hall to catch up with Cate as she approached the open west wing doors. The dogs trotted behind.

They approached the double doors. One stood partially ajar.

"I locked this!" Jack said, his brow furrowing.

"I watched you," Cate responded. The two dogs stared into the large hallway beyond the door. Bailey's tail gave another wag and the two of them barreled through the open doorway and down the hall, disappearing around a corner. "This must be where they're going. How long has it been open again, I wonder?"

"I've no idea, but I don't like this. I locked this door. And this is the second time we've found it open. And what are the dogs after in there?"

"Should we follow them in to find out?"

"Yes, I think so," Jack answered with a nod of his head.

Cate ventured in through the door with Jack behind her, still studying the unlocked and open door. He swung the door shut behind them and jiggled it. "Seems to latch properly."

"Perhaps the lock isn't working," Cate suggested.

"Even if that were the case," Jack answered, "how are the dogs opening it? It's latched." He jiggled the door again. "It's not opening even with me pushing on it. So a gust of wind blowing it open doesn't make sense. And besides, where would there be a gust of wind here? This wing is closed off."

Cate tried the door handle herself. It held firm. "It makes no sense. How is the door getting opened then?"

"I don't know. But I don't like it."

"Well, I suppose we won't solve that mystery at the moment. Perhaps we'll determine the source of the dogs' interest, though."

Jack gave the door another leery glance as he swung it open again and continued down the long hall with Cate. Large windows allowed light to filter into the massive hall-way. The chandeliers hanging from above remained dark as they continued to the corner they'd seen the dogs disappear around moments ago.

As they rounded it, the two furry animals raced toward them.

"Where were you?" Cate asked. While still excited, they were not as exuberant as they had been moments ago. Riley leapt onto his hind legs, placing his paws on Cate's thigh in a request to be picked up.

"Show me where you were first," Cate tried.

Riley pawed at her again. "Come on, buddy, what's so interesting over here?"

Bailey stood firm, glancing around but appearing uninterested in anything at the moment. Cate gave in and lifted Riley into her arms. "I suppose we'll have to explore on our own since neither of you are talking," Cate said.

Jack scooped up Bailey and patted him on the head. The little dog bared his bottom teeth in what Cate termed a "smile." "It looks like Bailey isn't going to help either."

Cate shook her head. "No, we're on our own. If we're lucky, maybe we'll stumble across whatever caught their interest and they'll perk up."

They wandered down the length of the hall. Cate peered into a few darkened rooms, but nothing stirred Riley, who lounged in her arms on his back like a baby. While Bailey curiously peered around from Jack's arms, he remained indifferent to their surroundings.

They continued around the hall, peeking into a music hall along the way. A large white sheet covered a grand piano near an ornate white and gold-trimmed fireplace. White walls, decorated with gold filigree and gold chandeliers graced the space.

Cate strode into the ornate room, gazing up at its tray ceiling decorated with gold trim, and the polished parquet floors, still gleaming despite the age.

"Wow," she murmured as she exited the space.

"Don't let Mrs. Campbell see this," Jack said, as he pulled the door shut behind them.

"No kidding," Cate said.

"She'll have ten concerts scheduled before the year is out."

"I'm surprised she hasn't mentioned exploring these wings for the Presidents' Ball," Cate mentioned, as they meandered further down the hall.

"Give her time. She's probably working on that right now.

You haven't met with her for over a week, so I'm afraid to find out what she has in store for your next meeting."

"I'm surprised she hasn't scheduled it already," Cate said, as they approached a set of ornate gold doors.

"She's probably texting you as we speak," Jack said.

Cate chuckled at the statement, mostly because it was likely true. She couldn't imagine making it through the week without hearing from Mrs. Campbell.

"Actually, I wouldn't be upset about hearing from her. I'd like to ask her about wartime Dunhaven. Sometimes she'll have a tidbit or two that will help us in our investigation."

"Aye, that she may," Jack said.

"And honestly, I'm not sure I would object to opening this wing for the party."

"Now you're talking crazy, Lady Cate," Jack objected.

"I'm not. That room is beautiful. It should be used!"

"So it was," Jack admitted. "Though I'm not certain I want strangers traipsing all over the castle."

"I think it's worth a mention to Mrs. Campbell," Cate said, as Jack swung open the curved gold door and they entered the large space. "Though I'm certain I'll regret it later."

Cate scanned the new space. Riley fidgeted in her arms as she stepped inside. "Wow," Cate said, her voice echoing off the golden walls. Accented in red and teal, large columns rose from the mirrored floor to hold the gold-paneled ceiling at bay.

In Jack's arms, Bailey also wriggled around. They each set the dogs down. Riley and Bailey pressed their noses to the floor and raced around the room.

"Is this the source of their curiosity?" Jack asked.

Cate's eyes still studied the room. Riley crossed the room and pawed at something, but left it within seconds in favor of pummeling Bailey, who offered a playful growl from his play-bow stance.

The two dogs frolicked around the room as Cate's brow furrowed. A scent wafted to her nostrils: musky, warm and sweet. Cate's mind scrambled to place the scent. Images flitted around on the edge of her brain, just out of reach.

CHAPTER 16

The golden room sparkled in front of her. Her senses dulled and a tinkling sound replaced the noise of dog claws scraping against the slick surface. Jack's voice echoed, sounding distant and static-filled.

Cate's body jolted. "Cate!" Jack said again. Cate blinked and sucked in a breath as the other world shattered to pieces around her.

The confused expression on her face deepened as she stared up at Jack. With his hands on her shoulders, his face was filled with concern. Riley and Bailey stood at her feet, peering up at her.

"What?" she inquired.

"What? What happened?"

Cate lifted a shoulder and dropped it in response. "I'm not sure what you mean."

"I asked you a question and you didn't answer. You were standing there like a zombie. I had to shake you to get any response."

"I don't remember any of that. Just…"

"Just what?" Jack asked as her voice trailed off, leaving the statement unfinished.

Cate's gaze fell to the shiny floor. She caught a reflection of herself in it. A flash of blue caught her eye. She tilted her head further, searching for the color.

"Cate!" Jack shouted at her again, grasping hold of her before she pitched forward, headfirst, toward the floor below.

"Huh?" Cate said.

"That's it. I think we should leave."

Cate swallowed hard. "I'm sorry," she said. "I thought I saw something in the floor."

"Saw something?"

"In the reflection. Blue."

"Blue?" Jack asked as he searched around the space. "Like the color there, near the ceiling?"

Cate shook her head. "No, blue. Like sapphire blue. It floated past in the reflection like fabric fluttering in a breeze."

Jack's eyebrows twitched as he shook his head. Neither of them wore blue, and no blue items existed within the space.

"I don't see anything blue, but like I said, I think we should leave. You nearly took a header into the floor, Cate. You were like a zombie again."

Cate scrunched up her face. "But why?"

"Maybe it's another attack from the music box?" Jack suggested. "Either way, I'd like to get you back to the main castle."

Cate shook her head as Jack stepped toward the exit.

"No. It's something about this room," she insisted. She spun to search it again. "But what?"

Jack approached her, eyeing her then the space. "Something about this room?"

"Yes," Cate said. "I..." Her voice cut off again.

"You what? What is it, Cate? Tell me whatever you're thinking so we can figure this out."

She sucked in a few breaths before shaking her head again. "It's gone." With a glance at Jack and a sigh, she added, "I can't remember anything now."

Jack rubbed the back of his neck as he considered the latest twist. "Come on," he said after a moment. "Let's get you back to the library. It's nearly time for lunch. We can discuss this while we eat."

He gently grabbed hold of her arm and tugged her away from the space. The two small dogs followed them as they closed the room again and threaded through the halls of the unused wing.

As they re-entered the main structure, Jack ushered the dogs through the doors and closed them. He tested the latch, ensuring it held as he pulled against the door. With another shake of his head, he said, "No sense in locking it, I suppose."

"No," Cate said with a sigh. "And maybe no sense in closing it. Someone keeps opening it and unless Riley and Bailey have discovered a way to open doors, it's not them."

Cate wrapped her arms around her midriff as she bit her lower lip and stared at the mysterious doors to the west wing. Jack wrapped his arm around her shoulders and led her away from the space. "Come on," he prodded.

Cate shook her head. "What is going on here?" she asked, her voice filled with worry. "Doors opening unexpectedly, a room that makes me a zombie…"

"I'm not sure, Cate. I hope our mysterious friends across the pond have some answers. Perhaps we should update them."

"Well, I guess we don't know for sure it's the room. Maybe it was the music box." Cate ceased walking and stared up at Jack. "Did you hide it there?"

"I'm not telling."

"I'm not trying to wheedle its location out of you. But if it's hidden near there, perhaps it's a proximity thing. And it could explain the door being open. If you accessed the west wing recently, perhaps the latch didn't work, or the lock stuck?"

Jack shook his head. "Sorry, Lady Cate. I wish that could explain it but no, I did not put the music box anywhere near that spot, and I did not go into the west wing since the last time we locked those doors."

Jack's admission dashed Cate's theory.

"And don't you go feeling proud of yourself for ruling out an entire wing to search for your music box. I could always move it," Jack said, wagging his finger at her.

The comment elicited a chuckle from Cate. "Duly noted. I just can't figure out what that room would have to do with anything. I've barely ever been in it. I think once when I went through the castle after I first moved here. I have no reason to be drawn to it. I can't make sense of any of this."

"We'll figure it out, Cate. Together. Just take solace in the fact that this time, no one is disappearing into other time periods." He grabbed her hand and led her further down the hall.

"That's some consolation. Though this time, I'm disappearing. Into some kind of trance."

"There you are!" Molly exclaimed as they rounded the corner, heading toward the library. "I brought your lunch and found the place empty!"

"Sorry," Cate said. "The dogs have been running around all over the place and we followed them."

"Oh? What were they after? I hope not another body."

"No," Cate said, with a wave of her hand and a chuckle. "No bodies. Though we never did figure out what gave them the zoomies."

"Hopefully they'll be ready for a nap so you can enjoy your lunch."

Cate ushered them in through the double doors with a nod in agreement at Molly's statement.

"Oh," Molly said to Jack as he passed her, "Mrs. Fraser said don't get used to this treatment. You're not lord of the manor."

Jack chuckled at her. "I would never," he promised. "Only when Lady Cate and I have pressing business."

Molly gave him an amused glance and nod before she disappeared down the hall, leaving them to their lunch.

"You know," Jack said, as he pushed a crouton around in his tomato basil soup, "I never thought I'd look forward to time travel, but I am!"

"Really?" Cate asked.

"Aye, if it solves your zombie problem, I am."

Cate scrunched up her face in thought. Jack reached over and patted her arm. "It'll be okay, Cate. I was only joking. Well, half-joking. If time travel works the way Damien seems to think it will, I won't mind. It's killing two birds with one stone."

Cate gave him a weak smile. "I don't know what to think," Cate said. "I can't believe time travel is a solution to whatever is happening to me. But Damien seemed certain."

"I suppose we'll find out."

"At least it will take my mind off of whatever is going on with me. I wish we had more clues."

"We'll find them, Cate," Jack assured her.

They finished their lunch and parted ways after delivering their trays to the kitchen. The task ahead rumbled through Cate's mind as she pulled on her 1940s style dress. What would they find when they arrived at the castle? And would they pull off their subterfuge with those they had met twenty years earlier?

Cate hoped to avoid the family as much as possible. Much to her chagrin, however, it appeared that would be impossible. With no information about Ruth Harper, they would be forced to speak with at least Rory to learn anything about the woman.

Cate slicked on her bold red lipstick and pressed her lips together to distribute the color. Perhaps they could claim fantastic genetics for why they remained youthful in their appearance. She hoped the changed hairstyle and makeup provided enough difference that they weren't questioned.

Perhaps her recent brush with death even added a few gray hairs and wrinkles. Cate's mind flitted to the encounter. She swallowed hard as she recalled the cold stone of the tomb closing around her. She sensed the weight of the necklace on her neck and the icy cold touch of Duke Northcott's fingers against her skin. His voice echoed in her mind.

She fought to steady herself as her mind began to slip toward the necklace and then the music box. Cate pressed her hands against her ears as tinkling music filled the air around her.

"No!" she shouted, with a shake of her head. She stared at herself in the mirror. Movement caught her eye. She spun to search behind her. As she broke eye contact with the mirror, her mind cleared.

The tinkling music died down and the sensation of the necklace pressed against her collarbones passed. Cate sucked in a long breath as a shudder passed through her body.

"What's happening to me?" she whispered aloud.

Tears stung her eyes, and Cate bit her lower lip as she fluttered her eyelashes. After blowing out a shaky breath, she risked a quick glance into the mirror for a make-up check. Finding nothing amiss, she heaved another sigh, smoothed the skirt of her dress, and pushed her shoulders back.

She and Jack had a murder to investigate. That should be

her focus. She stepped into her bedroom and grabbed her vintage purse before meeting Jack outside her suite.

"Ready?"

Cate gave a tight-lipped smile and a nod.

"You sure?" Jack asked.

"Yes," Cate said. "I can't wait, actually."

"Did something happen?" Jack inquired, as they traversed the halls to the secret passage outside of the library.

Cate swallowed hard and offered a sheepish grin. "Another incident where I really wanted to find the music box. It's almost all-consuming and I can barely think of anything else."

Jack arched an eyebrow. "Let's hope Damien is correct about the effects of time travel on enchantments." Jack ceased walking for a moment as they entered the hall containing the library. "Wow, I can't believe that statement even came out of my mouth."

Cate giggled at him. "You mean about hoping time travel solves our problems?"

"No, I mean about how easily I just mentioned time travel solving problems with enchanted objects. Lady Cate, before I met you I would have told anyone else all that was a bunch of hogwash. Now, I deal with it on a regular basis. And even more frightening, it's becoming normal!"

"Anyway, let's hope Damien's correct." She reached to the sconce and tugged on it.

They slipped into the secret passage, pushing the panel closed behind them. Jack toggled on a small flashlight and Cate held out the timepiece.

She set the date to September 17th, 1942. Jack closed his hand around hers and they activated the timepiece. As the secondhand slowed and 1942 settled around them, Jack blew out a breath.

"Well," Jack said, as he pointed his flashlight's beam toward the passage leading to the crypt, "here we go."

Cate drew in a sharp breath.

"You okay?" Jack asked.

"Yes," Cate said. "It's amazing."

"What is?"

"Always feel so clear-headed! Even if I think about the necklace and the music box, I don't experience that fuzzy headed feeling or the overwhelming urgency to seek it out."

Jack stared at her for a moment before he shook his head. "I can't believe that worked."

"Me either," Cate admitted. "But it's like night and day."

"Well, I suppose in addition to solving a murder, we also have found a temporary solution to your troubles."

Cate nodded as they reached the crypt. "Yes. I hope it buys us enough time to sort that situation out entirely. I really hate what it's doing to me."

"I can imagine." Jack reached above his head and tugged on the metal ring. The secret panel in the crypt swung toward them. They exited into the bright sunshine beyond. "Whew! I always forget we're going to fall, not spring."

"Yes, the new ability to travel to any date we want may become confusing."

"I was just getting used to the idea of traveling to the same date in another year, but a different day of the week..."

"And now you're faced with different day, date and season!" Cate said, lifting her eyebrows and offering him a coy grin.

"At least I'm faced with the old Cate Kensie! You're right, the difference is night and day!"

Cate sighed as they stepped onto the pathway outside the crypt. "I'm not sure if I find it encouraging or frightening that even you notice the difference."

"Let's take it as encouraging and leave it at that."

Jack gazed around as they made their way up the path. "Gee, I hope I don't run into Pap again."

Cate couldn't help but laugh. "I don't think it's funny, Lady Cate. He's likely to have me arrested. My own grandfather, turning me in as a Nazi."

"I'm sorry, but when you refer to that child as Pap it really makes me laugh."

"I'm glad it makes someone laugh. I, personally, am not amused that at five years old, Pap can still get over on me."

"He's probably already a better dancer, too," Cate said, with a coy glance at him.

Jack shook his head at her attempted humor. "What a comedian. I'm beginning to regret my statement about being faced with the old Cate Kensie."

They wound their way around the loch. Cate gazed at the large tent, shaded by Dunhaven Castle. "I hope Rory can provide us with some preliminary information," she said, as she watched several individuals bustle to and from the temporary canvas structure.

"Me too. I suppose the best course of action is to ask to speak with him first."

"Yes," Cate agreed, as they rounded the castle and approached the front door. "Let's hope we learn something."

Jack used the brass lion's head door knocker. "Here's the first test. If Benson looks strange at us, we're sunk."

Jack plastered a grin on his face as the door swung open before Cate could respond. A middle-aged man in a butler's uniform stood at the door. "Yes?" he inquired.

"Hello. Jack and Cate MacKenzie to see Rory MacKenzie."

The man's eyebrows raised. "Is Lord MacKenzie expecting you, sir?"

"No," Jack answered, "though I'm certain he'll recognize our name as we've met on several occasions before."

"Perhaps if you could check with Mr. Benson, he could

verify that my husband is Lord MacKenzie's cousin," Cate chimed in.

The man shifted his glance to Cate. "Mr. Benson has retired. I am the new butler, Smithers. You must have visited Lord MacKenzie quite a while ago."

Cate nodded. "Yes," she answered. "Nearly twenty years, actually."

"I see," the man said. "Please come in and I shall discuss the matter with Lord MacKenzie."

"Thank you," Jack said, as he ushered Cate into the foyer in front of him and followed her through the large front doors.

The man showed them into the sitting room, closing the doors behind them.

"I guess Benson won't be a problem," Cate said.

"Apparently not," Jack agreed as he sank onto the updated couch. He wiped at a bead of sweat forming on his brow.

"Take it easy, Jack," Cate said, as she plopped next to him and patted his knee. "Rory should remember us. And we don't need to explain our rather youthful appearances to him."

Jack nodded and they waited for several more tension-filled moments before the doors to the foyer popped open.

CHAPTER 17

As the doors to the sitting room opened, Cate stood, recognizing Rory immediately. His tall form, slightly more sturdy than lithe now, was hidden under a new style of suit. His once dark hair now had streaks of gray, though it remained unruly. And his piercing blue eyes were unmistakable.

He stood in the doorway, his face a mask of surprise and glee. A grin formed on his lips, spreading wider as he stepped toward them. "Jack and Cate MacKenzie!" he exclaimed.

Jack stood next to Cate, returning the man's smile. "Hello," he said.

"I'm amazed!" He studied them up and down. "When Smithers told me, I couldn't believe it was true! Yet here you stand! Oh, what a lovely surprise."

Cate smiled at Rory's enthusiasm. The picture of politeness and always the optimist, Rory's welcome gave her the boost she needed.

"I hope you don't mind us dropping in unannounced," Jack said.

"Not at all," Rory answered, still staring at them with a

silly grin. "After that spot of trouble you got us out of, I hoped to see you again. After years passed, I figured I wouldn't. But here you are again. One of life's little surprises!"

Cate smiled at him. "We're sorry it took so long but..." Her voice faded as she glanced to the open doors leading to the foyer.

Rory understood her silent signal and pushed the doors closed.

"Thank you," she said. "For us, it's only been a few months," Cate explained.

"How interesting," Rory said. "I'm not much of a traveler myself, but it's entirely fascinating to me that you're visiting me nearly twenty years later for me, though only a few months for you."

"We hope that doesn't cause any problems," Jack said with a wince. "Though it is rather unavoidable."

"Well, certainly no problems with me," Rory said. "And Anne is away at the moment visiting her parents in the countryside and will be for the next several weeks."

"Oh," Cate said, relief coursing through her, "that will make things easier."

"The only other person in the house with me is Oliver, and I doubt he'd remember you clearly enough to question your ages. Why the last time you saw him he must have been only a small boy."

"About ten, yes," Cate answered.

"And now he's approaching thirty!" Rory said, his eyebrows raised high. "Nearly an old man like me." He chuckled at his joke. Cate also offered a giggle, more so at the different views of age in a different era.

The conversation lulled for a moment and Rory took the opportunity to bring up the subject on everyone's mind.

"I assume you're here for a purpose?"

"We are," Cate said, with an apologetic glance.

"Please, you do not need to explain it to me, though I'll do all I can to help."

"Thank you. On that note, you mentioned Anne being away, but is Amelia here?"

"Funny you should mention that," Rory said, waving a finger in the air. "I received correspondence very recently from her. She is traveling to Dunhaven and plans to arrive tomorrow. What a coincidence you should mention her."

Cate held in another giggle at Rory's naïveté.

"Of course," Rory continued, "if you prefer to avoid her, I shall make no mention of your arrival to her."

"No, quite the opposite, actually," Cate said. "I hoped to speak with her."

"Oh!" Rory said with a nod. "Well, it seems you shall be in luck tomorrow then."

"Good," Cate said. "And if you wouldn't mind us 'staying' at the castle again…" Her voice trailed off as Rory waved his hand in the air at her.

"Oh, of course, of course. You needn't ask. I shall have the room prepared at once. I can arrange the one you used before, though will that pose a problem with returning to and from this time period? I'm not certain of the location of the time rip leading to this year."

"It won't pose a problem at all, thank you," Cate said, omitting the information about the latest developments with the time rips.

"Wonderful," Rory said. "I shall see to it then. And how I look forward to spending more time with you. Oh, I'm afraid dinners are a rather bleak affair these days what with the war effort, but we shall scrounge up something lovely, I promise."

"I'm sure it will be fine and of course, the draw is spending time with you and your family," Cate said. "And on that note, I spotted a tent outside. I understand it has something to do with the war effort."

"Oh, yes," Rory confirmed. "Yes, we're hosting several ladies and gentlemen who are working on those codes. Enigma machines I believe they're called. A terrible business, this war. It was the least we could do to provide them with a place to stay and work. They're a smaller branch of those working at Bletchley Park. My contribution, however small, to the war efforts." He shoved his hands into his pockets and offered a weak smile.

"It's more than small," Cate assured him.

"Would you like to see it? I could show you."

A smile brightened Cate's features. "If you have a moment and wouldn't mind."

"Of course!" Rory said. "Just allow me to retrieve my hat."

The man disappeared from the room, leaving Cate and Jack alone.

"Nice to see time hasn't jaded him at all," Cate said.

"Still the same old Rory, that's for certain," Jack agreed.

"I hope you don't mind the tour of the intelligence tent, but I thought it would be fascinating to see."

"Not at all, Cate," Jack said. "We can spend as much time as you like here."

Cate gave him a tight-lipped smile, understanding his meaning. He preferred not to return to the present where she suffered from some unknown ailment. She appreciated his sacrifice.

Rory returned a few moments later and led them from the castle and to the hut.

They entered the space. Temporary lighting hung overhead. A large board held a tacked-up map and several other pieces of information. Multiple tables were set up around the space. Paperwork covered most of the wooden surfaces. Men and women bent over the papers, pencils in hand, working to uncover patterns in the messages that could be used to crack the Enigma code.

Large baskets sat in the middle of the table with information waiting to be processed. A blonde woman, her hair styled in two large rolls and pulled back into a low bun, smiled at them as they entered.

"Hello, Miss Haverford," Rory said with a wave.

"Hello, Lord MacKenzie," she said, with a nod in a crisp British accent. "And again, please, Rita is just fine."

"Miss Haverford was one of our earliest transplants with the intelligence unit."

"How fascinating," Cate said to the woman. "How did you become involved with the work?"

Her red lips formed another curt smile. "I've always been good with mathematics. And with my knowledge of the German language, it was a good fit."

"Oh, you speak German," Cate remarked.

"I do," the woman answered. "My mother was German."

Cate gave her a nod.

"Fascinating work, really," Rory said to them. "I can't make heads or tails out of it, but they seem to be making some headway. Sadly, not enough to cease all the attacks on our allied shipments."

"No and the code has become rather tricky of late, but we'll keep at it," Miss Haverford added to Rory's statements.

"Thank you for letting us drop by," Cate said, as Rory led them from the tent.

"Well, it wasn't much of a tour, but I don't like to interrupt their work."

"Very important, yes," Jack said. "Thank you for showing us."

"Oh, of course. And I'll see you back tomorrow?" Rory inquired as they pushed into the castle's entryway.

"Yes," Jack assured him.

"Wonderful. I'll see to your room and look forward to visiting with you again tomorrow. Maybe then you can meet Oliver."

"We'll look forward to it," Cate said.

They said their goodbyes promising to return tomorrow. As Rory disappeared up the steps, Cate and Jack slipped into the secret passage to return to their time.

After changing into their normal clothes, they met in the library. Jack studied the puzzle as Cate meandered into the room. "I hate this puzzle," he announced.

"Maybe it'll grow on you, like time travel," Cate quipped, as she settled into the armchair and slid a few pieces around.

"How do you feel?"

"Fine," Cate admitted. "The time travel did remove the odd haze in my brain while we were there. When we got back, it's better than it was, but I feel it slightly."

"At least it relieved it somewhat," Jack said with a shrug. "Maybe the more you do it, the better it will be."

"I hope so," Cate said. "Although, I'll be on pins and needles until tomorrow."

"Oh? Over the idea that the haze may return?"

"No, over seeing Amelia again, and hopefully, meeting Ruth."

"I see."

"We're days before her supposed disappearance. And we have no information."

"I hope to find some soon," Jack said.

"So do I. Without it, we may never uncover the truth."

"No, but at least we'll have hopefully helped your issue."

"I'd like to do both," Cate said, as she finished one edge from corner to corner.

"I understand. Let's hope tomorrow's meeting is enlightening."

"If it isn't..." Cate paused and sighed. "We could be

barking up the wrong tree. We could be in the wrong year with the wrong woman entirely!"

Jack nodded. "Aye, that could be true. Though I hope it isn't. But you're correct. We have no real proof that this woman actually disappeared."

Cate gave him another sigh before returning her attention to the puzzle.

They spent the remainder of their rainy afternoon filling in the puzzle with Cate building toward the middle while Jack continued to frown over his edges, before finally fitting them together and finishing the outline. A celebration ensued over the small amount of progress.

With the rain turning to drizzle and finally ending as the afternoon hours waned, Cate took the opportunity to allow the dogs to stretch their legs before she returned to the library for dinner. With her current state of mind improved, Jack opted for dinner with the staff rather than eating upstairs with Cate.

Cate found her mind wandering more to the mystery in 1942 than anything else. Though it was a welcome change from her cloudy mind, her frustration over the lack of information bubbled inside her. They could be spending their time working an angle that had nothing to do with the body.

Cate frowned as she considered starting the process over again. But where, her mind pondered? Or when? With no reports of missing people fitting the description, they'd have no leads.

The mystery of their uninvited garden guest may go unsolved entirely.

A knock at the door returned her attention to her current surroundings. Jack poked his head in. "Everything okay in here?"

Cate smiled at him. "Yep," she said with a nod. "Just contemplating our mystery and hoping we solve it."

"Any haze? Overwhelming urges to roam around the castle? Music playing in your mind?"

"None of that! Damien was correct about the time travel helping."

"Have you heard from him?" Jack asked, as he eased the doors shut behind him.

Cate checked her phone. "No, nothing. And I hate to keep asking him about progress."

"Well, with the current upturn in your mental capacity, we probably can wait until tomorrow to see what they've come up with."

Cate nodded her agreement, and spent the rest of her evening in the library swapping her attention between a mystery novel and the puzzle. The combination seemed to keep any mental fog at bay.

She gathered both dogs as evening turned to night and headed to her suite with the hopes her garden guest mystery didn't keep her awake.

After saying good night to Jack, she continued to her sitting room, pressing the doors shut behind her. Riley and Bailey raced ahead of her to the bedroom. An excited yip sounded, and she heard the sounds of both dogs climbing onto the bed.

"You guys must be really tired!" Cate called, as she approached the double doors leading to her bedroom. As her large bed came into view, Cate ceased walking. Her heart skipped a beat and her stomach dropped. Her breath caught in her throat as her eyes widened at the sight.

With a furrowed brow, she took a slow step forward, her head shaking. "No," she whispered.

Riley and Bailey stood in the middle of the bed, staring at a collection of objects sprawled across the foot of it. Their attention flicked to Cate as she stepped inside. Riley's feather-like tail waved in the air and Bailey gave two clipped swats of his curly tail.

Cate's lower lip trembled as she approached the foot of the bed. Riley stretched out on his belly, his tail still waving. With a trembling hand, Cate reached out toward the objects. As her fingers caressed one, she pulled her hand back as though she'd been burned by it.

They weren't figments of her imagination. They were real.

On the bottom of her bed lay a red rose, the sapphire necklace, and the piano-shaped music box.

CHAPTER 18

$\mathcal{A}$ grimace formed on Cate's lips as she stared at the array of items spread on her bed. Her pulse raced and her breathing turned ragged as her mind shot in a thousand directions pondering the situation.

She spun toward her sitting room, intent on reporting the incident to Jack. As she took a step toward the other room, an icy cold breeze tickled her skin. The hair on the back of her neck stood up and her flesh puckered into goosebumps.

She ceased walking, her head slowly swiveling to glance over her shoulder. Her clenched lips parted slightly as she stared at the objects. She inhaled a deep breath and stepped toward the bed. Her fingers caressed the sapphires before she snatched them off the bed, clutching the necklace to her chest.

She twisted the winding mechanism and propped open the lid of the miniature grand piano. Soft tinkling music filled the air, causing the edges of her lips to curl upward in a slight smile.

She pulled the small music box onto her lap as she sank

onto the edge of the bed. A thought pervaded her mind. She had to find it. The blue dress. She had to find it.

Her mind made a mental inventory of the castle. Where had she put the dress? She had to find it. She rose from the bed and stalked across the room.

The music box tinkled away as she crossed her sitting room and flung open the door. She shambled down the hall as she considered the best place to begin her search.

A noise buzzed at the back of her brain. She wrinkled her forehead, attempting to concentrate on the music. The noise sounded again. Her footsteps slowed as she struggled to identify the sound. The tinkling music began to slow.

Cate's body shook. She blinked several times as her hand searched for the winding key.

"Cate!"

She recognized her name being called. It sounded like the speaker was far away and underwater. She shook her head and again searched for the winding key.

Her body jolted again. "Cate!"

She glanced up, finding a face in front of her. "Jack!" Her eyebrows shot up and she grinned at him. "You're back!"

Jack's brow furrowed. Cate flung her arms around him in a hug. She pulled back still smiling.

"Back? Cate?" Jack stared down at the objects clutched in her hands. "What's going on? How did you get those?"

"Now you can help me," Cate continued to babble. "I have to find it. I can't remember where I put it."

Jack grasped hold of Cate's shoulders. "Cate! Get hold of yourself! What are you talking about?"

"The dress. I have to find it. I have to find it before he comes."

The last few notes of music floated from the dying music box.

Jack shook his head at her as she turned the key again. He attempted to wrestle the box from her grip.

"No!" she shouted, yanking it back. "I need it! I've always loved it."

"Cate, what are you talking about? You just got this."

"No, I've had it since…" Her forehead wrinkled as she searched her mind for the detail. "Since…"

She shook her head, becoming perturbed by her memory loss.

"Cate," Jack said, squatting down to stare into her eyes. "Listen to me. There is some enchantment on this thing, and it's making you crazy."

"No," Cate argued. "No, it helps me. It relaxes me."

Jack swallowed hard and bit his lower lip.

"Will you help me?" Cate asked.

Jack narrowed his eyes at her. "Okay, sure. What do you need help with?"

"I have to find the dress."

"What dress?"

"My blue dress. For the ball. I can't remember where I put it." Cate continued down the hall.

"Where did you see it last?"

Cate's forehead crinkled. "I'm not sure." A pained expression crossed her face, and she stared up at Jack.

"Okay, it's okay, Cate. We'll find it." Jack held his hands out in front of him as though surrendering. "How about if we leave these things here, though? You can't look for anything when you're carrying so many things."

Cate glanced down at the music box and necklace. "But…"

"They'll be here when you come back. But it'll be easier to find the dress."

Cate's eyes slid sideways as she considered the proposition. Jack eased the music box from her hands and set it down on the floor. He carefully unfurled her fingers from around the necklace and laid it on the music box.

He breathed a partial sigh of relief as he wrapped an arm around Cate's shoulders and guided her away from the objects. He led her downstairs and into the library. Embers still glowed in the fireplace, casting the room in a dim, orangish light.

Jack guided her to the armchair near the fireplace and eased her into it. He perched on the edge of the table, keeping his hands firmly grasping her upper arms.

He studied her face.

"I don't think the dress is here," Cate said.

"No, but we need a break to think about where we should look."

Cate nodded.

"While we think, can you tell me what the dress looks like?"

"It's satin. Sapphire blue." Cate paused. Her forehead wrinkled again as she searched her memory for more details. After a moment, her breathing turned ragged, and a pained expression wrinkled her nose. Her face blanched. And she glanced to Jack with fear in her eyes. "I can't... the music box... I should get it."

"No, it's okay, stay here," Jack insisted, keeping his grip firm on her.

"Ugh," she moaned as she bent forward, rubbing her temples.

"It's okay, Cate. It's okay," Jack said, rubbing her arm.

After a few moments, Cate sucked in a deep breath and straightened. Her brow furrowed again as she glanced around the room then focused on Jack. She tilted her head at him, a worried expression replacing her pained one. "Was I roaming again?" she inquired.

"Cate?" Jack said, sitting up straighter. "Is it you?"

Cate pressed back against the chair behind her as she processed his statement. "Yes. Who else would it be?" Her eyes grew wide. "Jack, what's going on?"

Jack blew out a relieved sigh. "I'll explain everything in a second, just let me take a minute to be grateful you're back to normal you."

"You're scaring me," Cate said.

Jack blew out another breath. "Somehow you got a hold of the music box and necklace."

"What?" Cate asked, her voice incredulous.

Jack nodded. "I have no idea how. I hid it in the locked east wing. I won't say where beyond that. But there's no way you could have gotten it from there. But you definitely had it. You were wandering around the halls babbling about finding a dress."

"A dress?" Cate pursed her lips in thought. "That seems vaguely familiar. But beyond that, I can't remember anything. How did I get the music box?"

"What's the last thing you remember?"

"Going into my sitting room. The dogs ran into the bedroom and when I went in, I saw everything on the bed. The necklace, the music box, and a rose. That's the last thing I remember."

Jack swung from the table into the armchair next to her, still perched on the edge.

"Where is the music box now?" Cate inquired.

"I managed to wrestle it off you. It's in a hallway upstairs."

Cate shook her head. "Jack, if this music box keeps appearing, there's going to be no keeping me from it."

"I agree. No matter what we do, you end up with it. We're going to have to mitigate your symptoms as best we can while we figure this out, because there's no keeping it away."

Cate nodded.

"There's something else," Jack said, wringing his hands.

"What?"

"In addition to the strange comments about searching for your ball gown, you made a few other bizarre comments."

"Such as?"

"You said you needed the music box because you've always loved it."

"Always? I just got it."

"That's what I thought, too."

"Is there something else?"

Jack remained silent for a moment, staring at his feet.

"Jack?"

He shrugged. "Maybe it's nothing, but you seemed surprised to see me. You said I was back. I didn't know what that meant, but it was very odd."

"Perhaps because I was in a trance, I was surprised to see you, since it seems I'm almost closed into my own mind."

Jack shrugged again. "Maybe," he said. "And maybe I'm reading into things too much, but it seemed very, very odd to me. Though you may be correct. It took me a few minutes to get a response from you."

"Really?" Cate inquired.

Jack nodded. "Aye. I kept calling to you and finally you acknowledged me. But it took a few tries."

Cate shivered, more from the unknown than the cold. "What's happening to me?"

"I don't know, Cate, but we'll figure it out."

"How?" Cate cried.

Jack considered it for a moment. "As much as I hate to say this, we may need to let you slip into one of these trances and see what it is you're trying to do."

The worried expression returned to Cate's face as she considered the theory. "I'm not sure that's a good idea. What if you can't get through to me next time?"

"Perhaps we can use the time travel solution as our backup," Jack proposed. "If you don't snap out of it, I'll drag you into one of the time rip locations and we'll go back in time."

Cate remained silent for a few minutes. "This sounds like the worst plan ever."

Jack leapt from his seat and paced the floor behind them. "I know, Cate, I know. But I'm not sure what other choices we have!"

"Okay, okay, let's just calm down a minute," Cate said, noticing Jack's obvious agitation.

Jack continued his anxious pacing, biting his thumbnail as he marched back and forth across the room.

Cate rose and stopped him from his pacing. "Jack," she said, pausing to sigh before continuing, "we'll figure this out. I'm not sure how, but I know we will. Maybe it's best if we let things take a more natural course."

Jack tilted his head at the statement, setting his mouth in a firm line. "I really don't like to leave things to chance."

"I don't either, but I'm afraid if we force things..." Her voice trailed off and tears shined in her eyes. "Jack, what if I disappear entirely? End up locked in my own mind?"

"I won't let that happen, Cate."

"You may not have a choice."

Jack shook his head and pulled Cate into his arms. "I'm not going to lose you, Cate."

Cate sniffled as a tear fell to her cheek. She wrapped her arms around Jack's waist. "Thanks," she squeaked.

She spent a few moments with her head resting against his chest before she pulled back, wiping the wayward tear from her cheek. She blew out a shaky breath.

"How are you feeling now?"

"Okay," she admitted.

"Do you think you'll be able to get any sleep?"

"Maybe," she said. "I'll try."

"If you prefer to stay here, I'll wait up with you."

Cate shook her head. "No. But don't tell me which hall we left the music box in. And maybe you should lock the doors to my sitting room."

"Lock you in?"

Cate shrugged her shoulders. "I'd feel better if you did."

"Okay," Jack said. "Sounds like a plan."

They returned to the upstairs hallway and parted ways at Cate's suite, with Jack locking the door after she entered the room. She squeezed her eyes shut as she heard the lock engage behind her.

"Good night, Lady Cate," Jack's muffled voice called, before she heard him retreat down the hall and enter his own bedroom.

With a deep, steadying breath, Cate returned to her bedroom. The two dogs tossed the rose around on the bed. "Hey!" Cate exclaimed. "Stop that!"

She snatched the rose from them and collected the wilted petals that had fallen from the flower. She tossed them into her trashcan before changing clothes and climbing into bed. Her mind replayed the earlier events of the evening. She tossed and turned as worry consumed her.

Her mind focused on the music box after a while. She found herself calmed as she continued to concentrate on the item. She closed her eyes and pictured it in her mind. The tinkling music echoed in her brain.

Cate drifted off to sleep as the music soothed her frayed nerves.

* * *

Cate awoke the next morning feeling relaxed. She lounged in bed as the first hints of sunlight brightened the room. Cate rolled onto her back and closed her eyes, focusing on the tinkling music filling the room.

After a few moments, she rolled to her side, glancing at the piano-shaped music box perched on the edge of her nightstand. The music was beautiful. She reached out to caress the raised lid of the tiny piano as it played away.

A knock sounded at her sitting room door. Cate lifted her head to glance out of the bedroom door. She pushed herself up to sit and pulled her robe around her. As she slipped into her slippers, she hummed along with the music box.

She stepped into her sitting room as she heard the lock of her door disengage. The door popped open an inch. "Cate?" Jack called in.

"Come in," Cate said, waving him into the room.

"Good morning," Jack said. "How are you feeling?"

Cate shrugged, scrunching up her mouth into a pucker. "Another feel perfectly fine," Cate answered, "but there's been another new development."

Jack's lips formed an "o", and he paused for a moment before speaking. "I'm not certain I want to find out, but I suppose I have to."

Cate motioned for him to follow her. She stopped in the doorway leading into her bedroom. Both dogs leapt up at the sight of Jack, Riley's tail waving in the air at him.

Cate motioned toward the nightstand.

Jack's face whitened and he approached the tinkling object, staring down at it.

CHAPTER 19

*W*ith wide eyes, he shifted his gaze to Cate. "I would say this can't be, but I'm starting to learn it can with this thing."

Cate crossed her arms over her chest and nodded. "I found it there this morning when I woke up."

Jack stared at her. "You're not a zombie."

"No, I feel okay, actually. Well-rested and very content."

"And your door was still locked this morning," Jack noted as he rubbed his chin.

"Yep. I have no recollection of getting out of bed. And even if I did, I couldn't have gotten out of this room, unless my zombie-fied self knows of a secret passage."

"Anything on your cube camera?" Jack inquired.

"Let me check," Cate said. She stalked across the room and grabbed her cell phone. "No videos beyond the ones triggered this morning."

"Hmm, not even when the music box appeared?"

"Apparently not," Cate said. She flashed the phone's screen toward Jack. "Nothing listed overnight at all. Not even me rolling over in bed."

"I suppose we can view this as progress. You've got the music box here and you've not gone crazy."

"I don't see the necklace. Perhaps it's the necklace that causes my odd behavior."

"But it was the music box you were after a few times."

Cate leaned against the door jamb and shrugged. "I can't figure it out."

"Well, I hope you stay this way. It'll be one less thing to worry about," Jack said.

"Me too. I guess I'll get dressed. Hopefully, you don't find me wandering the halls soon."

Jack nodded. "Perhaps the time travel did do you some good. Hopefully, today's trip will help, too."

"Fingers crossed," Cate said, before Jack left her alone to finish her morning routine.

The little music box seemed to play on an endless loop without Cate winding it. She left it still playing its tune, ushering the dogs out of the room and down the stairs for a quick walk before breakfast.

Cate found herself surprisingly alert during the morning hours. Her phone jingled shortly after 9 a.m. Cate recognized Mrs. Campbell's number and accepted the call.

"Lady Cate!" the woman exclaimed through the phone's speaker after Cate picked up. "Why, I feel almost odd not having met with you in over a week!"

Cate chuckled at the comment, feeling as though she'd escaped an obligation. "With the way you streamline the process, Mrs. Campbell, we are well ahead of schedule for both parties."

"About those," Mrs. Campbell began, "I have several things we should discuss."

"Of course, Mrs. Campbell," Cate said, twirling her pen in her hands. "When would you like to meet?"

"Would Monday work? It's not our usual day but…"

"Yes, that will work fine. 9 a.m.?" Cate queried.

"Perfect!"

"Oh, Mrs. Campbell," Cate said, before the woman could end the call. "Could I ask you a quick question while I have you on the line?"

"Of course!" Mrs. Campbell answered.

"I've come across some information about World War II-era Dunhaven. Did you know there was an intelligence base here?"

Mrs. Campbell paused for a moment. "Oh, well," she stammered around. "Well, no! I most certainly was not aware of that!"

"Hmm," Cate murmured at the development.

"This is… well…" After a few moments of hemming and hawing, Mrs. Campbell exclaimed, "Quite frankly, I'm in shock! Where did you come across this information?"

"Oh, uh, a personal source from Rory MacKenzie, the estate's proprietor during the war."

"I can't believe this! I'm going to go through the information I've amassed. Surely there *must* be *some* trace of this somewhere!"

"I'd appreciate you sharing any information you find. I must admit I was surprised when I found out, too."

"Leave it to me, Lady Cate. I shall get to the bottom of it!"

They said their goodbyes and Cate ended the call as a knock sounded on the door. Jack peeked inside. "Still okay?"

Cate smiled and nodded. "Yep. I'm not sure you will be, though."

"What now?" he asked, slipping inside the door.

"That was Mrs. Campbell."

"Oh no," Jack said, his shoulders slouching. "Now what? A waterslide? Move a beach grain by grain for a luau? Shift the west wing out of the way for another garden?"

"None of those things, though she's requested another

meeting. She probably heard you telling me not to tell her about the west wing's music room, and now she wants to use it."

"Tell her it's gone missing."

"I'm not sure she'll buy that story, but listen to this. I asked her about the intelligence base here, and she'd never heard of it."

"Is it that surprising?"

"Mrs. Campbell not knowing something major about the castle? The poor woman was flabbergasted."

"You make a good point. Mrs. Campbell prides herself on being the end-all, be-all on information about Dunhaven Castle."

Cate nodded in agreement. "She had the scoop on Douglas, Randolph, and Rory's theft – but she didn't know there was an intelligence base here during the Second World War?"

"Well, she had most of her information wrong on all of those fronts."

"But," Cate countered. "She had information. Wrong or not. It seems odd that she has no information at all. Not even an odd rumor about it."

"Perhaps she'll find some," Jack said.

"I guess we'll find out. I meet with her on Monday."

"I'll prepare myself for the outrageous to-do list I'm certain she'll have."

"See you later this afternoon for our daily time travel trip?"

"I don't like when you say it that way, but yes, see you after lunch. If you need anything before then, I'll be in the back garden. The one without the body."

Cate nodded as Jack slipped through the door, easing it shut behind him. Cate spun to face her laptop. She hoped to track down some information on the intelligence base at the castle, finding it odd that even locally, it did not have a reputation.

After several internet searches, though, Cate began to wonder if her eyes had deceived her. Perhaps they'd entered some kind of alternate universe when they'd visited 1942 Dunhaven. No mention was made of the intelligence base. Outside of the famous Bletchley Park, the majority of the discussion about intelligence efforts in 1942 centered around the unreadability of the German code.

With a sigh, Cate closed her laptop and glanced at the two dogs lounging on the rug near the fireplace. "Want to head out for a walk?" she inquired.

At the special word, Riley and Bailey leapt to their feet, ready to go. Cate spent an hour outside with them enjoying the cool, but sunny, spring morning.

As they settled by the loch, Cate pulled her phone from her pocket. Accessing her messaging app, Cate typed a message to Damien: *Good morning, hope everything's okay on your side of the pond. A few updates here: that music box is persistent. It shows up in my bedroom no matter what we've tried. We've locked it in a safe, Jack's hidden it and we even left it in a hallway at one point. Every time it winds up back in my bedroom.*

She clicked off her phone's display after sending the message and wrapped her arms around her bent knees. White clouds floated by in the azure sky. Cate followed their journey across the sky in the reflective surface of the loch.

She turned her mind to another question. What was it about that room that excited both her and the dogs?

"Think, Cate, think," she murmured to herself, as she forced her mind to search for anything that happened during her zombie episodes.

"What about you two?" Cate asked the dogs. "What draws you to the west wing?"

Bailey climbed onto her lap and sat down, staring at her.

Riley settled next to her, laying on his belly and watching the loch.

"Not talking, huh?" Cate asked as her cell phone chimed.

She swiped at it and read the message from Damien. *Seriously? A persistent bugger, isn't it? Not much progress on our end. Enchantments can be really tricky, especially when we don't know what we're dealing with... well, we know WHO we're dealing with no matter what he says, but his knowledge is pretty extensive. I don't mean to sound so dire, we'll figure it out. At least nothing terrible has happened yet. I mean... I don't mean like this is trivial, but a reappearing music box doesn't seem too dangerous.*

Cate smiled at the babbling message. It brought a smile to her face. She could imagine nervous, introverted Damien attempting to get his thoughts across and be supportive, while also trying to stop her from worrying.

Cate sent a return text to him. *Yeah, nothing terrible so far. Is there something I should be watching for though? I've been wandering around the castle. When I wander around, Jack said I'm almost unresponsive like a zombie. He said I keep saying strange things.* She perused Damien's message again before adding: *And what did you mean by "no matter what he says"?*

She sent the text and laid back on her elbows. Her mind searched for answers as she detailed the situation to Damien and planned future texts to explain her meaning.

Two return texts followed in rapid succession. *Celine talked to the Duke again about the situation and he said it wasn't him... riiiight like I believe that.*

His second text said: *What types of strange things? Do you remember anything from your roaming?*

Cate answered both his questions, informing him of her lack of memory and her obsession with finding a dress and being ready for some unknown event, along with her surprise to see Jack.

As she waited for a response, she continued to ponder his

other admission. Celine had discussed the matter with Duke Northcott. Cate couldn't even begin to fathom how that conversation unfolded. To begin with, Celine could barely stomach the sight of the man when she'd last seen them together. Now, Damien acted as though they spoke regularly. And his denial of involvement floored her. How did people lie so easily? Then again, she and Jack were becoming pros at it, too.

Damien answered, seeming unsurprised by anything she told him. *Any idea what dress you're looking for or why? I'm not shocked you were surprised to see Jack. That's pretty common in what you're suffering from.*

Cate screwed up her face at his words. She responded: *Pretty common? I can't even begin to imagine the lives you and your friends lead, Damien. I'm worried about disappearing into my own mind. And I'm still stuck on the conversation with Duke Northcott. Did Celine just ask him straight out and he denied it?*

The web grew more complex at every turn and Cate's head began to ache as she strove to find meaning in what was happening to her or Damien's odd explanations. She began to long for her trip to the past to give her mind a chance to relax.

Damien's response further confounded her. His first message tackled her symptoms. *Celine went through a few episodes like this (she's fine, fully recovered). It usually means something or someone is drawing you to something. With Celine, it's usually the Duke, though we have seen a few other things. Can you do me a favor and give Jack my number in case he finds you unresponsive and can't pull you out of your trance? I know he has Michael's but I'd feel better if he texted me too.*

Cate's stomach turned at the message. She noticed his deliberate avoidance to address her worry about disappearing inside her mind. In fact, if anything, his message alluded to the fact that she could.

A second message appeared as she fretted over the first message's meaning. *Yeah, Celine asked him outright. He said "Whatever Catherine is experiencing is a result of her own doing" ... yeah, I'm sure you cursed yourself*

An eye-roll emoji followed the message.

Cate stared at the screen, her jaw hanging open. She read the words over and over again. *"Whatever Catherine is experiencing is a result of her own doing."* What did that mean? Cate had no hand in this. She did not enchant the necklace and she did not send herself the music box. She'd never seen it before it arrived earlier this week.

Tension pooled at Cate's temples as she struggled to make sense of the conversation. Perhaps she should return to the castle. She could run the conversation past Jack and see if he could offer any suggestions.

Gathering the dogs, Cate returned to the castle an hour before lunch. She wandered past the closed door to the west wing. Riley stopped at the doors to give them a sniff. Cate's hand hovered on the handle. With a flick of her wrist, she twisted the knob and pulled the door open.

The two dogs raced down the wide hall, disappearing around the corner. Cate followed them, hurrying down the hall. By the time she rounded the corner, the dogs had already scurried out of the second hallway.

Cate raced down the length of it, pausing at the end to listen for any sounds of the dogs. She gulped in a breath of air, holding it while she strained for any trace of a sound. A small yip drew her attention.

Cate swung a left and rounded another corner. Both dogs stood at the gold doors she and Jack had entered yesterday. Riley pawed at them and whimpered.

"Is this where you're always off to?" Cate inquired. The little dog glanced up at her before he pawed at the door again, offering another groan.

Cate pushed open one gold door. Both dogs dashed into the oversized space. Cate followed behind them. She scanned the room's decorative elements with a suspicious eye. She'd drifted away from reality yesterday when they'd been in this room. Had that been coincidence or not?

Cate pulled her sweater tighter around her as she watched the dogs frolic in the space. Riley zoomed around the room in large circles, his lips pulled back in an opened-mouthed grin. Bailey studied the floor with interest, pawing at it occasionally when he caught sight of himself in the shiny reflection.

Suddenly, both dogs ceased what they were doing and stood at attention. They stared at one wall, their eyes fixed on the same spot. Both of them raced toward it, standing and waiting while they stared at what seemed to be nothing. Riley whined at the wall, tilting his head as though expecting something to happen.

Cate's breath caught in her throat. The tinkling music played in her mind. She inhaled a sweet, musky scent. The world around her seemed to fade. Colors melted together as a new image formed. A windowless space. Warm light glowed overhead.

Cate glanced up as her eyes tried to focus. Stars twinkled over her head. Was she outside? Her fingers found her collarbone then glided across the large gemstones of a necklace. Cate glanced down as she clutched at a heavy jewelry piece.

She blinked a few times as she tried to make sense of what she saw. Sapphire blue material covered the length of her body. She could have sworn she'd put on a pink sweater earlier.

Cate shifted her gaze forward as she attempted to determine her location. Images swept past in a dizzying array. She worked to focus on what was in front of her. A blur of blue met her gaze.

Stepping toward it, Cate blinked hard and focused on what was in front of her. As the room's details filled in, she found a mirror facing her.

Clad in a sapphire blue ballgown, Cate stared into her own blue eyes. With her hair in an upswept style, she looked ready for an evening event. The large sapphires sparkled around her neck.

Another whiff of the musky smell passed under her nostrils. A shadow crossed behind her in the mirror. "I'm here," she murmured.

A muffled voice responded. She fought to understand the words. She spun to search behind her. The motion made her dizzy and the world began to go dark. "No!" she exclaimed. "I'm here!"

She experienced the sensation of falling, before her body jolted.

CHAPTER 20

Cate blinked her eyes a few times, finding one of the room's ornate columns filled her vision.

"Cate!" Jack's voice called. Her body shook again.

Cate twisted her head to face him. "I have to find my dress," she murmured.

"What? Cate! Snap out of it!"

"I have to be ready."

"Cate!" Jack shouted, giving her another firm shake.

Cate reached out to the pillar to steady herself. She fluttered her eyelashes as the room came back into focus. Nausea made her stomach somersault, and she gulped in air. With a deep breath, she glanced around. Jack stood in front of her, concern etched into his features.

"Cate?"

Cate grasped his forearm to steady herself. "I'm okay," she said, still gulping in breaths. "What happened?"

"I think I should be asking you that."

"After my walk with the dogs, I came here to explore. I don't know what happened after I got into this room." She furrowed her brow in concentration. "The dogs were playing, then suddenly, something caught their attention. And after that, everything went black."

"You don't remember anything else?"

"No, nothing."

"When I came in, I found you staring at this column."

Cate glanced at the pillar next to her. "This wasn't where I was when the dogs reacted to whatever they heard or saw."

"Where were you?"

Cate pointed to a spot several steps away. "Over there."

"Okay, so you were wandering again."

"But why here? Does this pillar have any meaning, or did I run into it or what?"

"I'm not sure," Jack said, studying it. He ran his hand along it in several places before he shrugged. "We should get back for lunch before Molly wonders where we are. We can discuss this over our meal."

Cate nodded and called the dogs to follow them. With a last wistful glance at the wall, Riley and Bailey followed them from the room.

Cate remained silent for most of the walk back to the library. Molly delivered lunch for her, and Jack and she settled into her armchair with the warm soup.

"Still feeling wonky?" Jack inquired.

"No, just wondering what is happening to me."

Jack pulled his lips to the side in a half-frown. "I'm not sure, but it doesn't seem we can prevent it, outside of time traveling." He twisted to face the camera that still sat on the library shelf. "But we can monitor it."

Cate followed his gaze, understanding dawning on her. "We can put the camera cube in the new location I seem to be so fascinated with."

"Aye, *and* I'll put the app on my phone so I will be alerted if you wander there. We can also use the collar cam. You probably should wear it at all times, and I should have access to the feed."

Cate rolled her eyes and slumped her shoulders at the suggestion. "Reduced to wearing a collar cam. What has my life become?"

"Well, if there's no stopping you from prowling around the castle, at least we'll try to learn something from it."

Cate sighed. "I don't disagree. I just... feel odd wearing the doggy cam so you can keep an eye on me like a wayward child."

"Maybe we'll solve the case and be done with this, and you can return to being an adult," Jack said with a wink.

They sat for another moment in silence before Cate spoke again. "What I can't understand is what is drawing the dogs there?"

"Maybe there's a can of Alpo hidden behind the wall," Jack said.

"That would explain it, but fails to explain my obsession with the same space."

"Do you like Alpo?"

"Not particularly," Cate answered. "Though in a pinch..."

Jack grimaced and Cate chuckled. "I'm only kidding," she said.

"Good thing. I thought you were serious. Given your proclivities toward cereal and peanut butter sandwiches, I worried you may have tried it for a quick meal."

"Going back to the subject at hand, Riley's extremely excited by whatever is there. Same with Bailey."

"Scent of another dog? Animal?"

Cate shook her head. "No, he acts like..."

"Like what?" Jack prodded as her voice trailed off.

"Like he does when he sees me or you after we've been gone. Whatever is there, Riley's extremely happy about it."

"I hope we find out soon."

"I updated Damien on the situation earlier."

"Oh? Did he have any insight?"

"Nothing that I could make heads or tails out of. His comments bordered on bizarre."

"No surprise there," Jack said with a chuckle. "Their lives are bizarre."

"Same thing I said. Wait, let me read you a few of his statements. Maybe you'll be able to decipher some meaning."

Jack nodded as Cate tapped around on her phone to pull up the messages. "Did he manage to make you feel any less anxious about what's happening to you?"

"If anything I feel more anxious," Cate said.

Jack winced. "Now, I can't wait to hear what he had to say."

"First, he says Duke Northcott denied any involvement, which blew my mind to begin with, because I'm still trying to figure out how they're having casual conversations with this man when Celine couldn't stand the sight of him last time we saw them together."

"They asked him?"

Cate shrugged. "He said Celine did and his response was… wait, let me find it. Here. *'Whatever Catherine is experiencing is a result of her own doing'.*"

Jack's eyes went wide, and his jaw dropped open. "What? What the heck does that mean?"

Cate shrugged again. "First of all, how is this your own doing? Second, why are they discussing it with him? And how…" Jack massaged his temples. "Never mind. I'm not sure I'll ever figure those people out."

"That's only the first cryptic thing. Not only is this my own doing, but when I mentioned what happens to me, specifically the zombie walking and the strange statements I've made, he answered that it was pretty common."

Jack's shocked expression failed to fade with the latest

revelation. Instead, his eyes darted around the room as though he searched for the meaning of the words.

"Okay, well, I suppose we could take that as a good thing."

"While I understand what you're saying, he then went on to ask that I pass along his number to you, and if you can't pull me out of one of my trances to text him and Michael right away."

"That sounds scary."

"Same thing I thought. That was after I asked him if I could disappear into my own mind. He didn't say yes, but he didn't say no either."

"You've really done it this time, Cate," Jack said, with a shake of his head. "And to think less than a year ago I thought my biggest issues were going to be time travel."

"I haven't done anything! Contrary to Duke Northcott's accusation, I did not do this to myself!"

"That guy has some nerve, huh? What an odd thing to say. Then again, I'm still shocked they went and asked him about it. Perhaps he was, too, and just lied to cover his tracks."

"I'm having a hard time imagining a man like Duke Northcott shocked about anything. He seems like the type of guy who always has the upper hand. What I can't figure out is why he'd do this to me? I have no importance in the grand scheme of things. Why?"

"Perhaps you're more important than you think, Lady Cate. You do own a castle that allows for time travel."

"True."

"Or perhaps he enjoyed tormenting humans. Maybe it's a favorite pastime."

Cate grimaced at the words.

"Sorry," Jack said. "Maybe once we get to the bottom of what's happening to you, we'll know the why."

They finished the last scraps of their lunch. "Well, what

do you want to do first? Set up my child monitoring system or go to 1942?"

"Decisions, decisions. Let's get the time travel out of the way and set it up when we get back. I don't want to take a chance on you disappearing into your mind again when we go back to that room."

Cate nodded. "Sounds like a plan." She shook her head as she stood from the chair.

"What?"

"I feel like I'm on the verge of remembering something and I just can't get there. My mind won't make the last connection. I remember nothing that happens to me during those blackouts, but I feel like I'm so close to remembering something."

"Maybe it'll come to you when you least expect it."

"Maybe. Well, I'll meet you in the hall as soon as I'm ready."

"See you then!"

They parted ways to change for their trip. As Cate entered her bedroom, her gaze fell upon the music box. It stood silent despite its little lid being open. Cate approached the small item and studied it. She lifted it in her hands and turned the winding key. Music filled the air.

The tinkling sound eased the tension from her temples. She smiled down at the little item as she set it down on her nightstand.

She slipped off her shoes and padded into her bathroom to ready for the trip. Her mind relaxed as the music floated through the air. She considered the task ahead of her. Would they learn anything today about the woman they suspected had been buried in the side garden?

They had a slim window in which to gather information. Cate hoped they could determine what happened. A piece of her wondered if they could prevent it. Would it change history? Would solving the murder be enough? If faced with the opportunity, could Cate let a woman be murdered and secretly buried without attempting to help her?

Questions blazed through Cate's mind as she pulled on her dark-colored dress. She stepped into her bedroom and pulled on her retro-style shoes. Cate stood and her gaze fell to the jewelry box. She crossed to it and pulled open the bottom drawer.

Cate pursed her lips as she stared down. Limned against the black velvet, the stunning sapphire necklace sparkled in the light.

"So, that's where you've been," Cate murmured as she caressed the item. Something in the large center stone caught her eye, and she leaned closer to study it.

Her mind sorted through images until it settled on one: a room with soft, twinkling stars casting a warm glow over-head. Mirrored panels were set between tall decorative pillars. A colorful floor painted the space with warm-colored images of unicorns sailing with the clouds. The music played behind her, and she experienced the sensation of twirling.

Cate blinked rapidly as the image faded away. The sapphire settled back to its dazzling blue color. She swallowed hard as she straightened and slid the drawer closed.

"Where is that room?" she whispered to herself.

A knock sounded at the doors to her suite. Cate grabbed her purse and hurried from the bedroom. Another mystery awaited.

She pulled the doors open to find Jack waiting in his 1940s-style suit. Two suitcases, packed earlier by Cate, sat just inside the door. Jack grabbed hold of them both. The grin on his face faltered as he glanced over her and into her bedroom. "Is that thing still playing?"

Cate gave him a sheepish glance. "I wound it."

Jack closed his eyes for a moment before responding.

"Before you say anything," Cate rushed to say, "I just…"

"Couldn't help it," Jack finished for her. "I know, Lady Cate. I know. If that little bugger can find its way back to you no matter where we put it, I can imagine we're fighting a losing battle."

"That's not all," Cate said, as she stepped into the hall with him, grabbing one suitcase. "The necklace is back, too."

Jack's shoulders slumped at the admission as Cate continued. "Safely tucked in the jewelry armoire where I've always kept it."

"I suppose at least you're still normal. Thank heavens for small mercies."

"There's still more," Cate said with a wrinkled nose.

CHAPTER 21

Jack side-eyed her with wide eyes.

"On an impulse, I opened the drawer and found the necklace. I thought I saw something in the large sapphire in the center. When I inspected it, an image of a room formed in my mind." Cate did her best to describe it. "Do you know of anywhere in the castle like that?"

Jack shook his head as he rubbed his chin with his free hand. "No, it doesn't ring any bells."

Cate sighed as they descended the stairs. "I thought if we could find it, maybe we could discover more about what's going on."

"I hate to say this, Lady Cate," Jack said, as Cate pulled on the sconce to open the secret passage. "But what if…"

"Yeah?" Cate asked, stepping into the darkened passage.

"What if it's a room only in your mind?"

Cate sighed as the darkness closed in around them when Jack pushed the panel shut. "I suppose if that's the case, you'd better keep Damien's number handy."

Jack flicked on his flashlight and reached out to squeeze

Cate's arm. "Let's hope it's not," he said. "And now, let's get to 1942 and solve our other mystery."

Cate and Jack activated the timepiece and slipped back to another era. Cate smiled at Jack, happy to leave the problems of the present time behind.

"Feel better?" Jack asked, as the timepiece finished its cycle, indicated by the second-hand crawling around the face.

"I didn't feel that bad before, honestly," Cate admitted. "Just a little...off." They followed the passageway toward the crypt at the other end.

"Maybe the curse you hexed yourself with is wearing off."

Cate rolled her eyes. "How ridiculous," she said. "How could I be the source of this?"

"You spent a good amount of time with Duke Northcott," Jack began.

"Don't remind me," Cate groaned.

"Were there any clues about this? Anything he said that could help us?"

"No," Cate said, flinging her arms out then letting them slap her thighs. "I've been over and over the conversations we had. I can't imagine why he'd waste time on me, to be honest."

"He seemed awfully interested in you in the 1700s."

"According to everyone else involved, he merely wanted to create a ruckus to draw Celine's attention to him."

"Perhaps he's trying that angle again?"

"Why use me an ocean away? Why not Damien or Michael?" Cate shook her head. "It doesn't make any sense."

"None of this does, I agree."

"The only thing that sticks in my head is when he told me to keep the necklace to remember him. It's so odd. But it really doesn't help."

They reached the end of the passage and Jack opened the

panel leading to the crypt. "The entire situation is odd. He's a warlock. That's more than odd. He kidnapped you for some unknown reason. Odd. He gave you a necklace likely worth thousands of pounds to remember what must have been the worst experience of your life. Only one word for it, Lady Cate: odd."

"You know what else is odd," Cate said as they exited the crypt into the sunny September day. "The fact that I can't find any information about this intelligence post."

"Maybe all these people are time traveling warlocks," Jack suggested as they walked the path toward the castle. "And that's why there's no information on them."

"I can't believe I'm about to say this, but you make a point."

"Cate, I was only joking."

"I know, but that's a fantastic way to check this out from another angle. I can ask for some names of those who work there and track them back through the records. Thanks, Jack! I'll work on that when we get back. Gosh, I hope I find something! This could be the key we're looking for!"

"Gosh, I hope we don't run into Pap. I've been sweating bullets about traveling to this time period ever since that first day."

"We avoided him once already, let's hope our luck holds out. And speaking of, maybe we should ask him about the intelligence base. He obviously knew about it."

"He was only five. He couldn't have known much."

"He knew enough to frighten you into not wanting to run into him again."

"Good point. I'll ask him when we get back. That'll be my contribution to the research."

"Invite him to dinner tonight," Cate said. "We can ask the whole group."

"Aye, that sounds like a good plan."

"Okay, one thing settled. Now, let's work on finding out who ended up in the side garden."

They approached the castle. Cate handed her bag off to Jack and used the door knocker. Smithers opened the door within moments.

"Mr. and Mrs. MacKenzie," he said with a smile. "Come in. Lord MacKenzie told me to expect you. Oh, please, sir, allow me to take the bags."

"I can…" Jack began as the man wrestled the bags from his grip.

"No trouble at all, sir. I shall inform Lord MacKenzie of your arrival and then place these in your suite. Lord MacKenzie informs me you stayed there in the past. I trust you can find your way there when the time is appropriate?" He phrased the last statement as a question.

"We can, thank you," Cate said, as she strolled into the sitting room.

"At least he was friendlier today," Jack said as he paced around the room.

"I thought you were going to fight him on the bags."

Jack offered a chuckle as their conversation was interrupted by Rory's arrival. "There you are!" the man said with a grin. "I wondered all night if I'd dreamt you. I'm so pleased you have returned. Has Smithers handled your things?"

"Yes, he took the bags up. Thank you," Cate said.

"I told him to inform Amelia of your arrival. I'm certain she'll want to see you. She arrived just before lunch."

"I'm looking forward to seeing her again, too," Cate said, her stomach flip-flopping at the prospect. Her great-grandmother would now be almost twenty years older, while Cate remained almost the same age. "It's a shame we won't be able to see Anne."

"Oh, yes, she'll be so sore when she finds she's missed you.

I'm quite surprised, actually, Amelia asked to visit and didn't elect to travel to Anne's parents' country home."

"Oh?" Jack inquired, prodding for more information

"Mmm, something about being in the area and wanting to show the property to her traveling companion." Rory waved his hands in the air. "In any case, I'm pleased to have her here. The castle is far too quiet with just Oliver and me."

A woman arrived in the open doorway to the foyer. Cate recognized her great-grandmother immediately. Streaks of gray at her temples and a few added wrinkles changed her appearance slightly from the last time Cate had seen her.

"Cate! Jack!" Amelia said, a smile lighting up her face.

"Amelia!" Cate said as the woman rushed toward her and pulled her into an embrace. She pushed away, holding out Cate's arms and giving her a once over.

"My goodness, you look splendid. I'd swear you haven't aged a day, Cate," Amelia said before pulling Jack into a hug.

"Oh, it's been more than a day," Cate said with a nervous chuckle.

"And you, you handsome devil," Amelia said to Jack. "You two must be living the right kind of lives!"

Smithers appeared at the doorway.

"Tea," Rory requested, before motioning for everyone to take their seats.

Jack issued a nervous glance toward Cate. They'd pulled off their subterfuge for now. Amelia chalked up their youthful appearances to a trick of time.

"How lovely for us all to be together again," Amelia said. "Such a shame Anne couldn't be here."

"Mmm, I said the same," Cate said, as she sat across from the woman. "Rory tells us you're here to show someone the estate?" She hoped the question wasn't too obvious, but she desperately needed information quickly.

"Oh, yes, Ruth Harper. She's a traveling companion of

mine. Lucas insisted I have one, what with the war going on. He works in the Ministry of Defense now, you know. And he absolutely detested the idea of me traveling alone, though I had to get out of London."

"Oh, I hadn't realized Lucas did that type of work. And I agree, a smart move to leave London," Cate said.

"Whereabouts are you now, Jack? Still in land?" Rory questioned.

"Oh yes," Jack answered. "Though I suppose in a bit of a lull given the current state of affairs." Cate offered him a smile and a nod as he gave her a sideways glance to check his story.

"Oh, I can imagine. How dreadful this all is," Rory said, wringing his hands.

Smithers arrived with the tea and Rory busied himself playing host. Cate attempted to steer the conversation back to Amelia's traveling companion.

"Has Ruth been with you long?" Cate inquired.

"No, only a few months," Amelia said. "She's quite a smart girl, very personable. I'm very much enjoying working with her."

"Working with her?" Cate questioned.

"You know, traveling and such. We get on well and so on. You'd quite like her, Cate."

"I'm certain I would. I'd love to meet her."

"We'll have to arrange it."

"Ask her to join us for dinner tonight, Amelia," Rory said. Cate's pulse quickened as she awaited Amelia's answer.

"Oh, shouldn't we keep it family?"

Rory shook his head as he responded. "Some of the wonderful folks from the base will be joining us. The more the merrier."

"Oh! How lovely. I shall definitely invite her then."

Conversation turned to their activities over the years.

Cate's grandfather, Amelia's son, Charles, returned to a boarding school in the English countryside for the term. He'd finish his final year there before going on to university.

Cate and Jack made up a few interesting tidbits about travel to fill in gaps in the conversation. The party broke up in the mid-afternoon with promises to continue their discussions over dinner.

Cate and Jack retreated to their bedroom suite. Jack tossed himself onto the chaise and scrubbed his face.

"Thank heavens Amelia thinks we've just got good genes," he said.

Cate paced the length of the room, lost in her thoughts.

Jack propped himself up on his elbows. "Cate? You haven't gone funny on me, have you?"

"No," she said as she twirled around to amble in the opposite direction.

Jack raised his eyebrows as she spun to face him again. "Anything you'd like to share?"

Cate puckered her lips. "Amelia said she enjoyed working with Ruth."

"So?"

"Why phrase it that way? That was odd."

"You're reading into things. I mean, the girl is literally an employee. She just accompanies Amelia wherever she goes for pay. So it's not that odd of a phrase."

Cate's mind continued to churn. "Even if you don't think the phrase is odd, think about the timing. Amelia loves working with her. And in two days she'll leave for another position. Something doesn't add up here."

"Amelia likes working with Ruth. We don't know Ruth likes working for Amelia."

Cate sighed. "I guess. I can't wait to meet her. I'm going to try to pry some information from her so I can track her down."

"Go get 'em, tiger," Jack said with a grin.

Cate glanced out of the window. "Want to take a walk?"

"I was comfy where I was," Jack protested.

"Okay, I'll leave you lounging. I'm going to poke around the intelligence tent." Cate strode to the door with a determined step.

"Are you serious?" Jack asked, bouncing up from lounging to sitting.

"Yes. Maybe I can find something out that will further my research."

"Wait, wait," Jack said, groaning as he pulled himself up to standing. "I'll come with you."

"You don't have to. I'll be perfectly fine."

"Famous last words. The last time I let you out of my sight on one of these trips a warlock kidnapped you."

"Let's hope that doesn't happen again," Cate groaned, as she pulled the door open.

"I'm going to hedge my bet," Jack answered her.

Cate and Jack strolled through the halls and wandered into the bright sunshine outside. As they rounded a corner of the castle, a small boy leapt from a tree across the property.

"Oh, no," Jack groaned. "Hurry up before he spots us."

Cate couldn't help but chuckle. "Too late," she said, as the little boy's face scrunched up as he shielded his eyes and glared at the pair of them. He raced up the hill toward them.

"Great! I should have stayed behind."

Cate patted Jack's arm. "Let me do the talking."

The little boy skidded to a stop in front of them and poked a finger toward them. "You two again, eh?"

CHAPTER 22

Cate winced at the little boy in front of them, holding up her hands. "Guilty."

Stanley raised his eyebrows. "Have you come to join the others at the base?"

"That's where we're headed right now."

"Oh, lollygagging, huh?"

"What?" Cate inquired with a small laugh.

"You don't seem to be in a hurry. Haven't you got work to do? My Da says they're having a terrible time with the codes. And another convoy was attacked as a result."

"That's terrible. I'm not certain we'll be of much assistance. We're actually visiting Jack's cousin, Lord MacKenzie."

"Oh. I didn't realize you were MacKenzies."

Cate smiled and nodded. "Yes, we are."

Stanley eyed Jack head to toe. "You don't look like one," he said. "In fact, you remind me of my Da."

Jack chuckled nervously. "You don't say, laddie."

Stanley stood firm in his words. He crossed his arms and stared at Jack again. Suddenly, his expression changed. "Got to go!" he shouted. With a twirl, he was gone, racing down to the tree and scampering up into its limbs.

"I saw that!" a Scottish accent said behind them.

Cate and Jack spun to find Lachlan Reid, Stanley's father, and Jack's great-grandfather, striding down the path toward them.

"Jack and Cate," he said, recognizing them. "Rory told me you were here. Wonderful to see you again."

"Thanks," Cate said with a grin as Jack shook Lachlan's hand.

"I see you've met Stanley." He pointed to the tree.

"Aye, we did."

"I hope he hasn't been too much of a bother. He can be a little prickly."

"I'm used to it," Jack said.

"Still irascible in your time, is he?"

"Oh, you know it," Jack said with a chuckle.

"Well, I won't interrupt your walk. Hope to see you again, though."

With a wave, Lachlan strode toward the tree, leaving Jack and Cate to continue their walk to the tent.

They overheard him demanding Stanley come down from the branch he perched on and that he hoped he hadn't been bothering the MacKenzies.

"I was not!" they heard the little boy shout as he shimmied down the tree.

Cate couldn't hold in a giggle. "He really is a character," she noted as they approached the canvas hut.

"You'd almost suspect he's a MacKenzie with that cheek," Jack said, with a shake of his head.

"Very funny, Jack. We're not that cheeky of a bunch."

"Oh, really?" Jack questioned playfully. "Tell me that again when we're in our own century. It's thanks to you cheeky buggers that we're able to do this, after all. Jamie was thoroughly against it if you recall."

"And it's a good thing we can," Cate said. "Look at all the good we've done!"

"Yeah, I'm just waiting for the moment something terrible happens."

"Don't be a negative Nellie," Cate warned, as they closed the gap and arrived at the tent. Cate pushed through into the interior, blinking as her eyes adjusted from the bright sunshine to the dim light inside.

A few people worked away at the tables; others bustled around the make-shift room. A blonde man passed them, slowing his step and staring at them.

"Can I help you?" he asked in a British accent.

"Hi," Cate said. "Maybe. I'm Cate MacKenzie and this is my husband, Jack." Jack waved and nodded. "We're cousins of Lord MacKenzie. He showed us the base yesterday. And I was wondering if anyone could provide us with more information."

"Oh," the man said, his brow wrinkling as he scratched his head, "well, I'm afraid there isn't much information I can share. It's all classified, you see."

"I don't mean the messages, but just some information about how you came to be here."

"Oh, right. Well, I suppose I can share that much. Actually, we come from all over. I'm from Kent. My parents emigrated from Germany when I was six. So, I grew up speaking German. And I'm very good at pattern detection. At least I'd like to think so." The man gave an awkward laugh.

"How interesting," Cate said. "So, are you a mathematician?"

"Yes, I was recruited out of a college by the Defense Ministry at the start of the war. Initially, I was based in London, however, with the blitz, several of us were moved."

"So, all of you came from London originally?"

"No, just Victor and me. I'm Hans, by the way. Hans Schmidt."

"Nice to meet you, Hans," Cate said. "It must be difficult moving here and working with a new group."

"It can be, though everyone here is quite professional. A large portion of our group went to Bletchley Park. We were split in the event that something should happen. A sort of a 'don't put all of your eggs in one basket' approach."

"I see. Very smart."

Hans smiled and nodded. "Well, we won't keep you from your work any longer," Cate said. "Thank you so much for explaining everything."

"You're very welcome," Hans said with a nod of his head. He strode away, taking a seat at the table and shuffling through several papers.

Jack and Cate exited into the bright sunshine. "Well, did you learn what you wanted to?" Jack inquired.

"Hans didn't give me much to go on, but he did say some of them came from London."

"How does that help?"

Cate shrugged. "Maybe it doesn't, though we do have one name and half of another. Perhaps I can track information on Hans and use it to link to Ruth in some way."

"Do you believe they're connected?"

"It's a long shot, but we have to start somewhere. And if Ruth disappeared and ended up murdered and buried in the garden, someone here killed her. So, someone is connected to her."

"Could have been a crime of opportunity," Jack suggested.

"As in a random person here is a killer and kills Ruth for no reason?"

"Sure. She's in the wrong place at the wrong time, maybe."

Cate considered it, then shook her head. "It doesn't add up. There has to be a motive beyond it."

"Maybe she saw or heard something she shouldn't."

"Okay, so the killer has no prior connection to Ruth, but she overhears or sees something she shouldn't and he…"

"Or she," Jack added.

"Right, he or she strikes, kills Ruth and buries her in the garden."

"The garden burial suggests it wasn't pre-planned."

"I agree. It suggests the killer acted in haste and dumped the body in the most readily available space. It wouldn't be questioned because there's planting being done there."

"So now that I've blown your tenuous chance at tracking down information to bits, what would you like to do?"

"You haven't blown it to bits," Cate said with a chuckle. "I can still use the information Hans gave me to try to ferret out a clue as to what Ruth may or may not have heard."

They slipped back inside the castle. "And let's hope we gather even more information at dinner tonight. Then, I can track down all the leads when we get back."

"Wait for dinner, then," Jack concluded from Cate's statements.

"Right," she said with a nod, as they threaded through the halls and back to their suite.

Cate spent the short time before the meal pacing the floor. "It's amazing how reliant we've become on the internet," she lamented as she made her twelfth trek across the floor. "I feel practically helpless here."

"What did they do in a time before Google?" Jack asked.

"It was called a library, I think," Cate joked.

"I suppose we could have gone into town to the library. I wonder if there's a 1942 version of Mrs. Campbell there, waiting to spring a random party on an unsuspecting castle owner." Jack rubbed his chin in faux thought.

"There may be, in which case we'd draw too much attention. Plus, we don't have enough time before dinner." Cate checked the clock on the mantle. "I suppose we should be getting ready, in fact."

After a change of clothes, Jack and Cate made their way to the sitting room, finding Amelia there with a woman. Her dirty blonde hair was pulled back in a neat bun. Large eyes and red lips were set in a round face. Cate pegged her to be in her mid-thirties.

"Jack, Cate! I hope the rest of your afternoon went well," Amelia said.

"It did," Cate answered, hoping she wasn't too obvious when eyeing Ruth.

"This is my traveling companion, Ruth Harper. Ruth, this is Jack and Cate MacKenzie, distant cousins of Rory's."

"How lovely to meet you both," Ruth said.

Rory entered the room moments later, followed by Rita Haverford, Hans, and a tall, well-muscled, dark-haired man. Rory introduced the unknown man as Victor Richard. Cate assumed he was the Victor mentioned earlier by Hans when they'd visited the intelligence hut.

As Rory introduced Hans, Cate said, "Nice to see you again."

"Oh, I hadn't realized you two knew each other," Rory said.

"We met earlier this afternoon," Cate explained. "Hans was kind enough to tell us more about the formation of the base."

Hans smiled broadly at her. "Well, I'm afraid I wasn't very much help, but I'm glad to know I provided you with some information."

After a few more minutes of small talk, they shuffled into the dining room. "We're evenly split between genders, so seating should be simple," Rory said. "Anne would be so proud of me."

"I shall be sure to inform her of your balanced dinner prowess when I see her next," Amelia said as they sat down.

Cate found herself sandwiched between Hans and Victor. Jack, across the table from her, sat between Amelia and Rita. Cate flashed Jack an "oh well" look as they both found themselves separated from Ruth.

Cate began her pre-meal discussion with Hans. "Hello, again, Mrs. MacKenzie," he said with a shy smile. "I do hope you are enjoying your stay at the castle."

"Yes, I am. And what about you. You said you're from London originally?"

"Oh, no, Kent."

"Oh, right. Yes, your initial base was in London."

"Yes, that's right."

"This must be quite a change for you then."

"Oh, quite. None of the conveniences of the modern city, though also none of the drawbacks."

"So, you're enjoying the quiet countryside?"

"Well, it's quieter. We still have the occasional flyovers. In fact, there was a dog fight nearby recently." The man pulled his lips into a thin line. "I'm sorry," he said, after a moment, "bad memories from London."

Cate offered him a consoling glance. "Forgive me for bringing it up. We don't have to discuss it further."

He twisted the corners of his mouth into a tight smile, though a pained expression still shined through his features. Amelia turned toward Jack for a conversation, and Cate took the opportunity to end her awkward discussion with Hans and turn her attention to Victor.

"Hello, I'm Cate."

"Lovely to meet one of Lord MacKenzie's relatives. The poor man has been overrun by us of late, I'm afraid."

"I'm sure he doesn't mind," Cate said. "The work you're doing is so vital. I know Lord MacKenzie is very pleased to do anything to help the war effort. So, where are you from originally? Hans said you came from the London office. Was London also your home?"

"No, I'm originally from Leeds. Born and bred."

"Oh!" Cate furrowed her brow in mock confusion. "So, no German connection?"

"Heavens no!" Victor exclaimed with a chuckle.

"So, how is it that you can decipher the German missives. Or am I being short-sighted in terms of how the intelligence works?"

"Not at all. I took three years of German in my uni days."

"I see. Well, that explains it. And are you also a mathematician?"

"Yes, with a concentration in the study of codes."

"And Hans said you worked together in London?"

"Yes, we did. We were both in the London office since the start of the war until we moved here. Our building was destroyed in a blast."

"Oh, I'm so sorry to hear that."

Another awkward end of the conversation as Smithers entered with a footman and the first course. Cate glanced across the table, her eyes widening at the scene. Rita leaned indecently close to Jack. With her elbow propped on the table, she rested her chin in her hand, her head cocked flirtatiously. She batted her eyelashes at him as she lifted a shoulder and offered him a pout, letting her free hand fall onto his forearm.

Cate narrowed her eyes at the woman. Jack glanced at Cate. She offered him an unimpressed glance. Jack offered her a "what?" expression and a shrug. Cate puckered her lips and shook her head.

"Oh, please tell Mrs. Bakewell the soup smells divine," Rory said.

Cate softened her expression and smiled at Rory. Perhaps now the conversation could include the whole table and she'd learn more about Ruth. She was certain Jack didn't learn much from Rita beyond how quickly the woman could flutter her eyelashes.

At the first break in the conversation, Cate interjected a question for Amelia. "Have you been traveling very much, Amelia?"

"Mmm, quite a bit, yes."

Cate found it odd given the current state of affairs. Usually, in wartime, activities were quelled. "And do you enjoy the traveling, Ruth?" Cate inquired.

"I do, yes. I've always been a bit of a rolling stone, I suppose. So the travel suits me."

Cate smiled at her. "And where are you from originally?"

"Manchester," Ruth said, without skipping a beat.

"Are your parents still there?"

"No. They both passed away when I was nineteen."

"Oh, what a shame. Both my parents passed when I was young as well."

Ruth offered her a polite smile. Cate narrowed her eyes at the reaction. Given that information, she thought there would have been a reaction of kindredness between them.

"No other family?" Cate pressed.

"One brother. His plane went down over Germany last year, though."

"Oh, how tragic. I'm so sorry," Cate said. She returned to sipping at her soup. Her conversations were winding up awkward at every turn. At this rate, she'd never discover any information.

She allowed the rest of the dinner conversation to be led by Rory and Amelia. Cate detected no awkwardness between Amelia and Ruth that would suggest the woman would suddenly leave her position. Amelia had told the reporter she left for a better job. What position would be "better," particularly when she'd indicated her love for travel?

Cate mulled it over as the conversation continued around her. The party broke up early, with the codebreakers turning in for a long day of work the following day. Cate and Jack chatted with Amelia and Rory for another few moments before excusing themselves for an evening walk.

They returned to the crypt, entered the secret passage, and in short order were back in their own time period.

"Meet in the library as usual?" Jack asked, as they took the back stairs up to the bedrooms to change.

"Sure," Cate said.

Jack narrowed his eyes at her curt response as they wound through the halls. "You feeling okay?"

"I'm fine," Cate said, attempting to keep her annoyance in check. "See you soon."

Cate slipped into her bedroom, making her way straight to the music box. She wound it and set it on the nightstand to play as she changed back into normal clothes. The music soothed her frayed nerves.

Her conversations had been a bust. She hoped whatever small details she'd gleaned could lead them to a breakthrough, though she didn't hold out much hope. She wondered if Jack had learned anything. Her eyes narrowed, and she frowned as she recalled buxom blonde Rita gushing over him at the dinner table. The nerve of the woman to openly flirt with someone else's husband. She reminded herself she and Jack weren't married, though Rita wasn't aware of that fact.

Perhaps they could solicit some information this evening at the staff dinner. As she finished dressing, Cate closed her eyes and let the music melt away any tension. Her odd statement to Jack was proving true. She did love the music box.

Reluctantly, she left the tinkling object behind and made her way to the library. She found Jack wrestling with Riley over a toy, while Bailey gnawed on the ear of a stuffed moose.

Cate collected a notebook and pen before collapsing into her armchair. She began jotting notes.

"This looks promising," Jack said.

"I'm just jotting down names and the few bits of information I got from them to help me find information." She finished her list and glanced at Jack. "Did you happen to get any information from Rita, or was it all batting eyelashes and rubbing your forearm?"

An amused expression crossed Jack's features. "Why, Lady Cate, whatever are you talking about?"

"I'm talking about Rita Haverford shamelessly flirting with a married man."

"I wouldn't call it flirting."

Cate screwed up her face. "What would you call it?"

"She seems very friendly."

"I'll say."

"I'm starting to believe you're jealous, Lady Cate."

"I just don't like the type of woman who would flirt with another woman's husband. Especially when the woman is right there!"

"Oh, right."

"Look who's talking. I still haven't heard the end of calling Grayson Buckley handsome."

"Nor of your budding relationship with a certain shipbuilder of yore turned modern-day computer scientist."

"Anyway," Cate said, getting the conversation back on track, "did you learn anything from blonde and buxom?"

"Yes. She told me how much she enjoys long walks on the beach and roses."

"You're kidding?"

Jack chuckled. "Yes, I am. She wasn't that obvious."

"I should hope not!"

"And to answer your question, no. I did not find out much from Ms. Rita Haverford. She had a way of steering the conversation back to me at every turn."

"And neither of us were sitting near Ruth, so we couldn't grill her."

"I'll try tomorrow if she's at dinner. And I'll keep away from Rita before she ruins our marriage." Jack made a frightened face.

"I'm certain Anne would feel the same way if she saw the looks Rita gives Rory."

"Really?" Jack questioned.

"You didn't notice her perk up yesterday when we went to the tent? That demure smile she gave him? And with her behavior earlier, I'd say she does this a lot."

"Maybe she's just a flirt."

Cate tapped her pencil against the notepad. "Well, this isn't much to go on, but I suppose it's a start. I'll have to work fast, though, we don't have much time."

"Maybe we'll learn more tonight at dinner."

"That's my sincere hope."

"Until then, let's set up the cameras for later."

"Good idea."

They spent the remaining time before dinner adding the camera apps to Jack's phone and testing them. Jack also placed the camera from the library in the large room the dogs and Cate continued to frequent, suggesting Cate stay away from the space for the time being.

With the collar cam attached to a bracelet, they were set to monitor any of Cate's movements overnight.

As they finished the tasks, a knock sounded at the door. Cate ushered a waiting Stanley Reid into the foyer.

"Hello there, lassie," he said, as he removed his hat.

"Hi, Mr. Reid. I'm so glad you could make it."

"I'll never turn down Emily's cooking," Stanley said. "And I hear the whippersnapper from across the pond isn't so bad at it either."

"Molly is a fantastic cook and baker," Cate agreed.

"We should head down," Jack said.

"Oh? I thought I was early," Stanley said.

"I'm hungry, though," Jack answered.

"Okay, okay. Though I doubt you'll hurry Emily along if she's not ready."

"I can try," Jack said.

"And how are you feeling, lassie?" Stanley inquired of Cate. "Jackie said you were having some issues?"

"Oh, I'm okay. Just experiencing a few strange incidents stemming from the necklace I returned with from 1792."

"From that odd Duke fellow?"

"Yes," Cate said, as they descended the stairs.

"Well, I hope you sort it out soon. And keep me in the loop, especially if I can be of any help in figuring things out. I love a good mystery."

"What's a mystery?" Emily said as they entered.

Stanley winced and shot Cate an apologetic glance.

"An intelligence base at Dunhaven Castle in World War II," Cate answered, covering their conversation.

Mrs. Fraser stopped in her tracks, her brow furrowing. "Well, that was before my time, but I cannae say I've ever heard of it."

Mr. Fraser concurred. "Aye, me neither."

"I've come across a reference to one," Cate mentioned. "It would have been during Rory's time. But Mrs. Campbell hadn't heard of it either."

"Well, there's your answer, Lady Cate. If the busybody herself doesn't have the scoop, no one does," Mrs. Fraser said with a nod, setting a salad on the table and greeting Stanley.

"How about you, Pap?" Jack said. "You go back that far. You remember an intelligence base here at the castle?"

Stanley wrinkled his face in thought. "You know, for the longest time as a child, I thought there was. But my Da said no."

Cate and Jack shared a glance. Young Stanley Reid had most certainly been aware of the intelligence base. They'd discussed it.

Stanley chuckled for a moment before he continued. "I must have made up a fantastical story about that. Years later, well after the war, I asked my father about it. 'There was no intelligence base here, you daft bugger,' he said to me.

"And I said, 'Yes, of course, there was. In a big tent behind the castle.'" Stanley chuckled again. "He said my little mind was making up stories. For the longest time, I really believed Dunhaven was the center of intelligence for the Crown. Ah, the stories a young laddie will make up to entertain himself."

Cate's mind processed the information. She smiled at Stanley as the conversation turned to another subject. Why had Lachlan lied to Stanley? As a child of only five, his memory may be hazy enough to pull it off, but Cate was well aware of its existence. And of Lachlan's knowledge of it. What were they trying to cover up by denying it existed? Was it murder?

ate and Jack walked Stanley upstairs after their dinner. "Where's your car, Pap?"

"I walked," the man said, raising his chin with pride.

"Why?" Jack said. "Now you've got to walk back.

"Aye," the man said. "Good exercise for me."

"And good exercise for me worrying something will happen to you on the way back."

Stanley gave Jack a roll of his eyes. "I'm not a wee child, Jackie. A little walk won't hurt."

"I'll drive you."

The man waved away the offer. "I'll send you a text when I get there."

"No," Jack said. "I've got enough worries without adding to the pile. Come on, you can get your exercise walking to get the car with me."

"If you don't mind, I'll tag along," Cate said. "There's something I'd like to discuss with you."

They stepped out into the cool spring air. "What is it, lassie? Your troubles with that madman?"

"No," Cate said as the gravel crunched beneath their feet.

"I know what it is," Jack said, with a glance at both of them.

"Oh, do you, smart guy? Do you mind sharing it?"

"It's about the intelligence base," Cate said.

"I already told you. There was no intelligence base on the property. Sorry, lassie."

"But there was," Cate said. "We've seen it."

"And even better, Pap, so have you," Jack said.

Stanley ceased his walking and shifted his gaze between them. "What?"

"As a matter of fact, we talked to you about it," Jack said.

Stanley's face turned into a mask of confusion.

"You probably don't remember," Cate said. "You were only five. But we've spoken to you about the tent in 1942. You told us it was an intelligence base."

"Right after you asked me if I had flat feet or if I was a Nazi," Jack added.

"And Rory MacKenzie confirmed the tent was an intelligence base. We've been inside it. We've spoken to the people who worked there."

Stanley took a moment to process the information. He stared into space as he started to slowly shake his head. "But Da said…"

"I know what Lachlan told you, Pap, but there was an intelligence base there. One he was very much aware of."

"Why would he lie?"

Cate shared a glance with Jack before she turned her gaze back to Stanley. "I'm not sure. But there was most certainly a base on these grounds in 1942."

"Can I ask what you two are doing in 1942?"

"Investigating a murder," Jack said, as they reached the garage.

"We think the body from the garden was buried in that time frame. We started with that year since a woman went missing from Dunhaven Castle. It was explained away, but we didn't have any other leads. When we arrived, we found an intelligence base. What I can't figure out is why there is no record of it. And now I'm further baffled by the fact that your father told you it didn't exist."

"I don't know what to say," Stanley said, as they slid into the car and Jack pulled down the driveway. "I just can't believe Da would have lied to me."

"Perhaps he didn't have a choice. But the question is why did they have to keep it secret? It couldn't have been confidential information," Cate said. "People would have been aware of its existence. Why deny it?"

"I wish I could tell you, lassie, though if you learn anything, I'd appreciate hearing about it. So, all that time I thought there was a base, I was right. Oh, why did you lie, Da?"

Cate flicked her eyes to Jack. "Don't get too upset over it, Pap. It could be for any reason."

"Perhaps a similar reason to why you couldn't share the information about the time travel secret with us when I first came. There must be a reason. As soon as we find out, we'll let you know."

"Thank you. I appreciate that, lassie."

They dropped the older man off at his cottage and started their return trip to the castle. "Gosh, I feel terrible about bringing this up to your grandfather," Cate said as they pulled away from the small house.

"Why?"

"Well, his father lied to him. I shouldn't have pushed it. He thought he'd just made it up in his mind, and now he is wondering why Lachlan lied to him."

"There's a reason, you can be sure of it. And I'd like to know what it was. We need to get to the bottom of this."

"I agree. Do you think the covering up of the base could be connected to the murder?"

"As in, they shut down the base and didn't speak of it again after the murder?"

"Yes," Cate said with a nod.

"That seems a stretch, even if they were related. Surely, they would just remove the person responsible and keep the base operational."

Cate pursed her lips as she considered it. "Yeah, you're probably right. So, we may have two mysteries on our hands here."

"Looks that way," Jack said, as he eased the car into the garage.

"Well, I hope we can solve one or the other soon," Cate said, as they wandered back to the castle in the waning light.

"I'd also like to solve our present-day mystery," Jack said.

Cate sighed as she considered heading to bed for the night. She wondered if the camera app would awaken Jack as she wandered around the castle babbling nonsense.

She rubbed the back of her neck. "I just hope we like the ending."

Jack wrapped his arm around her shoulders. "It'll be okay, Cate. I won't let anything happen to you."

Cate gave him a nervous smile and a nod. Though she worried they may not have a say in the final outcome.

* * *

Cate heard the tinkling music emanating from the music box even before she opened her eyes. Despite the trepidation it caused, she found herself enjoying the music and feeling comforted by it. She rolled over and stared at the music box on her nightstand.

The music began to slow. Cate pulled herself up to sit and

grabbed the small object, turning the winding key again. Odd that it played all night long but sometimes needed wound to continue. She set the musical item on her nightstand and rose from the bed. As she lifted her hand from the piano, her fingers brushed against the tiny keys.

The small keyboard lifted up before clapping back into place with a small thud. Cate cocked her head at the piano and squatted down to study it at eye level. She reached her thumb toward the keyboard and gently pushed it upward. The keys swung upward revealing a small cubby.

A yellowed piece of paper lay within the well. Cate carefully lifted the scrap of paper from within the piano's hiding spot with her thumb and forefinger.

She unfolded the small paper fragment. Her eyes bulged at what her brain registered on the page. She dropped it, scrambling back a few steps and clutching her abdomen. The small sliver fluttered to the floor, landing face up.

Cate continued to stare at the black ink on the page. "You've always loved this," it read. Cate recognized the statement as something she'd imparted to Jack in one of her trances. She also recognized something else about the note. It was written in her own handwriting.

Damien's text flashed through her mind. She recalled his quote from Duke Northcott. "Whatever Catherine is experiencing is a result of her own doing."

She sank onto the bed and allowed her mind to dwell on the only question she could come up with: what was going on here?

A knock sounded at her door, and she hurried to open it. "Good morning, Jack. Did I wake you last night?"

"No," Jack said. "You were surprisingly quiet. I'm shocked, actually."

"Perhaps it was because of the time travel," Cate said.

"I almost hoped you had woken me last night."

"Why?"

"We're no closer to a solution."

"That's not exactly true," Cate said.

"Oh? Something happen that I don't know about?"

Cate nodded and motioned for him to follow her. "This morning, I woke up to the music box playing. Surprise, surprise. Anyway, I touched it, and the keys moved. Upon further inspection, I found a hidden compartment." Cate snatched the paper from the floor where it had fallen moments ago while the dogs raced to Jack's side.

"Good morning, boys," he said, ruffling their fur.

"This was inside." She passed the note to Jack.

He read it aloud: "You've always loved this." He screwed up his face. "That's almost exactly what you told me while you were in your trance."

Cate nodded. "I know. And here's an even creepier part."

Jack studied the note for another moment before flicking his gaze to Cate. "Which is?"

"That's my handwriting."

Jack's eyes shifted back to the note. "Are you sure?"

"Positive. I recognize my own writing. Which makes the statement Damien passed along from Duke Northcott even more disturbing."

"Cate," Jack said with a tilt of his head. "You can't be serious. You aren't doing this to yourself."

"How do you explain this then? The same statement I made to you, written by my own hand."

"Impossible. This looks old. Look at the paper."

"I know that, but…"

"But what? You wrote that note to yourself a hundred years ago?"

"It's not like we don't have that capability, Jack."

Jack pursed his lips. "But you haven't done it. You don't remember it. You couldn't have done this."

"Then how do you explain it?"

"That warlock probably can pull this off with the snap of his fingers. It's a trick. To play with your mind."

"Why?" Cate asked.

"That I don't know. But I know you didn't do this." He handed the note back to her. "And I'm glad the effect of this thing seems to be waning. I'd venture to say this little note is a desperate attempt to try to revive the effect this thing has on you."

Cate rubbed her fingers along the text. "I hope you're right."

"Well, think about it. You didn't sleepwalk last night. You didn't even get up to get the necklace from the jewelry armoire. Let's hope this thing has run its course."

Cate nodded. "Fingers crossed."

Jack squeezed her shoulder. "I'll let you get dressed for breakfast. See you downstairs?"

"Yep," Cate said with a smile.

She dressed to the strains of the music box. Her conversation with Jack played over in her mind. Perhaps he had a point. Her wandering through the castle at night had become less frequent.

Still, something nagged at her. Could it be that easy? Could the enchantment have simply "run its course?"

This may be a question for Damien. After Cate let the dogs out, she sent a quick text to Damien. Still the middle of the night in Maine, she doubted she'd receive an answer for several hours.

Just as an update, no weird sleepwalking last night. Jack suggested the effect could be waning. Is that possible? Thanks!

Cate shoved the phone into her pocket and shooed the dogs into the castle. She planned to take her breakfast to the library and begin work on tracking down any leads from those she'd met in 1942.

Cate pulled her laptop open the moment she got to the library. She began a search for Ruth Harper using the little bit of information she'd listed on her notepad. She found no record of a Ruth Harper with a brother, older or younger, from Manchester between the ages of twenty-five to forty.

Cate expanded her search to find a male and female with the last name Harper who passed away between the years of 1921 and 1936. She found no deaths matching the description.

With a sigh, she moved on to the next name on this list. She searched for Victor Richard from Leeds. It quickly led to a dead end.

She began to wonder if Jack's theory, however fantastic it sounded, was true. Perhaps these people were time travelers or immortals.

Halfway through her search, her phone chimed. Damien must also be an early riser, she thought, as she spotted his name on her phone's display.

I'm glad to hear things have settled down. Umm... I'd keep an eye out still, don't let your guard down.

Cate typed back: *That sounds ominous. Do these things not wane?*

She received a quick response. *I've never seen that happen. There's usually some culmination. That being said, I'm still a newbie to this world, too. It very well could happen!*

Cate bit her lower lip as she typed her response. *You say Celine suffered from a few similar incidents. What was the culmination of those?*

Three dots appeared as Damien typed. They disappeared with no message replacing them. They appeared again. The dots toggled on and off three more times before a message finally came through.

Ummm, well her situation was sort of different, so I'm not sure we can directly compare the two. In fact, it may be best not to. Do you happen to have a doctor there who can hypnotize you and see if you can tell them anything while you're under?

Cate stared at the odd message. "Hypnosis?" she questioned aloud. "Is he serious?"

With a shake of her head, she typed back: *No, I don't have a doctor like that.*

She tapped the phone against her chin as she considered his message. She typed another message and sent it. *It seems like you're avoiding telling me what happened with Celine.*

Damien responded: *No, just hard to explain over text.*

Moments later, she got another message: *I can call if you have a minute?*

Cate blew out a long breath as she typed an affirmative and waited for her phone to ring. She answered it on the first jangle.

"Hey, Damien," she said. "Thanks for calling, and sorry if that message sounded rude or pushy."

"Hey, Cate," Damien's voice answered her. "No, it's no problem at all. You're almost as good as Celine at catching me when I'm not being completely upfront."

"I just wanted to know if there's anything I should look out for. You said Celine has experienced this. How did it end for her?"

"Well, I mean, she is completely different from you. And she's experienced things similar to this, but not exactly identical."

"What were the similarities and differences?"

A knock sounded and Cate peeked at the door. Jack waved. She motioned for him to enter. "Hey Damien, before you start, can I put you on speakerphone? Jack's here."

"Sure, Cate." Cate toggled on her speakerphone.

"Hi, Damien."

"Hey, Jack. Uh, so similarities and differences between your situation and Celine's. Well, in one instance when she had these sort of trancelike blackouts, she was poisoned, and you haven't been, so that's not similar."

"Wait," Jack said. "Are we sure she hasn't been poisoned? How can we be sure?"

"Um, well," Damien stammered, "pretty sure because you'd be dead already."

"But Celine didn't die," Jack said.

"Celine's not human. Anyway, um, the other time she didn't really have trances, but she kept having these attacks. Physical symptoms where she'd get headaches or nausea. Again, not similar to yours in symptoms."

"Well, I have had some of that, but I'm not certain it's related to my trances. I think it's related to stress. Mostly I've just been wandering around in a trance. What happened to her in that instance?"

Silence met her question.

CHAPTER 24

"*D*amien? Are you there?" Cate questioned when he didn't respond.

"Yeah," his voice squeaked. "Uh, that time she was kidnapped by the Duke."

"What?" Cate said, her eyes going wide.

"Yeah, umm, it was proximity to him causing her attacks, until he finally just nabbed her."

Cate shot Jack a glance.

"Okay, so could that be what's going on here?" Jack inquired.

"No. I mean, the Duke's not there. He's here, so it's not proximity."

"If he disappears, can you let us know? He's kidnapped Cate once already. I don't want him to do it again."

"Sure thing, no problem. It's too bad you can't get a better handle on this through hypnosis."

"Is that a typical approach you use?" Jack said.

"Yep. Millie – she's a doctor, she lives with us, she does it all the time. You try to induce the trance in a controlled setting and see what happens."

"We'll keep that in mind. I was hoping this was blowing over," Jack said.

"Yeah, that's what Cate said. Though these things tend to come in waves, so I'd stay vigilant for now. But like I said, the Duke was completely unhelpful, which isn't surprising. But if he suddenly disappears, you'll be the first to know."

"Thanks, Damien," Cate said. "By the way, time travel did alleviate some of the symptoms."

"Oh, really? That's great! Well, you can always do that until we can figure this thing out! Oh, the other thing you can try is asking Cate leading questions when she's in a trance."

"Leading questions?"

"Yeah, like why she thinks you wouldn't be there or what year it is. That kind of stuff. It's sometimes helpful in determining what you're dealing with. Not like crazy helpful, but it may give you some ideas as to what's going on."

Jack nodded. "Okay, I'll try that, though I'm hoping I don't find her in any trances."

"Fingers crossed, but if you do, you have some strategies."

"Okay, yeah. Well, thanks for the call, Damien. I'll keep you informed," Cate said.

"Sounds good. Hang in there, Cate. We'll figure this out."

They said their goodbyes and Cate ended the call.

"Great, time travel is our solution to this!" Jack exclaimed, as she shoved the phone in her pocket.

"Or hypnosis."

Jack shook his head. "So, he thought there was no chance it was just running its course?"

"He didn't seem to think so. That's what I texted him about. Your theory. I figured if anyone knew if that could happen, it would be Damien. And once again, after speaking with Damien, I feel worse."

Jack put his hands on his hips and drew his lips into a thin line. "Could we try the hypnosis thing?"

"What?" Cate inquired. "Are you serious?"

"How hard could it be?" Jack asked. "Look at the sparkly thing and relax, I'll count backward. You're hypnotized."

"I'm not certain it's quite that easy."

"Let's try it."

"Are you serious?"

"Why not? What's the worst that can happen? I fail miserably."

"Fine. I'm not getting anywhere with the research anyway," Cate said with a huff.

Jack pulled out his phone and performed an internet search on hypnosis. "Okay, I'm ready. Ah, give me your timepiece."

"This is ridiculous," Cate said.

"Just give it to me." He wiggled his fingers at her, signaling her to hand it over.

Cate removed the chain from her neck and passed it to Jack. "Okay, now you sit here in your chair. Get comfy. Just relax. And now look at the pocket watch. Focus on the pocket watch." Jack set the timepiece into motion, swinging it back and forth like a pendulum. "You're getting sleepy. You're feeling very relaxed. Close your eyes."

Cate's eyes drifted closed.

"You're feeling more and more relaxed. I'm going to count backward from ten. And when I reach one, you'll be completely relaxed." Jack began his countdown. When he reached one, he asked, "Are you relaxed, Cate?"

Cate sat motionless in her chair. After a moment, one eyelid popped open. She shook her head.

"Damn it," Jack said with a sigh. "Okay, it's not as easy as it looks."

Cate opened both eyes and chuckled, as Jack collapsed

into his chair and passed the timepiece back to her. She looped it over her head. "Don't feel bad. When I first came, I considered holding a seance."

"That does make me feel better, actually."

"Damien makes a few compelling points about the differences in what I'm experiencing. So, there's a chance you're still correct. We have no idea what's going on here."

Jack sighed. "Well, on to another subject. You haven't found anything in your search?"

"Nothing but dead ends. No Ruth Harpers matching anything she told us. No Victor Richard either. I was about to move on to Hans and ravishing Rita."

Jack chuckled at Cate's nickname for the blonde looker. "I'll check back with you later. As long as you're feeling okay."

"I feel fine. The time travel really does seem to have helped," Cate said.

"See you before lunch for a progress report."

Cate nodded and sank into the desk chair as Jack disappeared from the room. She began her search with Rita, finding no one matching her description in any records. With a deep sigh, she tried Hans's name. Much to her surprise, several records popped up. She found a birth record for Hans Schmidt in Germany along with immigration paperwork in 1920 showing their move to the United Kingdom, settling in the Kent area.

Cate tracked the man through the 1921 and 1931 censuses. The next census would not take place until 1951 due to the war. After another hour of searching, Cate managed to find him alive and married and living in post-war Kent with his wife and two children. She traced him through history until he died in 2005.

Cate noted all the information, pleased to have found something. At least they could verify one person was a normal human who lived a normal life. But where were the others?

Cate let her pen tap her lips as she considered the latest development. Why could she find Hans and no others? Was there some credence to Jack's theory that they were not humans? Was that possible? Just how many supernatural creatures were lurking around the globe, Cate pondered?

She picked up her phone to text the question to Damien, feeling slightly guilty about bombarding the poor man with questions. She stared out the window for a moment, contemplating her next move. She hated to bother him, yet he had encouraged her to use him as a resource. And he seemed eager to help. And he was far more knowledgeable than either she or Jack in these matters.

She decided to text him and pulled the phone toward her. As she toggled on her display, she caught movement in the reflective surface. Cate twisted to glance behind her. She found nothing.

She clicked off the display and stared into it, searching for the source of the movement. As she was about to give up, she caught sight of a dark figure behind her.

Her heart stopped and she spun to search behind her. With ragged breathing, she scanned the room. Nothing. Her brows knit tightly together, and she glanced into her phone's dark display again. The room appeared normal.

A chill passed through her as she settled back in her seat to text Damien. She wiggled her shoulders as she clicked on her display. She bit her lower lip and rubbed the back of her neck. Her skin turned to gooseflesh.

She shook her head and tossed the phone onto the desk. She rose from her chair and wandered from the library. She made her way upstairs via the main staircase and took the most direct route to her bedroom.

When she entered, she twisted the winding key on the

piano music box before she stalked across the room and retrieved the sapphire necklace. She clutched it in her fingers and held it to her chest as she closed her eyes.

The tinkling music filled her mind and she swayed to the music. Snippets of images flitted through her mind. A glimpse of a sapphire blue dress swinging in the air. The sapphire necklace sparkling under warm lights that glowed from above her. A hand reached for hers. Fingers stretched toward her.

Her lips curled in a smile at the memories. She opened her eyes and stared down at the sapphires in her hand. They sparkled in the light. She spun and eyed the music box. After she clasped the necklace around her neck, she collected the music box from her night table and wandered from the room.

* * *

Cate awoke in the west wing. Jack hovered over her. "Cate!" he shouted, worry creasing his face.

"Jack?" she inquired in a hoarse voice, as she lifted her head.

"Yeah," Jack said, "it's okay. You're okay."

Cate pushed up to sit.

"Easy," Jack said, his arms outstretched in the event that she collapsed.

"What happened?" she asked, glancing around. The dogs crowded around her. She stroked their fur as she attempted to recall anything that happened. Her fingers found the sapphires around her neck after a moment. The music box sat in the middle of the room. It wound down, tinkling out its last few notes.

Jack collapsed to the floor next to her and blew out a long breath.

"Jack?" Cate prompted.

"What's the last thing you remember?"

Cate pursed her lips, considering it. "Uh, I thought I saw something reflected in my phone's screen in the library. Then after that, I couldn't settle. I went upstairs, wound up the music box and picked up the necklace. That's the last thing I remember." She looked around again. "How did I get here?"

Jack pursed his lips and hesitated before he responded. "Perhaps it's best I show you."

He tapped around on his phone for a few seconds before he brought up one video. "I got an alert on my phone that you were moving." He swung the display toward her and showed her the collar cam feed. The camera bobbled around before falling to her side. She approached the music box, at the camera's level, and picked it up.

She crossed her bedroom and walked through the suite. The door swung open as she approached the hall.

"Cate?" Jack's on-screen counterpart inquired. "What are you doing?"

"I have to go," Cate said.

"Go where?" Jack inquired.

"I have to go," Cate repeated.

"Why are you wearing that necklace?"

That question did not garner a response. "Can you tell me the year?"

The question stopped Cate in her tracks. Her brow crinkled before she took another step forward. Jack grasped her arm. "Cate, what year is it?"

Cate considered it again. Her eyes searched around her as though she wasn't sure.

"I have to go," she said again.

Jack shook his head but allowed her to continue. She wound through the halls as the music box continued its tune.

Jack followed her, reaching into his back pocket for his cell phone. He toggled into his camera and hit record.

"Okay, this video may show a better view," he said. He swapped the video for the one he'd recorded himself.

On-screen, Cate continued her wandering down the hall. "It's 11 April," he narrated. "It's about eleven in the morning. I found Cate nearly unresponsive. As you can see, she has the music box and the sapphire necklace. The only thing she'll tell me is she has to go. She hasn't said where she's going. I asked her the year; the question seemed to give her pause, but she didn't answer it."

Jack followed her down a set of stairs. She aimed toward the west wing's doors. Both dogs sat at attention at the entrance. She pawed at the door and pulled it open. The dogs raced ahead of her as she continued her slow shamble.

After a few moments, they wound around to the large room they'd entered on many occasions before. The dogs already stood inside. They sat staring at the far wall as though it held a secret.

"Okay," Jack continued his narration, "we're at a room in the west wing. She's come to this room several times. I found her in one of these trances here once before."

Jack kept the camera trained on Cate as she shuffled across the large space. She stopped in the room's center.

"I'm here," she said. "Where are you?"

"Cate, who are you looking for?" Jack tried.

Cate spun in a slow circle, searching the space. After two and a half full rotations, she stopped. Her eyelids slid open and closed in slow motion. After she set the music box down, she stalked to one pillar and circled it.

She stopped on the side facing where Jack stood. She stood for several moments staring at the pillar. After a moment, she reached out and touched it. She stood frozen with her hand pressed against the pillar. Unblinking and unmoving, she appeared statuesque.

Jack paused the video. "Cate…" he began.

"What?" Cate asked.

"It gets a little weird after this."

CHAPTER 25

$\mathcal{C}$ate flicked her gaze from the screen to Jack's face. "*This* is where it gets weird? What, the weird slow blinking as I spin in circles and my best impression of a statue isn't weird enough?"

Jack licked his lips as he offered an amused scoff. He cocked his head and nodded. "It gets weirder. I'm just warning you."

Cate inhaled deeply and bit her lower lip. "Okay, warned." She turned her attention back to Jack's phone. He tapped the play button and the video continued.

The camera angle shifted as Jack circled around Cate. She remained still, her hand pressed against the pillar and a blank expression on her features.

After a moment, she lowered her arm and turned slightly toward Jack. Her expression softened and her lips curled into a smile. Her gaze lifted slightly above her. She raised her arms, her right floating in the air near her face and her left cupping an unknown object with her palm facing her belly.

Her feet moved as she held her arms in position. She

circled around the room in a waltz with some unknown partner.

Cate covered her mouth with her hand as she watched herself float around the room in time with the tinkling music. The video followed her as she made wide arcs around the large space, twirling a few times between box steps.

She continued the waltz for two minutes before she began to slow.

Jack clicked the video off. "And that's about it."

"Jack," Cate said. "How did I end up on the floor?

"Doesn't matter," he said.

"It does," she answered. "I can take it. Please, I need to see it."

Jack huffed but gave in and played the video.

On-screen, Cate continued to spin for a few more seconds, slowing her motion. Her smile was replaced by a worried expression. She stopped spinning and her brow furrowed.

"No," she said.

"What's wrong, Cate?" Jack inquired.

"No, I'm not ready." She glanced down at her clothes. "I need the dress." She puffed out a breath. "I need the dress. I need the dress. The dress. I... need... " Her words slowed before slurring. Her eyelids grew heavy, and her eyes rolled back as she began to slump to the floor.

The camera bobbled and pointed at a blurred floor as Jack raced toward Cate. He caught her before she hit the floor and eased her to the floor. "Oh, Cate," she heard him say, as the video shut off.

"That's it," Jack said. "You woke up a few moments later."

Cate sighed and shook her head. "What is happening to me?"

Jack clutched his phone and climbed to standing. He pulled Cate to her feet. "I'm not sure, but I'm going to send this video to Damien. But first, I think we should get you back to the library."

Cate nodded. They began the walk back with the dogs trotting behind them. "I don't know how I feel about sending that to Damien," Cate admitted on the walk.

"It sounds like he's seen stranger," Jack said.

"Still," Cate said, "it's sort of embarrassing."

"It's not. And it's proof of what's happening that they may be able to use to research more."

"I know," Cate said. "It's just odd."

They returned to the library and Cate collapsed into her armchair. Her fingers found the sapphire necklace. With a frown, she unclasped the necklace and tossed it onto the coffee table.

"So much for this waning," she lamented.

Jack tapped around on his phone. "One thing's certain. For once, I can't wait to time travel."

Cate offered a sharp laugh at the statement.

"You okay?" Jack inquired.

Cate nodded. "Yeah, I'm fine. No residual effects from the strange experience."

"Okay, video sent," Jack reported.

"Thanks, Jack," Cate said. She reached for his hand. He grasped hers and squeezed.

"We'll get through this, Cate. I promise."

"Thanks for your help," Cate said with a smile.

"Hey, we're a team," Jack confirmed. "Reids and MacKenzies. Centuries-worth of problem-solving is on our side."

Jack's phone chimed. He pulled his hand from Cate's and swiped at his phone. "It's Damien."

"Anything?"

Jack's thumbs tapped a response. "He asked if either of us have any idea what dress you're looking for. I said no."

"A blue dress," Cate murmured. "Sapphire." Cate stared

ahead at the necklace as snippets of the dress floating in the air flashed through her mind.

Jack wiggled his eyebrows. "How do you know? I thought you didn't remember anything."

"I catch visions of it now and again. There's more just beyond that, I know it, but my brain can't access it."

Jack stared at her. "When did you see the dress?"

"I think I've been seeing it on and off. I think in addition to the dress, there's a room I'm searching for. I just get snippets of it."

"It's not the room you've been going to?" Jack inquired.

"Not to my knowledge, but it has to be connected."

Jack sent another text to Damien, recapping the latest from Cate. He received a reply immediately. Jack reported the message to her. *"I'm showing this to Celine and Alexander and passing along the other details. Will let you know what we come up with."*

Jack settled back into his chair, a pensive expression on his face. After a while, he said, "Well, I suppose there's one good thing to come out of this."

Cate shot him an incredulous glance. "And that is?"

"You're waltzing skills are coming along nicely, Lady Cate."

"Too bad the same can't be said for your comedy skills," Cate retorted, an amused grin on her face.

"Well, I suppose we should have our lunch and then do our duty and head back to solve our other mystery." Jack rose to his feet with a groan. "I never thought murder would be the more innocuous of the two issues we're facing."

"I'm not certain it's the more innocuous, but it may be the one with the lower stakes. At least for me, personally. I'd love to know who is in the grave, but I'd also love to stop losing my mind."

"You're not losing your mind, Cate," Jack said, with a squeeze of her shoulder.

With a faint smile, she grasped his hand and squeezed. "Thanks, Jack. Enjoy your lunch."

"You want me to stay?"

She shook her head. "No, I'll be okay. And you can monitor me in spirit with my doggy cam." She offered him a wink.

"Aye, so I can. Okay, enjoy your lunch, then," Jack said. He strode from the room as Molly slipped inside.

"Perfect timing, I see," she said. "Jack's leaving to let you enjoy your lunch."

"Thanks, Molly," Cate said.

"WHOA!" Molly exclaimed. Her eyes widened as she stared down at the coffee table, her mouth forming a wide "o." "Where'd *that* come from?"

"Oh," Cate said, swiping the necklace from the table. "Ah, it's a really old piece given to a MacKenzie in the 1700s. I considered giving it away for an auction item."

Molly's jaw dropped. "Are you serious? I can't even begin to imagine what it's worth."

"Well, it's worth some sentimental value, too, and I decided I couldn't part with it."

"I don't blame you," Molly said. "I'd *never* give that up. It's absolutely stunning."

"Thanks, Molly," Cate said. "It really is a beautiful piece. And don't worry, I'm not giving it up."

Molly smiled and nodded at her. "Hey, how about a road trip tomorrow?" she questioned as she set the tray down. "I've got the next place on our list all ready."

"Oh, uh," Cate stammered.

"You should go, Cate," Jack called from the doorway where he still hovered.

"See, even Jack agrees," Molly said with a smile.

"Well," Cate hedged. "I should…"

"Oh, come on, Lady Cate," Jack heckled her. "Live a little."

Cate glanced at him, and he gave her an encouraging nod. "Okay, then. I just didn't want to hone in on your day off."

"Nonsense!" Molly exclaimed, with a wave of her hand. "I can't wait for a nice girls' trip."

"And leave the dogs with us," Jack said. "We'll watch 'em. Both of the Frasers and I will be here, so we've got it handled."

Cate smiled and nodded. "Well, looks like it's all set, then!"

"Great!" Molly said with a wide smile. She spun on her heel and pointed out the door to Jack. "Out, you. Let Lady Cate enjoy her lunch!"

Jack raised his hands in defeat. "Okay, okay. Just remember who was instrumental in convincing Lady Cate…" she heard him reply as they made their way down the hall.

Cate pulled the lunch tray onto her lap. Her eyes fell onto the sapphire necklace. What was happening to her? Why did the music box and necklace seem to affect her so strangely sometimes, but in others she remained completely normal, even soothed by the items?

The Duke's words rang in her mind. "Whatever Catherine is experiencing is a result of her own doing." What did it mean? Was it him she searched for? Was it him she called out to when in her trances? But why?

* * *

Cate stared out of the library's window at the garden beyond. Her mind struggled to find the meaning in any of the muck she waded through concerning any of her mysteries. The chiming of her phone pulled her mind from its wandering. A text from Damien showed on her preview screen.

Hey Cate, how you feeling?

Cate smiled at the simple message. He'd gotten the video of her and thought enough to check in with her after to see how she felt. She sent a return message: *I'm okay. I feel fine right now. Thank you for checking. How embarrassing to have to send that video over.*

Cate added a face-palm emoji to the end of her message.

A quick response answered her: *Not at all! Don't feel that way. Also, you're an awesome dancer!*

The comment gave her a chuckle. *Jack said the same thing. I guess there's my silver lining!*

Damien answered: *Seriously, Cate, don't feel bad. This helps a lot because we can see exactly what's happening and research it. We'll get some answers soon. In the meantime, maybe plan a time travel trip to ease your nerves!*

Cate responded: *Way ahead of you... Jack and I are doing a little traveling this afternoon!*

That's awesome! Get your mind off all this and enjoy!

Cate replied with a "will do!" before returning to her lunch. After a few bites, her phone jangled next to her. Assuming it was Damien, she grabbed it. "Wow, did he find something already?" she murmured, as she swiped to answer the call without glancing at the display.

"Hello," she said.

"Lady Cate!" Mrs. Campbell greeted her.

"Oh, hello, Mrs. Campbell," Cate said, surprised to hear the woman's voice when she expected Damien's.

"I hope I'm not catching you at a bad time," the woman said, noting the confusion in her voice.

"No, not at all. I'm just having lunch."

"Oh, well, I'm sorry to interrupt your meal, but I did want to pass along a smidge of news I found after digging into the intelligence base rumor."

"No interruption at all. What did you find?"

"Well, straight after our discussion, I delved into any records I could find. None of them had any references to an intelligence base."

"Hmm," Cate murmured, as her mind pondered why all references were squelched from the records.

"But I am not a quitter! I called a friend with access to the Ministry's records."

"No mention there either?" Cate inquired, questioning her own sanity in the matter.

"Yes and no," Mrs. Campbell said.

Cate's brow furrowed at the statement. "That sounds intriguing."

"Very. And what I found out from my friend is even more so."

"Oh?" Cate inquired.

"It seems an intelligence base did reside on the grounds of Dunhaven Castle for a short time in 1942."

Cate's heart skipped a beat. So there had been a record of it somewhere. She wondered why the references were so obscure.

Mrs. Campbell continued, "It was dissolved in September of 1942 after it was discovered to have been infiltrated by a German spy!"

"What?" Cate cried, shock apparent in her voice.

"Yes," Mrs. Campbell said. "Quite an affair apparently, and very quickly disbanded and forgotten about. No one mentions it as it was considered quite a black eye on the intelligence community, and Dunhaven, too. A spy living at Dunhaven Castle! Can you imagine!"

"I can't. I'm quite surprised," Cate said. "Did they identify the person?"

"Not to my knowledge. That's all the information my contact could dig up. But anyway, I wanted to pass it along because I thought perhaps you'd want to leave it out of your book. For the reputation of the castle."

"Yes, thank you, Mrs. Campbell, that's quite interesting and very helpful."

"Oh, you're very welcome. And rest assured, Lady Cate, I will not breathe a word of this to anyone," Mrs. Campbell said.

Cate held in a chuckle at the statement, realizing by this time next week, everyone in the Highlands should know about the botched intelligence base at Dunhaven Castle.

The two women spoke for a few more moments about their upcoming meeting before Cate ended the call. As she took the last few bites of her lunch, Cate mulled the latest information. German spies at Dunhaven Castle during the war? This could explain several things, including the lack of records on some of her targets.

Someone, or more than one someone, was a German spy. Someone wasn't who they said they were. The question was: who?

CHAPTER 26

$\mathcal{C}$ate pondered the question as she slid her tray onto the coffee table in front of her. The necklace caught her eye again. She pocketed it as Molly strolled into the room to retrieve her tray. Moments later, Jack slipped in.

"You okay?" he asked as she sat with her chin in her palm.

"Yeah," she responded. "Damien checked on me while you were out."

"Oh? Did they find anything?"

"No, but he wanted to make sure I was okay after what he saw on the video. And he assured me they'd get to the bottom of it."

"Well, so far they've got a good track record. They fixed Douglas's problem and ours, too."

Cate nodded. "I got some other information, though, that you'd be interested to hear."

"Really? Did you find something on one of our forties friends?"

"Yes, I did," Cate said. "But there's even more than that."

She rose and retrieved her notes from the desk. "I wasn't

able to find anything about Ruth, Rita, or Victor, but I did manage to track Hans from birth to death."

"Okay, Hans is human. Now, what about the other three?"

"Well, I may have an explanation for that, and it doesn't involve immortality."

"I'm all ears."

"Mrs. Campbell just called me. I asked her to look into the intelligence base."

"And?"

"She has a friend…"

"Of course she does," Jack groaned.

"Her friend looked into some records and found there was an intelligence base on the grounds in 1942 for a very short time. It was disbanded in September 1942."

"Why?"

"Because it had been infiltrated by German spies."

Jack's eyes went wide. "Spies?"

Cate nodded, a grin on her face. "Which explains why at least one of these people has no records!"

"Because they're lying about who they are," Jack said.

Cate bobbed her head up and down.

"So, are all three of them spies?"

Cate lifted a shoulder in response. "Mrs. Campbell had no information on the individual accused. It could be one of them, or all three of them. I'm not sure. But it marks progress and explains a number of things."

"Aye, it does. And it explains why Lachlan lied to Pap. They likely did not want that news out, especially during the war. It really makes the intelligence effort look bad."

Cate nodded. "Perhaps we should let Stanley know what we think then head back and see if we can crack this spy ring!"

"Okay," Jack said, pulling out his phone. "Though I have to point out that we should be extra cautious. We're not equipped to be in the middle of a spy ring, Cate. And this murder very well could be related to it."

"I agree," Cate said. "Though I'd still like to go back. As Damien pointed out, it may help with my mania."

Jack chuckled. "Don't call it that. You're not a madwoman."

"Yet," Cate said.

"We'll call it mania when I have to lock you in the tower."

"Let's hope it doesn't come to that."

"Okay, I sent Pap a text and explained the spy situation. Ready to go?"

"I am," Cate said.

"Oh, where's the necklace."

Cate patted her pocket. "Here. I swiped it before Molly spots it again."

"Good thinking. The last thing we need is her innocently trying it on and beginning to suffer from the same fascination as you have."

Cate nodded in agreement as her fingers caressed the necklace in her pocket. "I trust Molly wouldn't do that, but she may pick it up to take a closer look. I don't want to take the chance that something happens to her."

Jack nodded at her assessment.

"I'll dump it back in my jewelry armoire."

"Okay. Well, I'll go change and knock when I'm ready."

They made their way upstairs and Cate entered her suite. The piano-shaped music box, last left on the floor in the west wing, sat in its usual spot on her nightstand.

Cate sighed at it as she slipped the necklace into the bottom drawer of the jewelry armoire. The little music box was quite persistent in returning to her, magically showing up on its own like an obedient boomerang. The idea she had the ability to enchant an object to continuously return to her bedroom almost made her chuckle. How ridiculous, she thought as she styled her hair.

She pulled on a pink dress and peep-toe mules. Music began to float from her bedroom. The music box had engaged itself and began to play. Cate stepped into her bedroom as she readied her purse and stared at it. Why did it only affect her at certain times?

A knock sounded at her door. With another mystery to resolve, she hurried across the room to meet Jack. They made their way down to the secret passage and set the time-piece to September 19, 1942. Within moments, they stood hidden inside World War II-era Dunhaven Castle.

After sneaking through the passage to the crypt, they stepped into the gray day. Angry storm clouds rolled across the sky. "Looks like a storm's blowing in," Jack noted. "We'd better hurry."

Cate agreed and they hurried across the property in search of the safety of the castle. Wind whipped wildly as they pushed through the doors into the foyer.

Large raindrops pelted the roof and windows as thunder rumbled. "Just made it!" Cate said, as Jack pushed the doors closed.

"Aye, good thing, too. This looks to be a bad one."

"Indeed," a male voice said behind them. Cate spun to face the speaker, finding a man near thirty behind her. With medium brown curly hair and dark eyes set in a round face, his resemblance to Rory made Cate certain he was Oliver MacKenzie. "You must be Mrs. and Mrs. Jack MacKenzie."

"We are," Cate answered with a smile.

"Oliver MacKenzie," the man said, extending his hand to Jack.

"Jack MacKenzie, your very distant cousin, and my wife, Cate. Please, call us Cate and Jack."

"Lovely to meet you. My father has nothing but good things to say about you."

"We met you once before," Cate said, "when you were about ten."

"I have very little recollection of it, I'm afraid."

"I wouldn't imagine you would have much memory of us," Cate said, as they strode to the sitting room. "I believe we only spoke for a few moments."

"Ah, memory of you specifically, no, but knowledge of you, yes. My father still discusses how you saved the day with the missing jewelry."

Cate smiled. "I was so pleased we could help."

"Well," Oliver said, "can I offer you anything before I depart? I'm off on some business. Too bad the weather had to turn nasty. It will make the driving treacherous."

"No," Jack said. "We're perfectly fine, thank you. We may spend some time in the library to pass the hours before dinner this evening. Will you attend?"

"No," Oliver said with a shake of his head. "I shan't return until day after tomorrow. But I am so pleased to have caught you before I left."

"We're glad to have had the chance to say hello again, too," Cate assured him.

The man said his goodbyes and left them in the sitting room.

"Okay, what do you really want to do?" Jack asked.

Cate shrugged. "I'd like to gather some information on our three suspects, but short of visiting the intelligence tent, I'm not sure where we'd find them."

Jack glanced out the window as rain poured from the skies and winced.

"I, too, would prefer to wait until the rain stops."

"Library it is, I suppose," Jack said.

Cate considered it, staring at the pattern on the area rug

below her feet as she contemplated it. After a moment, she raised her eyes to Jack's. "Wait!" she exclaimed.

"What?"

"I have an idea. It doesn't help us with solving the murder, but it may help with our other problem."

Jack furrowed his brow. "You mean your mania, as you call it?"

"Yes! I'm always drawn to a room in the west wing, and whenever I go there in our time, I have strange attacks, visions, trances…"

"Waltzing," Jack added.

"Right. And as a result, we've avoided the space as much as possible. But I may not be affected in this time period. Perhaps we should try to explore it here rather than in the present."

Jack pursed his lips as he rubbed the back of his neck while considering the prospect.

"Okay," he agreed. "We can try. But at the first sign of you going haywire, we leave. The last thing we need is a trance during a time travel trip."

"Deal," Cate said.

She looped her arm through Jack's, and they wandered through the castle halls and to the doors leading to the west wing.

"I wonder if it's locked," Jack said, as they approached the large, thick wooden doors.

"I don't suppose you brought your keys in case it is?" Cate questioned.

Jack reached in his pocket and flashed a set of keys. "Ask and you shall receive, Lady Cate."

"Oh! Prepared! Nice!"

"Did you expect anything less?"

Cate shrugged.

"Your lack of faith in me is a little disturbing, Lady Cate,"

Jack said, as he grasped the door handle and tugged. To their surprise, the door opened.

"Hmm, not locked in this era," Cate noted.

"I'm surprised. I didn't think the west wing was used much after Ethan's time."

"Still, maybe they didn't lock it until a later period," Cate said, stepping into the wide hall.

Jack side-eyed her. "Any weirdness?"

"Nope," Cate said. "I feel pretty good when I time travel. No haziness, no odd thoughts. But here's something interesting. When I went to my room to change, the music box was back, sitting on the night table as usual."

"After we left it in the west wing," Jack noted.

"Right. It appeared back in my bedroom. And it started to play on its own. But I had no issues with it. Nothing. In fact, it seems to be soothing to me. It helps me sleep, it eases my headaches, it oddly seems like I do love it. Like my note said."

"I'm not convinced that note is from you, Cate."

"It was in my handwriting."

"I'm certain a man who has the ability to throw lightning bolts from his hands can fake someone's handwriting."

"Good point," Cate said, as they turned the corner into another hall.

Jack ceased walking, cocking his head to the side as he scrunched his brows together. He pressed a finger to his lips. Cate inched closer to him, and her eyebrows shot up.

"Do you hear that?" Jack whispered.

Cate nodded. "Voices," she breathed.

They listened for another moment before Cate pointed a finger toward the music hall. Jack agreed with a nod, and they crept toward the double doors.

Cate motioned for Jack to inch the door open, but he refused with an emphatic shake of his head. Garbled voices floated on the air as they pressed against the doors.

Cate mimed for them to round the corner and listen at the second set of doors. Jack nodded and they crept down the hall and approached the other double doors.

The heated voices became clearer as they pressed their ears to the door.

"NO!" a male voice shouted. "This is wrong!"

A female voice shot back, "It isn't."

"You are mistaken," the man answered.

"Am I? Prove it."

After a moment, the man answered, "I can't."

"Just as I thought."

"No, it isn't at all what you thought. These people have become my friends. Though there isn't much to be done about it now."

"There is too much at stake for this second-guessing," the woman said.

Cate's eyebrows shot skyward, and she glanced to Jack. She mouthed the word, "spies," to him.

He nodded.

"I won't do it. I can't!"

"You must."

Another pause before the man said, "All right."

"Then we proceed as planned."

Footsteps punctuated the last statement and Cate and Jack scurried to the corner to peek around it. The doors burst open as the woman exited first. Cate's jaw unhinged as she saw Ruth stalk from the room. Several moments later, Hans strode out of the doors and down the hall.

Cate glanced at Jack. Had they just witnessed two German spies at Dunhaven Castle?

CHAPTER 27

"Let's head to our suite," Jack suggested as the supposed spies left the west wing behind.

Cate nodded, abandoning her plan to study the room to which she was drawn. They waited a few moments before they wound their way from the west wing into the main castle and up to their bedroom.

"Wow!" Cate exclaimed as Jack closed the doors behind them.

"My sentiments exactly, did we just witness a meeting of spies?"

"That's what I'm thinking!" Cate played the conversation over in her mind.

"So, what happened?" Jack inquired as he stalked around the room, rubbing his chin.

"Ruth and Hans are in on it together," Cate surmised. "He has admitted connections to Germany. He was born there. Perhaps he has family there, still."

"But Hans seems to be having second thoughts."

Cate nodded. "He talked about his time in London with

Victor briefly at dinner. Perhaps the time he spent with them made him rethink his allegiances."

"But Ruth is insistent on forcing his hand."

"It would explain why the code is indecipherable in this time. It's actively being destroyed by Ruth and Hans," Cate said.

"It also explains her position with Amelia."

Cate bit her lower lip. Jack added, "I'm certain Amelia had no knowledge of this." Cate nodded at his statement. "Ruth likely saw her position as useful to her cause."

"And perhaps even Lucas's ties to the Ministry of Defense," Cate said.

"Right."

Cate furrowed her brow again. "What I find odd is Ruth tying herself to Amelia, though. Surely she has less freedom because of it."

"But a great cover. And perhaps she is adept at manipulating Amelia without Amelia realizing."

Cate nodded. "Yes. Maybe I can get some information from Amelia at dinner. Or you if you sit by her. Ask where she's traveled and see if you can ferret out who suggested the places or how their trips came about."

"On it," Jack said with a salute.

"Hopefully you'll get a seat near Amelia. And ravishing Rita can keep her hands to herself."

"You know," Jack said, "when you had a male interest, I told you to use your female charms to gain information."

Cate offered an unimpressed glance. "Damien was not a male interest nor was he as licentious as Rita."

"Oh, right," Jack said. "He was a male. And he was interested. Plus, he still texts you! Talk about rakish!"

"Damien is far from rakish. He is a wonderful friend."

"I'm only teasing you, Lady Cate. Though I am starting to

think you may be a wee bit jealous. And I must say, it really is quite a boost to my ego."

Cate offered him a half-smile. "I'm so glad to be of service. Just be careful around her, I don't think she's as innocent as Damien."

"Don't worry, Lady Cate. I'd never ruin our marriage over the likes of her." Jack winked at her.

"I'd better change for dinner," Cate said, checking the time.

After they both changed clothes, Cate and Jack threaded through the halls and down to the sitting room. Rory, Ruth, and Amelia waited there for the others.

After greetings around the room, Cate and Jack sank onto the loveseat across from Ruth and Amelia.

"What frightful weather," Rory commented, as he poured drinks for Cate and Jack.

"Oh, yes, just terrible," Amelia commented. "What a shame Oliver had to travel in it."

"Mmm, yes," Rory agreed.

Cate used the comment as an in to discuss more with Amelia. "And will you be traveling again soon?" she inquired.

"Perhaps," Amelia said. "I'm waiting on word now from Lucas. If he's able to make a trip up, we'll stay. Otherwise, we may be off again!"

"And have you done much traveling before coming to Dunhaven?"

"Oh, yes," Amelia said. "We've done a great deal."

"You must be worn out!" Cate said.

"Not really, I find it invigorating. It's so easy to be down given all the events surrounding the war. It takes my mind off things."

"How do you decide where to go?" Jack inquired, picking up on Cate's line of questioning.

"Oh, wherever the wind takes us," Amelia said with a chuckle as Rita and Victor entered the room.

The conversation ended with the new arrivals. Rory suggested they head into the dining room.

"Oh, shouldn't we wait for Hans?" Cate inquired, hoping to have the opportunity to converse with him.

"He sent word he isn't feeling well and won't attend," Rory answered.

Cate knit her eyebrows at the development. She glanced at Jack then flitted her gaze to Ruth. The woman offered no reaction to the announcement.

They shuffled into the dining room and took their seats. Cate noted the way Rita slid into a seat next to Jack, nearly tripping Ruth to claim the seat. Ruth stepped two seats over, sitting on Jack's other side. At least one thing went right, Cate thought. She hoped Jack could learn something from the woman.

With the unbalanced party, Cate found herself seated between Victor and Amelia. She'd use the conversation to try to pry any information she could from Amelia.

Amelia began her conversation with Cate, including Rory in the mix. The addition of Rory slightly dampened any chance Cate had to inquire about Amelia's travel plans.

"What a shame the weather is so dreary," Rory said. "I hope it hasn't ruined anyone's plans."

"Not at all," Cate assured him. "Amelia, what about you?"

"No, I spent the day reading."

"Does Ruth enjoy days such as this or does she prefer to be on the move?"

"Oh, I'm certain she didn't mind. I believe she spent some time exploring the castle."

"You should have told me," Rory said, "I would have given her a tour."

"I'm quite sure she did not mind wandering about on her own."

Amelia glanced down the table, noticing Victor lacked a conversation partner. "Oh, dear, it seems Mr. Richard has been left alone!" Amelia noted to Cate.

Cate switched her direction to speak to Victor. She glanced across the table, noting Rita playing up to Jack, inserting herself into Jack's conversation with Ruth.

"Oh!" Cate exclaimed, loud enough to be heard across the table. "Had I realized Rita turned the wrong way, I would have included you in our conversation."

Rita gave Cate a cold glance before offering her an equally frigid smile and retorted, "Victor and I spend all day together. There's really nothing else to talk about."

"My mistake," Cate said, "I thought you'd be far too busy with code-breaking to talk."

"Perfectly fine, Mrs. MacKenzie," Victor said, ending the polite bickering between the two women. "After all, I'm certain you'd like to spend some time conversing with your family."

Cate smiled at him. "Do you miss yours very much being stationed here?" she inquired of him.

"Yes, though we must all make sacrifices in the face of adversity such as what we suffer."

Cate smiled and nodded at him. Throughout her degree work, she'd only read about the adversity faced during this time. It was another matter entirely to stare at it straight in the face. How much more difficult that adversity would be when someone sabotaged your efforts for the opposite side, Cate reflected.

Cate gazed at the empty chair, now dragged away from the table and the place setting removed by Smithers. Had Hans avoided the meal because of his confrontation with Ruth? Would that confrontation lead to murder?

If so, it was a murder never avenged, as Hans had lived his entire life normally, as evidenced by the records. Cate's eyes slid sideways to the man on her right. Why had she not found him in the records? Or Rita? Were their names changed to protect their identities after the base was shut down?

Dinner continued with little other discussion that would shed any light on the circumstances surrounding the upcoming murder. After a brief nightcap, Cate and Jack returned to their own time via the universal time portal in the secret passage.

"See you in the library," Jack said, as they parted ways to change.

"You bet!" Cate answered, darting into her suite.

The moment Cate set foot into her bedroom, the music box across the room began to tinkle. Cate shot the object a glance. "You're persistent, I'll give you that. But I've been time traveling, so your effects are diminished!" she shouted triumphantly, as she pulled off her dress and slipped back into her normal clothes.

After a moment redoing her hair in the bathroom, she reentered the bedroom with her eyebrows raised at the little device. "No time for a trance now; we're on to something!" she called, darting across the room and making her way down to the library.

The dogs stood on each side of Jack's armchair as he petted them both. "Well, that was quite a trip!" Cate exclaimed.

"Aye. And it's very nice to see you so chipper because of it."

"I can't believe Ruth is a spy. Poor Amelia. I'll bet she told the paper Ruth left for a better position just to keep everything hush-hush and save face."

"Aye, same reason they nixed any mention of the intelligence base overall."

"Do you think we can't find any information on Victor and Rita because their names were changed to protect them after Ruth's murder?"

Jack pursed his lips as he considered it. "Could be. Though was anyone aware of Ruth's murder?"

"Maybe not, though her disappearance could have led to the outing of the spy ring. Did you learn anything at dinner?"

"Not much. Ruth is extremely good at hiding what's going on."

"I'd imagine she would be. Also, I'm sure your conversation was squelched by Rita." Cate pursed her lips in a half frown.

Jack rolled his eyes. "You may have a point about our cheeky friend. She seems to have a real affinity for pushing herself in."

Cate considered it. While annoyed, she still found the situation odd. The woman went overboard to insert herself into a conversation with a married man. She exhibited extremely poor behavior. It seemed unusual. Perhaps subtly wasn't her strong suit.

"I wonder if there's another reason for her overly keen interest."

"Outside of my roguish good looks, wit, and charm? You may be reaching, Lady Cate."

"Well, she seems rather obvious. Even for a flirt."

Jack shrugged. "What would it be?"

"Do you think she's on to Ruth?"

"Oh, I wonder," Jack said as he considered it. "Perhaps she's the one who outs the discovery."

"I wonder what causes Hans to kill Ruth."

"Assuming that's what happens."

"Yes," Cate agreed, "assuming. He seemed exceptionally

upset with her today. Does he just snap? He seemed too gentle."

"I suppose that's why he's a good spy. He seems banal, innocent, safe. People confide in him, and he uses it to his advantage."

Cate shook her head. "I spent most of my dinner wondering how people could do that. I'm not sure I have it in me."

"I suppose they believe they're doing it for the right cause and their country."

Cate remained silent for a moment before Jack spoke again. "Cate, are you sure you want to pursue this?"

"We need to know what happened. Ruth didn't deserve to be killed and buried with no one knowing."

"She likely has no family looking for her and the man we suspected murdered her is dead, too. And she was a spy."

"I know. But she still didn't deserve to die. Plus the time travel is a great diversion from our other problem."

"Good point. Okay, well, I suppose we're off the hook tomorrow with your girls' day out. We can head back on Monday."

"That sounds good."

"You know, speaking of our other problem, I think your day out will do you good. That's why I encouraged you to go."

"I figured," Cate said. "I caught on when you insisted. At first, I didn't think it was a good idea, but maybe getting away from the castle will help."

"It can't hurt," Jack said. "I assume you won't drift into any trances and wander around someone else's castle."

"Let's hope not. That would be even more embarrassing than my waltz."

"Well, either way, I think you should enjoy your day off."

"I'll try," Cate said with a nod.

Jack climbed from his chair with a groan, leaving her alone for the remaining afternoon and evening hours. After a quick check-in before bed, Cate, Riley and Bailey headed to her suite. The now-familiar music already played in greeting. The dogs settled in as Cate readied herself for the night.

With a pause at the jewelry armoire, Cate pulled the necklace from the drawer and continued across the room to climb into bed, still clutching the ostentatious item. As the little music box filled the air with its music, Cate drifted off to sleep, exhausted from the extra hours added to her day.

Cate awoke the following morning to the tinkling sounds of the music box. The little musical item had played throughout the night, though Cate had slept soundly. Her hand contained an indentation in the shape of the large central sapphire of the necklace.

Cate sat up, wiggling her fingers to loosen them. She reflected on her peaceful night as she eyed the small piano. There seemed to be no rhyme or reason to when the item affected her.

Though whatever triggered her odd affliction seemed to be worsening. She'd risen from retrieving the necklace and returning to bed, to roaming the halls, to full-blown delusions.

As Cate climbed from bed and padded to the bathroom, she tried to recall any details from her trances. Cate glanced into the mirror as she pulled her clothes on. Visions of the blue dress had pressed into her mind yesterday. Where had they come from?

And a room. She vaguely recalled a room. What room? She forced herself to recall details from the episodes. After a moment, another thought danced across her mind. She hurried to her bedroom and retrieved the sapphire necklace. She clasped it around her neck and returned to the mirror, staring at it.

"Think, Cate, think," she willed herself. She crinkled her brow as she focused on the necklace, her fingertips finding the central blue stone. She blinked slowly as her mind regressed to another memory. She swept her hair up behind her, holding it in place with one hand. Her head tilted as her mind's eye found what she sought.

A room. With mirrored walls and pillars between them. She wore a satin sapphire blue ball gown. Warm lights shaped as stars hung overhead. Music played and the room seemed to spin.

A cold, wet nose snapped Cate back into reality. Riley stood with his paws planted on her thigh, nudging her free hand.

Cate fought to keep the image in her mind as her focus returned to the present.

"Just a second, buddy," Cate said, as she raced to her bedside. She dug into the drawer of her nightstand and retrieved her journal and a pen. Shuffling through to the first empty page, Cate wrote the details she remembered in the journal that had been used to write about her nightmares of Duke Northcott.

A knock sounded at her door as she scribbled the last piece of information across the page. "Coming!" she shouted, a grin on her face as she perused her efforts to remember something. She hurried to the door in her sitting room and flung it open. "Come in!" she said to a waiting Jack. The dogs scampered over to offer Jack a hearty hello.

"Well, what a greeting! Lady Cate is chipper this morning. I suppose this is directly related to the excellent night's sleep you got last night?"

"I did have an excellent night's sleep, but it's more than that."

Jack's gaze fell to the sapphire necklace around her neck.

"Oh," Cate said, realizing she still wore it. She unclasped it and placed it on the side table near her chaise. "Not that. But related to that. I remembered something."

"Remembered something?"

"Yes, the vision or memory of the room I'm searching for. Remember yesterday I couldn't recall any details of it? But I did remember the dress was blue. Well, this morning, I managed to remember what the room looks like. I wrote it down in my journal."

She handed it to Jack, and he perused the description, his lips curling into a confused expression. "Mirrored walls with stars for lights?" he questioned.

"Yes."

"I don't know of any room like that in the castle," he answered.

"Neither do I, but it must be what I'm searching for. It was very clear this morning."

"Are you certain it wasn't a figment of your imagination? Something your mind created to fill in the gap?"

Cate shook her head. "I don't think so. I'm not that creative," she said with a coy grin. "I'll admit the vision of it I had was fleeting, but still I got enough to get a description."

"I'm not sure how it helps," Jack said.

"Me either," Cate admitted. "But I feel like it's a break-through all the same. At least I'm remembering something. What it means, I don't know."

"That's a curious statement," Jack said after a moment.

"What is?"

"You're remembering something," Jack said. "But, to your knowledge, you've never had this dress or been to this room."

Cate pondered it for a moment, her eyebrows shooting upward at his assessment. "You're right. I've never been in this room. Just as I have no knowledge of ever writing that note to myself or of the music box, yet I seem to think I've had it in the past. In my trances, I act like I have seen it before."

"Aye, and other details are distorted. Like you act like you're surprised to see me."

"But the vision I had this morning felt like a memory. It's as though I was remembering something that happened in my past. Like my graduation or a major life event."

Jack puckered his lips as he processed the information. "Are these false memories somehow planted in your mind?"

Cate's features fell into a frown. "From the time I spent with Duke Northcott."

"Did he do anything to you then?"

"No," Cate answered. "Well, not to my knowledge. But I was gone for sixty hours. And several times, I fell asleep after drinking tea."

Jack breathed out a deep sigh. "I wonder if he drugged it."

"And then used my unconscious state to slip false memories into my mind?"

Jack shrugged. "Could be."

Cate stalked around the room as she pondered it. "I suppose your theory could be correct. Though again, why?"

"That I cannot answer."

They spent a few moments in silence before Cate shrugged. "Well, I don't suppose we'll get any further with this. But at least we've made some progress. Very little, but some."

"More than we've made before," Jack agreed. "And now, we'd better get the pups outside and you to your breakfast. You've got a big day today!"

"Right. Maybe I should cancel. Spend more time…"

"Now, Lady Cate, I won't hear of it. This will be a nice break for you."

"Oh, well since you insist, then okay!" Cate said with an amused smile.

"I do. And you should listen!"

Cate saluted. "Aye, aye, sir!" she said, before calling the dogs and ushering them through the halls and outside.

After her breakfast, she piled into the car with Molly and waved goodbye to the dogs and Jack as Molly pulled down the drive. "Where are we headed today?" Cate asked.

"Ellon Castle Gardens," Molly informed her. "It looked pretty in the guidebook. I hope it's nice."

"I'm sure it will be."

"Though no match for Mr. Fraser's gardens, surely."

"He'll be happy to hear you say that," Cate said.

"You know, I'm not going to other places because I don't love Dunhaven," Molly mentioned.

"I know that, Molly," Cate answered. "You just love to explore. And the country is certainly beautiful enough to do that."

"I just wanted to make sure you know that."

Cate squeezed Molly's arm. "I know that. You love Dunhaven. Bodies in the garden and all."

"It's such a shame they never found anything else about that poor person."

Cate nodded. "Yeah, it is."

They continued along their journey, arriving in the late morning at the castle gardens. After their stroll through, Molly suggested they grab lunch. They settled on their choices and gave their order to the waitress. As she left, Molly tapped around on her phone.

"Looking for another attraction?"

"No," Molly said, as she slid the phone away. "Just checking the time."

They made conversation about Molly's upcoming plans, Cate's first-year anniversary party, and more as they ate. Molly checked her phone several times during the meal. Cate found it odd. Molly usually never fiddled with her phone, preferring the human contact, and not needing the crutch of technology to achieve it.

"How about dessert?" Molly asked, as they finished up their meals.

"Sure," Cate said, assuming Molly had her eye on something scrumptious.

Molly checked her phone several more times as they ate the dessert. She pushed the pie slice around on her plate, dragging out the experience rather than digging in.

"Coffee?" she asked afterward.

"No, thanks. I'm about to burst. But if you'd like some, I'm happy to wait. I don't have any plans today!"

Molly gave her a nervous chuckle. "Uh, no, it's fine."

As the waitress returned to their table, Molly reversed her decision, requesting coffee. She meandered through the cup, sipping at it as if she hoped to make it last as long as possible. As she finished the last of it, the waitress returned with their check.

Cate paid the bill, despite Molly's protests, and they left the restaurant. After a quick consultation of her phone, Molly slid behind the wheel. "Mind if we take a bit of a drive? I'd like to see more of the country out this way. Unless you're in a hurry to get back."

"No, no hurry here."

They spent the early part of the afternoon driving around the eastern coast near Aberdeen. Molly pulled over several times to snap pictures. It didn't escape Cate that she also checked her phone outside of her camera app, too.

After an hour and a half of seemingly aimless driving, Molly said, "Well, I guess we should head back."

"Okay, sounds good to me."

Cate settled into the passenger's seat and let Molly program in Dunhaven Castle as their next destination. They pulled into the driveway in the late afternoon.

Cate made her way to the library, finding Jack, Mr. and Mrs. Fraser, and both dogs waiting there.

"Hi," she said as she entered. "Helping Jack with that puzzle?"

"What puzzle?" Mrs. Fraser inquired as Molly appeared at the door. She glanced at Jack and raised her eyebrows. Jack gave her a slight nod.

"Lady Cate," Molly began, laying a hand on her shoulder.

"Yes?" Cate asked. A sinking feeling welled in the pit of her stomach. Why did this seem strangely like an intervention? Perhaps Jack was more concerned about her behavior of late than he let on. Did he tell the others?

CHAPTER 28

She glanced around at the others who had risen to stand. A nervous smile crossed her face and she swallowed hard. "Your one-year anniversary as Countess of Dunhavenshire is coming up. And we know it's not until June, but…" Molly continued.

"We couldn't wait any longer," Mrs. Fraser jumped in. An excited grin filled her face. "And we didn't think you should have to wait all the way until June."

"Wait for what?" Cate asked.

"We got you a gift," Jack said.

"A gift? You didn't have to do that." Cate's shoulders slumped in relief.

"We did," Mrs. Fraser insisted with a curt nod.

"That's the weird vibe you've been getting from us the past few months," Molly said.

Cate lifted her chin and pressed her lips together as understanding dawned on her. Memories of odd, interrupted conversations floated into her mind.

"Aye, we were picking out the perfect one, discussing it

and deciding on everything and so on," Mrs. Fraser said. "Then young Jack had to order it."

"It arrived a few days ago and we hid it. Then we had to get it ready. Hence the long drive around the Scottish countryside today," Molly said with a laugh.

"That's why you kept checking your phone."

"Yes," Molly answered. "A certain two someone's took longer than I bargained for."

"It had to be perfect," Mr. Fraser said.

"And I had to drive practically back to the States to give you time to get it there," Molly teased with a tongue-in-cheek grin.

"Anyway," Mrs. Fraser said. "It's ready. But you'll have to go outside to see it."

"Okay," Cate agreed.

The group gathered in front of the castle.

"Close your eyes," Jack instructed.

"Really?" Cate inquired.

"Yes!" Molly insisted.

"All right," Cate said, with a roll of her eyes. She squeezed her eyes closed.

"It's a bit of a walk," Jack said as he scooped her up.

"Whoa!" Cate exclaimed.

"And no opening your eyes."

"I voted for a blindfold," Mrs. Fraser said.

"I'm keeping them closed!" Cate exclaimed, as she hung onto Jack.

They walked for a bit before Jack carefully set her on the ground. Molly's hands covered her eyes as her feet touched the ground. "I'm not peeking!" she insisted.

"Just in case," Molly said. "Ready?"

"I've been ready since you made me close my eyes at the front of the castle," Cate said with a chuckle.

Molly removed her hands and Cate blinked her eyes open. They stood at the loch. Under the large tree nearby sat a beige two-seater bench.

Cate's jaw dropped open and her eyes lit up at the sight. "You got me a bench to sit on!"

"Aye, no more sitting on the ground," Jack said with a grin.

"And," Mrs. Fraser added, giving it a push, "it rocks."

A smile beamed from Cate's face. "It does!" She ran her hand along it.

"And it's made from Polywood, making it impervious to weather," Mr. Fraser chimed in.

"Give it a try, Lady Cate!" Molly exclaimed.

Cate rounded it, noting the final touch. "It has my name on it!" she said as tears pricked her eyes. Engraved in one of the Plywood planks was the message: *Lady Cate's thinking spot.*

She slid into the seat and set the glider in motion.

"Thank you, everyone," she said with a smile. "Though you didn't have to do this. And you didn't have to keep it a secret. Poor Molly had to drink cold coffee just to drag out our day."

Molly chuckled. "It was terrible. But all in the name of the secret!"

"We did so have to keep it secret," Mrs. Fraser said. "Though I was the one who suggested we give it to you early. Not only because you could use it, but because I doubted some of us could keep quiet long enough." She eyed Molly and Jack.

Molly shrugged. "I can't help it!"

"Well," Cate answered, as she set both dogs on the bench next to her, "I certainly can use it, so thank you. And I love it!"

She rose from the bench and gave each of them a warm hug and another thank you.

"Well, I suppose we should go and allow Lady Cate to enjoy her new gift in peace," Mrs. Fraser suggested.

"No," Cate said. "As excited as I am to sit and look over the loch, I'm coming back with you."

"You still have some time before the sun sets," Molly said.

"I know. And I'm very excited to use my gift. But I'd rather spend the time with the people who got it for me. Who's up for a little ice cream to celebrate?"

Cate spent the rest of her day enjoying time with her friends. After insisting on a pizza order for dinner and following up with ice cream, they spent the time talking, laughing, and even making some progress on Mr. Smythe's puzzle of Dunhaven Castle.

The smile hadn't faded from Cate's face even as she climbed into bed. The little music box added to her jovial mood, providing lovely background music as she slid between the sheets.

She turned onto her side to stare at the outline of the piano, limned in the moonlight streaming from the window. With the sapphire necklace clutched in her hand, she closed her eyes and drifted off to sleep.

* * *

Cate startled awake. She gulped in air as she glanced around the room, trying to orient herself. She was curled in her armchair in the library, a blanket draped across her. A fire glowed in the fireplace. Jack snored softly in the armchair next to her.

Cate struggled to recall how she came to be here. As she fidgeted in her seat, Jack shifted, his eyes opening. He blinked a few times, then straightened in his seat. "Cate?" he said, rubbing his eyes, sleep still lacing his voice.

"What happened?" Cate inquired. Her hand found the sapphire necklace clasped around her neck.

"You were in another trance," he answered, as he rubbed his eyes and stretched.

"What did I do this time?"

Jack grabbed his phone and pulled up his camera app. "The app notified me of your movements. I found you in the hall." He tapped the play button.

Cate, clad in her robe and slippers, wandered down the hall. The necklace was already clasped around her neck, its sparkling sapphires and diamonds peeking from under her robe's collar. She held the music box in her hands. "At least I had the good sense to put on my robe and slippers," Cate said with a sigh.

On-screen, Jack asked Cate where she was going. "I have to find it," she murmured.

"What are you looking for, Cate?"

Cate rounded a corner. "Cate? What are you searching for? I'd like to help."

"I have to find the dress," on-screen Cate answered.

"That dress again," Cate said, as she watched herself on the video.

"Keep watching," Jack said.

Cate wandered around the castle, stopping at a few doors before she shook her head and continued. After a few stops, she ducked inside a room and rustled through a trunk.

"Where did I put it?" she lamented.

"Do you remember where you saw it last?"

Cate stood still for a moment, unresponsive. "Cate? Do you know what year it is? Can you hear me?"

Cate approached a mirror and stared into it. Jack crossed

behind her. Cate caught sight of him, spinning to face him. "Jack! You're here!"

"Yes. I'm here, Cate. Do you know where here is?"

"Of course, I do." The smile faded from her face. "I have to find my dress."

"I'd like to help you."

Cate held up a finger. "I have an idea!"

The video bobbled as Cate spun on her heel and hurried from the room. Jack raced behind her. She threaded through the halls, arriving at the stairs leading to one of the turrets. Cate stared up the stairs before she hurried up them.

Jack followed her. Cate flung the door at the top open and scanned the room. The large wardrobe stood against the opposite wall, as it had for centuries. Trunks and boxes littered the rest of the space.

Cate scanned the room before she hurried to the wardrobe. She pulled it open. Inside, a neatly folded sapphire blue dress sat. Setting the music box down in the wardrobe, Cate grasped it and pulled it from the wardrobe. A smile lit her face.

"I found it!" she said as she spun to face Jack. She held up the dress in front of her with a wide grin. Red roses embroidered with chenille thread trimmed the silk sapphire dress. With short sleeves and a silk ribbon under the bust, the skirt flowed down into a flowy, trumpet bottom.

"It's lovely, isn't it?" Cate asked.

"It's very pretty, Lady Cate," Jack answered.

"I looked pretty in it when I wore it last," Cate said.

"When did you wear it last?" Jack inquired.

"To the ball," she answered.

"What ball, Cate? When?"

Cate's brow furrowed as she considered the question. "It was..." The crinkle in her brow deepened. Her breathing turned ragged, and a pained expression crossed her face. She shook her head before she clutched at it. "I can't..." she croaked.

She slid to the floor, still clutching the gown. The video cut off.

"You passed out and I carried you here. I didn't know what state you'd wake up in, so I didn't want to leave you alone."

Cate sighed. "Thank you. I'm so sorry to have ruined your night's sleep."

"It's no bother, Cate," Jack said.

"So, I found the dress." She pulled the phone from Jack's hand and rewound the video. She paused it as she held the dress against her and stared at the image frozen on the screen.

"Appears so. Have you ever seen it before? I haven't, you didn't wear it to any of the balls you've hosted."

"No," Cate answered as she studied it. "It looks like its early 1800s, maybe a decade or so after the turn of the century."

"Could it be before the turn of the century? Maybe the 1790s?"

"It's hard to say without a better look, but I'd say this looks later than that. The puffed sleeves and length suggest that. Though I can't be sure. Even so, I never wore this dress when we traveled to 1792."

"No, you didn't. The color is similar to... never mind." Jack waved his comment away.

"It's okay, you can say it. It's similar to the dress Duke Northcott gave me."

Jack nodded. "Aye."

"A fact that hasn't escaped me," Cate said. "Is it still in the tower?"

"Aye," Jack said. "Should I move it?"

"No," Cate said. "No, I don't want to spend more nights roaming the castle in search of it."

"But perhaps giving it to you will make this worse."

"And perhaps it will bring us more information."

"Or maybe a trance you don't come out of."

"Either way, hiding it or moving it doesn't seem to work. If it's anything like the other items involved, it'll just show up in my bedroom."

"Good point. We're fighting a losing battle."

"Did you send the video to Damien?" Cate inquired, changing the subject.

Jack shook his head. "No, I didn't think it shed any additional light, but I can if you'd like."

"It may not matter." Cate glanced to the clock on the mantle. It read 5:47 a.m. "It's the middle of the night there now. We can wait."

Jack nodded.

"I suppose it's time to get up for our day, though," Cate said after a moment.

With a yawn and another stretch, Jack agreed with a nod.

"You feel okay to go back to your bedroom?"

"Yep. Other than a mild haze, I'm fine. It's so odd."

"Okay, see you at breakfast, then."

Cate climbed the stairs to her bedroom. Both dogs still lounged in bed, barely moving when she crept into the room. The music box sat on her nightstand again. "Made your way home, huh?"

Riley lifted his head and gave her a sleepy glance before he collapsed back onto the bed. Cate removed the necklace and stowed it in the jewelry armoire. It appeared the dress hadn't wandered to her bed mysteriously. She supposed she should retrieve it and put it somewhere closer to avoid roaming around the castle in a trance.

She'd do it later in the morning, she decided. First, she

planned to have breakfast with her staff, followed by a long walk and a relaxing rock on her new gliding bench by the loch.

After her leisurely breakfast and stroll, Cate climbed the tower stairs. The door at the top still stood open from her escapade last night. With some trepidation, she climbed the final few stairs and glanced into the tower room.

Across the room, a silk dress lay sprawled on the floor. Cate drew in a deep breath as she stared at it, before crossing to pick it up. The fabric, soft and silky, was of a high quality. The dress must have been expensive in its time. Cate studied it again, pulling her cell phone from her pocket and comparing the features of the dress to photos of dresses from various eras. She narrowed it down to the 1810s, as she suspected.

She shoved her phone back into her pocket and swept the dress into her arms, carrying it down to her suite. She pushed into her sitting room and wandered to the bedroom. Standing in front of the full-length mirror, she held the dress in front of her.

The blue brought out the blue in her eyes. The neckline seemed to be tailored to perfectly outline the sapphire necklace. Cate wandered to the jewelry armoire and pulled the necklace from the drawer. Returning to the mirror, she held it up with the dress. It matched perfectly in shape and color.

She stared into the mirror. The image of the room entered her mind again. The world around her began to transform. A musky scent filled her nostrils. Candlelight lit her face. She wore the dress and the necklace. Her hair was pulled up with curled tendrils framing her face. A blue silk ribbon and strand of pearls decorated the elaborate curls arranged on her crown.

A garbled voice spoke to her. "Ready, my dear?" it said.

Cate turned to the side and stretched out her arm, reaching for whoever spoke to her.

"Cate," Jack said.

Cate's eyebrows squished together as lightheadedness swept over her. She shook her head, making the dizziness worse. Her knees began to wobble, and her legs turned to jelly. She stumbled forward a step before her world went black.

CHAPTER 29

Cate awoke on her bed with Jack's concerned face hovering over her. "Cate?" he questioned as her eyelids fluttered open.

"Jack?" she questioned, her voice hoarse. "What happened?"

"You were staring in the mirror holding up the dress and the necklace. And then you collapsed."

Cate attempted to sit up, but a wave of dizziness passed over her. She collapsed back to the pillows.

"Easy, Cate." Jack palmed his phone and tapped around.

"What are you doing?"

"Calling Damien."

"No," Cate said, placing her hand on his. "I'm fine, just a little lightheaded."

"Cate, this is getting more and more serious by the minute. Now you're passing out every time you experience one of these trances."

Cate eased herself up to sit. "The dizziness is passing," she reported as her mind churned.

"What is it?" Jack asked as she sat pensively.

"Can I see the video from last night?"

Jack opened his camera app and handed it to her. She replayed the video three times. She swiped back to the previous video, speeding through her waltz around the west wing's massive space. She grabbed her phone, opened the camera cube's app, and found the video from her bedroom camera today. She played it twice.

"What is it, Cate?"

"Every time I collapse, it seems to be when I'm trying to recall details or physically trying to reach something in the trance."

Jack considered the statement, rubbing his finger along his chin. "What are you saying?"

"That my passing out is related to a break in continuity in my trance. When a question is asked that I can't answer or there is an object that I can't reach, it must cause some issue with my mind and I just implode, for lack of a better word. Fainting is the body's way of 'resetting,' like rebooting a computer."

"So, your brain is resetting because it can't access whatever it needs to."

"Right, that's my theory."

"I think we should pass that along to Damien."

"Okay," Cate said. "I'll text him."

Jack blew out a long breath as Cate typed out the message.

"I can't believe I'm saying this, but I can't wait until we time travel after lunch. At least then you're normal and I don't have to worry about you passing out."

"No, we only have to worry about figuring out if Hans killed Ruth and why," Cate said.

"Never thought I'd see the day where murder was the least of our problems."

"Things sure have taken an odd turn since we met the

Buckleys," Cate said, as she slid off the bed and stood.

"You okay?" Jack inquired.

"Yeah, no dizziness or weak legs." Cate crossed the room and snatched the dress and necklace off the floor where they'd landed when she's taken her nosedive. With them both put away, Jack walked her down to the library for her meal.

As she ate, her cell phone chimed with a message from Damien. *Seems to be getting worse but the good news is we may be getting closer to a solution. Will let you know more when we have it. In the meantime, any chance you can stay in the past for a bit?*

Cate chuckled at his message. The idea of asking Jack to stay in the past for longer than a few hours at a time was almost comical. Cate answered by thanking him and telling him she'd be spending at least a few hours there today.

They continued with a brief conversation as she finished her meal. Jack met her immediately following lunch and they headed upstairs for the normal routine of changing clothes and meeting outside her door, before traversing into the secret passage and slipping back to September 20th, 1942.

"At least the weather's better," Jack said, as they stepped into a cloudy, but dry day.

"Yes," Cate said. "One day before the disappearance."

"I suppose we should keep our eyes on Ruth. See if there are any additional clues to why Hans murders her."

"Perhaps he decided not to go through with the spying. He didn't seem keen on it yesterday."

"No, but that's what makes it even more curious."

"How so?"

"If he's opposed to spying because he feels these people are his friends, you'd think he'd object to murder."

"Perhaps she forced his hand. Or it was an accident and he panicked."

"We'll do our best to find out."

Cate nodded as they reached the castle and entered.

"Hey, we never got the chance to check out the room in the west wing yesterday," Cate said.

"Want to try it now? We've got some time to kill."

"Sure," Cate said.

They threaded through the halls on their way to the west wing and entered through the large double doors. "Didn't need my keys again," Jack noted.

"Rory seems like he wouldn't lock up unused wings."

"You're right. He has a rosy view of the world. He probably doesn't see the need."

They wound toward the room Cate seemed drawn to in the present. As they passed the music hall, Cate inched to the doors and pressed her ear against them.

"Just checking," she said, as she flicked her gaze to Jack. After a quick peek inside, they continued down the hall.

Voices floated through the air as they rounded the corner. The door to the large hall stood open a crack. Cate stopped walking, her eyes widening as she glanced at Jack.

He held a finger to his lips, and they crept forward. Cate peeked through the crack in the door. Ruth stood inside, her arms crossed as she stared up at a man. To Cate's surprise, the man was not Hans. Victor Richard stood inside the room, his hands clasped behind his back as he stared at Ruth with a sour expression.

Cate's jaw unhinged as she glanced at Jack. Jack returned the surprised expression, and they returned their attention to the conversation in the room.

"How did this happen?" Ruth inquired.

"I don't know," Victor answered.

"You were supposed to prevent this from happening!" Ruth exclaimed. "Hans never should have had access to those communiques."

"I've done my best. I can only do so much before people begin to suspect."

Cate furrowed her brow at the conversation. Was Victor also a part of the spy ring?

"Tell that to der Fuhrer when he demands to know why the code, which has gone indecipherable for months, has now suddenly become readable to the British."

Victor wrinkled his nose at Ruth's statement. "I'll handle it," he growled.

"You'd better. Because if that message ever reaches Bletchley Park, it will ruin our chances for victory."

"It won't," Victor spat.

"We'll see. If it does, it'll be you whom I hang this noose around. Your days with the Reich are finished!"

Ruth took a step toward the door before Victor grabbed her arm. "Careful who you threaten, Brigitta. I worked hard for my place in the party. I'm not going to let it all go for naught because of you."

Cate began to fall backward as Jack tugged her away. They hurried as silently as possible down the hall and Jack pushed her through the doors into the music room before easing them shut behind them.

"OMG," Cate mouthed to Jack.

He nodded but held his finger to his lips again. High-heeled shoes clicked off the tile floor as Ruth, or Brigitta, stormed past the room. More footsteps followed, signaling Victor's return to the main castle.

They waited several more moments in silence before Jack inched open the door and peered into the hall.

"Looks clear," he said.

Cate nodded and they navigated through dugh the halls to their suite in silence. "OH MY GOODNESS," Cate burst, as Jack closed the doors behind them.

Jack shook his head in disbelief.

"What is going on here?" Cate inquired, as she sank onto the chaise.

"Victor is a spy, obviously," Jack said.

"Yes, and so is Ruth. Or Brigitta, or whatever her name really is; that much is clear. But what is Hans?"

"Also a spy?" Jack inquired.

"He can't be. He's the one who discovered whatever the Reich didn't want him to."

Cate pondered the latest information. "Yesterday, we assumed Hans and Ruth were the German spies. But today it seems like it's Ruth and Victor."

"Oh! I've got it!" Jack exclaimed. "Ruth is a double agent!"

"Possibly, yes. But which side is her true affiliation with? And what did she want Hans to do that he seemed to refuse so vehemently?"

"Maybe they're both spies – Hans and Victor – and she's playing them against each other for her own gain," Jack suggested.

Cate bit her lower lip. "This is becoming very tangled. And now it is much less clear who killed her."

"After the conversation we just heard, it very well could be Victor."

Cate nodded in agreement. "Yes, in fact, I'd say he may be the more likely culprit. And it would explain why there's no information on him. Victor Richard is not his real name."

"Neither is Ruth Harper," Jack noted. "I wonder if you'd get anywhere with Brigitta."

Cate fell silent as the facts bounced around in her head. "There's one other person whose name I couldn't find anywhere either. Rita. Could she be connected?"

Jack threw his arms in the air as he paced the floor. "How many bloody spies are there here?"

"I'm not sure, but I think we should speak with Amelia."

"And tell her what? Your traveling companion is a Nazi spy and so are a few other people, we're just not sure who yet?"

"Something like that," Cate said.

"Cate! We can't!"

Cate's shoulders slumped. "Jack, if they succeed, this could ruin the war efforts."

"They don't succeed, though, right? We know this."

Cate considered it. "Yes, eventually Bletchley Park managed to work through whatever stymied their efforts in the early parts of this year and decipher the Enigma code, but…"

"But?"

"But what if that was only because whatever message Ruth said couldn't get to Bletchley did get to Bletchley?"

"Because Ruth was killed," Jack said.

"By Hans!" Cate exclaimed. "Hans kills her to make sure the message gets through."

"A likely scenario. And one we shouldn't disturb by talking to Amelia. In fact, I'm leery about disturbing things more than we have already."

"Do you want to go home?"

Jack considered it. "I don't want to go if it'll mean you'll suffer from another trance."

"Okay," Cate said. "Then let's stay for dinner as we planned and head back after."

Jack nodded. "Okay."

They bided their time, pacing the floor of their suite as they waited for the dinner hour to approach. As Jack escorted her down to the sitting room for cocktails, Cate felt unease creep into her shoulders. They were immersed in a web of spies, secrecy, and deep state secrets big enough to commit murder over. She offered a nervous glance and fleeting smile at Jack before they stepped into the sitting room.

They were the last to arrive at the party. Cate swore a pall hung over the room. She sipped at her sherry as she eyed the four suspects in the room. Which of them were allies? Which were foes? And which would turn out to be a murderer?

Cate found herself distracted through most of the dinner. Conversation was stilted on her part by her general unease. With Rory on one side of her and Hans on the other, Cate struggled to make polite conversation as her mind churned through the latest developments.

Across the table, Cate noted Rita managed to wrangle the seat on Jack's left again, while Amelia sat on his right. That left Ruth sandwiched between Hans and Victor. The irony did not escape Cate as she watched the woman converse with both men. Which was she betraying? Which would murder her?

Cate and Jack retired shortly after dinner and returned to their own time.

"Whew," Jack exclaimed, as the second hand returned to normal speed, indicating their arrival in the present. "What a day."

"I agree. I'm exhausted just thinking through the possibilities."

"Should we talk through them and then a plan for tomorrow?"

"Okay," Cate said.

They parted ways, reconvening in the library after they returned to their normal duds.

"My mind is racing in a thousand directions," Cate admitted, as she plopped into the armchair.

Jack sighed. "Yep. We thought we had this all figured out and then Victor decided to be a spy."

"I couldn't help but notice the irony of Ruth sitting between Victor and Hans," Cate said.

"And here I figured all you noticed was Rita finagling a seat next to me for the third night in a row."

"That didn't escape me, either," Cate said with an unimpressed glance. "And speaking of Rita, what is her deal? How is she involved?"

"Maybe she isn't," Jack suggested.

Cate narrowed her eyes at the statement. "Doubt it," she retorted. "I couldn't find her in any records, either."

"Working off that theory, perhaps Hans is British intelligence and isn't our murderer."

"Because we found him under his real name?"

"Aye. The others are using assumed names, obviously."

"Which you think makes them the more likely suspects for the murder," Cate surmised.

Jack nodded.

"So, what's our next move?" Cate asked.

"Well, I suppose we should go back and at least ensure whatever message must get to Bletchley from Dunhaven makes it there via Hans, or whoever."

"And hopefully discover a murderer, too."

"We'll head back tomorrow, same time as today?"

"It seems to be the most active time."

"Okay, sounds like a plan," Jack said.

* * *

Cate spent the remaining afternoon hours searching for any information on German spies in the World War II era. In particular, she searched for any names that may be familiar, such as Brigitta. She found little information and gave up in favor of dinner and an evening walk.

She stared up at the castle on her return trip. Would they solve the mystery in 1942? And would she experience another trance tonight?

What if she became stuck in it this time? With the dress, music box and necklace, did she have all the components she needed to be sucked into her own mind? Worry grew in her and her shoulders tensed as she approached the castle's facade.

With a deep breath, she pushed inside. Whatever she was dealing with, she'd have to face it one way or another. She just hoped she liked the outcome.

CHAPTER 30

Cate's eyelids fluttered. She blinked slowly as her senses began to return. With bleary eyes, her gaze darted around as her pulse quickened and she gasped in breaths.

"Easy, Cate," Jack said.

She clutched his arm, her head in his lap. "What happened?" she whispered.

Cate recognized her surroundings. She laid on the floor in the large hall in the west wing. Jack sat with her cradled in his arms.

"You had another episode," Jack said.

Cate glanced down at her attire. No longer clad in her pajamas, she now wore the sapphire blue dress. The necklace hung around her neck. Her hair had been pulled up into an upswept style.

"Looks like it was a doozy," she said, as she surveyed her attire.

"Outside of your rather formal attire, it was much the same as it was before. I caught up to you in the hall. You wandered here and started pawing at the pillar. You kept saying you had to find it."

"I must be searching for the room," Cate said, pushing herself up to sit.

"Easy."

"I'm okay. And I feel ridiculous laying on the floor. Why do I think the room is here?"

"I'm not certain. I've checked that pillar and I don't see anything odd on it."

Cate reached her hand out. "Help me up," she asked.

Jack climbed to his feet and pulled Cate up to stand. She approached the pillar and studied it, reaching out and touching or pushing various pieces.

"I don't see anything either," she admitted. "What snapped me out of it this time?"

"You got exceptionally upset about 'finding it' – or rather not finding whatever it was you were searching for. You were near tears and then you collapsed."

Cate inhaled deeply. "I wish I would have found it. This is getting old."

"Cate, I'm not sure I want you to find this room or whatever you're looking for. I'm afraid of what's going to happen when you do."

"Maybe I'll finally snap out of this nonsense."

Jack approached her and took her hands in his. He shook his head, worry creasing his forehead. "Cate, I'm afraid of what may happen to you," he said, his voice just above a whisper.

Cate squeezed his hands. "That's not going to happen."

"Isn't it? How do we know that?"

"Damien never mentioned it as an outcome."

"That doesn't mean it won't happen," Jack said.

Cate sighed as Jack pulled her into an embrace. "I'll always fight to come back," she said.

She glanced up at him. He stared down at her. He cupped her face in his hands. After a moment, he said, "We probably should go."

Cate nodded as she reached up to squeeze his hand. "With any luck, we can get a few more hours of sleep."

"Again, I find myself looking forward to going back to the past. It's the one place you're safe."

They strode from the room. "I'm safe here, too, Jack," Cate reassured him. "I'll always be safe with you here. Reids and MacKenzies, remember?"

"I appreciate the vote of confidence, Cate. But I feel like I'm failing miserably at protecting you."

"You're not. We'll be okay. As long as we're together." Cate gave his hand another squeeze before they parted ways.

As Cate closed the door to her suite, she collapsed against it with a heavy sigh. Her mind spun to the future. She squeezed her eyes shut as Jack's statement rang in her mind. What would happen once she found that room? Was Jack correct? Would she disappear into her own mind?

* * *

Cate arose early the next morning. She hadn't had much luck sleeping after the incident with the dress. She spent most of the remaining wee hours of the morning pacing the floor of her suite. She'd removed the collar cam from around her wrist so the camera would not alert Jack to her restlessness.

She dozed off on her chaise for a few moments before the sun rose over the moors. The moment the light began to paint the morning sky brilliant shades of pink and red, she rose and dressed for her day. Anxiousness filled her, not only about her current issues with the west wing and sapphire dress and necklace, but also concerning their trip to 1942.

What would they find? Could they ferret out the

murderer? Questions surged in Cate's mind as she took the dogs for an early morning stroll, settling on her new bench to watch the sun rise higher into the sky.

Jack strolled to her location by the loch before she'd returned to the castle.

"Morning," he said as he approached her.

She offered him a weak smile. "Good morning." She patted the bench next to her.

Jack eased onto it, searching her face for any clues about her well-being. "I'm fine," she said before he could ask.

"Did you get any sleep?"

"Not really. You?"

"I stared at my phone all night in case you needed me."

Cate drew her lips into a thin line. "I'm sorry."

"It's not your fault, Cate," Jack said, as he settled back onto the bench and stared at the sunrise.

Cate blew out a long breath. "I can't wait to go back to 1942, though I'm afraid of what we'll find there, too."

"Like I said, at least in 1942 I know you're safe. Now, we better be getting back for breakfast before Mrs. Fraser starts to worry."

"We do not need that," Cate said with a chuckle. "Come on, boys."

She and Jack returned to the castle and Cate collected her breakfast and headed to the library. She toyed with the puzzle pieces as she attempted to focus on something other than the two major issues looming in her life. As mid-morning approached, her phone chimed.

Cate found a message from Damien. *Hey Cate, how are things?*

Cate smiled at the message, though her smile quickly faded as she considered her answer. *Thanks for checking. Things have been better. I had another episode last night.*

Damien responded quickly. *Sorry to hear that. What happened?*

Cate typed up the gory details, sending a message containing as much information as she could. *I put the dress on, pulled my hair up, put on the necklace and headed for that room in the west wing. Jack said I kept insisting on finding something and became really upset when I couldn't find whatever I was searching for. Then I passed out. I have no memory of this at all. I woke up on the floor.*

Damien responded a few moments later. *I'm sorry this is happening to you, Cate. Can I ask you a few questions about it? We may be on to something here. If you're not up to it, that's fine.*

Cate answered: *I'll answer anything you want, ask away! And THANK YOU for all this help.*

A message came back a moment later: *Of course, Cate! We're happy to help. Alexander and I have been pouring over his reference library and we found a few leads. I just need more information to narrow it down.*

Another text came shortly after the first. *Any headaches?*

Cate searched her memory. *Not consistently. In a few of the trances, I seem to have experienced some pain but nothing before or after the episodes or in general, no.*

Damien answered a few moments later. *Okay, next question. Dizziness?*

Cate nodded as she typed into her phone. *Yes. I did experience that after collapsing the other day. I had to lay down for a few moments after the episode. This last time Jack wouldn't let me sit up until I had fully recovered so I'm not sure.*

Damien responded: *Okay, noted. Nausea?*

Cate shook her head and typed: *No (thankfully!).*

Damien returned her message with a smiley emoticon followed by another question. *Lack of focus or clouded mind?*

Cate answered: *Yes, definitely. It does clear with time travel but sometimes I can't focus, and it seems like those are the times when I've slipped into a trance while awake. Much of the time, I slip into them when I'm asleep.*

Damien answered: *Okay, so most instances are nocturnal.*

Cate typed: *Yes, though I have slipped into them while awake a few times.*

Damien sent another message to clarify. *And you've lost time in every instance, right?*

Cate confirmed the lack of memory or "time losses" in every instance. She also included the details of what she recalled in terms of what the room she sought, and the other odd comments she'd uttered during her trances.

She followed up with a final message stating: *I don't understand why I seem to have "memories" that aren't mine?! These feel like memories, but I've never had a dress like this, never had this music box, never went to the 1810s. Why am I acting like I have?*

After a few moments, Damien responded: *It may be connected to what's happening to you. I don't have any more questions right now, but this will help us sort through the possibilities. We have a few leads. I'll get back to you as soon as we search them all out INCLUDING solutions!*

Cate sent a "thank you" back in all capitals before returning to her puzzle. She found herself unable to focus, though she wasn't certain that it was a side effect from whatever she was suffering from or the general tension of the two mysteries.

Cate rubbed at the back of her neck as her mind shot in several different directions. She considered returning to the west wing to seek answers while she was more awake and cognizant. The concept of disappearing into herself before she ever determined what happened in 1942 stopped her.

Instead, she frittered away her hours with another walk outside and a long contemplation near the loch. She forced her lunch down and sat drumming her fingers on the desk as she awaited Jack.

He appeared in the doorway moments after Molly collected her tray and she leapt from her seat. "Ready?"

"Uh, I guess," Jack said. "I hoped to find out how you were feeling and how your morning went first."

"It was okay. I talked to Damien. He asked me a bunch of questions about my symptoms. He said they had a few leads and would be back to me soon with an answer and a few solutions. Here's to hoping!"

Jack nodded. "Let's hope. Okay, I guess we can get going then."

Cate led the way and they separated to change clothes, meeting in the hall and heading to the secret passage and 1942.

Cate blew out a long breath as the timepiece slowed. "Moment of truth today," she said.

"Aye. Should we head to the west wing again?"

"Maybe third time's the charm," Cate said. They reached the end of the passage, and exited the crypt into the bright sunshine beyond.

Jack nodded and they started up the path to the castle. After a moment he puckered his lips and flicked his glance to Cate. "Wait, did you mean third time's the charm for exploring that room, or getting information about our spies?"

"Either? Both. Doesn't matter, it'd just be nice to move forward on some front."

"I agree. Boy, I hope we don't find Rita and Ruth engaged in an argument there."

"Why?"

"Because then we'll have another suspect, and we may never know who did it. There'll be too many to keep an eye on."

"Who's our first priority to track?"

"I'd say Victor," Jack said. "He's definitely on the German side."

"Which may also be Ruth's side."

"Good point," Jack said. "So maybe it should be Hans."

Cate nodded. "Though he really doesn't seem the murderous type."

"So, Victor?"

Cate opened her mouth, flicking her gaze to Jack. "No," he answered.

"I didn't say anything yet."

"We're *not* splitting up!"

Cate grimaced. "I didn't suggest that."

"No, but you were about to. And that's not happening. Every time we have ever split up it's been a disaster."

"All right. It's just like you said, there are too many people to keep an eye on."

"So, we'll have to go with the most likely suspect. Which I still say is Victor."

"I'd agree," Cate said, as they pushed into the castle.

"Oh golly, I've won a debate with Lady Cate. I'm in shock."

"That's very funny, Jack. Come on," she said, leading him through the halls toward the west wing.

"You know, I have to say, this is the first time I'm enjoying time travel with you."

"Oh really? Is it because there're bathrooms and electricity?"

"No, it's because I've won a debate *and* you are normal in this time."

"Sorry I'm abnormal in the present," Cate lamented, as they strolled down the wide entrance to the west wing.

Jack put his arm around Cate's shoulders and gave her a

squeeze. "I like you either way. I just like not having to worry about you here."

They slowed as they approached the first entrance to the music hall. Cate pressed her ear to the door before easing it open. They stepped into the empty room, their footsteps echoing off the large space.

"On to the famous grand hall!" Jack said.

They left through the second entrance in the music hall and snuck down the hall. They stopped several feet from the golden doors and strained for any sounds. None came so they continued toward the doors, still moving as noiselessly as possible.

Cate pressed her ear against the door then shook her head at Jack. She eased one door open, peering inside. After shifting her gaze around as much as the crack allowed, she eased the door back further. They found the room empty.

"I'm not sure if I'm pleased or not about finding no one here," Cate said, her voice echoing in the large space as they stepped inside.

"Feel okay?" Jack inquired, shooting her a sideways glance.

"Yep. This room doesn't seem to have any weird effects on me here." Cate shrugged as she approached the pillar she seemed to be drawn to in her time.

She studied it again. Nothing new jumped out at her. Jack joined her, feeling around on the pillar for any secret triggers or compartments.

"I don't see anything, Lady Cate."

"Neither do I," Cate admitted. She sighed and glanced around the space, searching for anything to clue them in to what she sought in this room.

"The dogs were at this wall," Cate said, stalking across the room.

She ran her hand over it, hoping to find some clue as to what was behind it. Jack approached and pounded against it. "This is an interior wall," he said. "There could be something behind it."

"I don't see a trigger," Cate said.

"How could you with all this gold covering the walls?"

Cate shrugged as she tugged at a wall fixture. After a moment, she frowned and spun around, leaning her back against the wall as she crossed her arms and huffed.

"Maybe the trigger is somewhere else in the room?" Jack said, phrasing it as a question.

Cate lifted her eyebrows. "Maybe," she murmured. "Though why am I drawn to that pillar?"

"Cate, you're in a trance. Who knows if you're thinking straight?"

"I'm thinking straight enough to come here!" she countered. "To put on a necklace, and to get dressed!" Cate shook her head in frustration.

"I know you're frustrated, Cate, but we'll figure something out."

She nodded, her arms still folded tightly over her chest and flicked her gaze across the room. Her brow crinkled and she cocked her head. "What is that?" she questioned.

Across the room, a dull spot broke up the otherwise shiny, reflective flooring. "What's what?" Jack inquired, following her gaze.

"That spot on the floor," Cate answered as she stepped toward it.

As she approached, she discovered it to be a small scrap of newspaper. Cate snatched it from the floor. The side facing her contained a partial date: *ber, 21, 1942.* An imprint indicated a message had been scrawled on the back. She flipped it over to read.

Meet me at 10 p.m. in the folly. Urgent. Mission-critical.

ate's eyes went wide, and her eyebrows shot toward her hairline. "Jack!" she exclaimed as he joined her, peering over her shoulder at the note.

"Do you think this was from today?" Jack inquired.

"Yes," Cate said, flipping the paper over. "It's from the paper printed today."

"Aye, so it is. Who do you think it's from?"

"I'm not sure," Cate said. "But this is our first solid clue as to where we may learn just what happened to Ruth Harper."

"Guess we'll head to the folly tonight and unmask a killer."

Cate nodded her agreement. She glanced at Jack's watch. "It's almost half-past three. We've got a few hours to kill."

"Aye, I suppose we'll do that in the comfort of our suite. Unless you'd like to continue poking around in here."

"I don't see the point. And I don't want to be in here if a pair of spies attempt to use it for a meeting spot."

"Good point. Let's go."

They threaded back through the halls and slipped into the

privacy of their bedroom suite. A note from Rory awaited them.

"Oh, no," Jack groaned as he read the note.

"What is it?" Cate asked, her stomach somersaulting. She leapt from her seat on the chaise. "Is it Ruth? Have we missed it?"

"No, he's canceled dinner."

Cate puckered her lips in an unimpressed expression.

"He says we can request a tray be brought up, but Amelia's plans are up in the air, and she may be leaving tonight or tomorrow morning."

Cate furrowed her brow. "Leaving? Do you think this sudden change in plans is due to whatever is going on with Ruth?"

"I'd say it's tied together. She must be a master manipulator to get Amelia to do her bidding."

Cate sighed. "And we won't have a chance to discuss this at dinner." She bit her lower lip as she stared into space, her mind churning. "Perhaps we should seek out Amelia. Maybe she'll give us some information."

Jack considered it for a moment. "We may gain some information as to why Amelia is leaving and what prompted it, but I'm not sure it helps us."

"I'd like to try," Cate said.

"I don't want you going alone. Though I suppose it would look odd for us both to go."

"Well, in the interest of saying goodbye, you could tag along."

"You may get more information out of her if I wasn't there. How about this, I'll walk you to her suite and leave you there. Only if you agree to come straight back here when you're finished."

"I promise," Cate said.

"No racing after clues on your own," Jack warned.

"I said I promise!" Cate exclaimed.

"Yes, I know. But I also know if you get a whiff of a clue, you'll go darting off after it and I'll be left out of all the fun."

"I won't dart after anything. But I would like to say goodbye to Amelia, even if I don't get any information from her."

"I understand," Jack said with a nod. "Well, come on, then."

Cate slipped her hand into the crook of his arm, and they proceeded to the suite Amelia usually occupied when they stayed at the estate. The door opened a few moments after Cate knocked on it. Ruth stood inside.

"Oh, hello, Ruth," Cate said. "Is Amelia here? Rory left a note saying you may be leaving soon, and I hoped to speak with her."

"Oh, yes, she's here." Ruth stepped aside to allow Cate to enter.

"I'll see you later, dear," Jack said, as he waved to her and departed down the hall.

Cate swallowed hard as she stood face to face with the woman who so easily lied to those around her.

"Amelia!" Ruth called into the bedroom. "Cate is here to see you."

Amelia emerged carrying a dress a few moments later. "Cate! How lovely to see you."

"Sorry to interrupt, I realize you must be quite busy, but Rory said you're leaving?" Cate phrased the remark as a question, hoping to solicit some information.

"Oh, it's no bother. I would have asked to have a tea since we'll miss dinner this evening, though, you're usually out in the afternoons. Ruth, would you be so kind as to ring for tea?"

"I'll request it straight from the kitchen. I have a few things I need to take care of."

Amelia nodded at the girl as she slipped from the room. "Come in, I'm just throwing a few things into the suitcase. Then we'll sit down and have a nice cuppa when the tea arrives."

Cate followed her into the bedroom. "Can I help with anything?"

"Oh, no, I've got it all under control. I am so used to traveling, this is becoming second nature to me."

"What prompted the sudden change in plans, if you don't mind my asking?"

Amelia offered her a shrug as she continued to fill her suitcase. "We had no definite plans when we came. An opportunity came up to meet with Lucas on some travel he'll be doing, and we decided to take it."

"Oh, how nice. It's too bad Lucas's business couldn't bring him here. We would have loved to see him again."

Amelia gave her a brief smile. "I'll pass along your regards. I'm certain he'll be sore he missed your visit."

A maid arrived with tea and Amelia gave her packing a break as she settled onto the settee in the sitting room with a warm cup of tea. Cate sat next to her, considering ways to tease more information from Amelia.

"So, where are you off to now?"

"We'll meet Lucas in Northampton."

"Oh, you've got quite a ways to go then," Cate said.

"Yes, hence our rather dubious plans about the time at which we'll depart. We'll only have a short window to catch Lucas, so we must plan accordingly."

Cate furrowed her brow at the statement. "Oh, my, it sounds almost as rigid as a train schedule."

Amelia gave her a hearty laugh. "Close," she said, still chuckling. "Such are the times. What about you and Jack? How long will you remain at Dunhaven?"

"We'll be going in short order, as well. I'm so pleased we had the opportunity to see each other again."

"As am I. Lucas will be so jealous when I tell him who I've seen!"

Cate smiled at her, wishing she had the opportunity to see her great-grandfather again, too. Amelia used Cate's silence to transition into other topics as they finished their tea.

"Well," Amelia said as they finished their tea, "I suppose I should get back at it. I'm just waiting on word from Lucas, so I'd like to be ready."

"I understand," Cate said, setting down her empty teacup and standing. Amelia pulled her into an embrace.

"Oh, it was lovely to see you again, Cate. And I do hope we'll be able to get together after this terrible business is over with and truly enjoy each other's company."

"I do, too," Cate said. She gave Amelia's arm a squeeze, before she offered her a final smile and backed away. With a last wave, she disappeared into the hall.

With a tear-filled sigh, Cate navigated through the halls back to her suite. She found Jack napping on the chaise. Cate took the opportunity to pace the floor in the bedroom, not wanting to wake Jack from his slumber.

After forty-five minutes, Cate heard movement from the sitting room. As she approached the doorway, Jack sat up and stretched. He yawned before he smiled sleepily at her. "Oh good, you're back."

"I've been back for almost an hour. I didn't want to wake you since I've been doing a wonderful job of keeping you awake at night."

"I'm just pleased you came straight back! Did you learn anything?"

Cate shrugged. "Not much. According to Amelia, they're

leaving because they have a chance to meet with Lucas in Northampton."

"So Amelia is the one who made the decision?"

"Seems to be."

"Hmmm, that wasn't what we suspected."

"No, but now that I think about it, perhaps that's what precipitated this note," Cate said, unfurling the paper she had stuffed in her pocket. "Maybe Ruth sent a message to one of the men to up the timeline of their mission given her imminent departure."

"Could be. Wonder what causes whoever to kill her then?"

"I'm not sure, but her death must be the reason Amelia is still here in a few days."

"Aye, her plans must change after Ruth disappears."

Cate sighed. "Well, I suppose we'll find out tonight. But for now, should I ring for dinner?"

"Best idea I've heard all day."

* * *

Cate and Jack spent the early evening hours eating sandwiches sent up from the kitchen, taking turns staring out the window and pacing the floor as the sun lowered in the sky.

At promptly 8:30 p.m., Jack suggested they make their way to the folly. "We'll have a long wait, but I'd rather be there and hidden away in case anyone arrives early."

"I agree," Cate said. "Plus I couldn't stand being cooped up in that room anymore. I just want to get going."

"It's not going to make time go any faster, Lady Cate."

"I know, but at least I feel like we're moving now!"

"And now we're going to stop moving," Jack said, as they approached the folly. He glanced around the surrounding area to check for any watchful eyes before they ducked inside. As they entered the darkened enclosure, Jack flicked on his flashlight.

"We can hide here," he said, motioning to a partial wall separating the interior.

Cate grimaced at it. "Shine the light behind there before I go in."

"Why?"

"I'm afraid of critters."

Jack swept the beam behind the wall. "Just a few wayward leaves and dirt."

Cate, still frowning, kicked around the leaves before she squatted behind the wall. "Don't trust me?"

"I don't trust rodents," Cate said. "Can you see me?"

"No, totally hidden," Jack said, before clicking off his flashlight and settling onto the floor.

After twenty minutes, Cate fidgeted.

"Stop squirming around," Jack whispered.

"I can't help it! My legs are giving out."

In the dim light, Jack screwed up his face, glancing at her.

"Sit down!" he breathed. "Are you going for the world's record for squatting?"

"I was…"

"Afraid of critters, right," Jack noted. "Do you want to sit on my lap?"

"No," Cate said with a groan. "I'll brave it." She sank to the floor. Latticework at her eye level allowed her to see through into the main chamber of the folly.

They waited another twenty minutes before footsteps on the stone steps outside sounded. In the waning light, Cate grasped Jack's forearm and squeezed. She hoped she could hear over the loud thudding of her heart in her ears.

In the dim light, the form of Ruth appeared limned in

dying twilight. It couldn't be that close to ten. Why had Ruth come so much earlier?

As she entered, she flicked on a lantern, holding it high as she glanced around the space. Cate held her breath as Ruth spun in a slow circle. She focused on the half-wall, studying it for a moment before stepping forward. Jack slid his arm up and squeezed Cate's hand in his.

Shoes sounded on the stone outside. Ruth spun to face the incoming party. Cate pursed her lips to stop herself from gasping as the bright lantern shone on Hans's face. He held one hand up to block the bright light, his other hand clutched something.

"Did you bring it?" Ruth asked.

He nodded, still holding his hand up to the light. Ruth held her hand out. "You're doing the right thing," she assured him.

He shook his head as he lowered his hand. "I can't believe it," he choked. "He saved my life when our apartment building was hit."

"Of course he did. He needed you," Ruth said, a coldness in her voice.

"Anyway, I put everything in there you requested."

Ruth nodded. "And Victor?" she inquired.

"I gave him the fake report as you requested."

"Good," she said.

He pursed his lips, staring at the ground. "You've done your country a great service," Ruth added. "I'll certainly pass that along."

He gave her a slight nod. "Dismissed," she said with finality.

Hans turned on a heel and disappeared through the opening. Ruth set the lantern on the half wall directly above Cate and Jack. Cate winced at Jack as they tried to stay out of sight.

She shuffled through the papers. After a moment, she pulled her blouse from within her skirt. Stretching behind her back, she wiggled an identical folder from under her chemise. She set it on the stone bench and slid the folder received from Hans under her camisole. She quickly tucked her blouse into her skirt and adjusted the sweater she wore.

After the swap, Ruth perched on the edge of the stone bench and checked her watch. Cate glanced at Jack and shrugged. She pointed to her bare wrist in a silent question. Jack motioned the time to be ten to ten.

Cate nodded. Her mind screamed with the details of the incident. So, Hans did not kill her. The killer must be the person she was meeting at ten. The killer must be Victor.

Time seemed to stand still, but at long last footsteps sounded again on the steps outside. Cate's heart pounded in her chest. If they were correct, they would soon witness a murder. Jack must have sensed her apprehension. He reached out and grasped her hand. She clung to him, suddenly unsure she wanted to be here. She fought to keep her breath shallow and steady.

Ruth stood as the figure appeared in the doorway. Victor wandered inside.

"You summoned me, Brigitta?"

"I have intercepted the report from Hans." She waved the folder in the air. "I will destroy it and pass along a fake, thus meaning the code will remain indecipherable."

Victor wiggled his eyebrows at her. "So you managed to pull it off."

"I did. And now your cover can remain intact. I expect you to do a far better job in the future with making sure the code remains unreadable."

Victor narrowed his eyes at her. "I don't imagine I'll be here long."

Ruth raised her eyebrows at the statement. "Oh?"

"No. Not when I deliver the information you were supposed to retrieve. Give me the folder."

Ruth offered him a harsh cackle. "I am capable of doing my job."

Victor removed a gun hidden in his jacket. "That may be, but I prefer to see the job through myself."

Ruth remained calm despite the pistol being aimed at her. She flicked her gaze from the gun's barrel to Victor's face. "Put that away."

"Give me the folder."

"Fine," Ruth said. She passed the folder over to Victor. He glanced through it then tucked it under his arm, training the gun on Ruth again.

"You got what you wanted. Though don't think I won't report this little incident to our superiors."

"That's where you're wrong, Brigitta."

Ruth cocked her head, and Victor smirked at her.

"I have high aspirations. And I won't have them ruined by a little tufthunter like you. I don't trust you, you see. So, I think I'll up my chances of success."

Without another word, Victor fired his weapon. An expression of shock covered Ruth's face as she glanced down at her blouse. A wet red spot bled through the cloth. Ruth pressed a hand to her stomach. Blood glistened on her fingers as she pulled it away. A moan escaped her lips and she collapsed to the ground, slumping to the floor.

CHAPTER 32

Cate's muscles stiffened and Jack cupped a hand over her mouth. "Shhh," he whispered in her ear, as he pulled her closer to him.

"Goodbye, Brigitta, or whoever you are," Victor said with a sneer, as he stowed his gun in his jacket. "Now, I'll be the hero."

A voice sounded behind Victor. "I'm sorry, Victor. But I can't let that happen."

With furrowed brows, Victor spun to face the newest addition to the party. Rita stepped into the light from the lantern, gun drawn and pointed at Victor.

"Rita," he said.

"Oh, come now, Victor. I'm certain you've already deduced Rita Haverford is not my real name."

Cate's eyes went wide, and she squeezed Jack's arm.

Victor raised his eyebrows. "I've never suspected you of anything disingenuous."

"Well, then I'm very disappointed in you. I thought you were smarter than that."

Victor glanced back to Ruth. "I suppose you were in league with her."

Rita shook her head. "No."

"Well, then maybe you'll be interested in discussing a partnership. I'm certain we can come to some arrangement that will be mutually beneficial for both of us."

Rita pressed her lips into a thin line and shook her head. "Sorry, Victor, but there are larger things in motion here. And unfortunately, you're collateral damage."

With that Rita squeezed the trigger of the gun. The muzzle flashed as the bullet discharged. Victor grunted as the bullet struck him square in the chest. Rita aimed a second time and fired again as Victor dropped to his knees.

This one hit him square between the eyes. He flopped forward, his eyes still staring blankly ahead. Cate squeezed her eyes shut as a tear rolled down her cheek. With Jack's hand still clasped firmly over her mouth, she managed to keep her shocked squeal inside.

Two men appeared as Rita pulled the folder from the floor. "Bury him in the side garden."

"What about her?" one man asked.

"Leave her. Let her partner find her. They'll assume Victor killed her and fled, leaving us undetected."

The man nodded as he grabbed Victor under one arm. The other man grabbed him under the other and together, they dragged him from the folly, his feet making a sickening smacking sound as they slapped off the stone steps outside.

Rita spun on her heel and departed from the folly, leaving the lit lantern still shining inside.

Cate's chest heaved as she tried to gasp in breaths. Jack kept a firm hold on her for several more moments until he was certain no one would return.

"Stay quiet," Jack cautioned as he released his grip on her.

"What just happened?" Cate whispered, as she wiped at her tear-stained cheeks.

A groan interrupted any response Jack could offer. With wide eyes, Cate shuffled on her hands and knees around the half wall and over to Ruth.

Cate rolled her onto her back and stared down at the blood spot as her hands searched for her carotid artery. "Oh my God, Jack," Cate exclaimed. "She's alive! We have to help her!"

Jack pulled off his jacket and shoved it against Ruth's wound. "We've got to keep pressure on the wound."

"One of us has to go for help," Cate said.

"No, we can't split up, Cate," Jack insisted.

"Jack..." Cate began when a shout interrupted her statement.

Both Jack and Cate spun to face the entrance. Amelia stood in the doorway, her hand covering her gaping jaw. She rushed forward. "What happened? Is she alive?"

"Yes," Cate exclaimed. "Yes, she's alive. She's been shot. By Victor Richard. He's a German spy! And he was shot and killed by Rita. We have no idea who or what she is!"

"I know about Victor," Amelia answered, as she pulled Jack's hands away and ripped open Ruth's blouse. She shoved up the chemise to assess the wound.

"She'll need surgery," she said matter-of-factly. "We'll need to get her to a hospital as quickly and quietly as possible. Jack, I'll need your help."

Jack nodded, prepared to carry the woman. Before he could lift her, Ruth's eyelids fluttered open. She moaned in pain.

"Sarah? Sarah," Amelia said, leaning forward to stroke her hair. "Easy. You've been shot."

"F-F-Folder," Ruth stuttered.

"Shhh, don't try to speak," Amelia said.

Ruth gave a hard shake to her head. "Hans, folder. Must deliver."

"I'll handle it, Sarah."

"She had a folder from Hans. She hid it behind her back under the camisole," Cate explained.

"What?" Amelia said, as Ruth's eyes fluttered open and closed. She rocked, attempting to move. "Help me. Gently roll her."

Jack eased her over and Amelia reached to her back. She pulled a folder from a small wrap around her midriff. Amelia paged through it as Jack eased Ruth back to the floor.

"Oh my God," Amelia said with a gasp. She flicked her gaze to Cate. "And you say this is from Hans?"

Cate gave her a shaky nod. "Yes," Cate said. "Hans gave that to Ruth or Sarah or whatever her name is. Then she took another folder identical to this one from under her blouse and replaced it with this one. She gave the other folder to Victor. That's who shot her."

"Jack, Cate, I need you to do something for me."

"Anything," Cate said.

"Name it," Jack added.

"I need you to take this folder and deliver it."

"What?" Cate answered, her eyes wide and her eyebrows squashed together.

"This contains the information needed to decipher the Enigma code. This must get to Bletchley Park. Sarah and I were supposed to deliver it, that's where we were going. Obviously, we can't go now. You must take it. Please, it could decide the outcome of the war."

Cate flicked her gaze to Jack then back to Amelia. Was she hearing correctly? Was her great-grandmother a spy?

Cate's lower lip bobbed up and down as she tried to formulate a response. Amelia continued in the absence of her response. "I'll contact Lucas, let him know the change of plans."

"Lucas?" Cate finally managed to squeak out.

"Yes," Amelia confirmed. "Lucas, Sarah, and I work for the intelligence effort. We suspected a German spy ring operating here at Dunhaven. Victor Richard, aka Victor Richter, works for the enemy. He attempted to keep this information from ever being discovered. Please. You must deliver it."

Cate's head slowly nodded. "Okay," she said.

Amelia nodded. "Come along. I'll get you along your way."

"What about her?" Jack inquired.

The question was answered by the appearance of Rory and Hans.

"Oh, Rory, Hans, thank goodness. Please help me with Ruth. Cate and Jack found her here. She's been shot. She needs immediate medical attention, but we must keep the matter private. I must attend to something else immediately."

"I understand," Rory said, as he took over for Jack.

"Cate, Jack, come with me," Amelia said.

They followed Amelia from the folly. She led them to the garage, grabbing the keys to one of the vehicles. She led them to it before she spun and held the folder out to Cate. She pressed it into her hands and squeezed.

"Take this to Bletchley Park. Ask for Alan Turing. Give it to no one but Alan. Stop for no one. Watch your backs. There are many people who want to ensure this never reaches Mr. Turing and his fantastic machine."

Cate nodded as she stared down at the folder, speechless.

Amelia set her foot on the running board of the vehicle and hiked her skirt. Cate's eyes bulged as her great-grandmother pulled a weapon from her garter. She passed it off to Jack. "Take this. Stay safe."

Jack nodded as he accepted the weapon, sticking it in the waistband of his pants.

"Be safe, Cate and Jack." Amelia pulled open the door and loaded Cate into the passenger's side, as Jack slid in behind the wheel. Amelia hurried from the garage, returning toward the folly as Jack eased the car onto the gravel drive and aimed for Dunhaven.

Cate sat silent and stunned as Jack drove. After a moment, she gasped out, "What just happened?"

"I'm not one hundred percent sure," Jack answered, "though I am certain driving this is not going to be as easy as I hoped."

Cate glanced at him. "No power steering," Jack commented.

"Right," Cate said. She glanced at the folder in her lap. "Jack, Amelia… my great-grandmother is a spy."

"Aye. I did not see that one coming," Jack answered as the gears ground. Jack winced. "Haven't driven a manual in a while."

Cate continued to parse through the details of what they'd just witnessed. "So, Amelia and Lucas are spies. And Ruth or Sarah worked with them."

"And Victor was a German spy."

"Right. Ruth must have been a double agent, ferreting out the German spy embedded at Dunhaven."

"Aye, that seems right."

Cate paused a moment. "So, who is Rita?"

"That I'm not sure. She didn't seem to have a side. She didn't care what happened to Ruth or Victor."

Cate's brow furrowed. "She killed Victor and Ruth is still alive."

"Right," Jack confirmed.

"But…" Cate paused as she put together the pieces. "But the person in the grave we found was a woman. Ruth's height. Victor is a man and much taller. Yet he's the one buried in that grave now."

Cate's eyes bulged and she sucked in a gasp as she glanced sharply at Jack. "Jack," she said, breathlessly, "did we just change history?"

Jack considered Cate's question. With a sigh and a shake of his head, he responded, "I don't know if we did, but Rita definitely did."

"Why? What happened? Who is Rita?"

"I'm not certain," Jack answered, his eyes never leaving the road. "What did she say to Victor about suspecting Rita wasn't her real name?"

Cate bit her lip, trying to recall the details. The conversation happened less than an hour ago, yet it felt as it had happened ages ago. "She said there were larger things in motion. What does that mean?"

"I'm not certain, but for now, we need to focus on getting that folder to Bletchley Park."

Cate glanced down at the folder in her lap and nodded. "Yes. I can't believe this. We're delivering a piece of intelligence to Alan Turing. This is…"

"Frightening."

"I was going to say amazing, but that word works, too."

"So, this Turing guy…" Jack began, his hands wiggling the wheel to keep the car steady.

"Is well known for his work in deciphering the Enigma code," Cate answered. "His work led to the development of modern computer science."

"I see," Jack said, glancing in the car's mirror.

"To meet him will be…" Cate struggled to find the words. "I'm speechless."

Jack didn't respond.

"Sorry, history geek stuff," Cate added, glancing at him. "Is the driving really difficult?"

Jack shook his head, glancing in the mirror again. "No, but I swear this car has been following us since we left Dunhaven."

Cate glanced back behind them, finding a pair of headlights shining toward them. "Maybe it's a fluke."

"Maybe," Jack said.

Cate tried to keep her pulse in check as Jack veered off onto another street and the headlights followed. She flicked her gaze to Jack who studied the lights, too, and winced.

"I don't like this," Jack said.

Cate stared down at the folder in her lap. "Neither do I," she said. "Not when we're carrying information that could affect the outcome of the war."

"Aye, that's my thoughts exactly."

They continued along their route, making their way south toward London. As they reached a lonely stretch of road, the car behind them inched closer. Jack pressed the accelerator, speeding up as much as the car would allow. The tail car kept pace with them.

"Great," Jack muttered.

Cate removed the papers inside the folder and stuffed them into the blouse of her dress as the car veered around them and fought to gain on them.

"Cate, hang on to something, he's going to hit us."

Cate clutched for anything to brace herself. In a car with no seatbelt restraints, a wreck could be devastating.

The other car pulled level with them. Jack tried to drop back but the car swerved, crunching their front bumper on the driver's side. Jack swerved to maintain control from the hit.

"Hang on," he said through clenched teeth.

"What are you going to do?"

"I'm going to hit him back," Jack announced, as he mashed

the accelerator to the floor and swerved toward the other car.

The sickening scrape of metal-on-metal tore through the air, causing Cate to wince as her body jarred from the impact. A moan escaped her, and Jack flicked his eyes to her before returning them to the road.

"You okay?"

"I'm fine," she gasped.

"This guy isn't going to stop."

Cate shook her head. "No," she cried, and swallowed hard. "I'm not sure what to do."

"How good are you at jumping from a moving vehicle?" Jack inquired as they continued to drive neck-in-neck with the other car.

"Are you serious?" Cate asked incredulously.

"Yes," Jack said. "We need to get out of this car. He's not going to quit until we're…"

Jack's statement was interrupted as a bullet smacked into their hood. Jack cursed under his breath.

"Yes, I can jump from a moving car," Cate said, her eyes wide as she stared at the bullet hole.

Jack nodded. "There's water coming up. I want you to jump out now. I'm going to drive the car into the lake. I'll meet you back here as soon as it's clear. Stay off the road and out of sight."

"Jack!" Cate exclaimed.

"No, Cate. We can't risk those papers getting wet. You go now."

Cate nodded and swallowed hard. "Okay. Good luck," she said, squeezing his arm.

She spun and cracked her door open. The ground passed underneath her at a dizzying clip. She bit her lower lip hard and flung herself out, rolling across the ground and knocking the air from her lungs. Jack continued on as though she'd never budged. Her door swung shut as the car continued to barrel down the road.

As soon as she was able, Cate scrambled off the roadway and into the field beyond. She hurried across the darkened landscape, running low to the ground until she found a large tree. With some difficulty from her t-strap pumps, she managed to scurry up into the cover of the full leaves.

The two cars careened down the road. Jack took another hit as the car smacked into him again. The car flailed as though he couldn't maintain control. It swayed dangerously close to going off the road. The other driver took advantage as they entered a curve and swerved toward Jack. The other car hit Jack's car hard. He failed to recover from the hit, and his car rode roughly up over a small embankment, crashing through a wooden fence, before it sailed airborne over the edge of the hillside and smacked into a small loch.

Cate winced at the sight as she clutched the tree branch under her. The other car ground to a halt, then reversed. A man hopped from the passenger side and scurried up the embankment. Cate's heart dropped. She heard the crack of a pistol as it fired four shots.

CHAPTER 33

*C*ate covered her mouth as a horrified squeal emerged. "Jack," she breathed, as she watched the other man wait a few moments before he returned to the waiting vehicle. The car sped off into the night.

Cate trembled as she sat in the tree, waiting to be sure the car did not return. When it seemed safe, she scrambled down, falling the last few feet onto her rear. She clambered to her feet and hurried to the loch, staying off the road.

"Jack!" she called in a hushed tone as she reached it. The car still bobbed in the water with only its rear end visible. Bubbles escaped around it as it continued to sink into the waters.

Cate hurried around the water's edge as she searched for signs of life.

"Jack!" she tried again. She searched the water in the dim moonlight. Her breathing ragged, she picked her way to stand on a rock nearby and search the area.

A dark figure approached from her left. Cate scurried off the rock and began to retreat, when she heard a familiar voice. "Lady Cate!" Jack whispered.

Cate's heart soared as the sound of her heartbeat filled her ears. A tear escaped to her cheek, and she hurried toward the figure, colliding into him as she flung her arms around his neck.

"Jack!" she exclaimed. "Oh, thank heavens. When he fired that gun…" Cate cried, pulling away from him.

"It's okay. He shot randomly. I stayed hidden for as long as I could to make him think I was dead. And two shots he fired on your side of the car."

Cate nodded as she pulled him into another embrace. She leaned back as the icy water from his soaked clothes began to penetrate her dress. "You're soaked."

"Aye. Thank goodness it's warm." Jack glanced around. "We need to find a place to hide while we regroup."

"There's a barn over there," Cate said, pointing behind Jack. "I saw it when I climbed into the tree to hide."

Jack nodded as they set off toward the barn. "Climbed a tree? Lady Cate, I can't believe it."

"I'll admit it was better than taking a dip in the loch," Cate said.

They reached the barn and slipped in through the partially open barn door. Jack pulled Cate toward a stack of hay bales and plopped onto the hay-strewn floor. Cate joined him.

"Now what?" Cate inquired.

"I'm not sure," Jack said with a sigh, as he wrung out the bottom of his shirt.

"We can't walk all the way to Bletchley Park."

"No," Jack admitted with a sigh. "But we'll have to figure something out."

Cate shook her head as her heart sank. "Should we walk back to Dunhaven?"

"We're too far for that, too," Jack admitted.

"Do you know how to steal a car?"

"No! Why would I know how to steal a car?"

"I don't know!" Cate said. "I'm just throwing out suggestions."

Jack sucked in air. "It's not a terrible one. I suppose if we find a car, I can try to steal it."

"In the name of national security," Cate said.

"For now, I think we should get some rest."

"Don't you think we should keep moving?"

"No, I think we should get some rest and move on in a few hours. We're in a safe spot at the moment, let's take advantage. We don't know the next time we'll be able to rest."

Cate nodded as they settled back against the hay bales. She bit her lower lip as Jack's hand found hers in the darkness and squeezed. "Lady Cate?" Jack whispered.

"Yeah?" Cate answered.

"Time to hit the hay," he said. She heard the small snicker from him.

"Oh, Jack," Cate said. "Your humor hasn't improved."

"I couldn't resist," he said.

Exhaustion crept over her, but every noise startled her. Eventually, her eyelids became heavy, and she drifted off to sleep, her head lolling onto Jack's shoulder.

* * *

Cate awoke with a start. It took her a moment to recall where she was. Dim light from the early morning sky filtered in through the small opening in the barn doors. She glanced down at Jack's sleeping form. Cate stretched and considered trying to go back to sleep, but nervousness prevented her from doing that. Instead, she gave Jack a gentle shake until his eyes opened. They darted around for a moment before they settled on Cate.

"Good morning," Cate said.

"Good morning, Lady Cate," Jack said with a sleepy smile.

"We should go," Cate said.

Jack pulled himself up to sit. "You're right. I don't want to get caught by an angry farmer."

Cate grimaced at him. "Yikes! You're covered in hay!"

"I wouldn't point fingers, Lady Cate," Jack said, as he pulled a piece of straw from her hair.

They rose and removed as much debris as possible from their clothes before they slipped into the brightening day and set off on foot.

"We should stay away from the road," Jack said. "In case they come back in the daylight to search for our bodies."

Cate nodded and shivered at the events of the night before. "Did your clothes dry?" she asked, as the sun rose in the east.

"Mostly," Jack answered.

"Looks like it'll be a nice day. I hope it doesn't rain."

"You and me both," Jack said. "I'd like to stay dry today."

They continued over the rolling hills as the sun crept up higher in the sky. As the hour approached 8 a.m. a droning noise filled the air.

"Do you hear that?" Cate scanned the skies as they crested a hill, shielding her eyes.

"Aye. Planes."

"There!" she exclaimed. "An entire squadron."

"Friendlies or no?" Jack inquired.

"RAF," Cate said as they came closer.

"Wonder where they're going?"

Cate stared at the several sets of planes in Finger-four squadron formation. "There's so many. They must be heading out on early morning patrols." She paused as a thought formed in her mind. "Which means…" She flicked her gaze to Jack, her eyebrows raised, and the corners of her mouth turned up in a slight smile.

"There's a base nearby," Jack said with her.

"Yes!" she exclaimed.

"And what better place to hitch a ride to Bletchley Park than at a Royal Airforce Base?"

"Come on," Cate said, pointing southeast. "They came from that direction."

They quickened their pace and hurried in the direction they'd spotted the planes coming from. The walk took the better part of the morning. The planes returned as the sun rose overhead and the lunchtime hour approached, flying low over their heads as they approached their base.

"Whew, this took way longer than I hoped," Jack said.

"Tell me about it. These are the worst shoes in the world," Cate complained.

"Do you need a break?"

"No, I just want to get there."

"Want me to carry you? You can hop on my back."

"I'll save that in case I can't make the last leg. We should be getting close. Did you see how low they were flying?"

"Aye," Jack said.

They crested another hill, spotting a large structure in the distance. "There," Cate said. "That must be it."

"Looks like a large estate."

Cate nodded. "They're probably using it as a base."

"Not too much further at least."

They continued, aiming for the large home on the opposite hill. They circled around the walled estate, finding two uniformed servicemen patrolling the entrance.

"Hey!" Cate exclaimed as she spotted them. "Excuse me! We need your help!"

Both men stiffened their postures as Cate and Jack hurried toward them. One held up his hand, signaling them to stop. "Ma'am, I'm going to ask you to stop right there. This is a RAF military base. We do not allow civilians."

"We're not civilians," Cate explained. "We're completing an assignment from the Ministry of Defense. We have information that must get to Alan Turing at Bletchley Park from the intelligence outpost at Dunhaven Castle."

The man narrowed his eyes, flicking his gaze to his partner before returning it to Cate.

"We were followed last night," Jack explained. "The base there has been infiltrated by a German spy. We lost our vehicle. But we need to get the information there immediately."

"What's the name of your superior?"

"Lucas MacKenzie," Cate reported.

The soldiers shared another glance, before one spun and faced the interior of the estate's grounds. He called to someone and waved them over.

"These two say they are carrying sensitive information to Bletchley Park. Say they're on orders from Lucas MacKenzie."

The new man nodded and sprinted back toward the manor home. After a few moments, he returned. "Commodore said to bring them in."

The patrolling servicemen nodded and waved Cate and Jack over. One held up his hand to stop them before they entered. "We have to search you."

"Okay," Cate said. The soldier paused as he reached the papers under her dress. "That's the papers we're delivering." The man raised his eyebrows at her. "If I may," Cate said, reaching into her dress and producing them.

The man nodded at her, and she stuffed them back into their hiding spot. "Go ahead in."

The third man led them up the long driveway and into the large home. A few airmen lounged in a sitting room off the foyer. The soldier they followed marched them down the hall to a small office. A uniformed man stood behind a desk, bent over a map with several other officers.

"Here they are, sir," the man reported with a salute.

"That you, Corporal," the man said with a nod, dismissing him. He eyed Cate and Jack. "Have a seat."

"With all due respect, sir, we don't have time to have a seat. We must get these papers to Bletchley Park. We're already behind thanks to an incident last night with German intelligence," Cate said.

The man narrowed his eyes at her.

"She's right," Jack chimed in. "There was an incident at the Dunhaven outpost. The woman originally set to deliver this information was shot by a German spy. When we received our instructions and left Dunhaven, we were followed, ran off the road and then shot at."

"That's quite a story."

"And you can confirm it all with Lucas MacKenzie. He is our contact in the Ministry of Defense. Please, sir, we must get this information to Alan Turing."

The phone rang as the man considered their story. He snatched the receiver from the cradle. "Yes?" He paused, his eyebrows flicked upward. "I understand. Yes." His gaze settled on Cate and Jack. "Right away. Thank you." He replaced the receiver and stared at Cate and Jack again. "It seems your story checks out."

Cate breathed a sigh of relief.

"Can you spare a vehicle then, sir," Jack asked," so we can continue on our way?"

"I don't think so, Mr. MacKenzie," the man said. "It seems the papers you carry could change the outcome of the war. It is imperative Bletchley receive them as soon as possible. We'll fly you there."

Cate swallowed hard. "Uh," she began, as the Commodore shouted to someone outside. The man hurried to receive the orders rattled off by his commander.

Wide-eyed, Cate glanced at Jack who shrugged. "I don't think we have a choice," he said.

Before she could say anything else, Cate and Jack were ushered from the room, outfitted in a parachute – which caused Cate's stomach to somersault as the airman fastened it to her – and hurried out the door to a frenzy of activity. Men raced around the yard, prepping planes, and scrambling to start them.

The airman led them to two turret fighters sitting side by side. A man in a flight suit offered Cate a wide grin and stuck his hand out. "Cate, I presume?"

Cate nodded, unable to get out any words. "You'll be flying with me. I'm Flight Sergeant Roberts. This is my gunner, Flight Sergeant Wilson. He'll be sitting this one out while you take his seat. I understand we're carrying quite a sensitive piece of intelligence."

Cate stared up at the aircraft in front of her. She crooked a finger toward the craft. "In that?"

Flight Sergeant Roberts patted the plane's side. "She's a good plane."

"Isn't there one where we could sit in the back?" she questioned as another pilot introduced himself to Jack.

"You are going to sit in the back, my dear."

"With the gun?" Cate yelled over the drone of engines springing to life.

"Don't worry, Cate. They're sending plenty of fighters with us. They can handle the Jerrys if we encounter them."

Cate stared up at the plane, unblinking before she flicked her gaze to Jack. He offered her a wide-eyed and frightened shrug.

"Let's get you in, Cate. Step right up here on the wing and scramble up in there."

Cate fought to steady her legs as she clambered up onto the wing and slid into the tight space of the gunner's seat.

Claustrophobia set in, and the plane wobbled as Sergeant Roberts scrambled into his seat. Cate's stomach flip-flopped as the plane rumbled to life. She glanced to Jack in the plane next to her, her face filled with the dread of leaving the ground.

Cate heard the radio spring to life as planes began to enter the air. "Section leaders, we are a go. Repeat we are a go."

"All right boys, we are escorting an important package to Bletchley. We cannot fail. Protect Yellow three and Blue three at all times."

Cate grasped hold of anything she could find, squeezing her eyes shut as the plane lurched forward.

The drone of the engines was deafening. Cate swallowed hard and squeezed her eyes shut for a moment.

"This is Yellow three, package is loaded. Ready to roll," Cate's pilot muttered into the radio.

"Yellow leader, ready to roll."

"Blue three with secondary package loaded. Ready."

"Blue leader ready."

From the conversation, Cate surmised she was in the plane referred to as Yellow three while Jack rode in the plane using the call sign Blue three.

"This is Red leader; we are ready to escort."

"Green leader, ready to escort."

Planes rumbled down the makeshift airstrip. Four planes took off, keeping to a Finger-four squadron formation. Cate's plane lumbered behind two others and in minutes, they were airborne, trailing on the right side of their squadron leader with a plane flanking them as a wingman.

A report of quiet skies came over the radio as the other planes joined them, forming a wall of aircrafts across the skies. An incessant buzzing filled the air.

"Let's hope it holds."

After five minutes, Cate began to relax, releasing her white-knuckled hold on her seat.

"How you doing back there, Cate?" the pilot called.

"As good as can be expected," she shouted back.

"That's a girl."

They sailed along through the skies for thirty additional minutes before a loud call came across the radio.

"This is Red leader, we got Jerrys coming in at our nine o'clock."

ate's muscles stiffened at the news, and she searched the skies in the indicated area. In the distance, a contingent of planes approached.

"Green leader, engaging." Four of the sixteen planes veered off their formation, taking off toward the Luftwaffe fighters.

"Red leader, engaging." Four more planes broke off.

The remaining eight planes stayed the course as fighting broke out to Cate's right. Guns blazed and planes rolled and dove as they tried to shoot each other down. Chatter came across the radio as pilots warned each other or congratulated each other on avoiding or shooting down a German plane.

Four planes approached them steadily. Cate sat up straighter as she noticed they were German, not RAF.

"We got incoming, look alive, boys."

The German planes buzzed past them. Muzzle flashes burst as they strafed the RAF fighters while passing over.

"Yellow two, let's get 'em," the squadron leader said, as the two planes broke off. "Yellow four stay with the assets."

"Blue two and blue leader engaging."

Planes shot around the sky, diving and rolling as Cate attempted to keep track of them.

"This is yellow four, I've got one on my tail."

Cate checked the skies to her left, noting the Luftwaffe plane tailing their wingman.

"I got 'em, in my sights. Hammer down," someone answered. Shots burst from a plane lined up behind the German fighter. "Hit!"

"Nice one!"

Black smoke poured from the German plane as it dropped from the sky. Cate swallowed hard, and let her head rest against the plane's side as she blew out a breath. Minutes later an explosion rocked their plane. Her eyes snapped open, and she saw flames off their wing.

Sergeant Roberts said, "We lost Yellow four."

"Blue four, get over there and watch Yellow's tail."

The plane, formerly flying as wingman to Jack's plane, zipped over behind them.

Three more German planes still zoomed through the skies. Enemy fire strafed past them again.

"Blue four, tailing one of these guys. Got him in my sights. Hammer down." Cate saw one of the RAF planes on the tail of a German 109. He fired, but failed to hit his target. The German plane seemed to slow before it shot skyward, flipping over in a wide arc, and ending up behind the RAF fighter. Guns blazed from the German fighter.

"This is Blue four, I'm hit! I'm hit! Going down!"

Cate glanced out of her window, spotting the black smoke trailing behind the plane.

"Blue four, ditching. Godspeed, gentlemen."

The plane dropped from Cate's sight.

"Blue three, you with me?" Sergeant Roberts inquired.

"Blue three, with you."

"Cate, you with me?"

"I'm here," Cate answered.

"I'm going to need you to transfer the guns to me," Sergeant Roberts began, before panicked chatter interrupted.

"Blue three, watch your tail. You've got a Jerry on your six. He's real close, boy, real close."

The plane carrying Jack shimmied, rolled, climbed, and dove. "I can't shake him."

"I'm coming for you," Sergeant Roberts said.

"You won't make it," the man answered. "Blue leader, can you assist?"

"Blue leader, I'm in the middle of it with two of them."

"Blue three's in trouble, can anyone assist?"

Cate spotted the plane on her left. It tailed Jack's plane closely. Gunfire blasted from the German craft. "I'm hit! I'm hit! He got my tail!"

"Blue three is hit. He's still got the Jerry on his tail."

The plane carrying Jack weaved in an arc, trying to avoid additional gunfire.

Cate stared at the thick bullets feeding into the turret gun.

"How do I use this?" she asked Sergeant Roberts.

"Cate…"

"We have no choice. Blue Three isn't going to make it much longer. Now, how do I use it?" she demanded.

"There's a release on your right, grab it, palm up and pull it back toward you." Cate found it and pulled it back. The heavy weapon swung free. "Aim using the crosshairs and fire. You'll want to lead him a bit. Shoot where he's going to be, not where he is. And for God's sake, don't hit Blue three."

Cate lined up the shot, trying to avoid anywhere near the allied plane, and squeezed. Her bullets went wide, peppering the sky behind the German plane.

"That's okay, Cate," Sergeant Roberts said in an even

voice. "Line it up again and fire. Remember to lead him a little."

Cate nodded, mentally noting the advice. She felt the plane slow. The other two aircrafts approached them.

"Take your time, don't panic."

Cate fought to control her trembling body and latched onto the trigger. She swung the heavy gun into place again. She aimed carefully, lining her shot up with the German plane's engine as it weaved behind the RAF fighter, then inching it to slightly lead the aircraft.

"Cate, have you got the shot lined up?"

"Yes," Cate said, "but I can't get a window to fire with Blue three's weaving."

"All right, team effort," Sergeant Roberts said. "On the count of three, Blue three break left, Cate fire."

"Roger," Blue three's pilot acknowledged.

"Got it," Cate said. She blew out a steadying breath.

"Three, two, one," Sergeant Roberts counted, "BREAK!"

The fighter broke left in a quick move and Cate squeezed the trigger, swinging the gun to match the movement of the German fighter. A flame burst from the enemy aircraft's engine and black smoke poured in a stream behind the plane. It swung off, diving sharply to the ground.

"She got 'em! By golly, she got 'em! Ho-ho! Great shooting, Cate!" Sergeant Roberts sped ahead and into a barrel roll in celebration. Cate's already shaky stomach somersaulted as they swirled through the sky, but she chuckled nonetheless.

"He's down, Jerry's down," someone reported.

"Whoa! Unbelievable! She gets a hit on her first time out!" another said.

"Boy, he's never going to live down being shot down by a woman."

"You can't count this one, Roberts, she's not your gunner."

"Like fun, I won't count it. Too bad for Wilson his tally will lag mine."

"Wilson may be replaced by Annie Oakley."

Cate bit her lower lip and smiled as Blue three pulled level with them. Jack's pilot saluted her. "Thank you, dearie," the man said. Jack gave her a wave. She returned the gesture to both.

The blue squadron leader shot down a third German plane.

"Last Jerry's bugging out," he reported, as he pulled back into formation.

The dogfight continued between the others until the report came through that the Luftwaffe pilots were either downed or fleeing. The remaining planes returned to the squadron.

"Squadron report."

"Yellow leader, asset intact. We lost Yellow four."

"Blue leader reporting, asset intact, Blue two and blue four down. Blue three sustained damage."

"Green two reporting, Green leader is down, Green three and four remain."

"Red leader, Red squadron intact."

"I'm behind Green three, he's trailing oil pretty bad."

"Green three will you make it to Bletchley?"

"This is Green three. I'm sure as hell going to try."

"Negative, Green three, return to base."

"I can make it."

"Green three, return to base, that's an order."

"Red four, requesting permission to disengage and go with Green three."

"Granted, Red four. Return to base with Green three."

The planes shuffled as two veered off, heading north. "Good luck, gentlemen."

"Let's press on, boys, and get these folks to Bletchley."

The squadron continued their flight uninterrupted. After forty more minutes of flying, the planes began to slow. "Breathe easy, Ace. We're almost there," Sergeant Roberts said to Cate.

"Hardly an ace," Cate answered with a chuckle. "But I'm glad I could help, and also glad we're nearly there."

Within twenty minutes, Cate felt the ground rumble underneath her as the plane's wheels bounced off the ground then rolled to a stop. Sergeant Roberts hopped from his perch in the pilot's seat and offered Cate a hand to climb from the gunner's nest.

"Here we are, my dear," he said, as he grabbed her around the waist and set her on the ground.

"Thank you," she said.

"I think the thanks goes to you, dearie," Jack's pilot said as he stalked toward her, his hand extended. "Let me shake the hand of the woman who shot a Jerry out of the sky to save my neck."

He grasped Cate's hand, nearly shaking her entire arm off. Jack followed behind him, still looking green around the gills. Cate hurried toward him and tossed her arms around his neck. He wrapped his arms around her waist, lifting her off the ground. "Thank you, Cate," he said, as he squeezed her.

"You'll never hear the end of this one from the missus," Sergeant Roberts said with a coy grin.

"You know it," Jack said.

"Jack! Cate!" A familiar voice called to them.

"Lucas!" Cate exclaimed.

The man hurried toward them, limping a bit, a sign of his older age. "You made it. Thank God."

Cate smiled and nodded as he reached them.

"Come along, we've got to get the information to Alan."

Cate nodded. "Just a minute." She stepped back to the pilots as they milled around. "Thank you."

"You can fly with me anytime, Cate," Sergeant Roberts answered.

"Not just for getting us here and in one piece. But for everything you do. Thank you. You're very, very brave."

"You're welcome. And I hope our paths will cross again once this is all over. I'd like to buy you a drink, assuming your husband doesn't mind."

"Sir, I believe we owe you one first," Jack said.

"Then we'll buy each other drinks," the man answered.

Cate nodded and waved as Lucas led them away. She glanced back at the pilots as they discussed their latest experiences. She'd look them up when she got back. She hoped they made it through the war unscathed. She couldn't imagine living through what they did on a daily basis. One flight proved enough for her.

"What's this I hear about you taking out a German plane, Cate?" Lucas inquired, as they made their way to Hut 8, where Alan Turing spent much of his time leading a team of cryptographers.

"Hit his engine," Jack said. "And likely saved my life."

"My goodness, Cate! Amelia will be so thrilled to hear she sent the right woman for the job."

"Speaking of, I am absolutely astounded by Amelia's work!" Cate said to Lucas.

"Ah, yes. She makes quite a good spy, don't you agree? She has easy access to much of the country, most don't question her travel. And she's quite smart and capable. I suppose the war has made fighters out of us all in one way or another."

Cate nodded at the sentiment as they reached the small green hut. Lucas led them inside. "Alan?" he questioned of another man.

"With the Bombe."

"Thanks. Come on," Lucas said, leading them to another hut. They stepped inside. A massive, wheeled box stood against the wall. At just under seven feet wide and six and a half feet tall and two feet deep, the machine was filled with 108 cylinders, called drums, in three sections.

A dark-haired man with deep-set eyes fiddled with the machine.

"Alan," Lucas said. "I have something for you."

He straightened and stared at Lucas before eyeing Cate and Jack. Cate removed the papers from under her dress and smoothed them. "Mr. Turing, I have these for you from the intelligence outpost in Dunhaven. Hans Schmidt is convinced…"

Alan snatched the papers from her hand and shuffled through them, biting his thumbnail. "Oh, yes, yes, of course." He grabbed a pencil and began scratching on the paper.

Lucas nodded and motioned for Cate and Jack to step outside.

"Oh, thank you," Alan said as they stepped out. "Very helpful."

They stepped into the late afternoon air. "He'll be working all night now," Lucas said. "He doesn't mean to be…"

"I know," Cate said. "He's brilliant. His mind doesn't operate the way ours does."

Lucas smiled and nodded. "Yes, others complain he lacks social graces, but I maintain he simply does not have time to process them."

He began a walk across the property with them. "I'm convinced we'll soon be able to decipher the Enigma code again thanks to your efforts."

"We're happy to help," Cate said.

Lucas offered her a smile, the corners of his eyes crinkling in wrinkles that didn't exist in 1925. "And now I'm betting you'd both like to return to Dunhaven posthaste."

"Oh," Cate said, realizing she hadn't even thought of how they would get home in the rush of the events. She flicked her gaze to Jack before returning it to Lucas. "I hadn't even thought…". Her eyes wandered toward the landing strip they'd used earlier.

"Oh, don't worry. We won't send you up in the planes again," Lucas said with a chuckle. "Though perhaps we ought to with your shooting skills." He offered Cate an amused grin. "I have a car. I'll take you."

Cate returned Lucas's smile at the announcement of their ride back, pleased she would not have a second flight in the fighter. Jack wiped at his brow. "I'm certainly glad for that offer."

Lucas gave him a tight-lipped smile. "Yes, I heard your journey was rather rough. Took a bit damage to the tail."

"Aye," Jack said. "And I'm not too proud to admit I was terrified we'd crash or worse."

"Thank goodness for Cate's bravery. Though that tends to be the trend among the Americans."

"I owed him," Cate said, slipping her hand around Jack's forearm. "He's saved me more than once."

"I'm not sure I've ever done anything as dramatic as shooting a plane from the sky," Jack answered.

"Oh, by the way, Cate, I thought you may like to know the pilot you shot down is alive. He was recovered earlier with minor injuries."

"Thank you," Cate answered as they arrived at a vehicle.

"Well, here we are. I'm sure you're both exhausted, so if you'd like to slip into the back and doze off on the long drive, I won't object."

Cate nodded and smiled as she ducked into the back.

"I'll sit up front, though I make no promises about staying awake," Jack said.

They settled in as Lucas slipped behind the wheel. Cate found herself too wired to sleep on the first leg of the journey. However as the sun slipped below the horizon and the stars peeked out above them, Cate found herself dozing off.

Her sleep was interrupted by the buzzing of planes. Cate startled awake, exhaustion clouding her mind. She breathed easy as she realized she still rode along in the car driven by Lucas. Jack sat next to him, his head lolling to the side.

"Okay, Cate?" Lucas inquired as she sat up and stretched.

"Yes," she answered, as she scanned the night skies in search of the planes while stifling a yawn. "Thank you for driving us back tonight. I'm sure you must be tired, too."

"Of course! Plus, with my missed connection with Amelia, it gave me an excuse to see her."

"It must be difficult to be separated, particularly at a time like this."

"Yes, quite. Though we're both making our contributions. I am so proud of the work Amelia has done to help. We've managed to save several convoys. And with your contribution, I'd wager we'll save several more."

"I'm honored to have been a part of the effort."

"I am also quite anxious to determine how Sarah is."

"She was alive when we left."

"Yes, I received word she was at a base hospital undergoing emergency surgery. I do hope she pulls through, though her spying days may be limited."

They spent the rest of the journey making light conversation. Cate found herself unable to sleep anymore. In the lulls, she calculated how long they'd been in 1942. They had arrived around 2:30 p.m. on September 21st. It was now midnight on September 23rd. They'd been here for nearly thirty-six hours. Of course, in their time only two and a half hours had passed. She wondered if they had been missed.

As they approached Dunhaven, Lucas inquired about stopping at the field hospital first. Cate preferred to so she could get information on Sarah, a.k.a. Ruth, firsthand.

They approached the camp and after a few words with the soldiers guarding the entrance, Lucas pulled through and parked the car. With another yawn, Cate climbed from the car and stretched. After a poke to Jack, he too, spilled out of the car and stretched.

"What time is it?" he inquired, as they strode to the medical tent.

"Just about half-past two," Lucas reported.

"Thirty-six hours," Cate whispered to him, as they ducked into the tent.

Jack nodded in response to her comment. Lucas scanned the area. Across the space, Cate spotted Amelia sitting at Ruth's bedside. She spun and caught sight of them. Her worried expression broke into a smile, and she hurried toward them.

"Oh, Lucas!" she said throwing her arms around him in an embrace.

"Amelia, I am so glad to see you," he answered.

Amelia pulled back from him and eyed Cate and Jack. "Cate, Jack, what a relief to see you both, too. I fretted over my hasty decision to send you. I felt simply terrible about the danger I placed you in."

"We understand," Cate answered.

"And we're more than happy to help," Jack added.

"The cause was far too important."

"Yes," Amelia agreed. "Yes, it was. I would have gone myself but..." She flicked her gaze to the sleeping form of Ruth.

"Fret no more, Amelia," Lucas said. "They survived it. And

even got to ride in a plane." He offered an amused grin. "And Cate shot down a Jerry!"

Amelia's eyes widened and her eyebrows raised as she stared at Cate, who shrugged.

"Believe me, that story will be told everywhere by the end of the week," Lucas said with a chuckle. "Now, how is Sarah?"

"Holding her own. The prognosis is good. She should survive it. She's quite lucky we found her when we did," Amelia reported. She glanced to Cate and Jack again. "Good thing you two happened upon her. Though, what were you doing in the folly?"

Cate swallowed hard. "We found a note that suggested meeting there about a critical mission," she explained. "I thought it rather curious, so I suggested we follow up on it."

"Ah, I see. Inquisitive as always," Amelia said.

"What about Rita?" Cate questioned. "Have you caught her? Is she also a German spy?"

CHAPTER 35

"That's the tricky bit," Lucas answered. "We had our suspicions about Victor. But Rita was a complete surprise."

"No hint of her true loyalties before this?" Cate asked.

Lucas shook his head as Amelia explained. "It's not that. No hint of her whatsoever. She doesn't seem to exist. She'd never been assigned by anyone to the Dunhaven base. When she showed up, everyone thought she'd been assigned there, but we've not been able to track down her existence."

"Perhaps the Germans sent her to keep an eye on Victor," Jack suggested.

"Then why kill him and disappear? I don't understand it," Amelia said. "Though I suppose we may never know."

"Well, I hope she won't cause any more trouble," Cate replied.

"Not at Dunhaven," Lucas said. "We'll be closing that base entirely. With the infiltration, we'd rather shut it down completely and speak no further of it. Nothing undermines the war efforts and morale like a spy debacle going public."

Cate nodded in understanding. After a few more

moments, Lucas said, "Well, I suppose we should be going on to Dunhaven. I'm quite certain Cate and Jack would like to rest."

They slipped out of the tent a few minutes later, despite Cate assuring him they could wait until he was ready. Within the hour, they arrived at Dunhaven Castle. The morning sky was already brightening when they strode through the door. Rory greeted them, popping into the foyer from the sitting room.

He pulled Lucas into a tight embrace. "Good to see you, brother," he noted.

Lucas offered a similar sentiment before he turned his attention to Cate and Jack. "And our intrepid heroes. Cate and Jack, you've come through once again."

"Pleasure to be of service," Jack said.

"How proud I am to call you family. Well, I suppose you'd like to crawl into bed. Unless you'd like me to send up a tray or have a nightcap?"

"No, thank you. We're exhausted and we're going to head up. But we'll talk again tomorrow," Cate assured him.

"Wonderful. Pleasant dreams, then."

Cate and Jack left Rory and Lucas to have their drinks and conversation and threaded through the halls, slipping out a side door and hurrying across the darkened landscape to the crypt. As they entered the secret passage, Jack let out a sigh.

"I will be so happy to go home."

Cate squeezed his hand and he flicked on his flashlight. "I hope you don't mind my promising to come back tomorrow, but…"

"No, I understand. We can't just disappear. And we need to pick up the luggage anyway. I was too tired to do it now."

"Me too. What a day. I'm not sure words can even capture what's happened in the past forty hours."

Jack shook his head. "No, and once we're back in the safety of our time, I will definitely need a post-time travel analysis to decompress."

"You and me both!" Cate answered as they reached the hidden interior of the castle. Within moments, they were back in the present time.

With the coast clear, they slipped out of the secret passage and hurried upstairs to change. Cate's mind raced as she slipped out of her clothes, mussed from days of difficult circumstances. She sank onto the tub's edge. The magnitude of the experience hit her when a piece of straw fluttered from her dress to the floor.

Cate blew out a long, steadying breath as images flitted through her mind. She fought through her emotions as she realized how close they had come to their own demise. After a moment, she pushed back her shoulders and stood.

She had other unanswered questions. She needed to consult her notes and she wanted to follow up on tracking several of the people she'd come in contact with in 1942.

Cate pulled on her clothes, fixed her hair, including removing a wayward piece of straw that still clung to the underside. As she put the finishing touches on her look, she considered how strange the shift in her circumstances really was.

With a deep breath, she left her bedroom behind and wandered through the halls to the library. As she pushed through, the dogs bounded to her, leaving a dozing Jack's side.

Tears stung Cate's eyes as she scooped both boys into her arms and ruffled the fur on their heads. Jack stretched as she carried them both over and settled into the armchair.

"I need to get my notes, but I need a minute," Cate said.

"A minute? I need more than a minute," Jack said. "You're

a bigger person than me. Then again, you did take down a 109."

Cate chuckled at him. "That really was quite the feather in the cap, wasn't it?"

"I'm still not sure I can process what happened."

"Me either. And then we come back here and live normal lives. That might be the most mind-boggling part."

Jack weighed the statement before responding. "I can't pick a most mind-boggling part. There's so much. This is just as bad as the time we came back from the 1700s and learned there were witches and warlocks."

Cate nodded. "And still so many unanswered questions."

"Who is Rita? I feel so used if she's a German spy."

"I told you she was trouble," Cate said with her eyebrows raised. She set the dogs on the floor and strode across the room to retrieve her folder. "Stemming from your question, if Ruth lived and Rita buried Victor in the garden, why did the detective tell me it had been identified as a woman?"

Cate shuffled through papers to the notes she'd scribble when she spoke with the detective. She sucked in a sharp breath.

"What is it?"

"My notes. Jack, they're different. Look!" She passed the paper over to him. Where it had once said *Adult female, 5'4", 70-80 years ago, blunt force trauma to the head* it now read *Adult male, 6'2", 70-80 years ago, bullet fracture in skull.*

"So, the body found is now Victor's," Jack said.

"Which means history changed!" Cate exclaimed.

Jack stared down at the paper. "Aye, history changed all right. And I'm not certain that's a good thing."

Cate shuffled through to the newspaper articles. "This article still reads roughly the same. Amelia claims Ruth left for another position."

"When we know she was shot."

"Maybe that was always the case, but that doesn't explain who was in the grave."

"Rita?" Jack postulated. "Perhaps Victor killed them both in the last set of events. That would explain why no one missed her. No one seemed to know who she was or where she came from."

"It could be."

"This had to have left a ripple through time."

Cate swallowed hard as her eyes darted around the room. "Come with me," she said, as she stood and hurried from the library.

"Where are we going?" Jack inquired.

Cate led him below stairs. The voices of Mrs. Fraser and Molly talked and laughed in the kitchen. Cate's heart leapt at the sound and continued down the hall.

"Hi, ladies! Mind if we snag a cookie or two?"

"Snag away, Lady Cate," Mrs. Fraser said, handing her the cookie tin.

"Everything okay here?" Cate inquired.

"Aye. What would be amiss?" Mrs. Fraser said.

Cate shrugged. "Baking gone awry. Riley stealing a steak."

"No, everything is just fine."

"Mr. Fraser's all good?"

"Of course, he is," Mrs. Fraser answered. "What's with you today, Lady Cate?"

"I had a bad dream last night. Probably silly, but I just wanted to make sure."

"Everything is right as rain," Mrs. Fraser assured her.

"Good." Cate waved the cookies in the air. "And thanks!"

Jack grabbed one from her as they strolled back down the hall. "Well, it looks like nothing has changed here."

"Nothing major," Cate agreed.

When they settled in the library, she grabbed her laptop.

A quick search of the internet revealed no major historical changes to the war efforts. The war ended as expected.

"So, history changed, but it left no noticeable difference," Jack said.

"It seems so," Cate answered as she pounded on the keyboard.

"What are you looking for now?"

"Information on our pilots," Cate said. After a moment, she smiled. "Sergeant Roberts lived a full and happy life, it seems. I see him in the census after the war and a death certificate in the early 2000s."

"What about Sergeant Williams?" Jack asked, inquiring about his pilot.

Cate tapped around, searching the records. "He was shot down in 1943 but survived. He returned to fly with his squadron after a few weeks, survived the war and lived to a ripe old age!"

"Wonder if that was always the case."

"I'm not certain," Cate said as she closed her laptop. "I wonder if we'll ever learn the truth about what happened."

"I hope we don't learn our presence changed things radically," Jack answered.

"It doesn't seem to have. Let's hope that trend holds out."

Jack slouched in his chair and yawned. "Oh, I'm exhausted."

"Me too," Cate said. "My nap in the barn and the car were definitely not enough."

"You'll sleep well tonight!"

"Oh, please, I hope so. I hope I don't have you up with my midnight roamings."

"You and me both!"

They spent another hour together in conversation over the events in 1942, deciding they'd return to 1942 one last time tomorrow afternoon to say their goodbyes to Rory, Lucas, and Amelia.

"Again, I'll miss them," Cate said. "Especially after all that."

"Well, you still have me, Lady Cate," Jack said, offering her a cheeky grin.

"That more than makes up for it," Cate assured him as Molly popped in with her dinner tray.

After her dinner, Cate found herself unable to keep her eyes open. She opted for an early night, taking the dogs for one last walk before she crawled into bed, exhausted.

Sun shone through the windows as Cate opened her eyes the following morning. She still laid in the same position she'd fallen asleep in. Had she remained in bed for the entire night? No traces of the necklace existed, though the music box tinkled away on her night table. Sheer exhaustion must have provided a temporary solution to her problem.

She stretched and climbed from the bed, feeling as though she could sleep the entire day away. The motivating factor, though, was their final trip to 1942.

She met Jack in the hall as she emerged from her suite with the two dogs. "Sleep okay?" he inquired.

"You tell me," she answered.

"I didn't get any notifications on my phone, though even if I would have, I was dead to the world last night."

"I think both of us were," Cate admitted, as they strode down the hall together. "I don't think I moved."

"Me either. I guess that's one solution to your problem," Jack said, as they stepped into the crisp morning air with the dogs.

"Spending three days in the span of two hours? I'll pass and hope Damien finds something."

"One more trip today and then we can get back to normal around here. I can't wait."

"I know what you mean, though saying goodbye is always hard."

"Let's plan to visit them when the war's over."

Cate smiled and nodded at the idea.

"Hey, do you want to go back earlier? Maybe this morning?"

"Anxious to get there huh?"

"I just figured we might have better luck catching everyone early in the morning. The place seemed deserted when we went in the afternoons."

"Outside of the spies, you're right. Okay," Cate agreed. "After breakfast?"

"Aye, perfect."

Cate spent her first meal of the day pouring over more internet searches to try to find something amiss or gather more information on the mysterious Rita Haverford. She found none. With any luck, they'd solicit more information on their final trip to 1942.

After changing and meeting in the hall, Cate and Jack slipped back to the past using the universal time portal. A nervous wave passed over Cate as they stepped into the bright sunshine of September 23, 1942.

Mere hours ago, they had returned to Dunhaven after an intelligence mission. As they ambled toward the castle, Cate noticed the intelligence tent already being dismantled. Items were being carried to a waiting truck as the base ceased its operations.

They strode through the front door and made their way to their suite. Cate packed the few things she'd brought, and they carried their suitcases to the foyer. Lucas emerged from the hallway.

"Leaving?" he questioned.

"Yes," Cate answered. "We were just about to find Rory to thank him for the stay."

"Oh, that's too bad we didn't get the chance to visit more, though I'm afraid I'm heading back to London today, myself."

Cate grabbed Lucas's forearm and squeezed. "Be safe, Lucas."

He nodded and gave her a tight-lipped smile. "I will. And the same goes for you both."

"Is Amelia here?"

"Mmm, yes. She'll stay on for several more days, so she has easy access to Sarah. She should be along soon; she plans to go back to the hospital early."

"Has there been any change in her condition?"

"She awoke a few hours ago. Confirmed the details about her confrontation with Victor."

Cate shook her head, reminded of the frightening encounter. "Oh, here's Amelia now."

Amelia wandered down the stairs, still latching her watchband.

"Jack, Cate! Leaving?"

"Afraid so," Jack said.

Amelia pulled Cate into a tight hug. "Do be careful. And we'll have to plan to get together after this mess is over."

Cate smiled and nodded as Amelia pulled Jack into an embrace. She grabbed both of their hands and squeezed. "Thank you for what you did."

"Thank you for what you're doing," Cate said.

Rory approached the foursome, glancing at the suitcases on the floor. "Oh, how I hate to see those."

"I'm having mixed emotions about leaving, too," Cate admitted.

"Well, you've been through a terrible ordeal from what I understand," Rory said. "Are you certain you shouldn't stay a few more days? Recover a bit more."

"I'm afraid we can't," Jack answered.

Rory nodded. "I understand, though I still wish you weren't going. Anne will be so sad to have missed you."

"Well, I've invited them back when the war ends," Amelia noted.

"Yes, yes, that would be lovely. Let's plan for that."

"Oh, about the car…" Jack began.

Rory waved him away. "Don't mention it. I never liked that car, anyway."

They chatted for a few more moments, before Cate and Jack collected their luggage and headed out the front door. Cate gave the castle a final glance as they approached the crypt.

"You okay?" Jack inquired.

She nodded. "It helps to know the outcome here," she said, as they ducked into the secret passage.

"I imagine so. We'll have to make good on that promise to visit them when the war is over."

"Wow! Jack Reid suggesting time travel!"

"You've earned the trip," he said.

Within moments, they had arrived at the time rip and returned to the present. Jack helped Cate carry the luggage upstairs. She emptied it and returned all the items to storage before lunch. The time spent with her staff helped ease the nerves she still had over their latest time traveling adventure.

She found herself smiling and relaxed as she hurried upstairs to begin penning a chapter on wartime Dunhaven. As she waited for her document to open, Cate checked her phone. A message from Damien had arrived while she ate.

Hey Cate, how's it going? Text me when you've got a minute.

Cate sent a message back, alerting him to her availability.

Within moments, she received a reply. *I think we're on to something here about what's happening to you… I mean with the wandering around and stuff.*

Cate raised her eyebrows at his message. Maybe now they

could put this mystery to rest, too. Another message came as she contemplated her response. *Tell me if this sounds like what's happening to you.*

She waited a moment as the screen indicated Damien's typing. A long message popped up with a list of symptoms. *Symptoms include: Time loss, often during a trance-like episode where the sufferer may walk, talk and function almost normally; incoherent thoughts or inability to concentrate; confusion, particularly about the order of events over a period of time; preoccupation with a specific moment or event; dizziness, particularly when a trance is beginning or ending; memory loss; loss of consciousness when transitioning between normal functioning and time loss periods*

Cate studied the message then typed back: *Yes, that sounds like it! What is it?*

Damien responded. *Temporalysis*

Temporalysis, Cate pondered. What did that mean? Another text appeared on her screen. *Time travel sickness.*

Time travel sickness, she questioned? What was that? She typed back: *I've never heard of that. What is it? How can I stop it?*

Damien responded: *Well, that's where things are tricky. This *sounds* like time travel sickness, but there's one odd thing that doesn't fit. It usually occurs when a human time-traveler hops between several different time points in a short period. Which, to my knowledge, you haven't done.*

Cate texted back: *No, in the past two weeks, we've only gone to 1942. Though in the past year we have visited four time periods.*

His response came quickly: *That's not enough. What I mean is, it has to be hopping through four or more time periods in a day or a week, something quick. Rapid succession travel to lots of different eras.*

Cate pondered his statement before she responded: *So, this isn't time travel sickness?*

Damien answered: *Well, we think it is. Weirdly, it can occur BEFORE you do the time hopping.*

Cate's brow furrowed. "Before?" she questioned aloud and wrote back: *So, I'm going to time hop in the near future?*

Damien replied: *It's a likely bet if our diagnosis is correct. We're still digging around to determine how to prevent this or stop it.*

Cate rubbed the back of her neck, growing uncomfortable suddenly. She fidgeted in her seat as she typed back: *Is it harmful? Beyond the obvious time loss and weird conversations.*

Dots popped onto the screen and disappeared, indicating Damien's typing and retyping a message. Finally, a message popped onto her screen. *It can be fatal.*

Cate's breath caught in her throat. "Fatal!" she exclaimed.

Another message chimed in. *Don't panic. We're looking for solutions. In the meantime, please don't time hop. You know the cause of it now, so try to avoid it.*

Cate's mind spun. If the sickness was already occurring, could she avoid it? She was destined to time hop for whatever reason. She already suffered from time travel sickness. How could she avoid triggering the ailment? Questions with no answers swirled in her mind and she rose to find Jack.

With her mind a blur, she plodded through the halls in search of him. When she stopped moving, she found herself in her bedroom suite. She stared at space. Jack. She had to find Jack. What was she doing here?

She blinked slowly as she stared at herself in the mirror. She knew what she was doing here. She had to find it. She had to find the room. The time was almost here. She had to find it.

Cate pulled her hair into an upswept style. She removed the sapphire silk dress from the wardrobe and changed into it. She pulled the necklace from the bottom drawer and clasped it around her neck.

"I'm coming," she murmured as she stalked through the halls. Images of the room she sought filled her mind. She descended the stairs and made her way to the west wing doors. They stood open, beckoning her to enter.

Cate plodded through them, winding through the halls to the large golden hall. Riley and Bailey waited, staring at the far wall.

Cate approached the pillar near the room's center. She pressed four of the decorative elements at once. A grinding noise filled the room and a screech followed by a whirring. Hidden in the walls, a mechanism sprang to life. Music filled the room. Cate recognized the music from the music box.

She glanced across the room where the dogs sat. The wall opened, splitting down the middle and swinging into the room.

Cate approached the new doorway and smiled. She'd found it. The mirrored walls stared back at her; soft light glowed from inside star-shaped lamps, and the floor spun.

Cate stepped onto the spiraling floor, careful to keep her balance. She smiled as the music filled her ears. She spun in a circle, despite the moving floor, her eyes searching the space.

"I'm here," she said. "I'm here, where are you?"

The scent of musk filled the air. A shadow moved behind her. She spun in search of it, reaching her hand out. "I'm here!" she called.

The room began to spin faster. The music distorted and Cate's legs began to wobble. "I'm here," she breathed out, as her eyelids fluttered, and her eyes rolled back in her head. She slumped to the floor which continued to spin.

* * *

A voice called to Cate in the darkness, sounding thick and garbled. Confused, Cate searched for the source in her mind. "Cate!" the voice said again.

She tried to speak but found herself unable. "Cate!" She recognized Jack's voice and fought to find it.

After a moment, her eyelids fluttered open. Blurred for a moment, she blinked to clear her vision. She lay in the west wing's large hall. Music still filled the air. Jack hovered over her as she lay on the floor.

"Jack?" she questioned.

"Hey, Cate," Jack said, a smile crossing his face.

"What happened?" she questioned, still feeling too dizzy to sit up. "What's that music?"

"You found your room. At least, I think so."

Cate's head lolled to the side, and she spotted the room. She pushed up to sit, steadying herself by grasping hold of Jack's arm. Music floated from inside as the floor spun.

Cate crawled over and sat on her haunches. "I found you here, passed out, spinning around in there."

"How?" Cate inquired.

"The dogs. They were carrying on something terrible. I followed the noise here and found you in there."

Cate pressed her palm against her forehead. "I don't remember anything."

"It's okay, Cate. You're back now."

"Wait! I do remember something."

"What?" Jack asked.

"Damien! He sent a message. He said I had something called temp... temporal something. Temporalysis!"

"Temporalysis?" Jack repeated, his voice questioning.

"Time travel sickness. He said I had time travel sickness, and they were searching for a solution. He sent a list of symptoms."

"It's caused by time travel?"

"Yes and no," Cate said. "It's caused by a specific form of time travel called time hopping where the sufferer visits multiple eras in a short period of time."

"What? We haven't done that, have we?"

"It was very confusing. I can read you exactly what he said. Well," she said, staring down at her dress, "after I change, of course."

"Of course," Jack said with a chuckle.

"I'll change and meet you in the library. Can you take the dogs with you?" Cate asked, staring down at the two furry faces who watched her intently.

"Sure. See you soon, Cate. And then we'll get to the bottom of this."

Jack pulled her from the floor, and she smiled up at him and nodded. They parted ways as Jack headed to the library with the two pups in tow, and Cate hurried up the stairs and through the halls to her suite.

With a deep sigh, she unclasped the necklace and returned it to the drawer. She shimmied out of the dress and pulled on her discarded leggings and tunic. As she zipped up her boots, she stared outside, her brow furrowing.

It had been a beautiful day earlier – now rain fell from the gray skies and thunder rumbled in the distance. She didn't realize it was supposed to rain.

With a shrug, Cate stood and smoothed her sweater. She crossed her bedroom and entered her sitting room. She stopped before she crossed that room, approaching the window instead of the door. She frowned at the scene outside, the crease between her eyebrows deepening.

Bright sunshine gleamed over the budding trees and bright green grass. She glanced up to the cloudless blue sky. Seconds ago, gray clouds had socked out the sun. How had they disappeared so quickly?

She hurried back into her bedroom and glanced out the

window. Not a dark cloud was in sight. "That's odd," she mumbled to herself. With a shake of her head, she abandoned her weather watch and headed for the library.

She toggled on her phone and pulled up Damien's message as she stepped through the doors. "Okay, here's what Damien…" She stopped when she found the room empty except for the two dogs.

A whine emanated from Riley as Cate entered. "Jack?" she called, despite it being obvious he wasn't in the room. She spun and searched the hall. "Jack?"

Where had he gone? she wondered, as she stalked back into the library. He must have stepped out for something, she figured as she crossed to her armchair. She'd wait for him here.

As she sank onto the chair, her eyes focused on an object laying on the coffee table. The local newspaper sat tilted toward her.

Her brow furrowed as she stared at it. Realization dawned and her eyes widened. Her heart skipped a beat, and her stomach somersaulted. She shook her head as though it would dismiss what she was seeing.

"No," she cried, as she grasped the paper with trembling hands. Her next mystery smacked her in the face. But it was a mystery she had never wanted to face. "Oh, no."

A tear fell to her cheek. Her lower lip trembled as she stared at the page. A picture of Jack stared back at her, framed above by the words: LOCAL MAN MISSING, PRESUMED DEAD.

* * *

Continue the series with *Missing at Dunhaven Castle*, Book 6 in the Cate Kensie Mysteries.

A NOTE FROM THE AUTHOR

Dear Reader,

Thank you for reading this book! *A Spy at Dunhaven Castle* explored one of my favorite historical periods in the 1940s!

I hope you enjoyed reading the story as much as I enjoyed writing it! If you did, please consider leaving a review and help get this book and series into the hands of other interested readers!

Check out *Shadows of the Past*, Book 1 in the *Shadow Slayers Stories* series! You got a taste of these characters already, keep reading to learn more!

If you'd like to stay up to date with all my news, be the first to find out about new releases first, sales and get free offers, join the Nellie H. Steele's Mystery Readers' Group! Or sign up for my newsletter now!

All the best, Nellie

OTHER SERIES BY NELLIE H. STEELE

<u>Cozy Mystery Series</u>

Cate Kensie Mysteries
Lily & Cassie by the Sea Mysteries
Pearl Party Mysteries
Middle Age is Murder Cozy Mysteries

<u>Supernatural Suspense/Urban Fantasy</u>

Shadow Slayers Stories
Duchess of Blackmoore Mysteries

<u>Adventure</u>

Maggie Edwards Adventures
Clif & Ri on the Sea

www.ingramcontent.com/pod-product-compliance
Lightning Source LLC
Chambersburg PA
CBHW070239200726
48293CB00005B/1697